THE GHOSTS OF ARDENTHWAITE

By Harriet Smart

The Butchered Man: Northminster Mystery 1
The Dead Songbird: Northminster Mystery 2
The Shadowcutter: Northminster Mystery 3
The Hanging Cage: Northminster Mystery 4
The Ghosts of Ardenthwaite: Northminster Mystery 5
The Echo at Rooke Court: Northminster Mystery 6
The Fatal Engine: Northminster Mystery 7
The Witches of Pitfeldry: Northminster Mystery 8
Moonshine and Mercury: Northminster Mystery 9
Tarleton's Coffer: Northminster Mystery 10
The Wounded Oak: Northminster Mystery 11
Mummer's Night: A Northminster Novella
Carswell's First Case: A Northminster Novella
Emma Vernon's Northminster Ghost Stories
The Dolls at Heron's Reach
The True Value of Pearls
The Daughters of Blane
Green Grow the Rushes
The Wild Garden
The Lark Ascending
Reckless Griselda
A Tempting Proposal

THE GHOSTS OF ARDENTHWAITE

by

Harriet Smart

Published by Anthemion

Fourth Edition

ISBN 978-1-907873-58-4

Made with Jutoh

Chapter One

April, 1841

They reached Ardenthwaite at dusk – a crisp, cool spring dusk, lit clearly after a day of sun. The wind accompanied them as they rode down the long avenue of chestnuts that led to the house, making the scanty new greenery shiver and whisper.

The old house soon lay in sight, the setting sun catching here and there on the ancient lattices, and the smell of wood smoke filling the air. The thought of a fire and a glass of wine was a pleasant one after the ride from Northminster, but Felix could not be sure how they would be received. The circumstances were awkward, to say the least.

Major Vernon had dismounted and given charge of his horse to Holt. Felix did the same, and as Holt rode off towards the stable yard, they stood for a moment looking at the house.

It had been nearly a year since Felix had last crossed the threshold. Once again he did not feel as if he had much claim on the place, but the fact remained: it *was* his house, and because of that he was obliged to be there and deal with this strange business.

"When we were last here," he said to Major Vernon, "did you see anything that you could not account for?"

Major Vernon did not answer, for a tall, thin man dressed in a green riding coat came striding out of the house. For a moment, Felix found himself blinking, for the man had in his physique and bearing a strong resemblance to Major Vernon – they might have been brothers. He was accompanied by two pepper-and-salt pointers, who were yelping and leaping with excitement. By his appearance, Felix surmised this must be Colonel Parham, his tenant.

"Gentlemen!" the Colonel said. "Very glad to see you, very good of you to come! Mr Carswell," he went on, seizing Felix's hand in both his, and shaking it with vigour. He then turned to the Major. "And Major Vernon. A great honour."

"The honour is ours, sir," said Major Vernon. "And thank you for allowing us to come and –"

"What else could be done?" said Colonel Parham. "What else? Exceptional circumstances demand exceptional remedies." He sighed and turned back to Felix. "It really is good of you to come, Mr Carswell. In your shoes – well, I don't know what I would have thought! Please do come in."

They went into the great flagged hall, and Felix glanced about him, irresistibly reminded of the scenes that had passed there – his own ghosts, he supposed he might term them, and could not help frowning. He had meant to be indifferent but he could not quite manage it.

"Dinner will be served shortly," said the Colonel. "Mostyn will show you to your rooms," he added, indicating a manservant who stood in the hall. "There is no need to dress. My wife is not here. In fact, we have been the only souls here – Mostyn and I – for some days now. My wife could not bear it, nor the children. And of course the servants..." he added with a shake of his head.

They followed Mostyn upstairs. Felix found he had been put in the room his parents had occupied, not the great tapestried bed chamber as before. No one was expecting him to play master of the house this time.

"It is a shame the others have all gone away," said Major Vernon, meeting him on the landing a few minutes later. "It would have been good to hear their accounts."

"So you can pick them all to pieces?" Felix said.

"I thought we decided to keep an open mind," Major

Vernon said. "I have met plenty of people – intelligent, sensible souls – who are entirely convinced by what they have experienced."

"That's true," said Felix. "My mother, for one."

"Quite," said Major Vernon. "So let us hear what he has to say and then make our judgement."

They went down to the dining room.

The Colonel received them warmly and they sat down to a substantial dinner, all laid out on the table at once, in the old-fashioned style.

"I apologise for the plainness of the fare," said the Colonel. "Mostyn is no French chef."

"Still, he seems to be very handy in the kitchen," said Major Vernon. "This is excellent. You are lucky he has strong nerves. It would be a shame to be deserted by him, I think."

"Mostyn would never desert me," said the Colonel. "He has been with me since I was a captain in the Eleventh. We have been through thick and thin together."

"And what would you say this business was?" Felix could not help enquiring. "Thick or thin?"

"You are sceptical, sir, of course," said the Colonel, "but I tell you now, I should not have dreamt of disturbing your affairs had not –" He broke off for a long swallow of claret. "Believe me, I have been struggling with this! This business is so – uncanny!"

He gave a slight shudder, refilled his glass and pushed the decanter towards Felix, as if to imply he would need it for courage. Felix took some, and another helping of the excellent kidney fricassee that had been placed on the corner of the table between him and the Major.

"Perhaps we should start at the beginning," Major Vernon said. "Your letter said that these events only began three weeks or so ago."

"March the fifteenth," said the Colonel. "I made a note in my memorandum book merely because it felt like a curiosity.

A trick of the light."

"And that was?" Major Vernon said.

"I was coming back from some rough shooting. It was about four. The light was fading, but it was still not dark. I was coming down the lime walk with the dogs, Hector and Hero. All of a sudden Hero started barking, becoming very agitated, and at the same time, I saw a figure in a black cloak standing in front of the house. I supposed, of course, that it was a visitor, so I quickened my steps to go and enquire, and then suddenly there was no one there and I was left scratching my head!"

"So you decided it was a trick of the light?" said Felix.

"Yes, at least in the first instance. But then Hero went running up to where the figure had been and went sniffing around as if she smelt something."

"Only the one dog?" said Major Vernon.

"Hector is old, and has a rheumy eye," said the Colonel. "Mostyn, you can clear the cloth now."

Port, half a Northminster blue cheese and walnuts replaced the claret and the dirty dishes.

"These walnuts are from your own orchard, Mr Carswell," said Colonel Parham. "Quite a remarkable crop."

"I'm glad to hear it," said Felix.

"My wife has never been happier than in that garden," said the Colonel. "It is a great shame, but I had to send her away. Her nerves were torn to shreds. She has always been delicate, but this –"

"Is she far away?" said Major Vernon.

"At the seaside. I thought that best for all of them. Are you in favour of the sea, Mr Carswell?" said the Colonel.

"As a cure?" Felix said. "It depends on the case. But it will be good for your children, whatever."

"I thought so," he said, passing the decanter of port to Major Vernon.

Major Vernon took his usual scant glass and passed it on to Felix.

"So the dog's behaviour made you wonder at what you had seen?" Major Vernon asked.

"It did," said the Colonel. "But I thought very little of it until the following day. It was then that my wife told me that one of the maids had given notice because on several occasions she'd seen a black figure in the upstairs passageway going towards the linen room, which then simply vanished before her eyes. It had made her too afraid to sleep, so she wanted to be let go."

"Did you talk to the girl?" said Major Vernon.

The Colonel shook his head. "She'd already gone. And my wife had not wanted to mention it because it had frightened her, and she did not wish me to know. But when I asked where the girl was, she had to tell me. She confessed that the story had felt like a cold hand touching her heart. And that was only the beginning. It was that night that it began with the bedclothes."

"Yes?" said the Major.

"We were sleeping at that time in the large room with the green bed-hangings and the tapestries."

"Where I slept last summer," said Felix.

"Well, I do not advise that you sleep there now. It is impossible to get a night's sleep. There is something there that does not wish anyone to sleep."

"What happened that first night?" Major Vernon asked.

"It was most curious. My wife and her maid went in first. I was still downstairs, and they were very surprised to find the bedclothes all disarranged, as if someone had been lying abed. My wife's maid had only been in there five minutes previously to make up the fire, and had naturally left it all in perfect order."

"And you are certain no one else had been in there?" said Major Vernon. "Or that the maid was not making an excuse for forgetting to make the bed?"

"It is unlikely. She is a steady character. She was angry

that someone had undone her work. We did not come to any explanation as to why it happened, but we tried to imagine some natural cause. It would not have been so significant if it had not happened every night for a week – always the same, and then with added touches of disorder. There were ashes on the hearth, and the fire smouldering, there were vases overturned, and books lying as if they were thrown across the room in fury, and clothes tossed about and so forth. Poor Betty was reduced to tears by it – she takes a great pride in her work, but it was as if a demon was tearing through the room. And of course when all the other servants heard of it, there was no keeping the matter secret. And then on the eighth night, after the room had been particularly thrown around, we said our prayers, got into bed, and put out the candle only to have the bed-clothes stolen from us repeatedly. After that we quit the room, and I have locked it."

"Could you elaborate on that, sir?" said Major Vernon. "The clothes stolen from you?"

"Exactly as I said. They were pulled from us. It happened four or five times that night. It was as if someone were in the room and stripping the bed while we lay in it. My poor wife – she was almost insensible with fear, and I am not ashamed to admit I was shaking through and through. I have never experienced anything like it!"

"It is such a shame your wife was not well enough to stay here," said Major Vernon. "I should very much like to hear her account of it. Where was it you said she had gone? Swalecliffe, I think you said, did you not?"

"I should very much prefer that she was not disturbed," said the Colonel. "It has been distressing for her."

"Of course," said Major Vernon. "I quite understand."

"So no one has been back in there since?" Felix asked.

"No," said the Colonel.

"And was there anything else?" he asked.

"Yes," said the Colonel. "There were bursts of clattering

and banging in the room above the night nursery, as if furniture were being moved about. It woke the children and their nurse, and my wife, because she went to sleep in there with them on the second night it occurred, as they were afraid. It was only observed on two nights, because after that I decided to send them away. I have not heard that for myself, however, although I have slept in there myself after they had gone, just to see."

"And no one sleeps or uses the room above?"

"No, it is just lumber in there. I asked all the servants particularly about it, but it was after they had gone to bed. It was most peculiar."

"So that was the last thing that occurred?" said Major Vernon.

"I saw the figure again," the Colonel said after a moment, "the day after my wife and children left. Three days ago now."

"In the same place?"

"No, in the house. On the main landing, somewhat near the door to the tapestry bedroom. And as before, I saw it, and it vanished. I had the idea it was a woman, very slight, wrapped in black. It was only for a moment that I saw her."

"What time of day was it?" asked Major Vernon.

"Late afternoon. I was about to go into the library. It was perhaps just from the corner of my eye, but I did see her and I felt that same coldness grip me. I was very glad to get to a fireside."

"And nothing since?"

"No, thank God."

Felix drained his glass and refilled it with port, which was quite delicious. He drank and tried to make sense of this extraordinary account. He was aware that Major Vernon was watching the Colonel carefully, and that the Colonel was aware of his scrutiny. He doubtless expected it. Even if he was telling the truth he would surely expect to have his word questioned simply because of the fantastical nature of what he had just told them.

"Did Mostyn see anything?" Major Vernon asked after a moment.

"Not that I am aware of. Apart from seeing the room after it had been disturbed, of course."

"It is all very strange," said Major Vernon.

"I never believed that such things were possible," said the Colonel getting up from the table. "Never. And yet – if you will just excuse me for a moment, gentlemen," he added, and left the room.

The door closed behind him and Felix said, "So?"

The Major did not answer for a moment; he appeared to be studying the candle flame.

"It is a good tale," said Felix.

"Yes, rather too good, don't you think?" said Major Vernon.

"You think he is lying?"

"We only have his word for any of it at this point. I find it hard to believe him without corroboration. He may be mistaken in what he saw, or deliberately lying, though I would hesitate to say the latter. But that is the nature of our business. We can never believe anyone is telling the truth."

"Quite," said Felix, swallowing down his port.

"However," Major Vernon said, "there may yet be corroboration. Who knows what will happen tonight?"

"Anything or nothing," said Felix, pouring another glass of port.

"I am going to propose to the Colonel that we spend the night in the tapestry room," said Major Vernon, getting up and leaving the room.

Felix was left with his wine, wondering if it could possibly be a lie. Would a man ever make up such a preposterous tale and expect to be believed, especially a man like Colonel Parham? Surely he would have made it less extreme if he were attempting to dupe them in some way?

He took another glass and found himself picturing a woman in a black cloak, noiselessly walking the creaking passageways of the ancient house. A slender woman, a shadow creature who then vanished without trace before one's eyes. One of the Ardens, he supposed – there always were such stories in old families, the sort that made for excellent fireside tales on winter nights. Was she an unhappy daughter or a mad bride? Perhaps the latter, throwing about the contents of her bridal chamber, desperate to escape. Perhaps, like the Bride of Lammermoor, she had even stabbed her husband on their wedding night.

He took a long drink of wine, relishing the richness of the taste, feeling its effects steal over him like a warm embrace. He felt drowsy and curiously at ease. He pushed back his chair and gazed into the fire, which was burning brightly. How fascinating were the intricate patterns and myriad of unusual colours formed by the long licking flames! He did not think he had ever seen such a colourful fire before. It was, he knew on some level, odd and therefore striking, yet he was not unduly disturbed by that strangeness. He accepted it quite as it was and enjoyed it.

"I could leave you to sleep here, if you like," he heard the Major saying.

"I was dreaming," Felix said, startled that he had not heard him return to the room. He found he was slurring his words. "The fire. It seemed so –"

"It's not much to speak of now," said Major Vernon. "It has almost gone out."

He was right. Only the smouldering remains of a log remained in the grate, and a moment later it had crumbled into a heap of grey and white ashes.

Chapter Two

Carswell, who had undoubtedly drunk too much port, climbed into the great bed and fell asleep in a matter of moments.

Giles was not ready to sleep, and he sat down by the fire, turning over the Colonel's perplexing story in his mind. The room had not been disarranged as he had described, and judging by the way Carswell was clutching at the sheets there seemed little chance of some supernatural hand clawing them from him. The house felt quiet and safe, just as it had done when he had been ill and had made it his refuge after Laura's death.

He did not like to doubt the Colonel's word, but it had to be done. The man was requesting a release from his tenancy on the grounds that the house had become uninhabitable. There was a substantial sum of money involved, for there was over six months to run on the lease. Mr Pye, the land agent, had said he had never had a lease challenged on such grounds in all his years in the business. He had been fairly put out by it, but there was such a polite gravity in the Colonel's letter it seemed impossible not to give him the benefit of the doubt, at least in the first instance. Furthermore, the Colonel had been anxious that Carswell come and see for himself what was happening at the house, and form his own opinion of the matter. And so Carswell had turned to Giles and asked him to accompany him. This the Colonel had accepted without demur.

If the man was feigning, would he really have accepted such a pair of visitors, who were both sceptics by profession? It was a dangerous strategy if the whole thing was a pack of lies.

He had been faultlessly hospitable. In fact the Colonel's plain fare had been rich, and the flow of wine liberal, perhaps too liberal. Carswell was now murmuring in his sleep and threshing about in the bed, in no fit state to be a rational observer. One down, Giles thought, as if they had been lured into some kind of trap. But then, in all honesty, what was the man going to do? Lay on a phantasmagorical show for them, as if they were at the theatre? It made no sense at all.

Perhaps the Colonel simply kept a good table and Carswell could not hold his liquor. The latter was true enough. Giles had observed it frequently and had endured all the self-reproaches the following day. Carswell had a weakness for an open decanter, no matter what resolutions he made to resist it.

Giles lay back in his chair, stretched out his feet to catch the warmth of the fire, and closed his eyes. He felt suddenly exhausted, as if he also had drunk too much, which he was sure he had not. He had drunk two small glasses of claret and half a glass of port. That was not enough to produce the extraordinary languor that now overcame him. Perhaps it was the rich food that was to blame – a creamy kidney fricassee and a Madeira sauce with the roast widgeon. They had been living plainly of late. Their current lodgings were not comfortable ones, and the cooking was on the dreary side. Perhaps he had, like Carswell, over-indulged.

Slightly annoyed with himself for it, Giles got up from his chair with some effort, rearranged the fire a little to prevent accidents, and went to join Carswell in the great bed. As he got under the covers, Carswell gave a great moan as if he were being attacked by demons. It is as well I am tired, Giles thought, given such a vocal bedfellow. And it was not long after he had put out the candle, that he found himself falling deeply asleep.

~

She was undoubtedly the most exquisite young woman Felix had ever laid eyes on.

Such was her perfection that he decided she was not mortal. How could she be mortal, anyway, appearing alone in that woodland glade, with the early morning sun catching every drop of dew, and turning it into dazzling crystal? For she was riding a milk-white pony, and was dressed in green while her hair flowed loosely about her shoulders, without a care for fashion. She was not of this world, certainly.

That hair – it was a brilliant fiery red, far brighter than Sukey's dark auburn tone, and to his mind at that moment, far more desirable, as was the fascinating pallor of her complexion. Her porcelain skin was scattered with freckles. Why did anyone consider freckles imperfections? They seemed only to add to the sum of her beauty.

She brought her pony to a standstill and seemed to be examining him with the same scrutiny as he had extended to her, as he stood there, bare-footed in the woods. But he could not read her expression.

"Who are you?" he managed to say.

"Who are you?" she responded, as if all life were a riddle to her, and she had stepped straight from one of the old ballads. Had she come from a palace under the hills, and in which case where was her retinue of fairy knights? He expected to feel a dagger at his throat any moment. It was surely dangerous even to have seen such a creature as this, let alone speak to her.

"I..." he began but found he could not finish. He was not entirely sure who he was at that moment, nor how he had got to this place. "These are my woods, I think," he said, managing to grasp at least this fact from his memory.

"I very much doubt that," she said. "You look lost."

"Are these your woods, then?" he asked, wondering into what curious realm he had strayed.

"Perhaps. I'm not sure."

"I would have thought you might know," he said.

"Why should I?"

"Because..." He hesitated. Was there not some etiquette to be observed with such dangerous creatures? It did not do to name them, that was it, especially not to their faces. He did not want to be taken prisoner and dragged under the hill, or at least he supposed he ought not to want that. There was a strong feeling in him that he would have liked nothing better than to be her captive. "You have a look about you – it makes me think that you might know everything," he said at length.

"Oh, do I?" she said.

"As if you are very wise," he said, taking a step towards her.

"Only a fool would say that," she said.

"Then that is what I am!" he said. "Given I don't seem to know anything about myself, and I am standing here in just my shirt in the middle of a wood which might be mine, but is probably not, and even if it is, is not really!"

"What?"

"It's complicated," he went on, feeling breathless as he spoke. "My father, who is not really my father, but who is, in truth, bought them for me, the woods, that is – but what do you care?"

"I think you are ill," she said.

"Oh, certainly I am," he said. "Why else would I be talking to you, Your Highness? Or is it Your Majesty?"

"Neither."

"Your Grace? My lady?"

"Miss – Smith."

"Smith?" he said. "That's a very poor alias, I must say."

"I am going to get help for you," she said, gathering up her reins. "You are raving. You must stay here, and I will get help."

He stepped a little closer.

"And you will take me to your people?" he said.

"Perhaps. I am not sure what ought to be done with you. A doctor is what you need, certainly."

"You have doctors in your realm?" he said.

"Of course," she said.

"That I should like to see. That's my profession, you see," he added, recalling now that this was the case. Her eyes widened at that. "You don't believe me?"

"Stay there, will you?" she said, and steered the pony past him, turning it neatly. "Do you promise me?"

"Yes. Yes. I would promise you anything, you know," he could not help saying. She did not answer this, and instead started off, trotting crisply along the track by which she had come. He watched her hair flapping on her back, catching in the light.

In a minute or two the sound of the pony's hooves became indistinct and he could see nothing more of her. He sat down, intending to keep his promise, and saw at the same time that his feet were bleeding.

It began to rain heavily and in a matter of minutes he was soaked to the skin and coming to his senses. He was startled and appalled to find where he was. How was it he was sitting there in the woods in only his shirt? How had he come to be outside in such a disgraceful state?

He staggered to his feet and began to trek back to the house, slashing his feet and legs on the bramble-strewn path.

It was a blessed relief to find himself stumbling though the gate which led to the orchard. Here, the trees in their new blossom were being pounded by rain, and he felt as fragile as the tiny flowers clinging to the branches as he made his way back towards the house.

It was at this moment he caught sight of Holt running towards him.

"There you are, sir!" Holt exclaimed. "Where have you been? Away with the fairies, by the look of it!"

~

Giles was aware he was dreaming. He found he was with Laura, who was dressed very beautifully in lilac silk, with a bonnet veiled in gossamer lace. In short, she was wearing the sort of expensive clothes he could not have afforded to buy her. They were in some grand drawing room – he did not know where it was but it somewhat resembled one of the great rooms at Holbroke, except that it was far larger and more opulent. They appeared to be at an afternoon party. There was music playing in another room, and all the windows were open. Beyond those windows, he knew without looking, were vast gardens, kept in a state of utter perfection.

A little girl of eleven or so came up to Laura. She was dressed in the style of thirty years ago, neatly and plainly, in white muslin, with a blue sash that exactly matched the colour of her eyes.

Giles recognised the sash, having long ago seen it laid by on a dresser, in his mother's room. She had brought it into the room, having left the women to their work of laying out the small body, dressing her in best Sunday dress. No doubt his mother had decided it should not go with her and had stood for a moment, smoothing out the creases. She had begun to fold it, her tears running down her face. It was then that she had seen him, hiding in the corner. He was not supposed to be there. He had expected to be scolded. He was supposed to be upstairs in bed. But she had not scolded him. She had taken him in her arms and kissed him.

"Won't you come and sit by me, Lizzie?" Laura said to the girl, who Giles knew to be his sister. "I'm your brother's wife." She patted the space on the sofa beside her.

"Johnny's wife?" Lizzie said. "How can Johnny be married?"

"No, I am married to your little brother, Giles."

"Giles?" said Lizzie incredulously.

"Oh, yes," said Laura. "Please, won't you sit with me? We should be friends, don't you think?"

"I should ask my parents," said Lizzie. "Do they know you?"

Laura shook her head, and looked up at Giles.

"I should know them," she said, "should I not? Go and fetch them, Miss Vernon. Your brother will introduce me."

"Is that you, Giles?" said Lizzie, turning and staring at him. "Is that really you?"

He had no chance to answer, for at that moment he woke, shaking as if it had only been a day since Lizzie had died, carried off by a spring fever.

Then, as he crossed the tide margin from the confused world of his dream and into reality again, he had a further surprise.

There was no sign of Carswell in the bed beside him, and a quick glance about him established that his clothes and boots remained in the room, as if he had left in only his shirt. Given the fierce chill of the room, this seemed curious. Giles at first supposed he was wandering about the house. Perhaps he had taken refuge in the library, as had been his habit previously, but not to have bothered to dress, even in the most rudimentary fashion, seemed out of character.

He got out of bed and began to dress. A few moments later, Holt came in with the hot water.

"Have you seen Mr Carswell?" said Giles.

"No, sir," said Holt.

"Perhaps he went out to clear his head," Giles said, going to the window and looking out at the rain-soaked garden. "But in only his shirt." Saying it aloud, the more curious it felt.

"What was that, sir?" said Holt.

"He's not dressed. I think we should go and look for him," said Giles, pulling on his boots. "I will probably be proved a fool for it but –"

"As you like, sir," said Holt. "And surely no Christian would go out in that in his shirt!"

Yet in a little more than a quarter hour, his intuition was proved correct.

It was Holt who discovered him, staggering into the orchard, in a state of near collapse and considerable confusion. His bare legs and feet were bleeding, his shirt was torn and dirty and his face and hair covered in mud.

Between them, Holt and Giles got him back to bed and bound up his lacerated feet as best they could, although he was scarcely a compliant patient. He was talking nonsense between bouts of retching, as well as swinging between shivering and sweating.

"I will send Mostyn to fetch Dr Hall," said the Colonel.

Giles agreed to this, although he suspected that Carswell would not think much of his services, even in his strange condition.

After a while, Carswell grew calmer and fell into a fitful sleep. He woke a little after noon, and sat up in bed, staring at his two unlikely nurses.

"What is going on?" he said.

"That's a good question," said Giles. "I hope Dr Hall will be here soon to answer it."

"That quack?" said Carswell, starting to climb out of bed. As he did, he winced, and looked down and saw his bandaged feet.

"You must have walked through a briar bush, sir," said Holt.

"When?"

"This morning," said Giles. "Do you not remember, you were in the orchard?"

Carswell thought for a moment, and then covered his face with his hands.

"Dear Lord..." he murmured. "I remember now. What the devil was I doing out there?"

"Your guess is as good as ours, sir," said Holt.

"Go and find some breakfast for Mr Carswell, Holt," said Giles.

Holt left, and Carswell got out of bed with some care, and walked across the room, wincing. He peered at himself in the looking glass, lifting an eyelid and grimacing.

"Dear God," he said. "What on earth is going on? Did I have a fever?"

"Yes, and you were retching."

"I cannot make any sense of it!"

"Perhaps when you have rested some more it will become clearer," Giles said, attempting to steer him back across the room to the bed.

"Last night," Carswell said, turning and gripping his forearms, meeting his gaze with a wide-eyed stare, "did you experience anything or see anything?"

"I was extremely tired and I did have some strange dreams, but that would be expected given the subject of our conversation."

"You didn't see her?"

"Who?"

"I did try and wake you, now I think of it. But you were out cold, like a corpse. She was here. The woman in the black cloak that the Colonel saw. Except it was a grey cloak. She was standing there as clear as day, with a candlestick in her hand. She spoke to me."

"She did?"

"She told me I had to help her. That if I went out I could help her. So I went outside and then –" He pressed his fists to his forehead. "Or at least I think that is what happened. I don't remember going downstairs or leaving the building. I found myself in the woods and there was another woman, and she was –"

"Ought you not try to rest?"

"I need to tell you this now, in case I forget. My mind is

so turned about and upside down! This other woman – a red haired woman on a white pony. No, a girl, she was little more than a girl, and the most beautiful creature I have ever seen in my life. Are you sure you saw nothing? These dreams of yours, what were they?"

"Just a jumble, as dreams often are. Now, Carswell, I think you should rest. I think your fever is still with you. What should I do about that?"

"I want my books," Carswell said. "I need to see what this is – if there is any natural cause, that is. Otherwise, I do not..." He stood in the middle of the room, clutching the stuff of his shirt in his hands. "They were both real, as real as you are now –"

"You should rest," Giles said again, taking his arm and leading him to the bed. He was a little surprised that he consented, but it was clear that he was struggling with himself. "See Dr Hall, see what he says."

Carswell nodded and then said, "I will, but I think we should leave here."

"You are not in a fit state to go anywhere, surely?"

"I cannot stay here," he said. "I cannot think."

Giles thought for a moment.

"Then perhaps you might go to Holbroke? I understand that Lord Rothborough is due back tomorrow. They will take care of you there." Carswell twisted up his face as if in pain, considering the point, and then nodded. "Holbroke it is, then. I will go over there myself and see to it. Holt is a better nurse than I am."

Carswell nodded again, and sat there with the covers drawn up over him, shaking with cold, but with sweat beading his forehead. His condition would be a very poor welcome back for Lord Rothborough, but it could not be helped.

Giles made his apologies to the Colonel, who was equally apologetic about the length of time it was taking to fetch Dr Hall.

The rain cleared as he rode the four miles over to Holbroke, and it felt at least that he was doing something useful by going there. The housekeeper Mrs Hope welcomed him with a warm civility which was flattering. The loyal retainers of such great families were often haughty with those they did not think the equals of their masters.

"I did not think there would be any great difficulty, Mrs Hope," he said. "Lady Rothborough is staying in Italy, I understand."

"Yes, sir, and who knows when she will come here again!" said Mrs Hope. "She never cared for us much," she added with a sniff. "Lady Maria is coming, but not Lady Augusta nor Lady Charlotte. She has gone to stay with Lady Dunbar, which makes it sound like a settled thing. Had you heard anything more on that, sir? We are all wanting to know what is what."

She was referring to the laboured saga of courtship between the Earl of Dunbar and Lady Charlotte, Lord Rothborough's eldest daughter.

"I knew she was going to Scotland," said Giles, "but no more than that, I'm afraid."

"They had better make up their minds once and for all!" said Mrs Hope. "I can't fathom what all the delay is about, sir. Lady Maria told me that she thought they were beautifully suited, and her opinion is good enough for me."

"Lady Maria always sees the best in every situation," said Giles.

"That is true enough, sir," said Mrs Hope. "She is the sweetest creature alive. She will be very distressed to hear about Mr Carswell, I think."

"With luck it will all prove to be a trifle, but I thought to be on the safe side –"

"His Lordship would not want it otherwise, I am sure of that, sir, quite sure. I will go and see to everything at once. And the carriage will be ready for you now, sir."

Driving back in the comfort of the carriage, he found himself closing his eyes and remembering the strange dreams of the night before. How vividly Laura had appeared, as if he could have reached out and touched her.

He had often dreamt of her, but she had always seemed somewhat remote, as if in another room. He had always known in those dreams that she was dead. Yet last night he had sincerely doubted it and now, as the carriage lulled him to sleep, he had the same undeniable sense of her presence. Indeed, she was sitting beside him.

She reached out and insinuated her hand into his.

"I am so glad to be leaving there at last," she said, and leaned against him, her head resting on his shoulder. He reached up and pushed up the little silk frill that trimmed the back of her bonnet, revealing the nape of her neck. In a moment he would kiss it.

He jumped back into wakefulness just as the carriage made the sharp turn into the long avenue leading to Ardenthwaite.

Chapter Three

Carswell was hardly a model patient, but Holbroke and its luxuries contrived to soothe his agitation, and the fever passed within a short time of his arriving there. This was succeeded by a profound exhaustion, and he asked to be left to sleep.

He was still asleep when Lord Rothborough and Lady Maria arrived the following afternoon, and the Marquis, although he sat for some time at his bedside, did nothing to disturb him.

"I cannot thank you enough for bringing him here," Lord Rothborough said to Giles later that day, after Giles had explained the circumstances.

"He would not stay at Ardenthwaite," Giles said.

"The Lord only knows what is going on at that house. It is a very bizarre turn of events. I should not have guessed at such a thing in a thousand years."

"You've had no dealings with Colonel Parham?" asked Giles.

"No. I haven't even met the man. Pye made the usual enquiries, of course – at least I trust he did. You think that something is not right about him?"

"I don't know. It is a strange claim, to say the least." He considered for a moment and then said, "This may sound like fuelling his fire, my lord, but are you aware of any stories about the house?"

"We have ghosts aplenty here, Vernon, so the stories go – and I have never seen hide nor hair of one. And I have never heard anything related to Ardenthwaite or the Ardens. It's curious. It has the look of a place which ought to be haunted."

"Exactly," said Giles.

"If it had been famous for its ghosts, I would have heard of it, certainly," said Lord Rothborough. "I had a tutor at one time, before I went to Harrow, who had quite a bent for these things. He was always scurrying about collecting such lore, and I went with him. It was most agreeable, as you may imagine. He was a charming man, but my Greek was not much improved. He is the Dean of Rochester now. I shall write to him about it. It is an excellent excuse for a letter. Besides, that and the university question, of course. Touching on that, by the way, your brother-in-law has been very useful to me on that account."

"He has?"

"Yes, while I was languishing in Italy we have been having quite a lively correspondence on the matter. We are extremely lucky to have such a sound man at the helm of the finances. The late Bishop could not have been more judicious when he made him a trustee. They were very close, I understand."

"They had the same interests," said Giles. "And at the end, I think my brother-in-law was one of the few people he could bear to see."

"If there were any justice in the world, then it would be your brother-in-law being installed as our new Bishop," Lord Rothborough said. "I did put his name forward, but it seems that neither good sense nor the virtue of continuity can prevail in this present climate of enthusiasm."

"I'm not sure he would have accepted," said Giles. "He is not ambitious, and my sister thinks the Palace a very inconvenient house."

"She's quite right about that!" said Lord Rothborough, smiling. "I am hoping that the new man and his family will realise that soon enough and move into Red Lodge, perhaps – then the Palace might be put to use for the University. There are ten children, I believe! Ten! But then these evangelicals are often monstrously fertile. One feels rather for their poor wives!" Lord Rothborough shook his head. "Have you met him yet?"

"No."

"But you are going to the installation?"

"No, I have not been invited. Captain and Mrs Lazenby will do the honours for the Constabulary. But I am going to the Guildhall."

"I shall be interested to know what you make of him."

"You've met him?" Giles asked.

"Just him, and only briefly. I cannot say I was impressed. He is glossy – that is the best word I can think for him. He may be perfectly sincere, of course, but with these people who make such a noise about their convictions, it always seems like insincerity to me. But he may grow into his mitre. He is only five-and-forty after all. He is very young for such a great preferment. One can but live in hope." Rothborough shrugged.

At this moment, James Bodley, Lord Rothborough's trusted manservant, who had been set to watch Carswell, came in.

"Master Felix is awake again, my lord," he said, "and has asked for his dinner."

"Excellent news! I hope you kept him to his bed."

"Yes, my lord."

They went up to his room and found Lady Maria already in attendance. Carswell was sleepy and a little bewildered, but clearly in better spirits than previously.

"I am trying to persuade Mr Carswell to stay here at least a week, Papa," Lady Maria said.

"Very sound," said Lord Rothborough. "And we will get Hall to have another look at you tomorrow."

"There would be no point. I intend to be back in Northminster tomorrow night. I am quite myself again, I assure you, my lord."

"That remains to be seen."

"Mr Harper is expecting me at the Infirmary," Carswell said. "I have slept it off, whatever it was!"

"Perhaps Mr Harper might confirm if you are fit for work?" Giles said. "You trust his opinion, I know."

"You would take leave if he told you to, I think," said Lord Rothborough.

"Yes," Carswell conceded.

"Then I shall write to him straight away," said Lady Maria. "And tell him what he must say."

Carswell looked alarmed at this for a moment, and then realised he was being teased.

"Mind you," Giles said, "given what you have done for him, Lady Maria, it is a favour overdue."

"What have you done?" said Carswell.

"My sister tells me that Lady Maria's efforts have swollen the Infirmary funds to almost monstrous proportions," Giles said.

"I simply wrote a few letters," she said. "And by no means all of them hit the mark."

"Enough of them did. It was quite an undertaking, I understand."

"Yes, she was at it night and day at one point," said Lord Rothborough.

"It was simply that I didn't care for Italy. I was homesick. It was a great comfort to write to people at home. I never feel quite myself except when I am here, to tell you the truth. And to be able to do something useful in Northminster even when I was away – it was a pleasure, and I shall always be grateful to Mrs Fforde for her suggestion that I do it. It was all her idea."

"She would say the opposite – that it was all yours," said Giles.

"It was a happy meeting of minds, certainly," said Lord Rothborough. "Your sister, Vernon, writes the most delightful letters – they were cherished in Florence by us all."

"Mr Harper has said nothing of this to me," said

Carswell. "If he had, then –"

"Oh, it's not supposed to be generally known," said Lady Maria. "And I hope, Major Vernon, you have not been gossiping about the town about it," she added with a mocking wag of her finger.

"No, of course he has not, Maria," said Lord Rothborough.

"I do not want to be put up as a plaster saint for writing a few letters, really I do not!"

"Then you had better go and break some hearts at the races," said Giles.

"Oh yes, that is a much better reputation to have," said Lady Maria.

"If we are allowed to have our races this year," said Lord Rothborough. "The new Bishop has preached against horse racing on several occasions, I understand. If he will not have the Bishop's Feast nor a ball, then I fear he will be agitating against that as well."

"He could not do that, surely, Papa?" said Lady Maria. "Entirely stop them, I mean?"

"He could if he puts his mind to it. Some of the land that the racecourse is on belongs to the Palace demesne – the far eastern quarter, to be precise. The rest is ours, of course, but it would be a poor sport without that stretch. Then where would I find anyone to take the tenancy of it, and make a living from three quarters of a racecourse?" He sighed. "But what will be, will be. Perhaps racing in Northminster is just another of those old customs that must fall away in the face of modern opinion. There are probably many good arguments to support our new Bishop, not merely that there is too much worldly pleasure in it. I am sure, Vernon, you can tell me what a den of thievery it always is."

"There will always be an element of that, yes," said Giles. "But I don't think that's reason enough to abolish it. If these occasions are carefully supervised and the availability of strong drink is regulated, then it could be a respectable entertainment."

"I am with the Bishop," said Carswell. "It is an excellent source of broken necks, if you ask me."

"You have clearly never won a shilling on a horse that no one else fancied," said Giles. "One that you picked out for its beauty alone."

"Yes, quite!" said Lady Maria. "Ah, here is your dinner, Mr Carswell. We shall leave you and go and eat ours."

So they left Carswell to his food, with Holt in attendance, and went downstairs to the family dining room for their own dinner.

Afterwards, Giles went back up to see Carswell, and found him sitting by the fire.

"Are you sure you will be fit to go tomorrow?" he said.

"I think so," said Carswell. "I managed to eat. There was a point I felt I would never eat again."

"And you cannot think what might have caused this?"

"Unless I accept that there are such things as phantoms, I can only think it must have been something I ate or drank that night. But you and the Colonel had exactly the same dinner – and nothing seems to have afflicted you. Or has it? Did you not say you had a curious dream?"

"Yes, but that's common enough, surely. You were raving, and violently ill. I was not."

Giles wondered if he should mention the strange experience he had had in the carriage coming back from Holbroke, and then decided it would only fuel Carswell's confusion. What he had felt was merely a waking dream brought on by fatigue and the feelings the previous night had stirred up in him. He added to that the business of being at Holbroke itself, where Laura had died and had been laid to rest.

"Perhaps there was something in the food to which I have an antipathy," Carswell went on. "You know how it is sometimes – my father will not touch rhubarb, for example. It gives him dyspepsia. But there is nothing I know of that disagrees with me."

"Except too much wine," Giles said, "if you don't mind me saying."

"No. But how much did I have, in truth? It was not an excessive amount."

"Perhaps we should write down exactly what it was we ate," said Giles, taking out his notebook.

"Artichoke soup," said Carswell, with decision, "and then trout, and then there was woodcock with that red sauce, and the fricassee, with kidneys and mushrooms."

"Madeira sauce," said Giles.

"Then there was a custard tart," said Carswell, "and blue cheese, walnuts and pears."

"Quite a feast for a so-called simple dinner. Now, did you try everything that was served?"

"Yes. Did you?"

"Yes, but I only had a small amount of the fricassee. I don't much like kidneys."

"You don't? It was excellent."

"And you took most of it, I remember that now."

"But such things have never disagreed with me before. Neither kidneys, nor mushrooms. I am very fond of mushrooms. Sukey used to –" He broke off and stared into the fire. "No, it cannot have been the food, it cannot, nor the wine, although I freely admit I may have taken too much. It has to be something else which we have not as yet identified. I was running about the woods in my shirt, for the Lord's sake, and I have no recollection of how I got there! None at all. It is utterly mystifying. Tell me what your dream was."

"I cannot see that it has anything to do with it," said Giles, and then said, "it was my wife. I dreamt I was in Heaven with her, and my sister, who died when I was five. I suppose I have had such dreams before. It is just that I do not remember them. This one was very vivid, yes, but I do not think it can have any relation to what happened to you."

"But I was dreaming, after some fashion. I cannot have been awake. I must have been sleepwalking or some such. The women I spoke to – the woman in the grey cloak and then the Queen of the Fairies – how could they be anything but dreams, no matter how real they seemed?"

"The Queen of the Fairies?" Giles said.

"The girl with the red hair," Felix said. "I was sure she was the Queen of the Fairies. I knew she was. Which is nonsense and therefore strictly for the realm of dreams which are always entirely void of reason."

"But full of desire," Giles could not help remarking.

"Why should I want to see the Queen of the Fairies?"

"You said she was beautiful," said Giles. "And she is famous for seducing young men, is she not?"

Carswell pressed his hands to his face.

"I am going back to bed. And I will let Harper look me over. You are right. He is the only medical man I trust, and he may have some good ideas."

Chapter Four

"Not the most pleasant return to work for you, Mr Carswell," said Mr Harper, drawing back the sheet that covered the body. "He died at just after six. As you can see, I performed a double amputation of the lower legs, at a little after two this morning, and the prognosis seemed quite good for recovery. However –" Mr Harper hesitated, as if annoyed with himself for his failure. "That was not to be. Of course, I did consider preservation of the limbs, but given the extent of the damage to the upper abdomen, not to mention his head –" He broke off again. "What kind of godless savage would attack another being like that? In all my years, I do not think I have ever seen anything like it."

"It is certainly methodical," said Felix, throwing off his coat and beginning a more thorough examination.

"I shall leave you to your work," said Harper. "My notes are here on the side, with his clothes. But be careful you do not over-strain your own health, Mr Carswell. I would have prescribed another day or two's rest if this business had not reared its ugly head."

"No, I shall not," said Felix. "And I am quite well again, sir, I promise."

Left alone in the icy basement, Felix wondered for a moment if this was entirely true. The extent of the injuries displayed by the dead man was shocking. He had thought he was to some degree hardened to such sights; but handling one of the amputated limbs, feeling for himself the shattered bones beneath the flesh, and seeing the regularity of the contusions where the assailant's weapon had repeatedly battered his victim, made him nauseous.

He took a nip of brandy and forced himself to continue his investigations, accompanied by loud peals of bells from the Minster. He was glad when Major Vernon joined him.

"Has anything come to light about how it happened?" he asked.

"Very little. We know where he was found and when, but I have not turned up any witnesses. Where are his clothes?"

"All there, on the table. I've not had a chance to examine them."

"Quite understandable," said Major Vernon, going to the table and starting to look through them. "Any idea how it was carried out? What kind of weapon?"

"Metal. Crowbar or poker, something like that. Very systematic. I should draw a diagram, should I not?"

"That would be helpful," said Major Vernon, handing him his notebook and a pencil.

Felix set about drawing an outline of a human body and then a rough schema of the contusions.

"There might be a little residue in evidence – a little rust, perhaps," he said. "But there will, no doubt, be blood and skin on the weapon, should we find it."

"And if it has not been wiped clean," Major Vernon said. "Interesting – his pocket book is still here. With four sovereigns in it, so not a common robbery."

"That will pay for his funeral," Felix said.

"His clothes seem quite decent," said the Major, picking up one of the brown leather top boots. "Well made. Not cheap."

"Here," said Felix, handing Major Vernon the notebook. "As you can see, the blows are all in the same direction, perhaps from someone swinging the bar with their right hand, and then working their way around, taking a limb at a time. Quite precisely done."

He mimicked the movement, swinging an imaginary rod.

"He must have been restrained in some way. Any sign of

that? Marks on his wrist?"

"Not that I can see," Felix said. "The odd thing is that his ribs were left intact."

"And that is odd why?"

"Because that would undoubtedly have killed him. A punctured lung and he'd been on the slab."

"What a very risky enterprise," said Major Vernon.

"Where was he found?"

"All Hallows Square. By the gate to the churchyard – but I doubt it was done there. It's well lit and no one apparently saw or heard anything untoward last night. It's a very quiet spot, and respectable, in a shabby sort of way. But I am sure someone will have seen something."

"He's a big fellow, and heavy. It wouldn't be very easy to move him."

"I imagine there would be more than one person involved in this," said Major Vernon, holding up the man's shirt. It was almost entirely covered in blood. "No initials to go on. But it's been well looked after."

He walked back to the uncovered body on the slab.

"What happened to his ear?"

"I think there may have been an earring. Ripped out, presumably because it would identify him."

"And what's that, on his left shoulder?" the Major said. "A birthmark? A bruise?"

Carswell came and peered at it. He reached for his hand lens and smiled briefly.

"It's a swallow, I think," he said. "That's one for your collection."

"I've never seen a swallow before. Nor such a discreet one."

"You just haven't caught a man with one yet," said Felix. "The odds are that this man has some criminal connection, given the circumstances in which he was found. Especially since they left the money on him."

"And that orders were being followed?" said Major Vernon. "And a degree of discipline imposed from above, perhaps? Opportunists would have taken the money."

At this moment one of the nurses came in.

"Mr Harper has ordered tea for you, sir," she said. "In your room."

Felix was glad of this excuse to be able to cover the body and leave.

"Ought I to be worried that you have a room here now?" Major Vernon said, as they went along the passageway.

"Wait until you see it," said Felix. "It is more a cupboard than anything. There is not enough of it to undermine my allegiances. Tolley, who is only the surgical dresser, has a much better room."

But when they went in, he knew Major Vernon had a point. He had been spending a great deal of time of late at the Infirmary. There had been a spate of interesting cases, and Harper had not hesitated to call him in.

The room, small though it was, had gained an accretion of his belongings: the shelf above the narrow bed bore a heap of new books on surgical techniques, while on the opposite wall he had gone so far as to pin up a mezzotint of a Scottish landscape that had caught his eye in the booksellers a few weeks ago. He even had a dressing gown to hand as well as a supply of fresh linen.

He poured out the tea.

"Harper is an excellent man," said Major Vernon, taking his cup of tea. "I have your letters for you. Here." He reached into his pocket and produced a large pamphlet along with his letters.

"What is that?" said Felix.

"A sermon by our new Bishop," said Major Vernon. "To commemorate his installation today."

"Oh, that's why the bells have been going infernally long," said Felix, taking the pamphlet and the letters from him.

The sermon, printed in dense text and unreasonably long, was accompanied by a full-page illustration entitled "Morning Prayer." This showed a wealthy, handsome young couple, their two small offspring and their female servants, gathered in a luxurious and fashionably fitted-out breakfast room. The father was reading from a large Bible and even the spaniel seemed piously disposed to listen to the word of the Lord.

"They are being distributed about the entire town," said Major Vernon.

"For use in many privies," said Felix.

"I rather fear so," said Major Vernon.

"The man is a fool," said Felix. "What a waste of money! What is his intention with this? It smacks of currying favour."

"If he had wanted that, he would not have cancelled the Bishop's Feast," Major Vernon said. "That will not have been popular. No, from what I hear of him, he wishes to deliver Northminster from evil. He may have a point, of course, if men are being left for dead in the street." He swallowed down the rest of his tea and went to look out of the window, resting his tall frame against the wall.

"Only one man," Felix pointed out.

"True. But one in that condition is quite enough."

"Do you have any idea who might be behind it?"

"Yes," said Major Vernon. "And I shall go and see what he has to say – if anything."

When he had gone, Felix sat down and looked through his letters, accompanied by the seemingly endless peal of the Minster bells.

There was little to surprise Felix in his correspondence. There was a long letter in his mother's tiny hand that he put aside for later. He looked in hope for a letter from Ireland, although it annoyed him that he should. It was a foolish, sentimental habit, and most unprofitable.

~

It had been a while since Giles had cause to visit the premises of George Bickley, liveryman, noted horse-doctor and timber-merchant, and it was clear his circumstances had changed for the better. In the first instance, the timber yard and stables were now surrounded by a fine new brick wall and the business seemed to have taken over the property next door. There was a freshly painted sign at the gate announcing in bold letters, "George Bickley, Building Contractor." Given how fast the city was expanding, this was a shrewd move, and it was clear that the new enterprise was doing well. A respectful young clerk, black-coated and not the least bit flash, received him in the front office and took his name straight into Mr Bickley.

"Not in the stables this time, Mr Bickley?" he said, when he was shown into his office. The last time they had met, Bickley had been in his shirt sleeves, massaging a thoroughbred. "I was hoping to get a glimpse of some of your fine animals." Today he was wearing a black frock coat and sober waistcoat and looked like any other man of business in Northminster, except for the knot of coloured ribbons in his buttonhole, and his jewelled cravat pin.

"Pressure of business, Major Vernon, unfortunately," said Bickley, getting up from his desk. "But for old friends, I am still available. In fact," he said, "let us go down there now. Are you looking for something in particular?"

"I might be tempted," Giles said.

"Did they put your stipend up?" said Bickley.

"No, I came into a little money," said Giles. "Of course, I should probably be investing it somewhere..." He shrugged. "But old habits die hard. A superlatively good horse is a pleasure it is hard to do without when the means present themselves."

Bickley smiled and opened the door to an external staircase. "This way, if you please, sir."

They crossed the busy yard, where carts were being loaded with supplies and men were running purposefully back and forth.

"You have a great deal in hand these days," said Giles.

"Sometimes Lady Fortune is kind," he said, and they turned into the immaculate stable yard. "Now, I have a three-year-old bay that might be just the thing for you. A friend of mine, about your build, thought him a good mount. An excellent hunter." He signalled to the stable boy. "Bring out Duke!"

"I don't suppose either of us have much time for hunting these days," Giles remarked.

"You still have your hunting," said Bickley.

"You might call it that."

"That's why you are here, I take it," Bickley said after a moment.

Giles declined to answer, and instead, as the horse was brought out, went forward and began to make a show of assessing his points.

"Very handsome indeed," he said. "Let's see him walk."

He went back to Bickley and they stood for a moment or two while the boy led the bay about the yard.

"Yes?" said Bickley.

"An excellent animal."

"But you're not here for that?"

"I've just been at the Infirmary," Giles said, after a moment. "There's a man there who has been savagely assaulted. Respectable-looking man, well-turned-out, good pair of boots."

"Robbed, I suppose?"

"No, that's the strange thing. There were four sovereigns left in his pocket."

"Why do you ask me?"

"He has the look of a sporting man. I wondered if you might know him."

"Why would I? This town is full of strangers."

"He has a tattoo on his shoulder, a swallow. And he's well built, like a pugilist. I know you have some connections in that world." Bickley made a slight incline of his head. "What puzzles me is how a fine, strong man like that ends up in such a condition, as if he had been entirely unable to defend himself."

Bickley said nothing but strolled forward, and taking the reins of the horse from the stable boy, began to extravagantly caress the horse's neck.

"I cannot help you," he said. "And why you think I might –"

"An earring ripped from his left ear," Giles went on.

Bickley shook his head.

"You'd be better asking this fellow for yourself than me," he said after a moment or two.

"I would, but he's dead," said Giles.

"You're wasting my time," Bickley said, pointing at him. "Why do you think I might have anything to do with this?" He gestured around him. "Why would I? With all this, eh? Your suspicions, sir, I don't care for them. Take him back in, Jack," he said to the boy.

Giles looked about him, at the immaculate yard, and then at Bickley, the king of his domain. He might have been wearing a frock coat, but it still had the sharp cut of the flash sporting man. Bickley had been a noted pugilist in his youth, and the intelligence was that he was still deep in the sport, with a stable of fighters in training.

But he was canny and careful. It had been impossible to make a concrete connection to him. And so it was with various other nefarious activities about the city. Bickley operated constantly at the margins of legality.

To Giles' certain knowledge, he had lately, in addition to

his horse dealing and doctoring operations, opened a large gin palace, according to the new fashion for such places, with glittering lights and dangerously cheap, strong gin. This had created a significant source of public disorder, as the many factory hands flocked there and then drank themselves into states of imbecility or savage-like violence.

As the horse was led away, Bickley strolled back to Giles, and said in the mildest tone, "Take care where you stray, Major. And what you say. You may have your notions, but they are mistaken."

"Thank you for your help," Giles said, and turned and walked away.

As he approached the gates, a man who was just entering caught sight of him, raised his hat to him and called out, "Good morning, Colonel – didn't know you were expected this morning! Come to look over the new filly for the boss? She's a sweet creature, don't you think?" But as they drew close to one another, he looked sheepish. "Sorry, sir, I took you for –"

"Yes?" Giles said.

"No one, sir," the man said, putting up his hands. "Good day to you," he finished and hastened away towards the stable yard.

~

Giles made his way back to Constabulary Headquarters. As he turned into the ancient inn yard, he wondered for how much longer the old building would stand. The lease on the place was due to expire in six months, by which time the combined County and City Constabulary would be moving to their new buildings on the Leeds Road. What then would become of the ancient Unicorn Inn, with its wooden galleries and sloping floors? A relic of an earlier time, it would be demolished and replaced by something modern and convenient, but lacking in character.

"Great progress, sir," said Inspector Rollins, coming to greet him. "We likely have our man. Picked him up at the corner of Bell Street. Had to have a bit of a chase to get him, but Constable Planter brought him down. He was running away weapon in hand and took immediate flight at the sight of a uniformed man."

"He's admitted to it?"

"Not yet. Do you want to talk to him, sir?"

"What's his name?"

"Horatio Baxter. He's downstairs."

"That's a memorable name. Is he known to us?"

"I didn't recognise him. And you are right about the name. Drew me up a little when he said it."

"An alias, then?" Giles said. "Let's have a look at this weapon first."

Rollins took him into his office.

"It's a nasty object, I must say, sir."

It was a wrought iron rod, about the size of a poker, but with more heft to it. It did indeed seem to match the description of the object that Carswell had described, and when he took it to the window and examined it, there seemed to be stains upon it.

"This needs to go down to Mr Carswell," said Giles. "At once."

"Certainly, sir. I'll take it myself," said Rollins.

Giles went down to the holding cells and asked the duty sergeant where he would find Horatio Baxter.

"Number three, sir," he said reaching for his keys.

"Has he said anything?"

"No, sir. Do you want to speak to him?"

"Not yet."

Giles went to the cell door and looked in through the

bars. A pair of wary eyes met his. Horatio Baxter was sitting on the bench, his fingers knotted. Giles took in what details he could of the man's appearance. He was dressed in shabby, dirty clothes, but his figure seemed at odds with his dress. He was well-built and adequately nourished. His hair was neatly cropped, and he was clean-shaven. He was also sporting a gold earring in his right ear.

Giles signalled back to the Sergeant to open the door.

"Stand up for the Superintendent!" barked the Sergeant.

Baxter pulled himself up reluctantly and his wary stare became contemptuous. The incongruity of his clothes became more obvious. He stood well, almost defiantly. Evidently he was not afraid.

"Take off your coat, Baxter," said Giles. The man complied, but slowly. He held it out almost as if waiting for an invisible footman to take it.

"Sergeant, take that," said Giles.

Beneath the coat he wore a ragged shirt of blue flannel.

"And the shirt, if you please."

He did this with the same contemptuous lethargy as before, revealing the taut upper body of a professional fighter. There was no doubt he would have had the strength to wield the iron rod with all the precision and force necessary to inflict such a set of devastating injuries. This was the body of a man who kept himself in good form, a man with great self-discipline. He was also a man who had put on dirty clothes for dirty work, Giles thought.

"Turn about now," he said.

The man obeyed and as he did, Giles caught sight of a mark on his right shoulder, which despite the dim light of the cell, seemed to be a tattoo.

"Now, is that a swallow?" he said. "That's very curious."

Baxter spun about, attempting to hide his back from him.

"Don't go asking about what don't concern you!" he exclaimed, attempting to grab back the stinking blue flannel shirt from the Sergeant. "I did it! That's all you need to know! You take me and hang me for it now! I wish you bloody would!"

"Do you wish to confess to something, Mr Baxter?"

"Yes, yes, I do. I want it all signed and sealed. All regular."

"And you think I will believe such a confession, Mr Baxter?" said Giles.

"You will have to believe it. You got me, didn't you, with the rod in my hand? Isn't that enough?"

"Give him back his shirt, Sergeant. You and I, Mr Baxter, will talk later."

"I want to talk now," said Baxter.

"And tell me a parcel of lies?" Giles said. "No, Mr Baxter, you can wait your turn and tell me the truth."

~

Giles left Baxter and went out into the yard, just as an open carriage drew up containing Captain Lazenby in his plumed hat and silver lace. He was returning from the service at the Minster, accompanied by his wife dressed in equal splendour, but looking pale and anxious.

"We are only passing through," Lazenby said. "Catherine needs to go home and rest if we are to manage the reception at the Guildhall later. The crowds were a little too much for her."

Giles suspected that Mrs Lazenby was with child again. Lazenby had been energetic in that department. There were twins born last year and three others in the nursery before that.

"I feel so silly," said Mrs Lazenby. "It was such an occasion and I really did not wish to miss it."

"I don't like crowds much either, Mrs Lazenby," said Giles. "How was the sermon?"

"Oh, so very passionate," said Mrs Lazenby. "Most inspiring. He seems such a sincere, good man. Oh, and Lord Rothborough was there – I never met him before today, but he was so kind when I was all at odds. And he said such things about you, Major Vernon, I think you would be horrified – no, that is not the word, what do I mean? Embarrassed."

"I hope you took it all with a pinch of salt, ma'am," said Giles, smiling.

"I did not," said Mrs Lazenby. "And I do hope he talks about my husband like that!"

"He does," said Giles. "Now, may I just steal him for a moment, ma'am? I have a little business that I need to discuss with him."

"Yes, yes, of course. In fact, why do you not just stay here, Henry?" she said to her husband. "I am better driving home alone, than sitting here waiting for you to rush through what should not be rushed, am I not?"

Captain Lazenby agreed to this plan, and he and Giles went back into The Unicorn, where Giles briefed him on the morning's events.

"So you think this Baxter is using an alias?"

"Yes. And he wishes to feed us a particular version of events."

"Even though it may hang him?"

"I think he is following orders. He is a loyal soldier prepared to sacrifice himself."

"Loyal to whom?"

"That is the large and troubling question. And one which we will need to devote considerable resources to answering, I'm afraid. I do not like any of the implications of this business. The injuries that were sustained were both brutal and considered. We are dealing with something well-organised and dangerous."

"Then do what you must, Major Vernon. But I beg you to be discreet, for the sake of public morale."

"I shall do my best," said Giles.

"Will you be at the Guildhall later?" said Lazenby. "You were invited, I think?"

"I may look in, if I have time," Giles said, without any real intention of going. After all, the riddle of Horatio Baxter and his willingness to be hanged seemed hardly likely to be solved by making small talk and listening to dry speeches.

He left Lazenby and was just approaching the main entrance gates when he noticed the figure of a woman standing in the street beyond. She was wrapped in a large drab shawl, but she was also wearing a pale, expensive bonnet with a white lace veil covering her face. He realised he had noticed her first from the corner of his eye when he had been talking to Mrs Lazenby in her carriage. The dark shawl was a poor match for that bonnet, and as he approached her and she moved away a little, the shawl flapped to reveal a pale lilac coloured dress that looked as if it were made of silk.

She seemed, in short, to be a great deal more fashionably dressed than Catherine Lazenby, so why was she standing at a dirty corner, covered with a dull cloak, outside the Constabulary Headquarters?

He gave her an enquiring glance, and she lifted up her veil and looked back at him as he approached. She was young and handsome, but appeared troubled.

"Can I help you?" he said, and crossed the road, at which point she picked up her skirts and began to walk briskly away.

Chapter Five

"Why are you following me?" she said, stopping halfway up the alley. She had a touch of the local accent in her voice.

"Because you wanted me to," he said. "And I wanted to know why you were waiting outside a police house."

"There's no law against stopping outside, is there?"

"No, but I wondered why you were waiting there. Did you want to speak to someone? Perhaps you have some information for us."

"No," she said. "I was just stopping."

"Are you certain about that?"

"Who are you, anyway?"

"Someone you can trust." She laughed at that, somewhat bitterly.

"I mean it," he said. "Why were you waiting there so long? You were there at least a quarter hour. I may be able to help you."

"I doubt it."

"Then why?"

She bit her lip and glanced around her.

"Who are you?" she said.

"My name is Vernon," he said.

"And you're one of them."

"By which you mean, the police?" She nodded. "Yes. And I know it's hard for you to trust me, but believe me, I will help you if I can. And I sense you want help of some kind."

Again she seemed to hesitate, her gloved hand twisting her expensive bonnet ribbon.

"Yes?" he said.

"Have you..." she began but then moved away, as if she

meant again to give flight. He reached out and caught her arm.

"Something is troubling you," he said. "Tell me."

She wrested free.

"All right, all right. But not here. And it will cost you. You need to look as if you are one of my punters. You look as if you could afford me, anyway. I don't pick 'em up. They come looking for me. They know where to find me."

"Oh, I see," said Giles, considering the usual haunt of high class prostitutes in Northminster. There were not many, and they kept to a very particular locale so that they could not be confused with other, less expensive women. They worked carefully and cautiously and rarely found themselves up before the Justices as a result. "Peacock's Lane, I suppose?"

She shook her head and he realised there was a degree of finish about her that not even the most expensive whores he had seen in Northminster displayed.

"No, not there," she said. "Nothing like that. Here, come with me. It will look better if you come back with me. If anyone asks, you are here for your health, yes?" He could not help smiling at such a euphemism. "Now, give me your arm."

He did so, and she led him into a secluded quarter of the town, with which, he realised, he was only slightly familiar. It was a district of plain, old streets, neatly kept up, but quiet, and all in the shadow of a venerable old parish church, St Mary Magdalene. That such a saint should watch over a previously undiscovered nest of vice seemed appropriate, to say the least. If that was where she was leading him, of course, rather than into some elaborate trap.

He decided that it was a risk worth taking.

Producing a key from her pocket, she stopped outside a gate in a wall and unlocked it, and then led him down a long, twisting lane, with high walls on both sides. They emerged into a court in which sat a couple of neat houses at right angles to each other with window boxes, painted shutters, and lace glass cloths decorating every window. There was even a fat tabby sunning itself on a well-scrubbed doorstep. It did not look like a bordello.

"Who –?" he began.

"No questions here," she said. "You are here for –"

"My health, yes," said Giles.

She stooped to caress the sleepy cat before unlocking the door. That cat would have made an excellent witness if it could speak and agreed to co-operate, Giles thought. But what cat was ever so obliging?

The house seemed to be in just as good order inside as out, and as they went in, she slipped off her shawl and revealed the full elegance of her figured-silk dress. She rustled ahead of him, up several flights of stairs and then along a passageway. There seemed to be no one about and he could hear no signs of life.

She unlocked another door, and took him into what appeared to be a sitting room, with a bedroom adjoining. It was elegantly furnished, with floral papered walls and matching curtains. There were prints on the wall of a mildly salacious nature. He noted how she locked the door behind her but left the key in the lock.

"Have some wine," she said, pointing to the table where a decanter and glasses waited. "Make yourself at home."

"Thank you. Will you have a glass?"

She crouched by the grate and lit a fire that had been carefully laid.

"It's always so cold in here," she said. "Half a glass. A cigar?" She offered a box from the mantelshelf. "These are... oh, I don't know. They are very good ones, I think." He shook his head.

"It would look better if you smoked."

"Do they all smoke?"

"Yes, usually."

He sipped his wine, and watched her take off her bonnet. She carried it away to the bedroom and then returned to take the glass he offered. She stood nervously and twisted the stem in her hand, glancing at the door.

"Are you waiting for something?" he asked.

She put her finger to her lips to silence him and sure enough, a moment later there was a tapping at the door.

"Kate?" said a woman's voice, refined enough but with a touch of the local accent about it. "Are you in there?"

"Yes, but I'm engaged."

"With who? At this time?"

"With the Colonel. I told you he was coming to town. Remember?"

The door handle rattled as the woman outside attempted to come in.

Kate went to the door, unlocked it and opened it a chink. "So don't be bothering us," Kate said to the woman outside.

The woman put her fingers about the edge of the door as if she meant to force it open.

"Now, Miss," said the woman. "I hope you are behaving yourself."

"Go away," said Kate, closing the door as if she meant to trap the woman's hand. "It's all as it should be. He knows all about it!"

"We shall see about that," said the woman, pulling away her hand as Kate smartly shut the door in her face. She stood with her back to the door, exhaled, and turned and locked the door again.

Then she crossed the room and came and stood very close to him, almost pressing herself against him.

"If I had any sense at all then I wouldn't have –" she said softly.

"Tell me," he said, wondering now who 'he' was and indeed who was the Colonel.

"In bed. I'll tell you then. Afterwards. And you'll have to do it, Colonel. She'll be watching us now."

"What?"

She pointed at the wall where, only just discernible as a result of carefully chosen paper, there appeared to be a peep-hole. He was surprised, having thought such things were found only in scandalous novels and in the fevered dreams of young ensigns.

So he kissed her with what he considered was sufficient fervour and moved to begin unfastening her bodice. "And there is one through there?"

She nodded.

He wondered how easy it would be to simulate the necessary act convincingly for the eyes of the spying woman. Kate, however, seemed determined that it would not be a simulation. She was loosening his cravat now, with practised fingers, and in a moment, she had tossed it across the room. She stood smiling up at him; her fingers were raking through his hair and although he knew this was a routine, her every movement as studied as a dancer, it was impossible not to desire her pretty face and figure. Her hand was now on the fall of his breeches and brushed across his fly.

Play-acting might be impossible, he thought. He was tempted – more than tempted. She was such a conundrum, playing the whore so professionally, in the manner he recalled from his youthful experiences when he had degraded himself and the women he had paid for their bodies. Those memories alone ought to have made him step away. Yet her uneasy pacing outside The Unicorn, her evident anxiety and the secret that she was so reluctant and yet determined to divulge – that weakened him more than the basic physical desire he felt for her.

After all, he was well used to continence. It was a fact of his life. He had got on very well for some time, barring one or two lapses. But now he could not think straight. He could only think that he wanted what was on offer.

In the minutes that followed, as he found himself naked on top of her in the bed, all too acutely aware of the spy on the other side of the walls, he knew he was taking pleasure from the situation for all the wrong reasons. It was meaningless for both of them, yet that sense of transgression, the wilful disregard of all the rules he attempted to live by, gave him a potent sense of liberation. He could not help but rejoice in the sheer sensual pleasure of this beautiful, vulnerable woman, who so obligingly lay beneath him and allowed him to exert himself with such fierceness upon her.

There was still a part of him which wished she would fight him or push him away and slap him and sit and cry in misery at such vile treatment, or better still berate him. He would have let her flog him raw with curses. But she did not. She endured it, as he supposed she endured all such encounters, and worse, for the sake of her bread. Worse still, it did not make him stop. He continued and took his pleasure to its natural conclusion.

It was pleasure that lasted only a moment. His heart beat faster and his limbs fell into a soft, warming paralysis as he climbed off her and lay beside her, catching his breath.

"Can you really help me?" she said, softly. "Can you?"

He rolled onto his side and looked at her. She had wrapped herself up in the sheet. This sudden modesty made him feel wretched.

"I will do all that I can," he said very quietly, wondering if they might be overheard as well as overlooked. "Why were you at The Unicorn? Is there someone there that you were worried about?"

She swallowed and said in a whisper, "Yes, and he'll be hanged."

He had known it before she said it. That sudden clarity of thought that he had often experienced after congress had made him glimpse the connection.

"Wrongly hanged?" he said.

"No, no, he did it, but he wasn't the only one, and he wasn't –"

"Horatio Baxter?" Giles murmured.

"That's not his name," she said.

"I thought not," he said. "What is his real name?"

"I can't tell you that," she said.

"Because you don't know?"

"I wish I didn't," she said. "No, because I can't. There are rules."

"I see," Giles said. "So your Baxter –"

"He did what he had to. He had no choice. He had to do it."

"That doesn't excuse him."

"I know, but, but –" She took a deep breath. "There are rules."

She broke away from him and got out of bed. She crossed the room and reached for a chemise hanging on a hook. Then, just as she slipped it over her head he saw it – a mark on her lower back, just above her buttocks. It looked familiar. A swallow?

"What's that on your back?" he said. "A tattoo?"

She came back to the bed and sat down beside him.

"My little swallow," she said. "I did that for him. He has one like it, so I thought... but he was so angry when I showed him. I thought he'd be pleased. What a fool I was. Women always are for men. I bet you have made a few women cry in your time, Colonel."

"I regret to say that's probably true."

She touched his cheek.

"It's no use," she said in a whisper. "I shouldn't have said anything. Forget it. There isn't anything to be done. He's going to hang and I'll never see him again."

"Where was that done?" he asked, putting his hand on her back, feeling with some pleasure the warmth of her flesh. "Can you tell me that, at least?"

She leant against him, and sighed.

"Oh God, this was a mistake. Such a mistake. I can't tell

you anything –"

"But you want to. You want to help your man. If he was forced into it, then there is help for him. It won't be easy, and you will need all your courage. But I think you have courage. You would not have done so much otherwise. So, who made your little swallow for you?"

"A woman up Bank Street way. You'll find her mostly in that fancy new gin place. You know the one I mean?" He nodded. "Ask for Eliza. But don't say it was me who –"

"No, I shan't," Giles said.

She slipped away from him and began to get dressed again. He noticed that she stood in front of the peep-hole to do this, as if to indicate to the watching eyes that the transaction was over. He gathered his own clothes and also began to dress.

"You can come and go as you please?" he said after some moments had passed. She had resumed her pretty figured silk and was at the glass of her sitting room rearranging her hair.

"Yes, mostly I can."

"Then I can meet you again – if they think I'm your Colonel?"

"Yes, if we take care."

"He'll want to see my money," he said. "Your governor or whatever you call him."

She shook her head and said, "The Colonel's on a tab."

"Lucky fellow."

She turned and gave him a quizzical look.

"No, lucky you," she said. "You married?"

"No." She looked as if she did not believe him. "Is your Colonel?"

"Of course."

"And he was introduced here by...?" She shook her head. "He has a tab. He must be a favoured customer."

"He spends a lot here, and elsewhere. The more he borrows, the better it is for business. You know how it works."

"Then not so lucky," said Giles, fastening his cravat, "to be in hock."

"He's a fool. But he wants what he wants. And his wife has expectations of an inheritance, so he gets credit."

"And why did you say I was he?"

"Because you'd pass for him. Tall and thin, and there's something about the look of you."

"When shall I see you again?" he said, taking up his coat. She helped him into it, with a sort of wifely care, smoothing his lapels and brushing away some imaginary dust. No doubt she did this with all her customers. It probably encouraged them to tip her.

"I go to Fairfaxes some afternoons," she said. "I might go tomorrow, but I might not be alone. About three." Fairfaxes was the largest and most expensive draper and silk merchant in the town. "I'll see you to the door – and don't you dare come back here without my say-so, will you?"

Chapter Six

Felix came back from the Infirmary to the Northern Office at about noon, and found Tom O'Brien sitting on one of the benches in the hall.

"Mr O'Brien! I hope you haven't been sitting there long. Do you want to see the Major? I am not sure where he is, or when he will be back."

"As a matter of fact I came to see you, Mr Carswell," he said. "If you have a minute?"

"I do," said Felix, somewhat surprised. "Shall we go down to my –"

"If you don't have a corpse down there," O'Brien said.

"Not at the moment," said Felix. "There will be one presently. I expect Major Vernon will want to talk to you about it."

"Dear God," murmured O'Brien, following him downstairs to his basement laboratory.

Felix lit the gas lamps and O'Brien stood looking awkwardly about him.

"I was going to have a whisky," said Felix, feeling as awkward as O'Brien. They had not seen each other for many months.

"Scotch whisky?" said O'Brien.

"Of course," said Carswell, putting the bottle on the table along with two tea cups.

"Just a small one," he said, "or Mrs O'Brien will smell it on me."

Felix nodded.

"And how is Mrs O'Brien?" Felix ventured.

"Very well, very happy, as a matter of fact," said O'Brien.

"Which is why I'm here. We had a letter this morning." He took his cup of whisky and sipped it. "Not bad."

"Thank you," said Felix, taking a larger gulp of his own, rather anxious now. "So, a letter – from Ireland?" he added.

"From Ireland," said O'Brien. He sighed. "There's no way of putting this but bluntly: Sukey is getting married."

Felix finished his whisky and said, "To whom?"

"A doctor," O'Brien said. "He's an old friend of the family. They've known each other since they were children. He was married to a distant cousin, and she died, poor soul, and there are three little ones needing a mother. He's doing well, and there's money in his family, and he's a decent man as far as I can judge. It's a good thing for her."

"Oh, I'm sure it is," said Felix.

"I thought you would want to know. It seemed only fair."

Felix nodded, but the contents of the letter were now beginning to affect him, like a blow sustained in the heat of a fight that does not start to smart until the fight is over. He felt a mixture of fury and pain. Sukey was to be married to some nameless Irishman, settled in his profession and with a good income. A widower with small children.

His mind conjured her up, surrounded by this other man's brats, her skirts constantly tugged at. He saw her living in some ugly, provincial house, in some rain-soaked corner of Ireland. He saw her lying in bed, being subjected to the conjugal embraces of this respectable widower. How on earth could she submit to that? He had asked her so many times to be his wife, and had always been rebuffed, being told every time that she would never marry again, that it was a wretched prison. But here she was, apparently willingly doing the very thing she swore she would not do. Was she in love with this man? Did she love him in a way that she had not loved Felix?

"And it's quite definite?" he managed to say.

"Quite," said O'Brien. "I thought I should tell you. Given that –" He broke off and finished his morsel of whisky. Felix grabbed the bottle to offer him another, but he covered the cup with his hand. "It's for the best," he went on. "It may not feel that way now –" He looked at his watch. "I'd best leave you to your work, if you have a new case in hand."

"I'll tell Major Vernon you were here," Felix managed to say as he departed.

Felix stared at the whisky bottle and the dirty cups. He was tempted to take another cupful and with some difficulty recorked the bottle and put it away. He sat down and began to work on his notes, while waiting for the cadaver to come from the Infirmary. It arrived, in due course, but he did not yet have the permissions to begin the post-mortem, so he sat, pen in hand, unable to muster any further concentration, his mind instead vacillating between deeply unpleasant thoughts of Sukey's marriage and the bizarre experience he had had at Ardenthwaite. On both subjects he failed to come up with any sort of explanation that satisfied him. Every question led only to far more unpleasant questions.

He was glad to hear the sound of footsteps on the stairs, and when Lord Rothborough came in, he could not help smiling at the sight of him.

"Ah, you are never happier than in the company of a cadaver," said Lord Rothborough, indicating the covered table.

"No, I am glad of the interruption," said Felix.

"Then you will not mind if I carry you off to the Guildhall?"

"That wasn't quite what I had in mind."

"No, I am sure it is not, but I think one of your patients might need you. Mrs Lazenby? This morning at the Minster she was on the verge of passing out. She is –"

"With child again, yes," said Felix. "She is not my patient. Peterson is looking after her."

"If he were, he ought to have told her husband to desist," said Rothborough, "or at least employ rational means! Lord knows, how hard is it? She is a delicate looking thing – one would think –" He broke off, smiling at himself.

"A new campaign, my lord?" said Felix. "Family limitation?"

"Yes, quite. And the higher classes need to set the fashion, instead of treating their women like brood mares, in the name of morality. It is quite disgusting! It would be better coming from you, though! If only you would stir yourself and write a paper or two. Or even a well-placed letter?"

"I ought to find as many occupations as I can," said Felix. "And you are right. It is disgusting and dangerous."

"You are alarming me now, Felix. I am not used to being agreed with."

"I'm still not myself," Felix said.

"That business at...?" he said.

Felix nodded, then pushed his hands through his hair.

"And Mrs Connolly is apparently getting married."

"Excellent," said Lord Rothborough. "We must send something to mark the occasion."

"What?" said Felix. "I think not."

"Her marriage is no slight against you," he said. "Your affair is long over. She is being sensible, as you should be."

"I need something to eat," Felix said, not wishing to pursue the subject. "And I will come to the Guildhall. But I need to go and change."

"Naturally. We will go by way of your lodgings. Have you succeeded in taming that landlady yet?"

"Major Vernon is working on her. The coffee is a little better, but as for everything else –"

Lord Rothborough nodded and gave him a sympathetic squeeze of the arm.

"It should be a fine affair at the Guildhall. There will be some good music. I made some suggestions in that direction. If we are not allowed to have a ball, at least we can have music!"

~

There was a time when Felix would have done anything in his power to avoid appearing at some great function at the Guildhall in the company of Lord Rothborough. The close physical resemblance between them had been a mortification he could not lightly bear. But that afternoon he scarcely felt it. It was almost a matter of indifference to him. He did not care what people might say or think. He gazed about the room, looking for familiar faces and enjoying the spectacle, which was as dazzling as Lord Rothborough had suggested.

The great reception rooms of the Guildhall had been decorated for the occasion with great swags of gilded leaves and the celebrated artificial flowers that were one of the notable products of the town, like the silk ribbons that hung from the garlands in equal profusion. Long tables groaned with elaborate food – fancy cakes and raised pies, and as a centrepiece, a stuffed peacock, its feathers on display. If the intention was to show the new Bishop where the real power in Northminster lay, then it could not be doubted.

"Have you ever eaten peacock, Lady Maria?" Felix said.

"No, and I never shall!" she exclaimed. "What a horrible fate for such a beautiful creature."

"It would scarcely feed a family of three by the look of it," said Lord Rothborough. "I have eaten peacock at Oxford, and also swan."

"No, Papa, you did not, surely?"

"It was a tad stringy, as I recall. I'd rather have a good French roast chicken," said Lord Rothborough.

There was a little stir by the door and a troop of fur-gowned, chain-bearing aldermen entered. They were accompanied by a tall, thin man in clerical dress, and his equally tall, thin wife, clad in black.

"The man of the hour," said Lord Rothborough. "And

his lady."

"I would have thought she might change her dress," Lady Maria said. "That black gown was all very well for the service, but for an afternoon party? But perhaps she knows how well she looks in black. It is certainly striking."

"I am sure you are right, Maria," said Lord Rothborough. "Otherwise it is false humility, and that is never pleasant. Oh, that's interesting," he went on. "The lady in blue, Maria, do you remember her?"

"Is that Lady Blanchfort?" said Lady Maria.

"Most unexpected to see her here. I wonder if Richard is here. That would be delightful! Sir Richard is a great friend of mine, Felix, but time and tide has swept us apart. But I should like nothing better than to see him."

Lord Rothbourgh set off towards the lady in question.

"I think he may be disappointed," said Lady Maria. "I heard a rumour that they are no longer... well, you know, Mr Carswell. It is very sad."

"Who is that with her?" Felix said, his mouth drying, as he caught sight of a face under a large brimmed bonnet, and a hint of bright red hair. "That girl?"

"Her daughter, I suppose," said Lady Maria. "I think there is only one. She is an heiress – the bank, of course. I am surprised she is here. They say that Lady Blanchfort keeps her under lock and key, to keep her away from fortune hunters. Mr Carswell, are you quite well?"

Felix was tugging at his collar, struggling to breathe and feeling as if there was no air in the room. He felt both sick and faint.

"Excuse me," he managed to say, and began to make his way, as best he could, through the crowd in the opposite direction from where the Bishop and the Aldermen had come in. He was sweating violently and his knees were on the verge of giving way under him. He could scarcely credit what he had seen under the broad brim of that bonnet.

He managed to reach an empty room. It appeared to be some sort of waiting room – long, high and narrow, with benches pushed against the walls. He forced open the window, gulped down some cold air and flung himself down on a bench, throwing his head between his knees in an attempt to stop himself passing out. Then, feeling that he was about to vomit up the little iced cakes upon which he had so thoughtlessly grazed, he sat cautiously upright again, and found himself facing none other than his Queen of the Fairies.

He threw out his hands, not to greet her, but palms forward, to defend himself against any sort of magical encroachment.

"Go away!" he exclaimed. "Whoever, whatever you are, go away!"

But she did not move. She stood there, observing him, looking for all the world as if she were flesh and blood.

He closed his eyes, and leant back, trying to steady his breathing, thinking about who he might consult about the violent disorder that seemed to have afflicted his mind. Because she was not real. She was the vision of that night, on her pony, with her milk-pale, freckled skin and fiery hair.

"Please," he added, not yet opening his eyes. He felt the brief touch of her hand on his forehead. "No, no..." he said, and attempted to push her away. He opened his eyes, and saw she was crouching over him.

"Let me help you," she said, "please. I could not before, but now –"

Again she reached out to touch his forehead, and he caught her wrist to stop her. He would have let go except that he was aware of her pulse beating strongly, which seemed excellent evidence for her corporeal reality. He counted the beats, and at the same time looked up into her face, which was only a matter of inches away. He could feel her breath and see the veins and blood beneath the surface of her pale skin.

"You are not well, sir," she said, moving away. "Let me

find you some help. This time I will not desert you, I promise. I would have come back for you, but –"

He got to his feet and went again to the window to catch his breath, before turning back to her.

This time he found he could look at her objectively. She was indeed real – a young woman of eighteen or so, small in stature and delicate in build, elegantly but simply dressed. On the ground was one of her gloves, and he stooped to pick it up. It was made of delicate glacé kid, dyed perfectly to match her pale blue dress.

"I am quite well, I assure you," he managed to say, holding out the glove to her. "But thank you for your concern."

When she had finished drawing on her glove again, she said, "May I ask you a favour?"

"Of course," he said.

"You will not say that you saw me that morning. If we are to meet, and perhaps we might, then we will be perfect strangers."

"That seems more than sensible," he said.

"I had better go or I will be missed," she added, and left the room.

~

Giles looked around the glittering crowd at the Guildhall, and wondered which of these men in their frock coats and aldermen's robes were paying for their pleasures in that discreet establishment near the church of St Mary Magdalene.

It was a very sophisticated operation, that much had been clear, and a professional one. How long had it been operating, and how had he entirely failed to discern any traces of it? He was angry with himself. He ought at least to have had some vague inkling of such a thing. It should have been on the list he kept in his desk of areas of concern and fields for future action. Such a large, luxurious den of vice – how had this been invisible to him? And was this business entirely confined to prostitution or were any of the concomitant vices involved? How far did this organisation reach into Northminster?

And who was the Colonel with his tab? The Colonel he had impersonated, the Colonel he had been mistaken for at Bickley's yard. Was he none other than Colonel Parham?

A footman was offering glasses of champagne. He drank one rather quickly, his mind churning. Why had this dead man turned up now, with the swallow on his shoulder? Why had the body simply been left on a public street? That was carelessness on somebody's part, surely.

Was something that had been carefully hidden now surfacing? Secrets and conspiracies could not be kept for ever. Human nature saw to that. Perhaps the operation had grown unwieldy or the person in command had become complacent and ceased to be vigilant over the secret. Or had the commander in chief become a tyrant and provoked mutiny among those under him?

Was rebellion, like the warm breath of spring stirring up the green shoots in the fields, making visible that which was previously invisible? Kate, in her wretched yet comfortable slavery, had been driven to desperate measures. What she had done was reckless and courageous. She had said frustratingly little, it was true, but the evidence of her surroundings was enough to raise the alarm.

Had Baxter, with his prize-fighter's physique and clear self-discipline, been an ordinary client to whom she had inadvisedly given her heart? That seemed unlikely, given the man's behaviour in the prison. It was possible he worked for the same organisation, and had been given the use of the whores as a benefit in kind.

Had he given his heart to her? Would her name even

mean anything to the brute who had wielded the iron bar? Giles hoped it would, and then wondered if Kate, that simple, plain name, was merely another alias, and that nothing he had seen was as it seemed.

Now, standing in the Guildhall with a glass in his hand, he began to take the measure of his true foolishness. He had made a spectacular blunder. He had been an utter fool in allowing her to seduce him.

It was late afternoon, and the great rooms of the Guildhall were filled with soft, spring sunshine, which covered everything with a glaze of warm gold. There was a concert in progress – a small orchestra and a pianist were playing and he could see his sister and Lady Maria sitting side by side listening intently to the music, looking calmly angelic.

Nearby sat the Bishop and his lady, both in black, looking like the Spanish King and Queen from some old story, perhaps Ferdinand and Isabella themselves. The Bishop had that morning proclaimed that Northminster was a sewer of vice. Who could deny that, Giles thought, when it seemed that the man in charge of purging it was so weak and wilful, taking his pleasure in the guise of searching out the truth?

He took another glass of wine and drank it, without pleasure, almost without tasting it. He felt he ought to remove himself forthwith, that he could not stay in this place which now uncannily resembled that great reception room he had seen in his dream about Laura and Lizzy that night at Ardenthwaite.

An air of unreality seemed to settle on him, as if he could not trust his eyes. He could still smell the girl's skin, and feel her warm flesh pressed against him, and it made him feel nauseous. In the meantime the pianist seemed to be playing the same rapid succession of notes again and again, as if in some sort of frenzy. The notes pounded his head, and reminded him of his own unconstrained assault on the girl, how he had used her, like an object, and how she had submitted in silence.

Then among the women standing listening to the music, he seemed to see Laura again, as real as she had been in the carriage that afternoon driving from Holbroke, but now she was not tender. She looked across at him and he saw the cold, hard look of reproach in her eyes. She was as angry as Kate had been submissive.

He turned away quickly, closing his eyes; the light in the room was unbearable, his head was aching and he felt he was going to be sick. He had not had a violent headache in some months but it seemed he was under attack now.

"Giles, are you quite well?" He heard his sister's voice, and felt her hand on his arm. "You look terrible."

"Just one of those heads –" he managed to say.

"Oh no, not again!" she said. "Lamb has gone for the carriage, which is just as well. You are coming home with us."

Chapter Seven

Major Vernon's headaches had been a cause of concern for some months in the wake of his wife's death, but he had not complained of them recently. Felix, still feeling unsteady himself after the events at the Guildhall, was shown into a cool, darkened bedroom at the Treasurer's House, where Major Vernon was lying flat on his back.

"Did you take some laudanum?"

"Yes, three grains at about seven o'clock, I think. Sally made a note of the time. And about a quart of green tea, which does seem to help."

"And how is it now?"

"If I lie still, in the dark, it is bearable. I think I have slept a little. What time is it?"

"About nine-thirty. I'm sorry I was not here sooner. I was at the Infirmary. I probably should not have gone; Mr Harper said as much," Felix said, sitting down in the easy chair by the bed. "I had a strange turn at the Guildhall as well." He reached for Major Vernon's hand and took his pulse, then stretched out and felt his forehead.

"You did?"

"Your pulse is regular, and there is no sign of fever at present. Have you felt unnaturally hot or cold?"

"No, not this time. Just nausea with the pain, as previously. It seems to be passing, though."

"You had better stay put, just to be on the safe side," Felix said. "Was there anything else, sir, anything you cannot quite account for?"

"Why do you ask?"

"Because of what happened to me at Ardenthwaite –

what I thought I saw. Some of which was explicable, it seems, but the rest of it – my strange behaviour, for example. Why I was driven out of my bed. I wonder if this is not related."

"Why?"

"Because you have not had one of these attacks for some time, and yet, here we are, a week after that business, which had me raving. Perhaps there was some effect on you after all. As if we had been poisoned."

"That is quite a wild hypothesis."

"Yes, but I have no other. It might be some substance that acts at different rates on different physiques and temperaments. I did drink a great deal that night. Perhaps that hastened and intensified the effect."

"A poison that could make a man act out of character? Are you aware of any such thing?"

"No, but there is plenty I don't know. I shall have to pursue it."

"Or, we put the fear of God into Parham," said Major Vernon, sitting up quickly, "and see if will he admit to anything! Oh dear Lord –" he exclaimed and lay down again, wincing.

"Steady now, sir," said Felix.

"Yes, yes," said the Major, breathing hard and closing his eyes. "I will not attempt that again. A poison of some sort. It makes a great deal of sense. I admit I've not been quite straight with you, Carswell. I think my mind has been playing tricks on me as well, and I certainly have not been –" He broke off and covered his eyes. "Today I think I lost my mind. I can't describe it as anything else."

"At the Guildhall?"

"No, earlier," said Major Vernon. "Of course, I may be clutching this straw you are offering me in order that I might excuse myself."

"Excuse yourself?" said Felix.

The door opened and Canon Fforde came into the room,

somewhat to Felix's relief, as he did not at that moment have any real wish to become a father-confessor to Major Vernon. The gravity of the Major's manner was alarming enough.

"I'm sorry to interrupt," said Canon Fforde, "but could you spare a moment to look at Tom, when you are done, Mr Carswell? He has – well, you will see soon enough."

"Is he all right?" Major Vernon said.

"I'll come at once," said Felix. "I've disturbed you enough, sir. Rest is the best remedy for this. Oh, and more green tea, perhaps?"

"I'll get some sent up," said Canon Fforde.

They left the Major in peace, and went upstairs to the boy's room. Tom was sitting on the bed in his shirt sleeves.

"It's nothing, Papa, truly," said Tom.

"Show Mr Carswell," said Canon Fforde.

The boy reluctantly took off his shirt. A makeshift bandage made from a handkerchief covered his upper left arm.

"It's nothing really, sir," said Tom, covering it with his hand, as Felix went to examine it.

"I'll be the judge of that," he said, gently removing the boy's hand.

"How's Uncle Giles?" said Tom.

"A little better," said Felix, untying the handkerchief to reveal a dirty wad of torn cloth soaked through with blood and pus. "Oh, that's charming," he said, and ripped it off. Tom cried out of the shock of it. "And this is – how did you manage to do this?" Felix said seeing, the wound beneath in all its glory. It was about three inches by two, and suppurating nicely.

"I must have cut myself on something," Tom said.

"You never could lie, Tom," said Canon Fforde. "Which I suppose is a sign of goodness in you."

"It's a wonder you haven't got lock-jaw and a fever," said Felix, picking up the candle and peering at it. "What did you do? It looks like you have been stabbing yourself with rusty needles."

"They weren't rusty," said Tom.

"You *were* stabbing yourself with needles?" said Canon Fforde. "Why on Earth...?"

"All the fellows at school are doing it," said Tom. "It doesn't usually go like this. I don't know what went wrong. Murray and Barnes – theirs came out perfectly."

"Doing what?" said Canon Fforde.

"Giving yourselves tattoos?" said Felix reaching for his bag. "Yes?"

"Like a sailor?" said Canon Fforde. "And that's the fashion at Rugby these days? Oh Tom, you –"

"Like a criminal," said Felix. "You should talk to your uncle about it. He's been collecting criminal tattoos."

"He has?" said Tom with awe in his voice. "Murderers and so forth?"

"So you want to look like a murderer!"

"No, Papa, it's not like that."

"And just because the rest of the herd is doing it, doesn't mean you have to!" Canon Fforde went on. "You have your own mind – at least I thought you did."

"It's not following the herd. It's a way of being distinguished. And it is Latin – it's a motto," said Tom.

"I don't care if it's New Testament Greek, it's still wilfully stupid!"

"I thought about having something in Greek. Or the Fforde family crest," Tom went on. "Hibbert has a whole coat of arms."

"If he hasn't died of blood poisoning yet!" said Canon Fforde.

"If I cauterize it," said Felix, "that should clear up any difficulty. It is just as well you have a strong constitution. Another day or two – well, who knows?"

"You could have lost your arm!" said Canon Fforde. "Or died on the table having it amputated! When your mother hears about this –"

"Does she have to know?" said Tom.

"Yes," said Canon Fforde.

"I'll never hear the end of it," said Tom.

"That's the least you deserve, Tom Fforde! Yes, cauterize away, Mr Carswell!" said Canon Fforde. "If that's what it takes."

With which he left the room, slamming the door behind him.

Tom look crestfallen. Canon Fforde was not easily angered.

"Will it hurt much?" he said, as Felix began to lay out his tools.

"I may be able to spare you that," he said. "It may be that if I clean it up properly and put a decent dressing on it, it will heal up of its own accord. But you are very lucky, you know. It is on the cusp of being extremely dangerous."

Tom nodded and glanced again at the closed door.

"I didn't think he would be so..." he said.

"He's just concerned about you," Felix said, dabbing the wound with alcohol. Tom screwed up his face.

"Perhaps you should cauterize it. Perhaps I deserve it. It's just that all the fellows are doing it, and I didn't want to look like a prig and say no, did I? And Hibbert's looks magnificent. They say women like them extremely."

"Women?" said Felix, smiling. "Aren't you a bit too young to be thinking about that?"

"I'm fifteen! And I bet that you –" He broke off, suddenly remembering himself. "Excuse me, sir."

"No, you're right, I did," Felix said. He had been fascinated by the fair sex from about the age of fourteen. At the same time he could easily imagine a fad for tattooing seizing the first year medical students at Edinburgh. At sixteen, he would have been first in line with the needles, especially if it was reckoned to make a man out of a lad. That had always been the great endeavour: to pass for men, when they were nothing but raw boys.

Chapter Eight

Although it might have been agreeable to unburden himself to Carswell, it could do no general good, Giles decided. It was just as well he had been called away. As for Carswell's theory that they had both been poisoned, either deliberately or inadvertently, he realised he could not use that to absolve his sins. The only way he could put this thing right, or at least find some means to justify his actions, was to bring down the secret edifice of corruption that he had stumbled upon.

He got up early, long before the household was stirring, finding his head much relieved. He left a note of thanks to his sister and brother-in-law and set out for the offices of the Northern Investigation Office.

No one was yet at work there, and he had the liberty to scour about for paper and pursue his thoughts unhindered by company. There was on the top floor a reasonably sized garret, well-lit by skylights, but inconveniently accessed by an awkward stair and a door half the height of a man. It had been decided that it should be used for lumber, and being generally disregarded and overlooked, it suited Giles' new purpose perfectly. He wanted a place apart, firstly to store and process what information came to hand, and secondly for the sake of discretion. It was important that they, whoever they might be, remained perfectly ignorant that the police had any inkling that they were being observed, to the extent that the police might even appear to be fools to them.

The fewer the people who knew what he was doing, the better.

Having furnished himself with a ream of foolscap, a thick, soft, carpenter's pencil, a box of pins and a cone of twine,

Giles knelt down on the bare boards (for there was no table nor chair) and began to make a list of likely criminal personalities. Some of these were easily eliminated as simply not being clever enough to oversee a business of such complexity as that brothel.

The one name that kept recurring was that of George Bickley.

So he wrote Bickley's name in capitals and pinned it on the wall.

On the adjacent wall he arranged papers inscribed with various names: Kate, Horatio Baxter and 'Swallow' (for the dead man). Then, he drew a rough approximation of the swallow tattoo, and pinned it above the names, and joined them with lengths of twine.

He sat on the floor and gazed at this for some time, wondering where best to begin, and indeed how, until he was interrupted by the sound of Carswell's voice, calling out for him on the landing below.

"I'm up here!" he called back.

A moment or two later, Carswell came in through the door, bent double as was necessary.

"What are you doing up here?" he said.

"Thinking."

"And you are recovered?"

"Certainly."

"I was just at the Treasurer's House. Your sister is beside herself. Your note –"

"I will speak to her, I promise. And I am quite myself again, I assure you. Anyway, I am glad to see you. I need to talk to you. We have a great deal to do."

"I was hoping for some breakfast first."

"You didn't eat at College Street?"

"She was still abed, and I wasn't going to risk her letting rip at me for waking her up, as if breakfast were a privilege and not what we pay our shillings for. I swear I am moving into

The Black Bull. It may be more expensive, but at least Mrs Wilkes will not let us starve!"

"You are right," said Giles, hauling himself up. "We will go and see what the Wilkes can do for us. We have left it too long. Holt has been grumbling at me. He will much prefer The Black Bull and I need to be comfortable. We have a lot of business coming our way."

"You won't be comfortable in here," said Carswell. "You can barely stand up. Were you looking for something?"

"No, this is our new campaign headquarters, strange though it may seem."

"Very strange," said Carswell. "What campaign is this, then?"

"I will tell you at breakfast."

Carswell was right about The Black Bull. Mr and Mrs Wilkes were more than happy to accommodate them, and at a reasonable price. The establishment was an old-fashioned, respectable one, in a quiet street near the Minster, and Giles was given a large sitting room with a small bedroom adjoining, with which he could not find fault. Carswell had a similar arrangement nearby, perhaps rather grander in scale, for Mrs Wilkes seemed to have some ancient connection with Holbroke and was inclined to dote on Carswell.

They were soon sitting down to a generous breakfast under a sunny window in Carswell's new quarters. The coffee was almost as good as that made by Mrs Connolly, but naturally Giles did not mention that.

"So what is this campaign?" Carswell said. "Are we at war?"

"Very possibly."

"Against who?"

"That's the great difficulty. I am not sure at present."

"I saw Bickley's name up there."

"He is a strong candidate."

"Because of the manner of the attack on our dead man?"

"There is a little more to it than that. There is a man in the cells at The Unicorn who has confessed to the attack, but it is a pat confession and I think he is using an alias."

"So you think someone else did it?"

"No, I think he probably was involved in it, but he is confessing to order. He is a willing victim, making a sacrifice for the greater good, perhaps – or taking a punishment."

"How on earth do you make someone do that?"

"He's no common criminal. He has self-discipline. He has, I think, a powerful allegiance to this unseen group – the sort of loyalty a good soldier shows his regiment. I will have to wear him down and see if I can get him to tell me more. Furthermore, he has a swallow tattoo, just like our dead man – and he was touchy about it."

"Oh," said Felix. "That's interesting. So they are from the same group? One executing the other, and the other taking the blame for the execution? I still find it hard to believe a man would do that. The instinct for self-preservation is so strong."

"Of course, I may be wrong that it is an execution," said Giles, refilling his coffee cup. "There may have been a quarrel between them over something else entirely – a woman, perhaps – and Baxter, our self-confessed murderer, killed out of anger, and this is his lieutenants turning him over to the authorities."

"They must be very confident that he won't say anything out of line, then," Carswell pointed out.

"True," said Giles. "Or they have a low opinion of our intelligence, which is justified, given that they have been operating under our noses for the Lord knows how long! And I have missed every sign of it!"

"You said it has been carefully concealed," said Carswell. "And this city is large enough, and getting larger all the time. Where do you think they might be at work?"

"Prostitution, in the first instance," Giles said. "Expensive prostitution. Women kept in luxurious duress and their actions spied upon, and by implication, the clients spied upon as well, giving them the perfect opportunity to increase their income by blackmail. If a man can afford to patronise such an establishment, he will have a reputation as a respectable man to maintain, and can be prevailed upon for more money. But I cannot believe that it is just prostitution, although there seems to be plenty of money in that. Gambling is another sure-fire way of raising large amounts of money from those who can not resist the lure of a wager."

Giles got up from the table and looked out of the window. There was a pleasant view of the rooftops, and in the distance the spire of St Mary Magdalene and the quiet neighbourhood where Kate had taken him.

"So where do we start?" Carswell said.

"We need to cultivate our sources," said Giles. "But in the first instance I need you to scour your books and find out what it was that made you so ill – and then, we must consider if it was deliberate or inadvertent."

"I have had a few further thoughts on that, last night," said Carswell. "There are some interesting cases in the annals involving a mould on rye bread that seems to have driven entire villages mad, to the extent of burning innocent women as witches. Perhaps there was something we ate that had some analogous effect upon us."

"We got off lightly, then," Giles said. "We have not burnt any witches yet."

~

Felix returned to the Treasurer's House and was able to reassure Mrs Fforde that her brother was quite well again. He did not tell her, however, that he was embarking on a war against an unseen criminal army, as that would alarm her.

Instead he told her that they had settled in The Black Bull and that they had given up their lodgings in College Street.

"A good idea. That place was quite disgraceful. I wonder how you both stood it so long, especially after being so well looked after by Mrs Connolly in Silver Street. It's a pity that she decided to go back to Ireland, but her duty to her parents must come first."

Felix managed to smile at this as best he could, and turned the subject swiftly to Tom.

He found his patient in the garden with his sister and another boy of about the same age as Tom, whom Felix did not recognise. They were playing with Celia's fancy rats. Tom was lying flat on his back on the lawn, encouraging the rats to crawl up and down him.

"I think they can smell the blood, Mr Carswell," said Celia. "This is Edmund Hughes, by the way. Edmund, this is Mr Carswell."

Hughes jumped up politely and put out his hand to Felix.

"How do you do, sir?"

"Are you related to the new Bishop, Mr Hughes?"

"Yes, he's my father."

"Welcome to Northminster, then. You have found yourself the best company here, although don't let Tom talk you into anything involving needles and ink."

"Edmund is not so stupid," said Celia. "Oh quick, Tom, get Dorcas, quick!"

"I'll get her," said Edmund, dashing after the rat and scooping it up. He presented Dorcas to Celia with a grin. She looked delighted at this act of gallantry.

"I need to have a look at your arm, Tom," said Felix. Tom got up from the grass. "Shall we go inside?"

"Will you be all right for a minute or two, Hughes?" said Tom. "Celia, don't bore Hughes, will you?"

"I shan't be bored at all," said Edmund, petting the other rat. "I want to see the trick with the rope again, Miss Fforde;

do you think we could get them to do it?"

"Oh yes, let's!" said Celia, and they went down the garden as Tom and Felix went back into the house.

"He doesn't go to school," said Tom. "His parents think that the public schools are hotbeds of satanic corruption. Honestly!" He stripped off his jacket and shirt. "It hardly hurt at all last night. You did a splendid job on it."

"Thank you," said Felix, taking off the bandage and removing the poultice. "It does look as if it is improving."

"Do you think there will be a scar?"

"Yes, probably."

"Oh good," said Tom.

"I thought it was a tattoo you wanted."

"A scar is just as good. I can pretend I got it fighting a duel one day. Like yours," Tom said.

"She nearly had my eye out," Felix said.

"I know! What a... and to think she was sitting in my mother's drawing room pretending to be so good, and all along she was a murderess. But that's always it with really wicked people – they are extremely good at pretending to be good, don't you think?"

"They are clever liars, yes, often enough."

"I can't lie to save my life," said Tom. "It's a nuisance."

"You won't have a career as a master criminal, then."

"No, it seems not. I shall have to think again!" he said. "Oh hello, Papa," he said, seeing his father come into the room. "Look how much better it is!"

"Goodness, that does look better. Thank you, Mr Carswell."

"Mr Carswell is a genius," said Tom. "Perhaps I should go in for medicine. What do you think, sir – would I be suited to it?"

"I don't know," said Felix. "But if you are anything like your sister who has a natural talent for dissection and anatomy, then perhaps."

"Where is Edmund?" said Canon Fforde.

"In the garden with Celia."

"I have to send him home."

"He only just got here," said Tom.

"He was only supposed to be bringing a message."

"Can't he stay for luncheon?"

"Apparently not. His tutor is here to fetch him. He has lessons."

"In the holidays?"

"Not for Edmund."

"How grim," said Tom. "I was going to take him over the Bishop's Meadows and up the valley to see the new viaduct being built."

"That will have to wait, I'm afraid."

"I don't think he ever has any fun."

"I'll go and get him," said Canon Fforde, going out into the garden.

"Have you been up there, yet, Mr Carswell?" said Tom. "The viaduct – it's going to be magnificent when it's done. Thirty-seven arches with spans of thirty foot each! What a feat!"

"I must go and look at it. Perhaps you should go in for engineering," said Felix.

"I had thought of that," said Tom. "I suppose a gentleman may do that now. And it would be a grand life, wouldn't it? There are moves to build railways across all the Americas, and the Continent is under way already, of course. Think how many viaducts and tunnels and bridges they will need. I should look into it more, should I not? I am far better at mathematics than Latin, after all."

Canon Fforde came in with Edmund and Celia just as Felix had finished redressing the wound, and the unfortunate Edmund was then delivered back to his tutor.

"Poor fellow," Tom said, pulling on his coat. "Papa, what do you think of my going in for engineering? I should have to leave school next year, of course, which would be wretched, for the First XI will never win anything without me."

"I am quite happy to take you from any place that encourages you to mutilate yourself," said Canon Fforde.

Chapter Nine

"Has Baxter said or done anything of note?" Giles asked the custody sergeant.

"No, sir, not a peep out of him all night. Didn't eat any of his breakfast, though."

This was unusual. Even if the breakfast provided for those detained overnight in the cells was not luxurious, it was adequate – a quarter pound of bread and a mug of tea – and it was usually devoured. The unfortunates who found themselves in custody were always hungry. Indeed, there was always the danger of making custody too attractive – there were those who courted arrest for the chance of a night inside, with food on offer. As a result Captain Lazenby had recently reduced the bread allowance to three ounces; Giles had fought him on the point, although it was not really his place to do so. However, he got the quarter pound restored. He had done this by arguing it was quicker, easier and ultimately less wasteful to split a pound loaf into four. He had been surprised that Lazenby had let him have his day over it. Perhaps the reduction had already been making his conscience queasy and he had been grateful to have Giles object.

"To understand crime, surely we have to understand the people who commit it?" Giles had said to him, aware he was speechifying. "And hunger is the commonest cause of petty crime. If we send them out again with their bellies full, they will perhaps desist from it for a little while at least."

He had gone away himself thinking that he did not really know how it might feel to be so hungry that he was tempted to steal just to satiate himself.

Horatio Baxter was not hungry – he had lost his appetite.

He was not a starving thief desperate for a crumb, even in the direst circumstances. He was a man who had admitted to murder, had been desperate to admit to it, but who refused to offer an explanation. Keeping to such a line would be like carrying a most exhausting burden, with no relief in sight except the hangman's noose.

Giles decided he would make him comfortable with coffee and a confiding tone. He would disconcert him with kindness.

He went to speak to the Inspector in the duty office.

"Get Baxter some hot water and some clean clothes. Shave him if that's what he wants, but don't leave him alone with a blade. I want the clothes he's wearing labelled and put in the evidence room. Then take him upstairs to the interview room, by the Chief Constable's office."

"Yes, of course, sir. I'll arrange for one of the clerks as well, shall I, sir?"

Giles nodded and went upstairs.

About twenty minutes later, Baxter was brought into the interview room, wearing a clean shirt and a pair of regulation trousers. He looked as if he had accepted the offer of a shave and although he was handcuffed, he held himself well. If he had been a recruit presenting himself, Giles would have been pleased at the sight of him. It was unfortunate that he had decided to join another sort of organisation entirely.

Giles decided to risk removing the cuffs. He had shown no signs of resistance or flight. He unlocked and removed them himself, and he detected a flicker of surprise on Baxter's face. The man then flexed his wrists and stretched his fingers, obviously glad to be free of the restraint.

"I think things will go easier without those," he said. "Sit down, won't you? Coffee?"

He poured out two cups and pushed one across the table to him, while taking up the other and sipping it.

"What's this?" said Baxter.

"You said you wanted to make your confession," said Giles. "This is your chance."

Baxter nodded and took up the coffee. He drained the cup in one go and then grimaced.

"Now, we have to begin with a few formalities," said Giles. "Full name."

"Horatio Baxter."

"No other names?"

"No."

"Place of birth?"

"Kirkwhelland, Lancashire."

"Where is that near? I'm afraid I don't know it."

"It's by Carnforth. About five miles north."

"I see. Father's occupation?"

"What?"

"His trade?"

"Oh, farrier."

"Church or chapel?"

He glanced over to Giles, puzzled again by the question. Giles repeated it. "Church, I suppose."

"Where you were magnificently baptised Horatio? After Nelson?"

"Yes, sir. After the great Admiral. My dad –" he broke off.

"Was an admirer. Yes, I understand. You didn't take your grandfather's name as well? That's the usual thing, isn't it?"

Baxter hesitated and said, "Not in our family." It was not said confidently. It had an air of invention about it.

"Date of birth?" Giles said.

"June seventeenth, eighteen twelve."

"And when did you come to Northminster, Mr Baxter?"

"Last summer."

"For what reason?"

"Mill hand."

"Mill hand? Where?"

"Taylor and Webb."

"Spinner or weaver?"

"Spinner."

"There are no spinners at Taylor and Webb, Baxter. It's a finishing house. And you don't look like a mill hand."

"What does a mill hand look like?" countered Baxter.

"Not so well built. You are used to having meat for your dinner, Baxter, not bread and broth. I don't think it's your line."

"It was just temporary," he said, with a shrug. "Between things. A man takes what he can find."

"Very temporary, since they don't employ spinners. So do you have another trade? Farrier's son that you are, you must have a bit of knowledge in that area."

"No," he said. "I didn't take to his trade."

"What did you take to, then?" Giles said mildly.

"Day labouring. Whatever I could get. Wherever. I've been about a bit. Here and there. Why does it matter?" he said. "I told you what I did –"

"You have told me nothing of substance!" said Giles, getting up. "Nothing of the truth of it. Now, listen – you will answer my questions honestly, Baxter, all of them, or I will continue to ask them until Kingdom come! And why are you afraid of a few questions anyway, a great brute of a fellow like you?"

"I'm not afraid, sir," he said. "I know what I've done and I'm prepared to take what is due. If you want to hang me now, sir, you can!"

"But I can't, Baxter, that's the point. I can't even send you in front of the magistrate to utter your plea of guilty until you tell me the truth. If you want to hang, then you have to talk. And it seems to me you want to hang, though God knows why."

Baxter looked away, massaging his wrist, and at the same time folding and then straightening his fingers. In any other situation Giles would have thought he was about to attempt to strike him.

"Just answer my questions," he went on. "That will be the easiest way. Just question after question and then it will all be over, and you can find your peace. For that is what you want, I think. Peace."

There was a long silence and the man looked up at Giles.

"I can't," he said.

"You can and you will," said Giles. "But I am going to let you think on it for a while. You will see soon enough it is the right thing to do." Giles took the drawing of the swallow tattoo and laid it on the table in front of Baxter. "We found this mark on the dead man's shoulder. Just like the one on your shoulder which so disturbed you when I saw it."

Baxter pushed the paper away.

"That's got nothing to do with anything," he said after a moment.

"We will see about that," said Giles.

~

Fairfaxes, on reflection, was perhaps not the best place for a discreet rendezvous. It was a large, fashionable shop, with a wide street in front of it, where a few carriages were usually drawn up.

Giles chose to wait across the street a little before three. He saw Kate come up the street and go in. She had changed the dull shawl of the previous day for a less work-a-day item, but there was nothing about her appearance to attract any attention.

The old codes of dress, which had clearly put all men and women in their particular place, were no longer to be relied upon. A respectable woman might dress like a woman of the streets, and vice versa.

So he waited until she came out again and then made himself obvious to her, without actually hailing her. She passed him and then set off down one of the streets to the side of the shop. He followed her, and she slowed her pace to allow him to catch up.

"This way," he said, steering her to the entrance of a lane which issued into the street.

"Where are we going?"

"Somewhere safe."

"No, I have to get back."

"You're not going back. It's too dangerous."

"It's dangerous if I don't go back. I was chancing it coming out today as it is. If I am not back within the hour –"

"We need to talk, Kate, talk properly. If you want to help your man, you have to talk to me, and that means you need to be away from that house. Yes?"

"I have to go back."

"Well, you can't, because I am going to arrest you for soliciting. I am taking you down to the Police House." He reached for his cuffs. "I can walk you down there in these, like a common whore."

"No!" she said, looking horrified at the sight of them. "Don't do that, for the Lord's sake! If they find out that I was –" She broke off, and Giles was pleased that his threat had hit the mark.

"Then come with me quietly now. It will be for the best."

"They will come and find me."

"They won't find you. I have taken precautions. You will be quite safe."

"I doubt it."

He led her up the lane and thence into Parkers Lane, behind West Street. Here was a slip of a house, of four rooms only, for which Giles had only just got the keys from Mr Pye. He had been surprised that Giles wanted to rent such a humble property, but was obliging. "And not a word about it to anyone, Mr Pye, if you would," Giles had said.

"Naturally, sir."

Holt was waiting for them in the ground floor parlour that was furnished with two chairs and nothing else.

"Not very cheerful, I'm afraid," said Holt, as Kate looked around her.

"Who is he?"

"This is Holt. He is going to be keeping watch on you."

"A policeman?"

"No, he's my manservant."

"My gaoler," she said.

"You are used to those. Let's go upstairs. It's a little more comfortable there."

The stairs lay behind a door, and led up to a fair-sized room, with an old four poster bed in it. In one corner a door led to a tiny closet.

"There are locks on all these doors. You will feel quite secure. There will be someone here at all times to keep watch. And no peep-holes."

"Anyone would think you were setting me up as your mistress," she remarked, sitting down on the bed and stroking the faded print of the counterpane. "Except no girl I know would stand for this. It smells damp."

"It will be better once Holt gets the fires going. I don't think anyone has lived here for a while."

"I can see why," she said, wandering across to the window and lifting the dirty muslin curtain. "What sort of a view is that?"

"I've seen worse. It's better than the view from a cell. Think of your poor Baxter."

She spun round.

"Have you seen him?"

"I was talking to him this morning."

"What did he say?"

"It's what he did not say. He is, like you, reluctant to tell the truth."

"You don't understand!" she exclaimed. "You can't!"

"I understand that you are tangled up in a net of untruths, the pair of you, and part of something very dark, something that threatens to destroy you both. Now, I am offering you a chance, Kate – think of that. A chance to get free."

She seemed to consider the point, walking up and down the room a couple of times, as if getting the measure of what he was saying.

"I wish you had told me. I could have gone back for my things."

"Then you would never have come back," he said. "And how would you have got away with your bonnet boxes and your stash?"

"What do you know about that?"

"I can't believe you don't have an old stocking stuffed with tips, hidden away somewhere. You're not stupid."

"And now I don't, thanks to you!" she exclaimed. "I don't have anything except the clothes I'm wearing."

"You have information, Kate, and you know the value of that. You wouldn't have waited outside The Unicorn or even spoken to me if you didn't realise the value of what you know to someone like me. And, in material terms, you have the contents of your reticule there. I don't suppose you ever shop in Fairfaxes on account."

"As if," she muttered and turned away back to the window. "Do you think you can do it?" she said. "Bring them all down?"

"I don't know," said Giles. "But it sounds as if someone should try."

"I hope you know what you are doing," she said. "Or else we are all damned, that's for certain."

He left her and went downstairs to Holt.

"Watch yourself with her, Holt," he said. "She is a tricksy

creature, to say the least."

"I can see that, sir," said Holt. "I suppose she tricked you."

"Careful now, Holt!" Giles said.

"Sorry, sir," said Holt, looking not at all reproved and highly amused. Giles let it pass. Holt's free manner was, in truth, one of his many virtues.

"So, sir," Holt went on. "What am I to say when I'm asked? That she's a –"

"That she's my mistress," said Giles.

Holt frowned.

"Are you sure, sir? That will stick badly, if you don't mind me saying."

"That's a risk I'm prepared to take," said Giles. "Now remember what I said. She is not to leave alone, nor talk to anyone. You have everything you need at present, I think?"

"Yes, I think we are pretty settled. Mr Wilkes at The Black Bull is sending over some supplies. It's going to cost you a pretty penny, this caper, though, sir. He was looking very askance."

"You need some more money, then?" said Giles reaching into his pocket.

"Don't worry, sir, I shall keep a proper note of it all, just as you told me," Holt said, pocketing the coins.

The door to the staircase banged open to reveal Kate, wrapping her shawl tightly around her.

"I thought you said something about a fire," she said.

"Just getting to it, ma'am," said Holt. "Coal or wood? What's your fancy?"

"What do I care?" she retorted. "Just get the fire going, will you? If I have to stay here, then I might as well be comfortable."

"I'm glad you are resigned to it," said Giles, but he was not at all sure that she was. While Holt went upstairs with the coal bucket, she walked about the ground floor room, with the air of a trapped animal. Then she turned and rushed towards the door to the street.

"Don't even think about it," Giles said, blocking her way. "I don't want to find you dead in a ditch."

"I'm as good as dead now!" she said, attempting to dodge past him, but he caught her by the forearms and turned her back towards the staircase.

"Upstairs," he said. "If you please."

He had to force her, and it was a most undignified process. She resisted all the way, and although he had the better of her in strength, her desperation made her fierce. In the end they stumbled into the upstairs room together, with her falling to her knees with a cry of frustration, and Giles almost falling on top of her.

"Oh, I do hope you bloody know what you are about," she said, getting to her feet, attempting to reassume her dignity. "You may think you do, but I'm telling you –" She broke off and stomped across the room, and threw herself down on the bed. "Let me be, will you!"

"With pleasure," said Giles, signalling to Holt.

They locked the door behind them.

Giles left, wondering if Holt would need reinforcements to guard her and if he had better not give Captain Lazenby a full account of what evidence he had gleaned and get the affair onto a more legitimate footing. Kate was certainly a valuable witness and he felt sure that she and Baxter together would lead them to the heart of the organisation. Their reticence suggested that they were involved at the highest level.

He was not sure if Lazenby would agree with his strategy, let alone with the way he had improvised it without any higher consultation. He was an excellent man, of course, and he liked to keep the pounds and shillings very straight, which was as it should be for a man in his position. However, Lazenby was not particularly imaginative and was very much one for doing everything by the book. He had not yet, Giles suspected, fully embraced the need for intelligence work, nor even specialised detective officers within the Constabulary. Giles had not yet pressed him for more money and resources, though he was conscious that for the sake of his own operations, he ought to assert himself. Perhaps given these discoveries, this was the moment to do it. The situation was grave enough to warrant it.

He mused on this, and how he might effectively present his case, as he walked back past Fairfaxes, towards the Minster by way of Angel Street, intending to call briefly on his sister. But as he reached the gate to the Precincts, he saw two familiar figures coming down towards him – namely, Lambert's brother-in-law Edward Fforde, and Lord Milburne.

"Major Vernon," said Lord Milburne, enthusiastically shaking his hand. "How very good to see you."

"I didn't know you were expected, my lord. The pleasure is all mine. And good to see you as well, sir," Giles said, shaking Edward Fforde's hand in turn.

"A rather impromptu visit," said Dr Fforde. "For various reasons."

"We were just going to the bookseller," said Edward Fforde. "I wanted a copy of Perry's new book of Essays. He has a very good stock, I find."

"It's for my mother," Lord Milburne said. "She hasn't read it yet. Have you, sir?"

"No, I'm afraid not," Giles said. "I have to confess I have not even heard of it."

"It has sold out in Oxford," Lord Milburne said. "I hoped we might lay our hands on a copy here. I lent mine to a friend and Dr Fforde has left his in college."

"Oxford is agreeing with you, then?" said Giles.

"It is," Milburne broke off, grinning with pleasure.

"A notable success," Dr Fforde said. "Charles has been put up for the Wenlock Prize. Quite an honour for a first year undergraduate, and none of my doing. I could not make a nomination in the circumstances. It would not have been ethical given the connection –"

"Give that you are to be my stepfather," Lord Milburne said and grinned broadly again. "There, Major Vernon, that is the great news. The reason for our visit. And it is excellent news, is it not?"

"Not quite the only reason," said Dr Fforde, "but the principal one, yes. Mrs Maitland has done me the honour of agreeing to be my wife."

Chapter Ten

"I am just going down to see Captain Lazenby," Major Vernon said. "I want to have my thoughts straight. Do you have anything further for me?"

"I have some ideas. But I want to go back to Ardenthwaite and talk to the Colonel again. Also, the place would merit a thorough search."

"My thoughts entirely. We will go tomorrow first thing, if that is convenient."

"Very. The earlier the better. That is the best time for a mushroom hunt."

"Mushrooms? You think mushrooms were the cause of this?"

"It's a strong possibility. There were mushrooms in that fricassee, were there not?"

"Yes, definitely."

"Mushrooms are the innocent perpetrators of much misery," said Felix. "They are quite a fascinating subject, all in all. Fortunately, Handley had this gem in stock. It's in German so I was struggling a little with my translation, but I think I have the gist of it."

"He really is an excellent bookseller," said Major Vernon. He opened the fly leaf and saw the price. "Not cheap, though."

"I think I'm keeping the place going," said Carswell. "When I last settled my account it was about half the rent on Ardenthwaite. Often he orders in advance what he knows I might want. And of course he is very excited about the prospect of the University. That will make his fortune."

"He should be asked to be a founder," said Major

Vernon, looking through the book. "These illustrations – how accurate are they?"

"Very, I trust. Why do you ask?"

"It's just at first glance, these things look so similar. How is one to tell one from the other, unless you are a great expert?"

"That is exactly my point. It is ignorance – admittedly of a difficult subject – that causes most of the mushroom-related poisonings. We are lucky, to be frank, that we are not dead. There is a morass of toxicity here. For example, if Mostyn, the Colonel's man, had chosen to add this one to our fricassee in error, mistaking it for a chanterelle, we should all be in our graves already."

"All of us who ate it, that is," said Major Vernon. "I cannot for the life of me remember if the Colonel took any. And that is the whole question here. Was there malicious intent or was this simply accidental?"

"Quite," said Felix. "For here we come to the really interesting thing. There is a class of mushroom that is known in both scientific circles and in popular lore to cause extraordinary effects on the human imagination. There are primitive tribes where they deliberately eat certain mushrooms so that they may feel closer to their gods. They believe that the mushrooms allow them to see the world of the spirits. At least I think this is what it says. It is all in this footnote here, but my German is so poor that I am a little uncertain I have got this entirely correct."

"You should give it to Mrs Maitland, then," said Major Vernon. "She's at my sister's house at the moment."

"She is?" Felix said, a little surprised.

"Yes, and Lord Milburne. They came back from Oxford with Dr Fforde. Mrs Maitland and Fforde are going to be married."

"Good Lord," said Felix. "And what do you feel about that, sir?" he ventured, thinking how he had felt on hearing Mr

O'Brien's news of Sukey.

"It is not my business to feel anything about it. Of course, it's a good match for them both. Milburne is clearly delighted with him as a stepfather and Fforde is a wealthy man, eminently respectable and almost her equal in intelligence. She will be the making of him. You'll have heard he is tipped to be the principal of the new University, I'm sure?"

"I had not."

"Lord Rothborough is backing it."

"Then it will –" Felix broke off. "Good match or not, it can't be pleasant for you to hear of it."

"She will be happy and well settled," he said. "That is all that can be said. And she will translate your German for you, I am sure. You can take it over to her tonight. We are asked there after dinner, remember?"

"Yes, of course," said Felix, sensing that the subject was closed. Major Vernon tapped the book with his finger and said, "So which of these are mushrooms that make us see spirits? Is that what we are dealing with? Do such things grow here?"

"It is quite possible. And the whole trick of such substances is the manner in which they are taken. The element of suggestion is apparently very important in these primitive religions. You are told what you are expected to see and then you see it."

"Is it perhaps like when one goes to the theatre?" Major Vernon said. "An absurd story can be accepted as real, and there are lights and music, and so forth."

"Exactly, exactly! We were told stories, were we not? We were told there were ghosts, and I saw them, because of whatever it was in that fricassee."

"Which suggests that the mushrooms were introduced deliberately," said Major Vernon. "Especially as the dish was placed between you and me, and not near the Colonel. He would have had to ask for it had he wanted to take any, which he did not."

"No, he definitely did not. And I ate most of the dish, and I was the one most strongly affected, at least in the first instance. I saw one creature who was plainly not there, and then mistook a living creature for the Queen of the Fairies. Although, in my defence, what she was doing roaming about the woods on her pony at that time in the morning, without a groom to attend her, I don't know, given that she turns out to be a respectable young woman."

"Then that must be some sort of comfort to you."

"I think it is, but I should rather it had been the Queen of the Fairies that saw me raving in only my shirt, rather than the daughter of some friend of Lord Rothborough's."

"You saw her again at the Guildhall, then?"

"Yes. And mercifully, she doesn't want me to say a word about having seen her there, but it makes me wonder again what she was doing there in the first place. And it was on my land, I am sure of that much."

"Your land?" said Major Vernon with a slight smile.

"I have quite fallen into the way of that, haven't I?" said Felix. "I am a reed in the wind. Yes, indeed, on my land, which may have these clever mushrooms growing on it. We'll go tomorrow and see."

~

"I'm sorry for the way this has happened, Giles," said Mrs Fforde, on the landing outside her drawing room, which was already busy with her guests. "I meant to come and tell you – and then... it was all such a surprise to us. I think Mrs Maitland is a little embarrassed, to tell you the truth, for it is not like Ned to be so impetuous. He never usually arrives without a proclamation in advance of him."

"It does not matter, Sal," said Major Vernon.

"If you are sure?"

"Quite," he said, but Mrs Fforde did not look very convinced, and neither was Felix. Major Vernon went on: "Now, who else is here? Is the Bishop here yet? You have quite a crush. You must be pleased."

"No, he's not. Lord Rothborough and Lady Maria are here, as you can see. We are unexpectedly dazzling, are we not?"

"Then probably the Bishop won't like it," said Major Vernon, "from what I have heard of him."

"You may have something there. But I'm determined they will be persuaded to enjoy themselves. If they cannot, I will consider myself a great failure as a hostess."

"They will be, I am sure; no one could resist you, Sal. Nor the curd tarts."

"There is no sin in a curd tart," said Mrs Fforde. "That would be tortuous theology."

"I'm sure Edward could set the Bishop straight on that if necessary."

"That would be excellent, if he could. For he will need to be firm if he is to conquer him, and that will be required if he is to get the job. Bishop Hughes is of course in favour of a low church candidate. A Cambridge man, I have heard." Sally sighed. "The old Bishop would not like that. He wanted a Salvator's man. That is the whole point." She turned to Felix and took his hand. "Enough of that. Now, I hope you are prepared to dance every dance, Mr Carswell. I have a great many handsome young women tonight looking for competent partners. I can promise you reels as well as quadrilles, for I know you have a taste for those. And you too, Giles – there will be no excuse for you not standing up frequently. You're not too old."

"Only if you will promise to dance a quadrille with me, Sally," said Major Vernon.

"I should be delighted. It has been too long since we danced together. Now you must excuse me; I must go and see to the musicians."

"If I didn't know any better," said Major Vernon, "I would think my sister was making a point insisting on having dancing tonight. And if anyone can make a bishop dance, it is she, don't you think?"

"He would not dare refuse her," said Felix, leaving his copy of 'European Fungi' on a side table in the hall, and surveying the crowd while the Major plunged in. He was not sure he was in the mood for dancing, but he knew he could not disappoint Mrs Fforde, and the truth was that enjoyment, in some form or other, would steal up on him, as it often did at the Treasurer's House. He only hoped he could remember all the figures of whatever quadrilles were chosen – it was a tricky business at the best of times. He decided he would ask Lady Maria to dance, if she was not already completely engaged, as she would be kind enough to discreetly remind him of the figures.

He saw her standing with Lord Rothborough, who beckoned him over at once. She was, as he had guessed, already engaged for the first dance with Lord Milburne, but he secured her for a reel.

"You should ask Miss Blanchfort," said Lady Maria. "I do not think she has a partner for the first dance. I will present you, if you like? If I present you, no one can object, after all."

"Is she likely to object?" said Felix, noticing that Lord Rothborough had frowned. "I have no wish to be objected to!"

"Lady Blanchfort can be a little inflexible," said Lord Rothborough.

"So inflexible, it seems, that poor Miss Blanchfort will have no partners at all," Lady Maria said. "She is objecting to everyone. It is very uncivil to accept Mrs Ffordes' invitation, Papa, and then not allow her daughter to speak to anyone, let alone dance. Why is she here, then?"

"You are right, Maria, she is uncivil. Yes, you should try your arm, Felix," said Lord Rothborough. "After all, Nell Blanchfort is a pretty girl, going to waste sitting in there with the old maids. I tell you what we shall do. I will engage the mother and you shall take on the young lady. Lady Blanchfort will not dare to refuse to dance with me. No, certainly she will not," he added, with a smile.

"Goodness, Papa, you sound as if you have something to threaten her with," said Lady Maria.

"Perhaps," he said. "Come, let us go and arrange this. Mrs Fforde is already assembling her sets."

Felix was dubious about this entire scheme given that it seemed to promise nothing but a nasty dose of drawing room humiliation for him. But Lord Rothborough was confident and determined, and so Felix submitted.

They turned into the adjoining sitting room, the haunt of the elderly ladies who always adorned these occasions, reminding Felix of the arrangements of autumn leaves that his mother loved to put about the house. Tonight, however, this gentle harmony was disrupted by the glittering splendour of Lady Blanchfort and her daughter, who were, as far as Felix could judge, overdressed for Northminster society. Lady Blanchfort was wearing diamonds, and her daughter pearls, and their pale, low-cut dresses dripped with lace. This was striking enough, but it was the resemblance between mother and daughter that he now saw with full force. At the Guildhall their bonnets had disguised it. Both had the same brilliant copper-red hair, Lady Blanchfort's only slightly dulled with age, and the same delicate physique and that remarkable porcelain-like skin. They looked like a pair of human-sized dolls, sitting on a window seat, the mother's arm protectively tucked into that of her daughter. Felix wondered whether this was an attempt at human disguise again. Was Lady Blanchfort the real Queen of the Fairies and Miss Blanchfort a rebellious princess riding in the woods at dawn?

The introductions were made and Lady Blanchfort responded with a polite wariness, which made Felix steel himself for a put-down. He was aware that Miss Blanchfort was flushing crimson, and that he was blushing himself, as if the effects of their last two meetings could never be overcome. Where was he going to find the words to ask her to dance, he wondered, as Lord Rothborough graciously prevailed upon Lady Blanchfort to stand up with him.

"Oh, I do not think –" she said.

"I insist, my lady," Lord Rothborough said. "We are needed to make up a second set. We cannot disappoint Mrs Fforde. And Mr Carswell will take Eleanor up to the first set. She will be in good hands."

"I am not sure that young man is quite the partner I would like for my daughter," said Lady Blanchfort.

"There is no harm in a quadrille in a private house, Ann," said Lord Rothborough, using, Felix supposed, an old familiarity as a weapon. What had gone on between them that he felt he could draw such concessions from her? Now he reached out for Miss Blanchfort's hand, and smiling, said, "Eleanor, will you dance with Mr Carswell?"

"Yes, of course, sir," said Miss Blanchfort, standing and allowing Lord Rothborough to place her hand in Felix's.

Lady Blanchfort rose and said, "One dance, Eleanor. One dance, and then we will go home." She put out her hand to Lord Rothborough. "If you insist, sir."

"I do," said Lord Rothborough. "And I make no apologies for it!"

~

Giles had not yet spoken to Emma Maitland, although she had

been within his sight several times. She had been with her fiancé, as was to be expected, and he had to admit the arrangement seemed to suit her as well as Dr Fforde. She was in excellent looks, wearing a wine-coloured dress that became her very well. He wondered if this was the moment to go and speak to her. She would be disturbed, he felt, until he had set it right. For that was his intention – to offer his good wishes.

Mrs Maitland was now alone, and Giles decided he would not put it off any longer. It would only be a short conversation, for Sally was already lining up her couples and he would be expected to take his own place.

So he went up to her, pleased to see her smile as he approached, and they greeted each other with perfect calmness.

"Will you and Dr Fforde be dancing?" he said.

"I hope so, but I have lost him for a moment," she said, glancing around for him. "Are you in need of a partner?"

"No, I am promised to my sister."

She smiled at that and laid her hand on his arm briefly.

"I cannot say how happy I am to be joining this family. I hope –"

"There is nothing that needs to be said," he said. "You both look very well. It seems to make perfect sense."

"Yes, yes, it does feel like that." She closed her eyes for a moment, smiling with relief. "Thank goodness you see it. I knew, of course, that you would understand, that you of all people would understand –"

"Hush," he said. "There is nothing to be said. No explanations. I am happy for you. Now, here he is come to get you."

He was aware, even as he said this, with his manner so cheerful and civil, that he meant not a word of it. Hearing her voice and seeing her expressive face was an intense pleasure for him, as was that brief touch of her hand on his arm.

Edward Fforde now took her hand in readiness for the

dance and said, "I should have mentioned this before, Vernon, but I have you to thank for this unexpected happiness. If you had not brought her to us, then –" he shrugged, and kissed her hand before leading her away.

Giles knew then that she had not told Fforde about what had passed between them. Perhaps there was nothing that could be said without causing pain and unnecessary embarrassment. It had been a still-born child of a love affair. She had allowed herself to have feelings for him, and had been rash enough to have told him about it; and instead of cherishing the possibility of it, like a fool, he had thrown it all back in her face. It was no wonder that Edward Fforde, wealthy and reliable, offering security and unwavering devotion, seemed like a better object for her love. It really was better that she should not love him any more, and whatever he might feel for her was irrelevant. He had not been worthy of her then, and he was certainly not worthy of her now. That it might feel like a punishment to see her on this other man's arm, looking so radiant, was the least that he deserved.

The set was almost assembled. Sally was signalling to him to join them. Lord Milburne and Lady Maria were already standing waiting, as eager to begin as a pair of high-strung racehorses. Next to them were Carswell and a handsome red-headed young lady, most elaborately dressed, and then Mrs Maitland and Dr Fforde forming the final couple of the set, standing directly opposite.

"Eight couples," said Sally, reviewing all her dancers as if they were a regiment. "How excellent."

"That's all this room will bear," remarked Lambert, who with his partner was leading the second set.

"We have plenty of room, if we are neat and careful," said Mrs Fforde. "Which I am sure you all will be. I propose we dance the First Set Quadrille, if that is agreeable to everyone? A little old-fashioned for some of you, perhaps, but it has the virtue of familiarity."

"An excellent choice," said Lord Rothborough.

"You are hoping the Bishop arrives in the midst of this, yes?" Giles said to Sally, as the introduction to the dance played.

"Would it be a wrong for him to see that dancing is a perfectly respectable activity?" she said, making her curtsey to him. "Indulged in by middle-aged people with perfect propriety."

But as they began, and he found himself facing and passing Emma Maitland, in the intricate moves of the dance, with the spirited, heart-lifting accompaniment of an excellent fiddler and pianist, he wondered if the preachers and puritans who condemned dancing had not got hold of some grain of truth. As graceful and sociable as it all was, with the ladies' skirts swaying as they skipped and chasséd, and turned with carefully pointed feet and nicely placed arms, he could not help thinking that all the gestures were calculated to rouse the senses into a state of heightened enjoyment that seemed like a prelude to abandon.

He was puzzled at himself, even as he enjoyed it, feeling himself seduced by the rhythms of the music and the elegant movements, watching Emma Maitland turn and twist, and move back and forth, sometimes touching his hand or catching his eye. She was smiling. Her pleasure was not to be questioned, and he could only think of what he had lost, and how much he desired her. It was not disinterested desire. He wanted her in his bed, and flushed and smiling at him in the same way.

They had come to the pastorelle figure, which required each of the gentlemen in the set to do a little fancy capering, as if to show the ladies what fine bucks they were. When he had first danced this as a young man in his bright new coat of regimental lace, it had been a great pleasure to indulge in this display, and he was amused to watch Milburne and then Carswell, of all people, making the most of the opportunity, the latter with flourishes that were distinctly Highland. Edward Fforde was quite sedate, as befitted his reputation, but having seen Emma laughing and clapping at Carswell's performance, Giles was moved to do a little graceful fooling of his own, hoping to remind her of the young officer she had watched dancing all those years ago. Then when it was done he caught her eye and she nodded at him, amused, comprehending, and suddenly it felt as if the door to intimacy with her might be opened again.

If it should be opened, he thought as the dance finished; and he wondered how he was going to resist going straight up to her and demanding she leave with him at once.

It was just as well that at this moment, the Bishop and his wife were announced.

Chapter Eleven

Miss Blanchfort stood and fanned herself with her hand ineffectually for a moment. Her cheeks were now a furious red, which he felt sure must match his own.

"We should find a cooler spot," said Felix. "It is close in here."

They went to one of the windows; the house was so ancient that they were set in deep embrasures, and partially covered by heavy curtains. It was a little like stepping into another room, and hid them quite from the view of the others. Felix pushed open the lattice as far as he could. She climbed up onto the window seat, leant out and breathed deeply, and he climbed up beside her.

"I wish I could stay for another dance," she said.

"Perhaps if Lord Rothborough commands it," said Felix. "You are not tempted to climb out, are you?" he said, noticing how she was leaning out rather precipitously.

"I should rather fly out of here," she said. "Do you think I could?"

"No. I am quite convinced you are mortal now, so I can't advise it."

"Oh, but how delicious it would be," she said, gazing out at the night again. "Oh, so delicious! Even more pleasant than dancing." She shook her head and then sat down. "I am glad for this chance to see you again. I wanted to apologise properly. I should have got you help and not abandoned you, but when I got back there was such a commotion, such a fuss about nothing, as ever!" She pressed her hands to her face for a moment. "I would have come back had I not been –"

"Were you in a great deal of trouble?"

"I am always in trouble. Nothing I do, nothing I say is ever the right thing! And I shall be in trouble again if I stay here any longer. I had better..." With which she jumped up and was gone.

Felix remained on the window seat, watching her progress across the room through the chink in the curtains, her white silk dress and copper hair glistening in the candlelight. It was just as well he stayed there, for Lady Blanchfort was coming to meet her, and as she spoke to her daughter she had the look of a woman recapturing an unruly dog and putting it on a leash. Miss Blanchfort appeared to droop a little, and then went off obediently with her to some other part of the room, out of sight. Felix felt a slight stab of disappointment that he could not talk to her any more, let alone dance, but decided it was for the best. He would not deliberately seek her out, he decided, for women were only a source of trouble and pain for him, no matter how alluring they were. Miss Blanchfort was too beautiful, vulnerable and strange to be anything but extremely dangerous.

He therefore remained idling on the window seat, watching the party through the chink in the curtains. After a few minutes he saw Major Vernon coming towards him, and he adjusted the curtain to show his hiding place.

"This is like a box at the opera," said Major Vernon, sitting down beside him. He was holding a glass of wine. "Who was your partner?"

"Miss Blanchfort," said Felix.

"Very handsome."

"Very dangerous, I think – well, for me at least," said Felix.

"Oh dear," said Major Vernon sipping his wine.

"I should go and find some of that," said Felix. "The quadrille was thirsty work. But I do not want to risk being presented to the Bishop."

"Here," said Major Vernon, passing him his glass. "What

is the man doing?"

The Bishop was going about murmuring to the ladies, apparently asking them to sit.

"It looks as if he is going to give a recitation."

"Or a sermon?" said Felix, draining the glass of wine.

A moment later, the Bishop had taken a commanding spot in front of the crowd and making a bow, began to speak.

"My lords, ladies, and gentlemen – no, my dear friends in Christ," said the Bishop. "You must forgive our rather late arrival. We had meant to join you all earlier but it seems that the Lord had different plans for us. We had just finished our dinner, when I was told that I had a visitor – a man I did not know, but who had told my butler that he was very anxious to speak to me.

"So I went out into the hall to see what it was he wanted and what sort of man he was. He was not the ordinary sort of visitor to a Bishop's Palace. Nor was he the sort of man who it is easy for respectable people to place in society, for he was well dressed, and clearly in easy circumstances, but his clothes were, most of you would concede, a trifle gaudy. His accent also proclaimed the most ordinary origins. But he spoke to me most respectfully and also to my wife who had come out of the dining room. He said that something of great importance had happened to him, that he felt he must talk to a member of the clergy and that having read my pamphlet, he felt I would understand what he was about.

"Naturally I said I would hear him, and indeed, I asked if my wife might join us and take notes, for I suspected even then, from the light in his eyes, and the excitement in his demeanour, that something wonderful had happened to him, that the power of the Lord was working strongly in him, and had brought him to our door."

"A sermon, what did I tell you?" said Felix, wishing he had another glass of wine.

"And so we went into my study and he began to tell me

his story. He was the son of a humble tavern-keeper just outside this city, and he had come to his present prosperity, he confessed, by means that were not always within the law. In his youth he had been a prize fighter, and had then discovered a talent for healing horses. This had been his principal occupation, operating a livery business, as well as getting a great reputation as a horse doctor, in which capacity I think some of you here may already know him. Now he had attempted, he told me, to put his youthful discretions behind him, and live what he hoped was a good and decent life, doing what he could for the poor and sick."

"Bickley?" murmured Major Vernon. "Can he be talking about Bickley?"

"And yet, even though he grew more and more prosperous, and built up his business, making himself very comfortable, he began to feel that there was an absence in his life. So he thought again of the simple lessons he had once heard as a child at his mother's knee. She had told him that Jesus was his Lord, and loved him very dearly. And he began to ponder on this more and more, all the while feeling that he was such a great sinner that the Lord could not love him, and that there was no hope for him, and the lake of fire and eternal damnation awaited him."

Major Vernon got up and went out from behind the curtain, standing in front of it, blocking Felix's view of the Bishop. In his turn, Felix climbed back onto the window seat and gazed out into the night air, and found himself picturing Miss Blanchfort taking flight.

~

The Bishop was now offering a prayer of extempore thanksgiving for the salvation of George Bickley, a most embarrassing procedure in a drawing room where most of the guests looked quite scandalised at his speech. Lambert was standing with Lord Rothborough, looking both mortified and furious, while Sally, on the other side of the room with the Bishop's wife, looked most uncomfortable, especially when Mrs Hughes fell to her knees, as if at the command of her husband.

Most people managed to bow their heads. Some even went on their knees, though hesitantly. It was clear that the power of the Lord was not working very strongly in the Treasurer's House that night.

The Bishop's prayer seemed to go on almost as long as his speech and contained nothing from the Prayer Book that Giles remembered. There followed an awkward silence following the muttered final amen, for what else was there to do but be awkward? It was surely what the Bishop wanted: to make them all uncomfortable. There could be no country dances or reels now. Lambert and Sally looked confounded and at a loss, as if their party had been overrun by a herd of bullocks.

In the end it was Lord Rothborough who managed to straighten the social cloth with an adept tweak. He went straight up to Sally, took her hand and kissed it, saying, "Your grace and hospitality, Mrs Fforde – I can never fault it. It has been a most delightful evening. Maria, do you not agree?" he added, stretching out his hand to his daughter. She joined him, and made a very graceful, deep and old-fashioned curtsey to Sally, as if she were far her superior. Sally responded by kissing her and that signal allowed the party to break up.

~

Three quarters of an hour later, Felix, the Ffordes, Major

Vernon, Mrs Maitland, and Lord Milburne were attempting to do justice to the very lavish supper that had been prepared for a multitude. Celia and Tom had been summoned from upstairs, somewhat astonished that the party had finished so soon, but pleased that they were allowed to come down and eat all the fancy cakes and ices they could. The servants had also been given their share, and Canon Fforde had sent the fiddler down to the servant's hall to entertain them.

"We should send some over to the palace nursery," said Tom.

"No, no," said Canon Fforde. "That would be –"

"A declaration of war?" said Major Vernon.

"War has already been declared," said Mrs Fforde, with a sigh. "I cannot believe it. What a business!"

"I think we should write to the Archbishop," said Edward Fforde. "The matter of the extempore prayer alone –"

"I do not know if his Grace would be sympathetic in the least," said Canon Fforde. "It is a pity there is no law against emotional vulgarity, which that was, pure and simple. Except that it was not the least pure and simple. If it had been remotely sincere I could have forgiven it, but it was calculated."

"I meant Canterbury, not York," said Edward Fforde.

"It might be politic not to tell him," said Canon Fforde, with a sigh, refilling his glass. "But what is to be done, I don't know."

Felix wandered out into the hall, having helped himself to another ice. Here he found Mrs Maitland and Celia waltzing together to the sound of the fiddle that was coming up from downstairs. Major Vernon was watching them, and then suddenly he stepped in and caught Celia's hand, and with his hand around her waist, whirled her about a few times, lifting her from the floor, much to her delight. Setting her down again he turned to Mrs Maitland, offering his hands to her. She accepted, and they proceeded, a little more decorously, but still with considerable intimacy in the arrangement, and with a certain forcefulness in the Major's manner as he swept her down the length of the hall.

The melody ended and they broke off laughing.

"I must say good night now," he said. "Carswell, will you get that translation from Mrs Maitland for when we see Parham tomorrow?"

"I am never to be idle when I am here!" she exclaimed with mock indignation.

"It will be a trifle for you. Good night, Celia," said the Major, kissing his niece. "Don't make yourself ill with all those cakes." She promised she would not, but went off in the direction of the supper table.

"We had better do as he says," said Mrs Maitland as the front door closed behind the Major.

"Perhaps if we went in here?" said Felix, taking up the book from the hall table.

They went into Canon Fforde's book room, where there was a good lamp burning, and Mrs Maitland sat down to make her translation. Felix sat on the sofa eating the rest of his ice.

Mrs Maitland finished reading the text.

"Well, this is rather startling," she said. "And you believe you ate these things?"

"It is possible. I was driven quite out of my wits, and the Major, to some lesser degree."

"I hope you are both quite recovered," said Mrs Maitland.

"I think so," said Felix.

"It seems that you might be, given your performances on the dance floor tonight."

"I have never seen Major Vernon dance before," said Felix.

"I have," said Mrs Maitland, taking up a pencil and smiling as she began writing her translation. Felix was quite sure it was not the text that was amusing her.

After a few minutes Dr Fforde came in, and looked a

little surprised to find his fiancée hard at work at his brother-in-law's desk.

"I shall not be a moment," she said, putting her hand up to him. "I have only one more sentence."

"What is this?"

"It is for Major Vernon," she said. "A case. Mushrooms with extraordinary properties. Listen to this: '*Agaricus semilanceatus* is occasionally found in Northern European woodland and low-lying scrub, often with a marshy aspect. In quantities above several ounces it is usually fatal, but in lesser doses it has been known to cause convulsions and visions, and in certain circumstances sleepwalking.'"

"It does say sleepwalking!" said Felix, jumping up to look at the text. "I guessed that it might, because of my own experience, but I was not certain."

"You were sleepwalking?" Mrs Maitland said.

"Yes. Quite an interesting experience, I must say. Perhaps if I find some of these, I should see if I can repeat it."

"That sounds rather rash, Mr Carswell," said Dr Fforde.

"All scientific enquiry has an element of risk. It is the nature of the beast. And if one could replicate the effect, then that would be the proof we need."

"It goes on to say," Mrs Maitland said, "'In the smallest doses the effects have been curious ones – often with an element of disinhibition involved. A taciturn man taking a pie containing the mushrooms was observed to grow unexpectedly voluble. Sometimes called the deadly milk-cap.' Oh, how interesting. I do hope you find your mushrooms, Mr Carswell." She finished writing out the text and then handed the paper to him. "With my compliments."

"Very much appreciated, ma'am."

She rose and said, "It was no trouble. Edward, was there something you wanted?"

"Just to know what you were doing."

"Assisting justice," she said with a flourish and a smile. "I am sorry, I did not mean to neglect you."

Sensing a little awkwardness between the lovers, Felix excused himself and said his goodbyes to the rest of the party. As he walked back to The Black Bull, he wondered if Edward Fforde had seen that impromptu waltz in the hall.

~

"We played cribbage, sir, and she took me for a shilling," said Holt. "She *is* wily."

"But she's gone to bed now?"

"I hope so," said Holt, stretching and yawning.

"And the door to her room is locked?"

"Yes, there was a lot of fussing and squawking about it, but I told her what was what."

Giles wondered if he should check on his charge and then decided he would leave it until the morning.

"I have two constables here for the night," he said. "You can go home. She didn't say anything of interest when you were playing?"

"No," said Holt. "She wasn't inclined to confidences."

Holt left and Giles gave his two plain-clothes men his instructions, before leaving himself. He would look in briefly in the morning before going to Ardenthwaite.

Instead of going straight to his bed, he went to the Northern Office, and lighting a lamp made his way up to the attic, where he sat on the floor and stared at the notes he had pinned to the wall, adding one new foolscap sheet which read: "Bickley has found his Saviour." How sincere was this repentance, that was the great question. If it was perfectly sincere then they had been handed a great advantage, for in such a state, Bickley might be persuaded to talk openly at last.

When Kate spoke of 'him' did she mean Bickley? Was he

the shadowy master, the rule-maker imposing exceptional discipline upon his underlings? From what Giles had seen of the man, it might be possible. He was meticulous and cunning. An intelligent criminal who saw crime as a business and did the thing properly. There was no sloppiness in Bickley's operations. That was why it had been impossible to find enough evidence to bring him down.

And now he was at the Bishop's Palace, on his knees, declaring he had found God. It was astonishing whichever way he looked at it. But from what Giles knew of Bickley, from the few occasions they had met, this conversion narrative felt fake and convenient. To go to the Bishop, who he would have noticed was an ardent self-publicist, and declare himself a repentant sinner, willing to be washed in the Blood of the Lamb, was a spectacularly daring thing to do. What would it gain him?

At length his mind clouded over, and he could no longer think clearly. He found himself thinking of Emma Maitland and her smiles, and how he would like to go home and find her in his bed.

Chapter Twelve

"You could write your memoirs," Giles said. "There was a woman in your profession who did that."

"As if I would," Kate said, with a pout. "I shall go out of my mind in here. It's so stuffy. Can't I even go for a walk?"

"Perhaps something can be arranged," he said. "But not today. I have to work. I am going to see your Colonel."

"What?" she said, her eyes narrowing.

"Have you any messages for him?"

"You are stirring it, aren't you?" she said.

"I mean to upset the pot," he said.

"Wouldn't you rather stay here and play the Colonel with me?" she said after a moment. "You didn't seem to mind that game the other day, did you?"

"It wouldn't serve any purpose," he said.

"But doesn't stop you wanting it," she said, coming close to him. He put up his hand to deter her, but she pushed against his outstretched palm. "You've got that aching, hungry look about you. A man who hasn't got his share. Furious for it, you were," she said, reaching out and touching his cheek. "Like a boy for the first time. No wife, you said. I know that kind well enough, and you are no different."

She walked over to the bed, and perched on the edge, her shawl falling away, and her chemise likewise, her pose calculated to entice.

"Wouldn't take long," she said. "For your health?"

"No," said Giles. "And if you have any sense you will not play these tricks with the men downstairs. Unless you want to end up in the Bridewell or a ship to Australia."

She got up from the bed and strolled across the room,

still displaying herself, as if she was very determined to tempt him to it. He was tempted, that he could not deny, for he had had nothing but the most lascivious dreams, involving this creature and Emma Maitland, and they had left him hungry, just as she had said.

She picked up the copy of The Bugle he had brought for her and studied its front page.

"Do you know George Bickley?" he said, pushing away these thoughts as best he could, and turning to business. She did not speak nor look away from the paper, but he thought he noticed her eyelids twitch for a moment. "Ever had any dealings with him?"

"Never heard of him," she said, and he felt almost certain she was lying. But he did not pursue the matter, as he was anxious to get on the road to Ardenthwaite.

~

The ride out to Ardenthwaite was a pleasant distraction, the exercise a good counter to his confusion. Even Carswell, usually cautious on horseback, seemed happy to take a brisker pace than usual, and occasionally urged his mount into a gallop as they rode through the extensive woodlands that surrounded the property.

Carswell brought his horse to a standstill, and gazing about him, said, "The Colonel – if he did poison us deliberately, then –"

"It would be a very serious matter if he did," said Giles.

"It seems a most elaborate scheme to get out of paying his rent."

"I agree, but if he was feeling pressure from elsewhere, then perhaps it becomes understandable? I suspect he is not entirely the blameless character he presents himself as."

"What have you found?"

"Nothing substantial. A scrap of gossip, really. But enough to unsettle him if it's true."

"These woods are the ideal habitat," Carswell said. "Though where to begin?"

He dismounted, and leaving his horse in Holt's charge plunged into the undergrowth on foot.

Giles and Holt rode a little further up the drive, before Giles himself dismounted.

"Go and see if you can find Mostyn," he said, handing the reins to Holt.

It was his intention to keep things absolutely mild and civil with the Colonel, with no hint of an accusation of anything improper.

He rang the bell but there was no answer. He could, however, hear the dogs barking furiously, somewhere within the house.

Giles tried the door. It was not locked. He opened it and called out to signify his presence, at which the dogs redoubled their barking.

He went into the hall. The great room felt cold and still. There was no sign of any recent fire in the hearth.

"Good day!" he called out. "Is there anyone at home? Colonel Parham? Are you about, sir?"

Still the barking continued. In truth it was more of a piteous yelping, a chorus of canine misery. Having tried a succession of doors, Giles opened one in the passage which led to the kitchen, and which he now remembered opened into a store room.

The two pepper-and-salt pointers, Hector of the rheumy eye and the younger Hero, both came shooting out of the darkness. They were highly agitated and panting for water. How long had they been locked in there, he wondered, noting a pungent smell.

They leapt delightedly up at him, desperate for

reassurance.

"No sign of Mostyn, sir," said Holt, coming through from the kitchen.

"And no kitchen fire?"

"No, sir. Not a soul about."

"Get these poor beasts some water and something to eat if you can find anything," Giles said, now down on his knees caressing the dogs.

Holt took the dogs into the kitchen and Giles began to search the house, feeling as every minute passed that this was not a simple case of flight. The Colonel would not have left his dogs – he had been devoted to them.

It soon became clear that most of the man's possessions remained in the house, with the exception of his guns, which were no longer in the rack in his study that Giles had noticed on his previous visit. Neither were there any papers on his desk.

He began to make a slow tour of the house, looking in each room in turn for signs of occupation. The same curious deadness of air remained.

He climbed up to the top story of the house and opened the door to a gloomy attic room. A disturbing smell of decay at once filled his nostrils, and the buzzing of a mob of flies broke the silence.

A second later he saw it – Colonel Parham dangling by the neck from an ancient cross-beam.

~

"How long has he been here, do you think?" Major Vernon asked when they had cut him down.

"Rigor is quite pronounced," said Felix. "But it's warm up here, and the fact he's been left hanging may have had some effect. I would say about three or four days."

"Tuesday or Wednesday, then."

"And this is definitely not suicide," said Felix. "Feel that. If you slide your hand there, you can feel that the second vertebra is broken. That never happens with suicide by hanging. This is a neat job. He will have died almost at once. It would have taken several men to do it, though, given his height and strength. You can see his hands have been bound from the rope marks on his wrists. They must have subdued him and then strung him up."

"A calculated affair," said Major Vernon. "So, are we supposed to see this as suicide, or is the point that it is an execution?"

"Given that it is straightforward for all but the most foolish medical man to distinguish suicide by hanging and murder by hanging, the latter, I suppose. But why make it so obvious that it was a murder?"

"To make a point?" said Major Vernon, getting up. He stood looking down at the Colonel's corpse. "A fearless demonstration of power."

"But to whom?" Felix said. "Who was their intended audience?"

"A good question," said Major Vernon. "So, a group of men arrive here and are apparently invited into the house by Parham – we can assume he knew them, or thought they offered no threat. They proceed to overpower him, drag him up here and hang him. Then they lock up the dogs, and take the guns and whatever valuables are lying around."

"They must have known that this room existed," said Felix, looking up at the beam. "To know that it was possible to hang a man here, of his height and weight."

"Good point. Someone among them knows the house. Mostyn, the Colonel's man – what's become of him? Did he bolt or leave with the others? Is he one of the others? We need to find him."

"Let's hope he's not dead as well," said Felix.

They went downstairs to the kitchen where the dogs were still howling with hunger.

"Not so much as a crust in the larder," said Holt. "I gave them some water."

"Nothing left to rot?"

"No, sir. The place has been quite cleaned out."

"Mostyn perhaps didn't leave in a hurry, then," said Major Vernon.

"Strolled away knowing his master was dangling upstairs?" said Felix. "A nice show of loyalty."

"Dangling?" said Holt.

"Colonel Parham has been hanged," said Major Vernon. "What did you think of Mostyn, Holt? You had more to do with him than we did."

"You think he hanged his master, sir?" said Holt. "The servant always gets the blame, is that it?"

"That is not what I said, Holt," said Major Vernon. "What did you make of Mostyn? How did he strike you?"

Holt thought for a moment.

"Now I think of it, he was a dull dog, all in all. He was busy making the dinner. Didn't make much in the way of talk. I had a hard time of it with him."

"He didn't say how long he'd been in Parham's service?"

"No, nothing like that. Nor talked about him much. But he had his hands full, and wasn't the type to talk."

"It would have been too convenient if he'd been indiscreet," said Felix, gazing at the drooling old dog who the Major was comforting with his hand. "I think these animals will eat us if we do not find them something."

"Holt, I want you to ride back to Northminster. I will have a few notes for you, assuming they have not taken the Colonel's ink pot as well. You can stop at the Inn in the village and get them to send some supplies up to us. Mr Carswell, we need to scour the house. These people may be careful, but they may have overlooked something of importance."

While Major Vernon wrote his notes, Felix went back upstairs to the attic, and attempted to trace the route by which the Colonel had been got up there. As a march to the scaffold, it was a considerable distance to travel.

"His boots are very scuffed," Felix pointed out when the Major joined him again in the attic. "He must have fought quite violently against being taken up."

"It's a grim end," said Major Vernon, "but clean and quiet, afterwards. There was no danger of that body being found in any hurry and no need for them to dispose of weapons, or clean themselves of blood. Just a rope left around his neck, and brute force. It's efficient, certainly."

"And Mostyn paid off?" said Felix. "Or one of them?"

"If we assume he poisoned us, being the cook, then it seems he may have such tendencies."

"Lord knows what Parham was mixed up in to come to such an end," Felix said. "You said you had a scrap of gossip about him?"

Major Vernon nodded, and said, "I think he may have been up to his ears in debt."

"Which would explain him wanting to break the lease," Felix said.

"Yes, and in debt to some dangerous people. He had bad habits – he liked expensive whores and gambling, for certain. I think we can place him in Bickley's establishment in some way or other."

"So you think Bickley is behind all this?"

"The miraculous repentant Bickley, yes, perhaps. He seems a very likely candidate to me for this kind of organised mayhem, but I don't have even a speck of proof. Just my intuitions, which may be quite wrong. And after all, if Parham was in debt to Bickley, why murder a man who owes you money? It makes no sense."

"Life insurance?" Felix said. "Could that work?"

"We shall have to go and talk to his widow in Swalecliffe," said Major Vernon.

They were interrupted by the sound of a carriage arriving.

"That was very prompt work by Holt," said Major Vernon, as they hurried downstairs.

They came out of the house to see Lord Rothborough's travelling carriage drawing up.

"This is a pleasure!" said Lord Rothborough, handing Lady Maria out of the carriage. "We thought we would call on the Colonel on our way back to Holbroke and unsettle him with an invitation for dinner."

"Unfortunately, it's rather late for that," said Major Vernon. "Colonel Parham is dead. Forgive my bluntness, Lady Maria."

"Good grief," said Lord Rothborough.

"How terrible," said Lady Maria. "How? Was he ill?"

"No, that's the worst of it," said Felix. "He's been murdered."

Lady Maria gave a little gasp and turned away to disguise her shock. Lord Rothborough reached out and took her hand.

"Poor soul," he said after a moment. "And to have such a thing happen here. Dear Lord! However, we will leave you to your business, and console ourselves with the knowledge that justice will be served, and promptly, if you are involved."

"Yes," said Lady Maria, moving back towards the carriage. "That is something, I think."

Lord Rothborough settled her in the carriage, and then, before he himself climbed in, said, "If there is anything I can do, please do not hesitate to ask, will you?"

"As a matter of fact, there is something," said Major Vernon. "Might you take charge of the Colonel's pointers? They have been left to starve."

"Oh no, surely not!" exclaimed Lady Maria. "That is dreadful. Yes, yes, of course."

Major Vernon went into the house and brought out

Hector and Hero who were then put in the carriage and instantly lavished with attention from Lady Maria.

"I wish I had his confidence in a speedy resolution," Major Vernon said to Felix as the carriage drove away. "I have an unpleasant feeling that the path ahead of us is a stony one. These people –" He sighed. "Well, at least we know our best witnesses are in good hands."

Chapter Thirteen

Giles returned to the little house in Parker's Lane, late in the afternoon, and found a domestic scene that would have made a fitting subject for a painter of ordinary life.

The table was littered with dirty tea things while Kate stretched out on the bed, listening as Constable Hale, in his shirt sleeves, read aloud to her from The Bugle. The fire had been made up to terrific proportions, and the room was uncomfortably warm. Lying beside Kate was a large tabby tom cat, flat on his back and clearly in an ecstatic trance from her gentle rubbing of his chin. Better that the cat was enslaved than Constable Hale, thought Giles.

Hale stumbled to his feet at the sight of him, and hastily put on his coat.

When Giles had dismissed him, Kate said, "He was glad to be off his feet. Sounds like you are a hard master."

"Where did that cat come from?" said Giles.

"He wandered in from downstairs. Lovely, isn't he?" she said. "You always know where you are with a cat."

"Put your bonnet on," he said. "We are going out."

"Just when I'd got comfortable," she said, not moving from the bed. "Shame to waste such a good fire. Can't it wait?"

"No."

"Where are we going?" she said.

He took her bonnet from the hook and held it out to her.

"To my office. Something has happened. I need you to identify someone."

She sat up now, squinting at him.

"Do you mean –?" She broke off and took the bonnet

from him. "Who is it?" she said, getting up from the bed. "You want me to look at a dead man, don't you?"

"I'm afraid so, yes."

She fell silent and put on her bonnet.

He took her in the carriage to the Northern Office, although it was very close. It was drizzling and he had not wanted to risk being seen with her in the streets.

They reached the gloomy little forecourt that fronted the building and as he handed her out of the carriage, she looked around her with some trepidation.

"Do I have to?" she said. "Isn't there someone else? I don't –"

"It won't take long," he said, ushering her inside.

They went downstairs to Carswell's laboratory. He was standing at his desk, writing up his notes, while the newly delivered cadaver of Colonel Parham lay under a sheet.

"Oh God, the smell –" Kate said, stopping on the threshold and covering her mouth.

"It won't take long," Giles said.

"I'll turn up the gas," said Carswell. "It's getting dark in here."

"Who's he?" said Kate.

"This is Mr Carswell, the surgeon."

She shuddered, but allowed Giles to bring her into the room.

"You're going to cut him up?" she said, pointing at the mound under the sheet.

"In due course," said Carswell.

"Show me him then, for God's sake!" she burst out. "Before I heave my guts up!"

Carswell folded back the sheet to display the Colonel's face.

"Oh, Christ in Heaven!" Kate said. Then she turned away, and began to retch.

Carswell got a pail for her, and took her out into the

lobby at the foot of the stairs, where she sat vomiting and crying for some minutes. A nip of brandy calmed her at length, and then Giles took her upstairs to his office, where she sat hunched and shaking on the chair in the corner.

"So who was he?" Giles said, handing her a cup of coffee.

"Was he murdered?" she said. "He was, wasn't he? Why else would he be here, waiting to be cut up?"

"Who was he, Kate?" he said, crouching down beside her, seeing her hesitate. "The truth now."

"The Colonel," she said and glanced away, choking back more tears. "How did he die?"

"He was hanged. Do you have any idea who might have done such a thing?"

"How would I?" she said, with a dismissive shrug that seemed to imply the opposite.

"Let's start from the beginning," Giles said, getting up and fetching a chair for himself. He sat down opposite her. "How often did you see him?"

"Once or twice a week."

"For how long had he been coming?"

"Two or three months. He'd do it for his health, like I said. I think he had a wife. She was delicate, the way ladies are, you know."

"And who brought him here?"

"I can't tell you that."

"But you said he had a tab. And liked to gamble."

"Maybe. Oh, I don't know. I don't know anything. I know you think I do, but I don't! Why can't you just leave it?"

"I can't. I've two men murdered, and you are going to help me. If you don't want to," he said, getting up, "I can always let the people you are so afraid of know that you did talk. That wouldn't be difficult to arrange and then you would be in trouble."

"You wouldn't dare!"

"I will do what I need to. So think about that. You are far

safer talking to me. And if you do, you will help your lover." She screwed up her face and looked away. "Tell me about Bickley," he ventured. She looked back at him now. "Is he your boss?"

There was a long silence and then she sniffed noisily.

"He's not going to like this," she said. "The Colonel was like a pet to him. They were always talking about horses and dogs and all sorts. He'd come into my room after we'd done it and then they would sit jawing on for hours. I used to fall asleep in my chair by the fire. Not that I am complaining about it – full belly, clothes on my back, no one bashing me about." She gave a great sigh. "Oh God, why did I ever open my mouth?"

"Because of the man you love," Giles said.

"Love is a fool's game. I've known that all my bloody life, and then along he comes and –"

"What's his name?" Giles said.

"Johnny," she said. "There, you might as well have it all. Johnny bloody Hopkins! There. But you won't tell them I've said this, will you? Swear you won't?"

"You've done the right thing," he said. "I know it isn't easy. And Johnny works for Bickley?"

"Yes."

"Thank you," he said. "And Bickley owns the place you took me to?"

"Yes."

"And there are gambling rooms, as well as girls like you?"

"Yes. It's more the gambling than girls. We're just the entertainment. It's good that way. You're not working all the time. Is that what you want?"

"It's a start. How did you come to be there?"

"I was working in Leeds. He picked me up. We had a night of it, and then he took me there saying I was too good for the street."

"Bickley did?"

"Yes. He's not rough, nothing like that, not with us girls. We get all we like to eat and ready money, and all that. It's a good place for someone like me. It was, but I won't be going back now, will I?"

"No," said Giles, but decided he would return at once.

He gave directions for Kate to be returned to Parker's Lane and watched as closely as before. Then he went down to speak to Carswell, who he found examining his cadaver.

"I'm considering having him taken over to the Infirmary," said Carswell, "given that the morgue there is a good deal cooler. This muggy weather is hastening decomposition and as I shan't get the necessary permissions until the day after tomorrow –"

"Yes, that's a good plan," said Giles. "And if you are at liberty tomorrow, you can come with me to Swalecliffe to see the widow."

"Oh Lord, yes, I suppose so," said Carswell, covering up the body again. "Poor woman."

"In the meantime, there is somewhere I want to go tonight. Will you come with me? I could do with another pair of eyes."

~

Major Vernon took him to a quiet corner of town which he had never visited before, the parish of an old church dedicated to the Magdalen. From underneath the dark and dripping shadow of an overhanging yew tree in the churchyard, a man emerged to greet them. It was Lloyd, one of Major Vernon's plain clothes constables.

"I'm glad you came, sir," he said. "It's been as quiet as the grave today. Not a soul going in nor coming out. Constable Martin will tell you the same."

"No lights in the windows, even?"

"Nothing, sir."

"That's very interesting. You can go home, now, Lloyd. Good work."

The constable left, and Major Vernon crossed the road and stood peering in through a locked gate which covered the entrance to an alley. Carswell joined him.

"I wish I had a better map of this district," the Major said. "It is hard to work out which property is which."

He was carrying a small lantern which he now hooked onto the gate. He lit the flame and then set to examining the lock.

"Would you care to attempt this one, Mr Carswell?" he said, handing Felix his set of skeleton keys.

"I'll try," said Felix. "What is this place?"

"Gambling rooms and brothel."

"Surely not? Here?" Felix said, matching the key to the lock and then inserting it. A few moments of gentle manipulation and the lock turned.

"I knew you would surpass me," said Major Vernon, smiling and taking up the lantern. He blew out the flame. "Shall we?"

The gate was well oiled and opened with a touch. The Major went first, for which Felix was glad. It was not fully dark yet but the brilliance of the lantern had made his eyes crave light.

They went down a twisting passageway, with high brick walls on either side, before turning into a courtyard that seemed to contain three terraced houses. There was no sign of life. The shutters were closed and no chink of light escaped from within.

"The cat's gone," said Major Vernon, trying the front door. He turned the lock successfully but the door would not budge. "It must be bolted from the inside. Are you ready for some serious housebreaking, Mr Carswell?"

"I don't know," said Felix.

"Those shutters haven't been fixed properly," he said, pointing to one of the ground floor windows. "If I break the glass, I should be able to get the window catch undone, and the sash up, as far as it can go. Then you can climb in."

Major Vernon stripped off his coat, and wrapped it about his hand to make a soft club with which he efficiently broke one of the astragaled panes of glass. He reached in, unhooked the catch and forced the window up a scant foot. He then pushed open the shutters.

"You are quite practised," Felix said, wondering how he was going to get through such a narrow gap.

"You will need a leg up," said Major Vernon, offering his clasped hands like a good ostler assisting a man onto a horse.

Fortunately there was a sofa under the window, and Felix found a comfortable landing as he slithered through. He rolled onto his back, falling off the sofa as he did. He blinked, trying to see what sort of room it was. There was a dull glint of gold and mirrors, and the flash of a chandelier above him. There was also a strong smell of cigars and spirits.

Catching his bearings, and feeling not a little terrified of discovery, he hastened out to the hall to draw the bolts and let Major Vernon in.

"I hope to God there is no one here," he said to him.

"I don't think there is," said Major Vernon, relighting his lantern. "I think..." he broke off, looking into the room where Felix had come in.

"If this is a den of vice," Felix said, glancing back into what seemed to resemble a drawing room that had seen better days, "it seems commonplace."

"Yes, certainly, but comfortable. Perhaps that's the trick of it," said the Major. "If you make the surroundings seem less strange, the sense of risk is diminished."

"If I was taking a risk," Felix said, "I would want to feel it. To get my money's worth."

Major Vernon crossed the room and opened a door to another chamber.

"I think this is where the real business takes place," he said. The room contained a large round table covered with a baize cloth. "Lord knows how much money got wasted here. All very nicely set up for the convenience of those enslaved by the cards and the dice. And so damned well hidden! I really should have guessed that there was something like this."

"Something that looks like a boarding house?" Felix said. "There are sentimental prints on the wall. How could anyone guess that this is a brothel and a gambling den?"

"Well, George Bickley is a cunning devil."

"Bickley? This is his place?"

"The same. It's no coincidence that this place is deserted. Bickley is taking no risks, and has closed down the operation. But how did they manage it so discreetly?"

Major Vernon left the room, and Felix followed him upstairs. They went up to the third storey and through a succession of interconnecting garrets.

"Ah, this explains it!" said the Major, stopping in front of a door and pulling it open. "I once saw this in another house in Horseferry Street. It's a precaution against fire, but of course, it works equally well if you wish to leave the building unnoticed. And they didn't remember to lock it, which was careless!"

"And that's another house through there?"

"Yes, in Butcher's Row, I think, if I have my bearings right. Which is quite a busy street, generally, and no one would notice a small exodus of light women and their band boxes."

He stepped through the door and Felix followed. They found themselves in a far tighter, lower attic, with ancient beams above them, and quite empty of lumber. A primitive stair that was scarcely more than a ladder led downstairs to another deserted room, and a final stair took them to what looked like a shop, with a counter and a shuttered window.

"A shop with no stock," said Major Vernon.

"And no more than ten foot wide," said Felix, looking about him.

"Most convenient," said Major Vernon, opening the shutter a crack and looking out into the gas-lit street. "And even a bed and a fire for the doorkeeper," he added, walking to the back of the shop, where an empty bedstead had been set up adjacent to the hearth.

Then he went back upstairs.

"How did you know this was all here in the first place?" Felix said, following him.

"That woman, Kate, that I brought in to identify the Colonel. She worked here."

"And he was one of her clients?"

Major Vernon did not answer. They were on the first floor now, looking at a long passageway, with doors opening off it. He pushed open one of the doors and went in.

"Yes," he said, as Felix came into what appeared to be a neatly furnished sitting room. The Major had set his lantern down on the mantel, and appeared to be examining the flowered wallpaper closely. "I told you I did something foolish," he said.

He snatched up his lantern and went through the door into an adjoining room, where a large bed and various large mirrors formed the principal furnishings. Again Major Vernon began to examine the walls.

"What are you looking for?" Felix said.

"Spy holes."

"Really? I thought they were only the stuff of indecent books," Felix said.

"And so did I," said Major Vernon. He stopped with his hand on the wall. "But it seems not. See."

Felix followed him into the room, and saw for himself a hole, a quarter of an inch wide, carefully placed on the opposite wall to the bed.

Major Vernon went back into the sitting room, and repeated the search until he found another spy hole. Having done so, he stood with his head bowed, and somewhat to Felix's surprise, gave the skirting a hearty kick.

"Sir?" Felix said.

"My best witness coerced me because of these wretched things," the Major went on, still addressing the wall. "Except that was not the case – I was tempted. That is the simple truth. They will have seen it all; and I have been blaming those damned mushrooms. Oh, how easy it is to find excuses!"

"Are you saying –" Felix began.

"Yes, we had congress!" Major Vernon said. "And yes, what the devil was I thinking?"

"I am sure you had good reason," Felix managed to say.

"I wish to God I did," said Major Vernon.

An uncomfortable silence fell.

Felix could easily imagine himself getting into such a predicament, but Major Vernon? But the woman had been extremely attractive, and it was no easy matter being continent. It was something he wrestled with daily – and he felt it to be harder than ever. In the brief period he had been with Sukey, his body had grown accustomed to the pleasures of the bedroom, and he felt the loss of them severely. Why should Major Vernon be any different?

Eventually he managed to say, "You are better not wasting your efforts on regrets, sir, given that we are dealing with such a man as Bickley. I am sure that is what you would say to me. The important thing is that you have him in your sights now."

"After a fashion," said Major Vernon. Then he put up his hands. "Yes, you are right. Excuse me. I apologise for burdening you with this. I have kept you from your dinner too long with this little escapade. Let's go home."

Chapter Fourteen

Given the number of lodging houses and hotels in Swalecliffe, it might have taken some time to discover where Mrs Parham might be living. However, a visit to the circulating library in Ship Street, where last summer Felix had subscribed on Sukey's behalf, yielded an address in Upper Swalecliffe, the newest part of the town. The proprietor was anxious to retrieve various volumes from Mrs Parham – he had been on the verge of sending his own boy. "Perhaps the gentlemen would be good enough to remind Mrs Parham about it? They are titles much in demand at the moment. Mrs Brundell's latest, especially."

They walked up to Upper Swalecliffe, along a newly-made road lined with modern villas, set into the hillside, with bay windows placed for a sea view and all with great flights of steps to the front door. Mrs Parham's was no exception, and as they went up the ten or so steps, a woman dressed as a servant came out into the area below and looked up at them.

"Can I help you, sir?" she said.

Major Vernon leant over the railing.

"Is Mrs Parham at home?"

"She's gone out."

"Will she be long? We need to speak to her with some urgency. It's important."

"Well, I don't know –" she began, and disappeared into the house, and after a few moments opened the front door to them. "She'll be back soon enough. If it's important – ?"

"It is," said Major Vernon.

She led them into the front room, where the blinds had been carefully drawn down to keep the sun from bleaching the very fashionable and shiny furniture.

"You can wait in here," she said.

"Were you with Mrs Parham at Ardenthwaite?" said Major Vernon.

"No, sir. I come with the house."

"But Mrs Parham brought her own staff with her – a maid, and a nurse for the children?"

"No children, sir, and no maids," said the girl. "Children aren't allowed in this house anyway. My boss –"

"Who owns this house?"

"Yes, sir. He won't let to people with children. It ruins the paintwork and furniture."

"I see. And your boss's name is –?"

"Hickman."

"And how long has Mrs Parham been here?"

"About a month. If you'll excuse me, sir, I have to get on. Mrs Parham shouldn't be long. She is usually back before noon."

Left alone, Felix sat down on the solitary sofa while Major Vernon went and pulled up the blind.

"That was really quite a tale that the Colonel spun us," said Felix.

"We may have the wrong Mrs Parham," said Major Vernon. "But it is not a common name. Ah, I wonder if this is the lady?"

Felix joined him at the window. Coming down the street, and then stopping at the foot of the steps, was a smartly-dressed woman leaning on the arm of an equally well-turned out gentleman. They were laughing, and both began to climb the steps together.

Major Vernon retreated from the window with a quizzical glance at Felix.

"We won't mention we are from the Constabulary just yet," he said.

Outside they heard the maid saying, "There are two

gentlemen to see you, ma'am."

"Who are they?" said a man's voice.

"I don't know, sir."

"Did you not ask for their names, you daft woman?" he said.

"No, sir. I'm sorry, Mr Hickman, it's just that they seemed, well –" She broke off as the door was pushed open and Mrs Parham entered, with a rather imperious sweep of her skirts.

"Yes, may I help you?" she said, with some hauteur.

"Forgive the intrusion, ma'am," said Major Vernon. "My name is Vernon, Major Giles Vernon. I am an acquaintance of your husband, and this is Mr Carswell, the owner of Ardenthwaite House. I am afraid we come here with very unpleasant news. Perhaps you should sit down."

"Unpleasant news? What do you mean?"

"Please, ma'am, do sit down. And perhaps," Major Vernon addressed the maid, "you might fetch some salts and some water."

"What has happened?" demanded the man, coming in and taking Mrs Parham's hand. "What is going on?"

"Perhaps you might confirm that you are the wife of Colonel Edward Parham, ma'am, residing at Ardenthwaite House?" Major Vernon said. "Just to save you unnecessary distress."

"I am," she said. "What is it? Has something happened to my husband?"

Major Vernon nodded and gestured towards a chair.

"Won't you sit down, ma'am? I'm very sorry to have to tell you such awful news – your husband is dead. He was found dead at Ardenthwaite yesterday."

"Dead? How?"

"It seems possible he has taken his own life."

"No! Oh dear God! No!" she exclaimed and threw herself into the arms of the man called Hickman who had followed her into the room. "No, no – surely not. You must be mistaken."

"I am afraid not. My deepest condolences."

She gave a sort of howl, broke from Hickman's arms, and ran out of the room.

"Suicide?" Hickman said. "You're sure they are saying that?"

"Quite," said Major Vernon. "I understand he was an unhappy man."

"Terrible, terrible news," said Hickman with a shake of his head.

"Is there anyone here, some woman friend that we can fetch to help Mrs Parham? It seems cruel to leave her here alone," Major Vernon. "Where are her family? Does she have any sisters, or are her parents still living? I'm afraid I don't know. The Colonel mentioned they had several children –"

"I believe they are with her sister," said Hickman. "In Warwickshire." He hesitated for a moment, and then shaking his head, said, "Suicide. That's shocking."

"Yes," said Giles. "I suppose you knew him?"

"Only slightly. I met him when he took the house. He sent her here for her health, you understand."

"Yes, quite."

"A kind, considerate gentleman, I would have said," Hickman went on. "But you never can tell. We all have our demons and sometimes, I dare say, they get the better of us."

"Why did you say it was self-murder?" said Felix, as they walked away from the house.

"I had an instinct about her – and him, for that matter."

"You think they might be involved?"

"It cannot be ruled out. Often enough it is the case that spouses murder each other. There is something about this arrangement that I don't trust. Walking home on her landlord's arm like that – he had a lover-like protectiveness about him, don't you think?"

"Yes, I suppose he did."

"I wonder how she pays her rent. And after all, she has had enough to put up with from the Colonel, with his gambling and whoring. Perhaps she is taking her revenge."

"By hiring someone to kill her husband?"

"Yes."

"So you said it was suicide to make her think she had got away with it? If she was responsible, that is."

"It can be convenient to make people feel the police are stupid," said Major Vernon. "What do you think of my theory about Mrs Parham? What did you make of her reaction to the news?"

"It may have been a performance," Felix said. "I cannot tell. She might be a very fine actress or it might be perfectly genuine."

"She turned away to cry," said Major Vernon, "so that we should not see if those were real tears or not. And given she retired so promptly – well, we shall see. In the meantime, let us talk to the neighbours and see what they can tell us."

The rain had now cleared away and revealed the magnificent view of the sea. Felix remembered he had once or twice walked up this road with Sukey when the houses were still being finished and plastered. It was extraordinary how it had become a settled district. A few enquiries at the neighbours revealed that Mr Hickman was responsible for a large part of it. He owned at least ten of the houses, and was letting them out at what seemed quite substantial rates.

"I wouldn't pay that much normally – it is very expensive for Swalecliffe – but the view is delightful," said Mrs Thompson, two doors down from Mrs Parham. She was a widow and was obviously glad to have callers in order to impart all she knew. "My birds love it!"

A pair of parrots strutted up and down on a rail in front of the bay window, sunning themselves.

"And have you had much to do with Mrs Parham at number twelve?" Major Vernon asked.

"Not very much, but she hasn't been here more than a month. Of course, I asked her to call. She was very pleasant, but I don't think she was inclined to be sociable."

"She seems to be quite sociable with Mr Hickman," Major Vernon said.

"Oh, well, yes, I have noticed them walking out together rather more often than one might expect."

"Does he live in the terrace?"

"I don't think so," said the widow. "It would be good if he did, for then he would know what the houses were like – and the best landlords, I've always found, know their properties inside out. But I suppose he is only trying to make as much money as he can, just as everyone is these days. It isn't as it used to be, wouldn't you say, Major Vernon?"

"Perhaps, yes, ma'am," said Major Vernon.

"Won't you have some more cake?" said Mrs Thompson, thrusting the plate towards Felix. "But I shouldn't criticize him for that, should I? He isn't entirely a gentleman, after all. I dare say you noticed that."

"Does he manage all the business of the letting himself?"

"Yes. He comes and takes the rent in person. I was rather surprised about that. It isn't how things are usually done here, but Swalecliffe is changing, just like everywhere is. For good or for ill, who knows?" she finished, and got up to pet one of the parrots which had hopped onto the back of a chair.

"And you have seen them together quite often?"

"Yes, yes, I have. I suppose she misses her husband. Some women never can do without a gentleman about to attend on them. But it does not look nice, if you know what I mean. Mrs Radcliffe and I were saying this only yesterday."

"That is the lady at number five?"

"Yes. You should speak to her husband, Major Vernon. They have had rather a bother with Mr Hickman. Their kitchen range has been quite shockingly badly put in, and he hasn't done anything about it."

"I shall. Will Mr Radcliffe be at home?"

"No, he works down in old Swalecliffe. He is a wine merchant – on the corner of Ship Street."

~

At Benjamin Radcliffe and Sons, Wine and Spirit Merchant, they were offered sherry instead of tea, and Mr Radcliffe expounded on the saga of the badly-fitted kitchen range at some length.

"Hickman is a devil," he said. "I cannot tell you how much I regret signing the lease on that house. The situation is marvellous, but how he got the land there in the first place, one can only wonder, because it belonged to the Brentwoods at Calesham Park, and they are the sort of family who never sell land – well, not usually. But he must have made them some offer he could not refuse."

"He's new to the town?"

"Yes. I think he comes from Northminster, but I don't know where he made his money. Throwing up houses and then charging a fortune for them. It's a fine game if you can get into it, of course! I am glad we are only there till the end of the year, I can tell you that, sir. It has been a wretched mistake as far as I'm concerned."

"Do you have his business address to hand?"

"Yes, he lives at the Pier Hotel. In some style, I am told. An acquaintance of mine told me he heard that Hickman had bought the whole place, but on the quiet." He shook his head. "That's the trouble with Swalecliffe nowadays, now the railway is here. Yes, we have more visitors and more money, but with that come the likes of Hickman! He is probably going to knock the place down and put up some monstrous confection which will only attract the worst elements. We already have a gin palace – have you seen that, sir? Shocking place. I wouldn't be surprised if Hickman were behind that. I did hear a whisper to that effect."

~

"That indeed is a disturbing development," said Major Vernon as they stood outside an elaborate shop front, ornamented by a clock and pillars, with large, many-paned windows. Inside, the walls were lined with huge barrels of gin while several elaborate gas-lit chandeliers hung from the ceiling.

"It looks exactly like the one in Blackfriars Street," said Felix. "In fact, isn't that called Merriam's?"

"Yes," said Major Vernon. "And I had Bickley down as the proprietor, or at least the money behind it. But perhaps not."

He pushed open the door and went in.

As it was early afternoon there were few customers at the bar. Later, if it was anything like the establishments in Northminster, the place would be crammed with all manner of folk, getting rowdy over a glass or two – or often enough, far more – of cheap, sweet, warming gin. The usual result of which, at least in Northminster, was a descent into mayhem and brawling later in the evening, with the worst affected being hauled off to the Infirmary or the Police House.

The barmaid did not at once turn to serve them but continued to polish and arrange the glasses on the shelves in front of her.

At last she turned and gave them an enquiring glance that bordered on the insolent.

"I'd like to talk to the proprietor," said Major Vernon. "Mr – ?"

"Cotgrave?" she said. Major Vernon nodded. "Who's asking?"

"Just fetch him out, would you?" said Major Vernon, with sufficient authority that she threw down her cloth on the bar and went scuttling off into the back.

"With luck she will take us for the Excise," Major Vernon said.

Cotgrave appeared a few moments later. Respectably, indeed soberly dressed, he nevertheless had the look of a hard man about him, a man who could break up a fight or as easily provoke one. He eyed them up warily, before taking a cut glass decanter from under the counter and three short-stemmed glasses.

"Madeira, gents?" he said. "I don't imagine you are here for the gin."

"No, nor Madeira, but thank you," said Major Vernon.

"Then what?" Cotgrave said, pouring himself a glass. "If you are from the Excise, let me tell you, there isn't a drop in this establishment that hasn't passed through the proper channels and paid the correct rate."

"I'm glad to hear that, Mr Cotgrave," said Major Vernon. "Tell me, how long have you been in business here?"

"Three months."

"And trade is good?"

"Trade is excellent."

"And who is Mr Merriam – the name above the door? Why is this not Cotgrave's? After all, I am sure you do most of the work."

"There is no Merriam. It's just a name the owner put up there."

"Mr Hickman?" said Major Vernon.

"Aye."

"Is he your landlord or your employer?"

"Employer," said Cotgrave. "But he lets me have a free hand. And you're right, sir, I have done most of the work building the business. There is more to a place like this than just the fitting out. You have to get the people over the threshold and then make 'em stay."

"He's lucky to have you in his employ, then."

"Yes, to be frank, he is and I'm not sure he knows it. But what's it to you, sir?"

"I'm considering making an investment in one of his enterprises. I like to get a feel of how a man manages things, the quality of the people he employs, that sort of thing, before I commit myself."

"Is he needing money?" said Cotgrave, and then leant forward confidentially, "I had heard that."

"I appreciate your confidence, Mr Cotgrave. Do you have any more detail for me?"

"Well, Mr – sorry, I didn't catch your name, sir?"

"Peters," said Major Vernon. "And this is my colleague, Mr Frazer," he added indicating Felix. "And any information would be very much to my advantage, Mr Cotgrave, and yours, if matters go ahead as I am intending they should. I would be only too happy to mention your name in the right circumstances. It would be a fine thing, certainly, to see Cotgrave above the door."

"Let's go into my office," said Cotgrave and took them into a cubby-hole of a room in the back.

"I don't like to be a teller of tales," he said, when he had closed the door. "But I have to think of my future. I have put my blood and my soul into building this place up – and with half the town sneering at me for it, as if I am the devil himself, and the other half queuing up for another, as if I am their saviour. So I reckon I'm on to a good thing and I want to stay in harness. He pays me nicely enough and there is a little extra to be made on top of that. So I am well placed and wish to remain so. And if Hickman is in trouble, that is trouble for me."

"Of course," said Major Vernon, "when he solicited me, he painted a very rosy picture of it all."

"It is, in places; well, at least this is rosy enough. You may look at my books, if you have a mind to, sir. But it's my opinion he's doing too much and too fast, what with the Pier Hotel and the bars in Northminster as well as here, and he is losing money hand over fist. His creditors are making a nuisance of themselves. He even brought one in here the other day, and took most of the week's takings out just to appease him. Caused me no end of trouble that did, but it's his money in the end. But why he should be so eager paying off a fellow like that, I don't know. Mostyn his name was. No idea what his line is, but it was serious business, that's for certain."

"Mostyn – are you sure of that?" said Major Vernon.

"Yes."

"Could you describe him to me?" said Major Vernon.

"A swarthy, dirty-looking fellow, with a manner about him. As if he were pretending to be a gentleman."

"And when he had been given his money, then what happened?"

"He went off, and Mr Hickman went off to see – well, his lady of the moment, up on the hill."

"Mrs Parham?" said Major Vernon.

"Somebody or other's wife, that's all I know. It always is with him, and the higher the flower, the higher he likes to reach." Cotgrave shook his head.

"Mr Hickman is beginning to sound like a risky proposition," said Major Vernon.

"Not if you were to take him over entirely," said Cotgrave. "I'm sure you could, if you had a mind to, Mr Peters. You have that air about you, sir, if you don't mind me saying. You might save him from himself, and save us all in the act!"

"I will bear that in mind, Mr Cotgrave," said Major Vernon.

Chapter Fifteen

"I never thought I could pass for a financier," said Major Vernon as they walked the long pier that led to the steamer dock. They had just submitted a description of Mostyn to the local police office.

"I suspect, though, that Mostyn will be long gone from Swalecliffe," Major Vernon went on. "It is too easy a place to get away from, with the steamer service to Newcastle and the railway to Northminster. Why on earth would he stay here? He has got his pay."

"Still, we have Hickman within our sights," pointed out Felix. "And he has every reason to stay here."

The Pier Hotel behind them was covered in scaffolding.

"But the curious thing remains," said Major Vernon. "Yes, pay a man to kill your husband, but to hang him? You need several men to do it. It could not have been Mostyn alone. Hickman must have got some others on the job – yet why not just have Mostyn dispatch him neatly? He could have poisoned him, just as he perhaps poisoned us. Why the hanging?"

"A show of power – that was your theory," Felix reminded him.

"And the Colonel was Bickley's pet," said Major Vernon. "We are back to Bickley again. Could that be it: Bickley versus Hickman?" He put up one clenched fist and then knocked it against the other. "Is this tit-for-tat? You murdered my man so I will murder yours."

"Lord, I hope not," said Felix.

"So do I," said Major Vernon. "For such people never stop at one murder apiece."

He stopped and glanced at his watch, then turned on the spot.

"As I thought," he said.

Coming along the pier behind them was a pony and trap; alongside the driver sat a well-dressed lady with her luggage.

"Is that not –?" said Felix.

"The widow Parham, yes. Catching the three-thirty to Antwerp," remarked Major Vernon. "Clearly, she has lost her nerve. I thought she might," and he strode down to halt the driver.

~

The Police House at Swalecliffe was formed of two ancient cottages adjoining an equally decrepit lock-up near the old harbour. Mrs Parham was thoroughly disgusted at being brought there, bristling with the sort of indignation that might betray a guilty conscience.

"Perhaps you would like to tell me the reason you are travelling to Holland, Mrs Parham?" Major Vernon asked, having taken her into the Station Sergeant's office.

"I was going to stay with friends in Brussels. Your news – it made me wish to be with my friends. And now I have missed the steamer – because of you!"

"Would not the usual thing be to write to them and ask if you might come to them? A day or two would have made no difference. But on the first boat to the continent, ma'am?"

"There is no law against impetuosity," she said. "And my friends would have understood."

"Oh, I am sure they would. But I find it very strange, all the same, this haste of yours to leave. Do you not want to go to Northminster and see your husband's remains? A proper leave-taking can be very beneficial to the curing of grief –"

"Am I to take advice from you on how I deal with my grief, sir?" she said. "How dare you! You have already misrepresented yourself to me and inconvenienced me grossly, and now this!"

"I apologise, but the circumstances of your husband's death require that you are inconvenienced. I cannot let you go flitting off to the continent," Major Vernon said.

"Flitting!"

"Yes, flitting. Your actions raise serious questions –"

"Only in your mind, sir. I am quite at liberty to do as I please."

"Your husband has been murdered. That puts a very different cast on matters."

"Murder? You said he had committed suicide."

"I have had new information."

She sat in silence for a moment. He could sense the calculation in it.

"But that is –" she began and broke off again.

"Do you know anyone who might have wished him dead?" Major Vernon said.

"No, no, of course not. It cannot be murder, surely not?" she said again.

"It certainly is. He was found hanged – and the evidence is very clear that it was not by his own hand."

She glanced away for a moment and then looked straight at him again, and said, "You must be mistaken."

"Why do you say that?"

"Because – because he had, unfortunately, threatened to take his life on several occasions previously. He was troubled. I have always feared that one day... but murder, no, that is impossible. You are mistaken, I am sure of it."

"The evidence is quite clear," said Felix. "The neck bones were broken in such a way –"

"Sir, I beg you!" she exclaimed, putting out her hand to silence him. "Have some pity!"

"I think we will leave it at that for now, ma'am," Major Vernon said. "Sergeant Barnes will escort you home now. Again, do not attempt to leave Swalecliffe, ma'am, if you please!"

"So it was murder that was supposed to look like suicide?" said Felix after she had gone.

"I think that was what she intended, yes, but it may not have happened that way. She perhaps chose the wrong man to organise the job."

"Hickman?"

"I think he may have promised her one thing and delivered another. He may have had his own reasons for disposing of the Colonel in such a way. Let's go and find him, before he leaves town."

It was five minutes' walk to the Pier Hotel, and there Major Vernon's fears were confirmed. Mr Hickman and his servant had left a little after noon, for the station. That they were seen boarding the one o'clock Northminster train was some comfort, but only a little.

"At least we can enquire at Merriam's for him," said Felix, as they boarded their own train back to Northminster.

"Yes, that is something, and his business interests may keep him in the city for a little while, with luck. But if I were him I would jump on the next train to London. We can only hope he has not done so already."

Chapter Sixteen

They returned to Northminster to find the city awash in a spring rainstorm that filled the streets with mud and sent the temperature plummeting. Giles ate a late, hasty dinner at The Black Bull, leaving Carswell at the table.

He made his way to the little house in Parker's Lane and was glad he had wasted so little time on dinner, for there he found Constable Hale sitting with a bleeding head and cursing.

"She just went at me, sir. I didn't stand a chance. She was like a fury, and before I knew it I was on the floor and she was out the door. Foley went after her, but I don't know if he has had any luck. She went off like the Devil himself, I can tell you!"

Giles reined in his annoyance that two competent men had been overwhelmed by a woman, and restrained himself from bombarding Hale with questions about how such a situation had arisen in the first place. That could wait, and it had to be borne in mind that Kate was no ordinary woman. She would have used some trick or other to get them to let her downstairs. She had used tricks on him, after all.

He therefore confined himself to asking when this had happened.

"About three quarters of an hour ago, at most."

He wasted no more time and set off to try and find her for himself, no matter how futile that attempt might be.

There was the advantage, although only a small one, that she was not a local. Her knowledge of Northminster would be limited to those places where she had been allowed beyond the confines of the gambling house. Given that she was mortally afraid of Bickley's retribution, she would, he supposed, steer clear of that district, unless she was very bold and determined to recover her stash. Perhaps she might even have concocted a story to cover her absence and intended to inveigle her way back into his favour. If she had discovered the locked empty house, then what would she do? It was a good place to shelter on a filthy night.

But that was merely a hypothesis. She may have thought that too dangerous. She would most likely have reverted to her former trade, and it was these areas of the city where Giles began his search.

He soon found that the weather had driven the bright feathered creatures inside from all their usual haunts.

He passed by one of the new gin palaces, not Merriam's, but one of the others that Giles was certain was owned by Bickley. This seemed an unlikely place for her to take shelter, despite the crowds. Yet it was the establishment that she had mentioned in relation to her tattoo, so he stopped and went in, first making sure that the few valuables he carried on him were securely placed in a pocket inside his waistcoat, entirely inaccessible to the most skilled criminal fingers.

There was a reason for the crowd, other than the rain. As he made his way past the great bar, with the wall of barrels behind him, he saw that the back room had been opened up to create an auditorium, with a platform at the far end, lit by glowing limelights that were better and brighter than anything the old Theatre Royal in Bridge Street could offer. On stage, three girls and a man, dressed in bright spangled costumes, were dancing and singing energetically accompanied by a small band. They were singing one of those inane but curiously unforgettable modern songs, with words that could be taken to be obscene or nonsensical according to preference. On hearing it once, Giles knew the tune would be spinning in his head for some time hence, whether he wanted it there or not.

He scanned the crowd as best as he could, standing with his back against the wall.

It was no wonder the place was popular: the gin was cheap, the lights were bright and the entertainment was free. Who but a fool would stay in their wretched rooms when there was this as a welcome antidote to hours of wearisome labour in the mills and manufactories? He knew that in his youth, he would have relished such a scene, embraced it, along with the dubious young women who were singing and swaying at the front of the crowd.

But there was no sign of Kate in her lilac silk dress.

He was about to turn away when someone tapped him on the shoulder.

He turned. It was inevitable he would attract notice. He was not dressed quite shabbily enough for the company.

"Yes?" he said.

"Looking for someone in particular?" The man who enquired was well turned out, with a look of the management about him – he wore a flash red silk waistcoat and a flowery cravat.

"Is this your place?" said Giles.

"What is it to you?" he said.

"I'm looking for amusement," Giles said. "I was told by a friend to enquire here."

"Amusement?" said the man. "What did you have in mind."

"A hand of cards? Something of that sort. I have it on good authority that there is a game –"

"No, no, you must be mistaken, sir," said the man. "Not here. Who did you hear that from?"

"A friend. His name need not concern you," said Giles. "I have the means, you know, there isn't a question about that, so answer me plainly. I really don't care to being made to wait about in such a fashion, do you understand? If your employer is not interested in such business, I can take my money elsewhere, but if I were you, my man, I should make him aware that I am interested."

"If you would come this way, sir," he said, suddenly deferential.

It occurred to Giles that if he did not like games of chance as played on baize tables with cards and dice, he did enjoy this sort of situation more than he ought. It was undoubtedly a reckless way to proceed, for he had no clear idea who might be waiting for him at the office at the end of the passageway. If it was Bickley himself, then it would be awkward, but perhaps the moment had come for a conversation with him.

"Your name, sir?" said the man in the red waistcoat.

"Peters," said Giles, deciding he would continue with his earlier impersonation.

Red Waistcoat knocked at the door and waited.

A woman's voice answered.

"Yes?"

"Gentleman for you, ma'am," said Red Waistcoat, opening the door and revealing a plushly furnished office, with a large mahogany desk, at which sat a woman with various large ledgers in front of her. Lace-capped, grey-haired, fashionable but sober in her dress, she looked for all the world like the mistress of a large country house. She looked up from her work with a look of mild, genial enquiry.

"Mr Peters," said Red Waistcoat.

"How do you do, Mr Peters?" she said, setting down her pen. "What may I do for you?" She had the accent of the city, but it sounded as though it had been gently sanded away by years in an expensive boarding school. "Thank you, Mr Hooper, that will be all."

"As you like, ma'am."

Giles studied her face with care for a moment and ventured, having seen no trace of a wedding ring, "Have I the honour of addressing Miss Bickley?"

She inclined her head.

"You know my brother?"

"I do. I could not help noticing the resemblance."

"Then I am very glad to know you, Mr Peters. What may I do for you?"

"I was told I might find some congenial entertainment here. A hand of cards with like-minded souls?"

She nodded, and said, "Yes, quite, but regrettably I have to disappoint you at present. That side of things has had to be given up, for various reasons too trifling to go into. But I can offer you a glass of wine, I hope, and perhaps a cigar? I am sorry not to be able to oblige you."

She got up, went to a cupboard and took out a decanter.

"That's a shame, and how unfortunate for you that your business should be interrupted."

"There is bad weather from time to time," she said. "Sherry?"

"No, thank you. I will not trouble you any more, ma'am. I can see you are deep in your books."

"It's no trouble," she said. "Please, take a glass with me." She poured out two glasses and handed one to him. "How do you know my brother?"

"We met at Doncaster Races, two years ago. We struck up a conversation about Blue Blazer – you know, that wonderful filly that Lord Hobart had running that season. From there, we found we had a lot of interests in common and he mentioned, if I should ever be in Northminster, I should look him up. I was directed here."

He hoped this sounded plausible.

"You're a racing man?"

"I have had some horses in the field, and I was in the training line for a while. My lords Maunsley and St John were kind enough to employ me. But I have been putting my assets into bricks and mortar of late. It seems sensible the way things are going. The old pleasures are being taken away from us. I had hoped to talk through a few ideas in that direction with Mr Bickley, to tell the truth."

"You are thinking wisely," said Miss Bickley. "This is a difficult time. Hence this establishment. We are doing very nicely with it. In fact, on the subject of bricks and mortar and investments," she said, "we were only speaking the other day of rebuilding here. Our theatrical arrangements here are rather makeshift. I was thinking it would be an excellent idea to knock down the room at the back and start again. With galleries and such. Then the better acts will be happy to come and play here. And one might sell tickets as well as gin."

"Your brother never mentioned he had a handsome little sister," he said. "A handsome clever little sister."

"Now you are being foolish, Mr Peters. I am far beyond the age of that sort of thing. I am a contented spinster, let me tell you!" But it was clear enough from her tone that the flattery had done some work.

"Do you have any drawings to hand?" he asked.

"Now, how did you guess?" she said, delightedly. "Oh, I can see why my brother liked you, Mr Peters. You are quite his type." She went again to the cupboard and took out a great roll of drawings. "I have asked for two architects to draw up a scheme for me. That is the usual thing, I think?"

"Very sensible, ma'am, very sensible."

"Now, what do you think of this one? This stage would be the largest in the North East, and would be able to accommodate the sort of spectacles usually confined to the West End. Imagine that, sir, in Northminster!"

After a glass of sherry and an extensive lecture on Miss Bickley's theatrical fancies, Giles managed to take his leave.

"If you come back before noon tomorrow, you will catch him, Mr Peters."

"I shall come then, most certainly."

"I will tell him you were here," she said.

It was still raining heavily as he left, and he then had a miserable walk through the less pleasant districts of the city in a futile search for any trace of Kate. He found nothing more of any interest, and made his way back to The Black Bull, soaked to the skin and bone tired.

If Kate was lost, he had at least discovered something else important about Bickley's operation. Bickley might be on his knees in front of the Bishop, pretending to be a repentant sinner, but his family were still firmly in control of his interests, and he was still firmly in control of them. It was a piece of showmanship that would not disgrace the great stage of Miss Bickley's imaginary palaces of entertainment.

But illusions could be destroyed, as easily as soap bubbles could be pricked. It was just a question of finding a pin.

He would need to talk again to Johnny Hopkins, alias Horatio Baxter. But that could wait until the morning.

Chapter Seventeen

Felix was surprised that Major Vernon had let him remain by the fire with a glass of wine and his letters. He had gone off with such urgency that he wondered if he ought to offer to assist him in whatever endeavour he had embarked upon.

He had not been sitting long when Mr Wilkes came in, asking if he would come and look at a newly arrived guest – a very great gentleman, apparently, had been taken ill.

"Or I should say, gotten worse," Mr Wilkes said. "For he didn't look in the prime of it when he arrived. I said to Mrs Wilkes that he looked in a dreadful condition. Apparently he was supposed to be travelling on today to his country property, but he couldn't face it after the railway. Hardly surprising, if you ask me – those things make me queasy to think about them – and yet you've been to Swalcliffe and back today, sir, I gather!" Wilkes gave a shudder. "Of course, Mrs Wilkes says I should be glad for the increase of trade, and she has a point, but I can't help thinking –"

He broke off as they reached the guest's door. He tapped it and went in.

"Here he is, Mr Field," said Mr Wilkes, addressing a black-coated man who was sitting at the table covered in paperwork. "Mr Carswell, the surgeon."

"Do you have much practice here?" said Mr Field, looking at Felix rather doubtfully. "You seem rather young, sir, if you don't mind my saying."

"A little," said Felix. "My work is principally with the County Constabulary."

Mr Field frowned. "My employer has been under the care of Sir James Rennison," he said.

"Then he has been in good hands," said Felix. "Perhaps if I might see him? I understand there was some urgency –"

"Sir Richard Blanchfort," said Mr Field.

"Lord Rothborough will be distressed to hear that an old friend is ill," Felix said. "He mentioned him to me only the other day."

"You attend Lord Rothborough?" said Mr Field.

"No. My father is a clergyman on his Scottish estate. I have known him since I was a child."

This was recommendation enough for Mr Field, whose whole manner seemed to change in a moment. Felix swallowed his amusement and went with him to the adjoining bedroom.

Here Sir Richard was lying in the vast, old-fashioned canopy bed that dominated the room.

It was as well the bed was broad, for the man himself was a giant. In good health he would have had an impressive physique, but now he appeared to be wasting away.

"Sir Richard, this is the surgeon – Mr Carswell," Field said. "Jackson and I thought it best to find someone."

"A clergyman might have been a better idea," said Sir Richard. "Carswell, did you say?"

"Yes, sir."

"Come a little closer, would you? You look most –" and then as Felix approached the bed, a mixture of puzzlement and pain crossed his face. "You look familiar – William, is it you? But how can –"

"Lord Rothborough was speaking to me of you only the other day, sir," Felix said, taking his hand and feeling his pulse. "He will be very concerned to hear of this. Perhaps a visit from him might help you."

"I should very much like that," said Sir Richard, grasping Felix's hand in return. "And you are – you are his boy, are you not?" Felix nodded. "The likeness is uncanny. You might be him when I first knew him! How strange is the hand of

Providence to bring you here now!"

"I hope I can help you a little if I can," said Felix. "You have not been well for some time, I understand. You have been seeing Sir James Rennison?"

"I am dying," said Sir Richard. "That is the plain truth of it. Sir James has done his best, and can do no more for me. I have very little time. I want to see my daughter. I must see her. If I can accomplish that, then –"

"I have met her," said Felix. "I danced with her the other night, here in Northminster. But I do not know if she is still in town. If she was, I would fetch her to you at once."

"You danced with her?" said Sir Richard, managing to smile. "How I wish I might have seen her dance!"

"You might yet partner her yourself, sir," said Felix. "With all respect to Sir James, you may have more life left to you than you imagine. We can be mistaken."

"You are kind to say so, Mr Carswell," said Sir Richard, "but I fear my remaining days are very few. If only I could find a little more strength. The pain is very exhausting, but I am afraid to take any more opiates in case they take me before I have made my peace with my daughter and my God."

"It is possible to mitigate some of the pain, without that risk," said Felix. "You should not rule it out entirely. And you must send for Miss Blanchfort."

"No, no, sending for her will not do. You must go and get her for me," said Sir Richard. "Just as you said. Her mother will never let her come here if I send a servant. You must go, Mr Carswell, and tell her that there is no hope and no time."

"I do not know if Lady Blanchfort –" Felix began, thinking it rather likely that he would be seen entirely in the light of a servant.

"Yes, yes, but you must oppose her. You must stand on your authority as a medical man," said Sir Richard. "She will not be able to refuse you that. And if she does, you will remind her that Lord Rothborough is Eleanor's trustee and future guardian, and that you are his representative."

"I will do my best," said Felix.

"Eleanor will come with you. Her mother may have poured poison into her heart but she will come if she knows the truth. She will want to come. And you will be a good messenger."

"I hope so," said Felix. "I will go at first light, I promise. In the meantime, perhaps you might let me examine you and do what I can to make you comfortable? You ought to rest as best you can so you will be in a good state to see her."

Sir Richard nodded, and sank back on the pillows, clearly too tired and in too much pain to speak any further. Felix examined him very gently and rather more superficially than he would have done in other circumstances, but even from such slight observations it was hard to dispute Sir James Rennison's grim prognosis.

Turning away from the bed a moment, Mr Field handed him a paper, saying, "I had Sir James write up his diagnosis in case we had to summon another medical man."

It made for sober reading and confirmed Felix's observations. A cancer of the stomach, which had spread into his bones and blood.

Felix did what he could to alleviate the pain, making him a mild opiate draft which he consented to drink. He then redressed the wounds where the skin had broken and applied soothing poultices where he could.

Eventually Sir Richard did pass into a form of sleep. In other circumstances it would have been far kinder to hope that this was the prelude to a gentle departure in the next dozen hours, yet the sense of the man's unfinished business hung in the air, like the lingering smoke of a recently extinguished candle. Felix left, hoping that Sir Richard would last long enough to see his daughter at least for a little while.

He left The Black Bull and went to arrange for a carriage to drive him at first light out to Hawksby Hall, where Lady

Blanchfort and her daughter were staying. He then walked round to the house in the Minster Precincts where Lord Rothborough generally stayed when he was in Northminster, and found on enquiry that his Lordship and Lady Maria were still at Holbroke. However, a servant was driving there first thing, with various items of business and shopping, so Felix sat down in Lord Rothborough's book room and added a letter of his own to the pile.

He sat there for a few moments alone, having sealed the letter with a stamp showing the Rothborough crest and given it to the servant. It was a crest that he also had in the form of a signet ring, which he never cared to use, let alone wear, but which Lord Rothborough had given him on his coming of age. He had struggled so hard to build his life free of the shadow of that crest, and yet now he found himself, willy-nilly, its representative. The hand of Providence, if one believed in such things, did indeed work in strange ways, and now it seemed to be determined to throw him into the society of that curious, red-haired young lady who he had decided it would be better for him to avoid at all costs. But a dying father's wish overturned all other considerations.

Chapter Eighteen

Hawksby Hall lay in the village of the same name that was, thanks to a spanking new road, a fast and easy drive from Northminster. Alongside this road quite a few houses were beginning to be built, making a sort of suburb of the outskirts of the village; but in its heart, beyond the ancient parish church, the old order was still evident.

The Hall, large, white and regular in form, was perfectly visible from the village green, but was set back behind a long gravelled forecourt accessed only by a pair of elaborate wrought-iron gates. These gates were locked and a bell had to be rung, and it was a few minutes before a manservant came running up from the house to enquire his business.

"I am on urgent business from Sir Richard Blanchfort. I must speak to Lady Blanchfort," said Felix. "This is my card."

"Urgent, you say, sir?" said the servant, examining the card.

"Extremely," said Felix.

"Very well, sir," said the servant, and opened the gates to him. Felix followed him across the gravel and up to the entrance of the house.

"If you will wait here, please sir," said the servant, showing Felix into the hall.

He was left to wait, with the distinct impression that envoys from Sir Richard were not very welcome. After a few moments he saw a mounted groom come trotting round from the back court of the house. He was leading a milk-white pony with a side-saddle on it, presumably meant for the young lady of the house for her morning ride. Felix supposed that Miss Blanchfort would be down imminently and she would be ready to go to Northminster at once. That, he hoped, would simplify matters.

Another five minutes or so passed, and Felix began to grow impatient. The groom outside with the horse nonchalantly took out his pipe and lit it. Felix would not have minded a cheroot of his own at that moment, when suddenly a door behind him burst open and Miss Blanchfort, dressed in her green habit, came striding out, with her habit skirt flung over her arm, her tightly-fitting riding trousers completely on view.

"I shall, and you shall not stop me!" she was saying to the older woman who came after her.

"You shall not, Miss!" said the older woman catching her arm. "Your mother has forbidden it. You –"

At this moment they both caught sight of Felix. The woman released Miss Blanchfort's arm, while she now bounded forward towards him, smiling.

"Mr Carswell!" she said. "What can you be doing here?" She put out her hand to him, and he could not resist taking it.

"I have bad news, I'm afraid. Your father –"

"Yes?" Lady Blanchfort's voice broke out from the staircase. "What is this urgent message, sir?"

Lady Blanchfort was coming downstairs in her dressing gown. She stopped a few steps from the foot of the stairs. "Yes?" she said again.

"It is Papa," said Miss Blanchfort. "Something has happened to him. Oh, Mama –"

"He is gravely ill," Felix said. "He wishes to see you at once, Miss Blanchfort, and I think urgency is in order."

"And he has asked you to come here and say this?" said Lady Blanchfort.

"Yes."

"Well, we shall see about that. Eleanor, please go to your room."

"Mama, did you not hear what he said?"

"Yes, and did you not hear what I said? Go to your room."

"I shall not!" she said. "I am going to see my father. He is very ill, Mama –"

Lady Blanchfort shook her head.

"I doubt it. Thank you, Mr Carswell, for your message. Please inform Sir Richard that his manipulations are of little interest to me."

"Manipulations!" exclaimed Miss Blanchfort. "Papa is ill, Mama, do you not understand what he is saying?"

"It certainly is not a manipulation, ma'am," said Felix. "I have examined him myself. He is in considerable danger. Sir James Rennison has said that there is very little hope, and, from what I have seen, I would have to concur."

"I think you had better leave, Mr Carswell. Come here, please, Eleanor," she said, putting out her hand to her daughter.

But Miss Blanchfort stood where she was, shaking her head.

"I will go with you, sir," she said. "I will not take such a risk, Mama, I cannot, no matter what you say about it!" She glanced at the door and then at Felix in a manner that he could only interpret as conspiratorial.

"You would not dare –" said Lady Blanchfort, coming down a step. "Miss Taunton, would you –?"

Miss Taunton was about to lay hands on Miss Blanchfort again, but the young woman was too fast for her. Before anyone could stop her, she had run out of the door and was dashing noisily across the gravel towards the gates and his carriage.

Felix took his cue and ran after her.

"Stop her, sir!" he heard Lady Blanchfort shouting after him but he knew he would do no such thing.

Miss Blanchfort had already leapt into the carriage.

"Back to Northminster!" he shouted to the driver and

jumped in behind her.

Miss Blanchfort was sitting in the corner opposite, in a regular furl of habit skirts.

"That is what I must deal with. Always! Always!" she exclaimed. Then she pressed her hands to her face. "How bad is it?" she said.

"God willing, there will be time," said Felix.

"And how long has he been ill?" she said. "I did not even know that. I do not get letters from him any more. Perhaps he writes, but she does not let me see them."

"I am sure he writes," Felix said.

"I write to him, but I am not allowed to send them. How I hate her! How can she be so wicked? My own darling Papa –" She looked away from him and out of the carriage window, the tears streaming down her face. "Just because she loathes him for her own wretched, unjustified reasons, I am always to be punished for loving him. He is my father! Oh dear Lord," she said closing her eyes and pressing her hands together. "Spare him, dear Lord! For my sake. At least for a little while."

~

Major Vernon was just on the verge of leaving when they returned to The Black Bull. He looked puzzled, as he might, to see Felix handing Miss Blanchfort out of the carriage.

"Miss Blanchfort's father is here, and gravely ill," Felix said to him. "I wonder, should I fetch Canon Fforde?" he added.

"I'll go and get him. My best wishes, Miss Blanchfort," Major Vernon said.

She nodded, as she stood in the doorway to the inn, wiping back her tears.

"Come," Felix said, and took her upstairs.

Outside, a fair spring day broke out, drying away the rain of the previous night. But inside the walls of the ancient timbered inn, Sir Richard's life slowly ebbed away. He could not speak much to his daughter, but the sight of her seemed to comfort him enormously, and she sat by the bed, her hands wrapped about his. Sometimes she bent forward and kissed him.

She no longer looked like the Queen, nor even the Princess of the Fairies. She looked pale and mortal and far too young to have to undergo this trial, without any close friends about her. Well-meaning strangers were all she had.

Canon Fforde came and gave Sir Richard communion, and read from the prayer book in his kindly, sober and intelligent manner. This seemed to both comfort and distress Miss Blanchfort, for it showed that there was little more to be done except wait for the inevitable, and indeed an hour or so later, his breathing wavered and struggled, and he was gone, her hands still wrapped about his.

She rose and looked across at Felix enquiringly, for he had been holding his other hand, feeling the cold of death creep up. He made the other necessary checks, closed his eyes, and returned her gaze with a shake of his head.

She nodded slowly, kissed her father's hand again, laid it on his chest and together they drew the sheet over him.

Then she rushed from the room.

Felix followed her, watching as she made her way down the passageway, unsteady on her legs, as if on board a ship. He caught up with her just as she almost collapsed, and steered her into his own sitting room, which was warm and full of morning sunlight. She sat in an armchair, gasping for breath.

"The windows –" she managed to say.

He opened the casements and in a moment she was standing beside him, breathing in the air in desperate lungfuls, her hands pressed to the window sill, her face turned up towards the sun.

"Godspeed," she said, softly, "godspeed, my dear Papa."

"Amen," Felix found himself saying.

She leant against him, her head on his shoulder, and he put his arm out to steady her as she dissolved into tears.

Chapter Nineteen

Having delivered his message to Lambert, Giles left the Treasurer's House and was surprised to meet Mrs Maitland and Tom crossing the Minster Precincts together. Tom looked as if he were struggling to speak, and was waving his arms about as if in frustration, closing his eyes and throwing his head back. As he came closer it became clear he was attempting to speak German, and Mrs Maitland was gently prompting him as he faltered.

He looked very pleased to see Giles, and gave him a long, enthusiastic greeting in the same language, which got an approving smile from his tutor.

"I am earning my keep by helping Tom with his German conversation," said Mrs Maitland.

"Uncle Edward and Charles have gone back to Oxford," said Tom, "so we have her to ourselves now, Uncle Giles."

The Minster clock chimed the half hour.

"Now, is that the time already?" said Mrs Maitland, whose expression showed a mixture of amusement and embarrassment at Tom's artlessness. "You had better go if you are to rescue Master Hughes."

"From what?" Giles asked.

"His tutor," said Tom. "He is allowed out for three quarters of an hour. I have a scheme that he should come and learn German with me. I'm going to put it to the Bishop himself, Mrs Maitland."

"Perhaps you should talk to your father first, Tom," said Giles.

"Yes, indeed," said Mrs Maitland.

"Do you think so?" said Tom. "Better from the horse's

mouth, I should say."

"Or *aus erster Hand*, as they say in German," said Mrs Maitland.

"Oh, that is good. I will write that one down," said Tom, reaching into his pocket and taking out a little memorandum book of the kind Giles always used. "You see, Uncle Giles, I am turning into you," he said as he scribbled. "In fact, I need your advice. I have been considering what I should do next. I have been looking into the Royal Engineering College at Woolwich."

"Hence the interest in German," said Mrs Maitland.

"Modern languages are a requirement for entry," said Tom. "And why should I waste any more of my time with a language no one speaks?"

"Given I was a very poor classicist, you should probably not ask me that," said Giles.

"You are exactly the person I should ask," said Tom. "Do you think I might cut it in the Engineers? I know it is not what one would consider a crack regiment, but then I remember you saying that half the battle is won by the Engineers, especially these days. I should far rather be useful than flash – as you are."

Mrs Maitland burst out laughing at that, as did Giles.

"Said by one who attempted to deface himself with a rusty needle!" Giles said, and moved as if to punch Tom in the upper arm. "If that was not flash, then –"

"I have reconsidered that!" said Tom, dodging his mock blow and covering his forearm. "I have learnt my lesson. I intend to be sensible and useful."

"Useful and not flash?" said Giles. "You make me feel miserable and old. Can I not be flash *and* useful? Perhaps I should buy a new waistcoat or two. I saw a magnificent specimen last night in crimson figured silk. It was decidedly gaudy."

"You would not have hesitated previously," said Mrs

Maitland.

"I think I should not hesitate now," said Giles.

"No!" exclaimed Tom. "That would look all wrong. Mama says you are the arbiter of discreet good taste in such things."

"It gets worse!" Giles said. "I really cannot have her holding me up as a paragon. I wish to be a bad example to you, Tom. I must work harder at it." Mrs Maitland was still laughing and he could not help but be pleased by it. "Now go and find your friend, Tom. I may see you later, as I must call on the Bishop this morning."

"I wonder what the Bishop will say to that," said Giles, when he had gone. "An onslaught from Tom is hard to resist, and I suppose German is godly enough."

"As a tutor, I may not be," said Mrs Maitland. "And there are certain theological texts in German that I am sure the Bishop will not care for. A rationalist school of thought that has been attempting to put our Saviour into an historical context. Some might say that such an endeavour rather chips away at His divinity."

"You have been busy at Oxford," said Giles.

"I had nothing else to do. My son was snatched from me and the bookshops are very good. And I heard a great many interesting sermons."

"They should give you a degree."

"The day is coming, I think, when that must happen. When it *will* happen!"

"Perhaps when Northminster gets its own university, you will agitate for women undergraduates?"

"It's already in hand," she said. "Edward is very aware of my views. He shares them. He did not originally –"

"Until he knew you, I suppose?" Giles said.

"No, I was not the cause of his change of mind. Perhaps I consolidated matters, though," she added. "Although I certainly did not need to agitate."

"If you are both of the same mind, then things can only go well with you," said Giles.

"I hope so," she said. "And thank you again for being so understanding."

He wished to say he did not understand at all, and that it was all an illusion created by good manners. In that moment, standing with her there in the pleasant embrace of the spring sunlight, hearing her laugh, he could only feel acutely the loss of that which he had so carelessly tossed away.

"I'd better go," he said. "I have a hundred things in hand, and if Celia catches me, I shall never finish any of them."

"She will have us dancing again," said Mrs Maitland.

"Yes, that was all much too pleasant for someone who is supposed to be useful," he managed to say, and quickly took his leave.

~

The Bishop was in a meeting, but his secretary informed him he would be done with it shortly, and showed him into the Bishop's library to wait. Here he found Mrs Hughes at work on a pile of correspondence.

"Forgive the interruption," he said after he had presented himself.

"No, no, I am very glad to know you, Major Vernon. I have heard quite a lot about you."

She was an elegant, rather beautiful woman, and her sober, grey, quakerish dress emphasised it.

"All good, of course," she added, showing him to a chair, and sitting down opposite. "Is there anything I can help you with, in my husband's absence?"

She said this as if he were about to request spiritual advice.

"I came about Mr Bickley. At the party at the Treasurer's house the other night – what the Bishop said was very interesting."

"I am glad to hear it. It was a remarkable thing, his coming here like that."

"That is my difficulty," said Giles. "You see, Mr Bickley is a person I have been watching for some time in my professional capacity, and recent events have only confirmed my fears about him."

"I don't quite understand you," she said, laying her hand on her breast. "Your fears? It is a matter for rejoicing, surely, that he was moved to come here and speak to my husband as he did."

"And you are convinced he is sincere?"

"Oh yes, absolutely. There was no doubt about it."

"I have been looking into Mr Bickley's affairs for some time, Mrs Hughes. He is an artful man, that much is clear. I suspect that he is associated with many criminal activities in the city, but I have never had enough clear evidence to make an arrest. Now, I believe you transcribed what he said to your husband the other night?"

"Yes, yes, I did make some notes. We were thinking of making it the basis of a popular tract. Such an eloquent testimony of God's purpose working in the heart of a sinner."

"A very great sinner, I am afraid."

"We are all sinners, Major Vernon. Even a newborn child –"

"That I can never believe," he said. "You will forgive me, ma'am –"

At this point the Bishop came in, saving him from a knotty theological conversation.

"Major Vernon is here about Mr Bickley," said Mrs Hughes. "He says he is a wicked criminal."

"Certainly his life did not seem to be regular or respectable," said the Bishop, "but I should not have imagined anything like that. There was wrongdoing, of various sorts, but it was all some time ago."

"I should very much like to see your notes, Mrs Hughes," said Major Vernon. "It may help me in pursuing him."

"You are pursuing him?" said the Bishop. "Why?"

"A man was beaten to death with an iron bar last week."

"And you think Bickley did it?" said the Bishop.

"No, I think he ordered it to be done. I would like to see exactly what he said to you. It may be that he let something slip that will be of use to me."

"Yes, yes, of course. Mary, do you have your notes to hand?"

"I will go and get them," said Mrs Hughes and left the room.

"So," Bishop Hughes said, "this moment of repentance may then have been prompted by the heavy knowledge of great wickedness. And perhaps he was not yet telling me the entire truth of the matter?"

"No, certainly he was not."

"I must talk to him again."

"I do not advise it. He is a dangerous man."

"I am not afraid of him. Not at all. No, I see now the work is half done. The Lord bless you, Major Vernon for coming here and telling us this. God be thanked for bringing you here today, to help me guide this poor wretch to where he ought to go."

"To my door, then?" Giles said. "He deserves a noose."

"What a strange business!" the Bishop said, "and wonderful. That earthly and divine justice should move hand in hand. I see now his conscience was reaching for the light, and he could only begin to speak. Yes, he must be judged and punished for his earthly sins, that goes without saying, but that the Lord is showing him that he must repent so clearly, that he has been moved so deeply by His redeeming love – well, it is a miracle of sorts, and it will be a great example to others!"

At this moment Mrs Hughes returned with her notes.

"These are all I have," she said. "I am afraid my hand was most unsteady. I was so moved by the occasion. You must make of them what you can, sir."

"I shall do, thank you very much," Giles said, taking them from her.

"Perhaps," said the Bishop, reaching for his wife's hand, "we ought now take a moment to offer our thanks –"

"Please excuse me," said Giles and made a hasty exit.

~

Mrs Hughes' notes were indeed sketchy. There were Bible references in them, and exclamation marks, but the text was heavily skewed towards the fact he was repenting, rather than listing any details of his sins. As evidence it was of little use.

The puzzle remained as to why he had done it. The Bishop and Mrs Hughes seemed in no doubt of his sincerity, but he suspected they were hearing what they wished to hear. He could not credit that Bickley, from all he knew of him, might have undergone such a transformation of character.

Yet, what did he really know of him? When they had met, the lasting impression had been of concealment, of a carefully cultivated façade, of disciplined deceit.

Perhaps Hopkins, alias Baxter, might yet come up with something useful. The time for another conversation was long overdue.

He therefore took a short cut back to The Unicorn, through a tangle of back alleys, and then emerged into the rag market in the lee of St Luke's Church. He was pleased to see a pair of uniformed constables on duty. This was a notorious area, and he scanned the crowds, wondering if he might spot any characters who might give him some useful scraps of information. As he did this he noticed a selection of bright silk dresses hanging from a makeshift rail behind one of the stalls. They looked smarter and more expensive than the usual fare of the market, and, as he approached, one of them looked uncomfortably familiar: a crisp, figured lilac silk.

"How much for that one?" he said, to the woman on the stall, who was eyeing him with suspicion as he looked it over. He was certain it was Kate's. He had, after all, helped her remove it.

"Guinea," she said, after considering it for a moment.

"Too much," he said. "Where did you get it?"

"Bought it. What do you think?"

"Nice piece," he said, looking at the other dresses. They were of the same quality, and in similar taste and size, as if they had been picked out by the same woman. Could he be looking at the rest of Kate's wardrobe, he wondered, that had made its way to a market stall after the gambling house had been closed down in such haste? "And these others. Where did you get them? Did you buy them from the same person?"

"Maybe," she said. "What does it matter to you?"

"I'll take the lilac one," he said, "and I'll give you ten shillings for it, if you will tell me who sold them to you."

"I don't know her name," said the market woman, getting down the dress, and bundling it up unceremoniously. "But she lives up yonder, in Croft's Building. She's a dressmaker."

"Does she often sell you stock like this?"

"No," she said, sticking out her hand, waiting for the money. Given she had accepted such a low price without a quibble, it suggested that she had not paid much for them.

"So you got it all very cheap?" he said, putting the coins into her hand.

"What business of that is yours?"

"You didn't think they might be stolen?"

"I just buys and sells," she said, counting the coins. "Questions aren't good for business. So mind yours."

He set off back into the maze of buildings, the crushed bundle of lilac silk under his arm.

Croft's Building was one of the famous buildings of old Northminster, a top-heavy, half-timbered merchant's palace of the Elizabethan era, now dirty and decaying and divided into a rat's nest of individual dwellings. It would probably have been demolished some time ago, for it lay in a convenient and prominent spot, but there was a long-standing dispute as to who actually owned the freehold, and until it was resolved, nothing could be done.

Exactly how many dressmakers might be eking out a precarious living in this ancient wreck, he was not certain, but as he made his way up the groaning stairs, he wondered if it was not an excellent place for Kate to be hiding. After all, her clothes had been made for her, and with considerable skill. A trusted dressmaker might well be a friend and ally in time of trouble.

A few enquiries led him to the door of a Miss Waites, who according to the neat-lettered paper pinned up outside, undertook "High class dressmaking of all descriptions." Giles could not imagine that many of her clients would visit her in such lodgings.

The woman opened the door to him cautiously. She was as neat in her dress as the handwriting on her sign: she was a curiously orderly figure for such a place. She looked him up and down carefully, taking in the bundle of silk under his arm.

"Might I have a word?" he said, and tapped the silk. "About this?"

She let him come in. The room was small, but meticulously clean and tidy.

"Who are you?" she said as he laid the dress down on the table. She said it with a boldness that could not quite disguise the fact that she was rattled by the appearance of the dress.

"Did you make this?" he asked.

"Who are you?" she said again.

"No one you need be afraid of," he said. "You sound afraid, I think."

She reached out and touched the silk.

"Yes, I made it."

"For Kate?"

"If that's what you want to call her, yes."

"And she was here?"

"Yes, but she's long gone. You're the policeman, aren't you? The one who –"

"Yes. So where is she now?"

"I can't tell you! I don't know!"

"But she was here recently?"

"Yes, but, but –" She broke off, her voice reduced to a nervous squeak, and stood twisting her hands together. "Please, sir, I can't tell you anything," she said at length.

"Don't you want to help her?" he said.

"I've got work to do," she said, crossing the room and picking up a piece of sewing.

"You can still talk to me," he said.

"I can't!" she said. "I don't know anything."

"You know Kate, Miss Waites," he said. "And you made clothes for her, and she came here and you have helped her in some way. Did she ask you to sell her clothes?"

"Yes, but what does that matter? I don't know where she's gone now. She didn't tell me. Why would she tell me? I don't know!"

"Has anyone else been here asking about her, Miss Waites?" She hesitated and then shook her head, forcefully. "Does that mean no, or that you don't wish to tell me?"

She gazed at him, stricken.

"I have to think about my livelihood," she said, at length.

He looked about the room, at the half-finished dresses hanging on hooks and at the neatly folded lengths of stuff, carefully stacked on a bench. A mixture of shades and weights, but none of it looked cheap or shoddy, as far as he could judge.

"You have a lot of work in hand," he said.

"Yes."

"And are these customers connected in some way to Kate, Miss Waite?"

"I have to eat," she said. "I can't –"

"Just tell me when Kate was here, and what she said to you. Can you do that much? You will help her if you do."

"She's past helping!" she burst out. "Oh, she's a daft girl and I did what I could for her, of course I did, but please, sir, I can't say anything more than that, not without –"

She turned her back on him and stood at the window, holding her work in her hand. It was a half-made bodice, in dark blue satin.

"I suppose Miss Bickley will be angry if she gets her dress late," Giles hazarded, thinking of how that lady had been dressed. "Yes?"

Miss Waites made a muffled sound that might have been a yes, and nodded.

"That's better," he said. "I shall ask questions and you can nod or shake your head. Then you will be able to tell them that you said nothing. Yes?"

She nodded.

"So you make dresses for Miss Bickley?" She nodded. "And for the women at the house behind Butcher's Row?" She nodded again. "A good business, then. You should be in better premises. A shop somewhere, with hands to help you, where all the other ladies in Northminster could come. A better reward than this."

There was a long silence and then the woman turned, and said quietly, shaking her head, "I'm lucky to have this. Given everything that has happened. I'm lucky. And I can't say any more than that, do you hear me?"

And, in her fierceness, for a moment Giles thought he saw something in her features that he had seen somewhere before – though where, he could not at once place.

“One more question, Miss Waites, only one,” he said. “Were you born in Northminster?”

“I’ll not say another word!” she exclaimed. “Not another word!”

Chapter Twenty

"It might be better if I were to take you home," Felix said, when her tears had subsided a little. "It would be more comfortable for you there, perhaps?"

"No," Miss Blanchfort said. "No, I do not want to go back."

"Do you not want your mother?" he said.

She broke away from him, shaking her head.

"No, that is the last thing I want. You saw how she was."

"Yes, but she was misinformed, and, if she knows the true circumstances, surely she –"

"She was not misinformed," said Miss Blanchfort. "She has known about this all along. She has known he was dying and kept it from me."

"You don't know that."

"You don't know her!" she said. "I swear it, Mr Carswell, that is exactly how she is. She loathes him so much – and she will be happy now, oh so very happy, now that –" She broke off and turned away from him.

"Maybe you should rest?" Felix said. "This has been a dreadful shock for you – you will need to recover from it physically as well as mentally. You cannot think straight at the moment."

"Perhaps," she said.

"You can rest on my bed, in here," he said, pushing the door open to the adjoining bedroom. "And later you can decide what you want to do."

"Do you mean that?" she said. "About allowing me to decide?"

"Yes, of course. And if you rest, you will be more likely to come to a sensible decision."

"You mean I will decide to go back to her," she said, with sudden sharpness.

"I did not say that, but in the circumstances, then –"

"And I thought you were different!" she said. "That you –"

"She is your mother," Felix said. "And I am sure, in her way, she cares about you."

"You saw how she was this morning," she said. "You saw that vile woman, holding my arm. I am nothing better than a prisoner and you wish to send me back!"

She rushed over to the window again. For a moment Felix thought she was about to hurl herself out of it.

"A prisoner?" Felix said. "Surely not."

"What can you know about it?" she said, turning to him. "You have had perfect liberty all your life to do as you like!"

"Not at all," said Felix. "And the world would be a fine mess if we all espoused perfect liberty."

"Have you had your every waking moment supervised, Mr Carswell, your day regimented by the quarter hours of the clock, with not a moment to think your own thoughts, and all the time told to be grateful that one is in a state of such slavery? And if I do not show gratitude, I am punished. I tell you, I am no better than a Negro wretch on some plantation!"

"That is an absurd thing to say," Felix said. "You have clothes on your back and food in your belly. No one is forcing you to labour for no wages, nor flogging you if you take some necessary rest. You cannot compare your privileged state with theirs!" He had spoken a little more forcefully than he intended, and he saw her lip quiver and she looked as if she were about to burst into tears again. "Excuse me for speaking so plainly, Miss Blanchfort. You need to rest. You will be able to think more clearly if you do."

"On this point," she said, choking down her tears, "I will be perfectly clear, I assure you, whether I rest or not!"

There was a knock on the door and Mr Wilkes came in with Lord Rothborough. The latter looked grim-faced and uncharacteristically at a loss.

"This is –" he began, but failed completely and sat down wearily. "My dear Eleanor," he attempted again, stretching out his hand to Miss Blanchfort. "I cannot begin to –" He covered his mouth and shook with his tears.

Lord Rothborough's distress moved him, but Felix was uncertain quite how he should behave. In the end he settled for laying his hand on Lord Rothborough's shoulder, a gesture which was received with a glance upward towards him full of pitiful gratitude.

"It was very peaceful," Felix managed to say. "Canon Fforde gave him Communion and there was no pain."

"I am glad to hear it," said Lord Rothborough, making an effort to right himself. He wiped his eyes, got up from his seat and went over to Miss Blanchfort. He took both her hands. "He was, at one time, the dearest of friends to me, Eleanor, but my loss is as nothing compared to yours. I promise you now, my dear, that I will do all I can to be a good father to you, for that is what he has charged me with."

He kissed her on the forehead and embraced her.

She looked up at him and said, "Then you will not make me go back to her?"

"Her?" said Lord Rothborough, puzzled.

"My mother," said Miss Blanchfort. "I will not go back there. I cannot. I swear I will go mad or destroy myself if I am made to go back. I cannot bear it any more, especially not now, sir, you must understand! Please –"

She was now on her knees begging him, and liable at any moment to sink further onto the floor in a mess of miserable tears. Sensing that she was likely to become dangerously overwrought, Felix intervened to help her to her feet and back to the armchair. She struggled somewhat at this, but eventually submitted.

"You are in a state of great shock," he managed to say, having got her to sit down. She was shaking with a mixture of frustration and misery. "Nothing needs to be decided yet. In the meantime, I strongly advise that you rest. In fact, I will give you something to calm your nerves if you like."

She pushed him away.

"No! I will not take anything. I know what you are trying to do, and I shall not. You are just the same as all the others!"

"My dear," Lord Rothborough ventured. "You should not be so quick to judge. Mr Carswell is trying to help you."

"No, he is not!" she said. "He is just doing what they all do."

"Has your physician prescribed something for you, Miss Blanchfort?" Felix said. "Did something disagree with you?"

"Disagree?" she said. "Is that how you put it, sir, when you starve a person of sensation with your vile concoctions that make them into a befuddled doll who cannot walk across a room without falling? All the while telling me it is for my own good!"

"Who has been attending you, Miss Blanchfort?" said Felix.

"A dirty quack called Cranstoun," she said. "I dare say she found him in the gutter begging for pennies, for he certainly is no gentleman. But she seems to think he is a genius!"

"Was this since you came here?" asked Lord Rothborough, "or when you were at Cheveleigh?"

"At Cheveleigh. Thank God he did not come with us, though my mother would have brought him if she could! But she brought his wretched potions. Of course she did!"

"I should be very interested to see what this stuff was," Felix said.

"So you can pour it down the throats of your own patients?" she said.

"No, of course not," he said. "It sounds as if the prescription has been ill-judged."

"Ill-judged!" she said. "Oh, how you quacks all pull together to defend each other!"

"Mr Carswell is no quack," said Lord Rothborough. "Eleanor, I know you are distressed, but really –"

"I cannot condemn him outright," Felix said, "because I have no idea what this man intended by his prescription. Until I know exactly what it was you were given, I have only your word against him and no more solid evidence than that."

"So you don't believe me?" she said.

"I do. It sounds likely you have been given something far too strong for your constitution, and I can perfectly understand your unwillingness to accept anything similar from me. So instead, I shall have Mrs Wilkes bring you some lime-flower tea, which is utterly harmless, and extremely pleasant, and you are going to rest, just as we discussed earlier. Yes?"

There was a long silence while she considered his words and then she got up from the chair and said, "If I must. I don't want quarrels at such a time."

"And while you rest, Lord Rothborough and I will go and see your mother," Felix added, glancing at Lord Rothborough, who nodded his assent. "And I promise you we will decide nothing further without your consent."

"You swear so?" she said. "I shall hold you to that, Mr Carswell, mark my words."

~

"You managed that extremely well, Felix," said Lord Rothborough when they were in the carriage heading for Hawksby.

"I should be doing a post-mortem," Felix said, as they passed the gates of the Infirmary.

"This guardianship is going to be a ticklish business.

When Dick asked me to do it – well, the girl was still a babe in arms, and I never thought I would be needed. I hoped she would be a middle-aged woman before her father died." He sighed. "I am glad you were able to help him, Felix, when I could not. And God knows, you are of far more practical use in these circumstances than I could ever be. I had not thought of that before, to tell you the truth. Your profession ought to stand by that of the priests."

"Certainly we should be above the lawyers," Felix could not help saying.

"Certainly!" said Lord Rothborough. "Opinion must change on the matter."

"It will, as our knowledge and skill increases," Felix said. "Take a man like Mr Harper at the Infirmary – no one could deny him a place at their dinner table on the grounds of his profession."

"Quite," said Lord Rothborough. "I'm glad to hear you say that. In fact, I was thinking of asking him to Holbroke for a few days – along with the Ffordes. I want to gather the University party together, and I think Mr Harper would be a useful addition. After all, there is a medical school to think of."

"In Northminster?"

"Of course. Why not?"

"No reason, I suppose," Felix said.

"Exactly. Why should the project be limited by the terms of the late Bishop's will? In fact, I think the spirit of the thing is there, if one reads it carefully."

"I thought it was mostly about training clergymen," said Felix.

"Additional funds would be required, of course," Lord Rothborough went on. "But that is a small matter."

"It would be no small matter to get Mr Harper to come to Holbroke," Felix said. "I can't imagine him allowing himself the indulgence of a holiday."

"You will have to work on him for me. I had

underestimated your persuasive talents until I saw you with Eleanor."

"Miss Blanchfort and Mr Harper are hardly comparable cases," said Felix. "He is the embodiment of reason, while she is – I won't say she's a fool, because she certainly isn't. No, she's a bundle of impulses, all at war with one another, as far as I can see."

"She is going to keep me busy, then," said Lord Rothborough. "What is to be done with her, that is a difficult question."

"I suppose she will marry someone," said Felix.

"And that is a problem. She is now one of the richest women in the country. If she were an ordinary, vulnerable girl with a few hundred to her name, then –" He sighed. "It's really no surprise her mother has kept her under lock and key!"

~

Lady Blanchfort was at first distinctly prickly on finding Felix and Lord Rothborough waiting for her in her drawing room, but the facts were soon laid out. The new widow sat ramrod straight, pale and apparently chastened by the news, and said, "I must see Eleanor. She will be..."

She got up from her chair and went to ring for a servant.

"I think it might be wise to wait a while," said Lord Rothborough.

"What do you mean?"

"She is very distressed, and –"

"Then I must go to her. I can't conceive why you did not bring her back with you."

"She is being well looked after, Lady Blanchfort," Felix said. "She was not ready to leave her father."

"Then I will go to her," said Lady Blanchfort. "A

common inn is no place for her at such a time. At any time!"

"It's hardly that," said Felix.

"The difficulty is," said Lord Rothborough, "Eleanor was adamant that she did not wish to come back here. Now, even accounting for her being in a state of shock, she was clear on the point, and this is not the time to distress her further by insisting upon something that would appear to cause her pain."

"She doesn't want to come back to me?"

"Of course, in normal circumstances, her place is with you, but these circumstances are hardly that. She feels –"

"She does not know what she feels. She is a child who does not know what is good for her. I cannot conceive why you are allowing her to use you like this, Rothborough."

"She is a young woman now, and I cannot dismiss her opinion entirely, Ann, even if it is misguided. As her guardian I must listen to her."

"And at once give in to her! What a poor father you must be, sir!"

"I must listen to her," repeated Lord Rothborough. "And make a judgement as to what will be best for her welfare. She is overwrought already. Naturally I suggested strongly that she come back here to you, but she would not hear of it."

"This is quite outrageous. Why did you not overrule her?"

"Because she is suffering enough as it is! Give it a little time, Ann, and all will be well. I shall take her to Holbroke for a few days. Maria is with me. And then –"

"No, no, I will not have this!" said Lady Blanchfort, throwing up her hands. "She will come back with me at once. I see how it is – yes, I see what it is you are doing, and I will not allow it."

"And what is that?"

"You are scheming, Rothborough, as you always do! But do not expect that I will not fight this. I shall take you to court, if necessary. You will not get her so easily."

"I am only proposing a few days at Holbroke until the first sting of her grief –"

"A few days which will turn into weeks and then months. I know how it will be, and she will be made a stranger to me!" said Lady Blanchfort.

"As you did with her father, I suppose," Felix could not help remarking.

"And then what will you do, Rothborough, marry her off to your little bastard here?" she said, flinging her hand towards Felix. "That is the plan, is it not? Sending him here this morning like that, when you know how impulsive and difficult she is! It is outrageous, utterly outrageous!"

"Very well," said Lord Rothborough after a moment. "If you are going to throw about accusations, ma'am, let me remind you that not everything in your own conduct would stand up to public scrutiny. You are on thin ice with this, remember."

"And you are trying to steal her from me!"

"No, no, I want nothing but peace between you and she, for the Lord's sake!" exclaimed Lord Rothborough. "Dick is dead, can you not remember that, and be decent for once? Our poor dear man is dead, and we shall not fight about this, I tell you. I shall not have it, for his sake, nor Eleanor's. She will come back to you, and in her own time, and you will be grateful for it when she does. In the meantime, let her grieve as she must, and perhaps spare a few of your own prayers for poor Dick. He deserved better than you, but he loved you, for all your sins against him!"

"How dare you!" she said. "I think you had better leave. But do not think you have had the final word on this."

She rose to show them to the door.

"There is one more thing," Felix said. "Miss Blanchfort mentioned a medicine she has been taking, prescribed by Dr Cranstoun. A sedative of some sort."

"Why do you ask about that?" she said.

"Because, to be frank, ma'am, it sounded dangerous. I wonder if I might have a sample of it?"

"No, you may not. You are impertinent."

"Very well, then may I strongly suggest instead that neither yourself nor anyone in the household takes any more of it? It is sometimes the case that servants take medicines not meant for them, and do themselves great damage. Please keep it safely under lock and key."

~

"Do you think the stuff might really be that bad?" Lord Rothborough said as they drove away. "Given how defensive she was about it – but Heavens, not even Ann Blanchfort would stoop to something that low, I hope!"

"It's impossible to say. It's more likely to be misguided than deliberate. I have read suggested treatments for nervous excitement and hysteria which I would baulk at attempting, but I do not know the full circumstances. It may be that Miss Blanchfort is –" He broke off, not liking to diagnose her so glibly.

"Whatever the case," Lord Rothborough said, "some time away from her mother will do her good, I think. Even though my lady will no doubt tell all and sundry that I have stolen her for my own devious ends."

"What did you mean about her own conduct?" Felix could not help asking.

"I shall not burden you with the details of that," said Lord Rothborough. He sighed and rubbed his face. "I only know it by chance, and to be frank I wish I did not. I do not care to use it as a weapon, but sometimes there is nothing else one can do. Poor Dick! And poor Eleanor!" He gave another great sigh. "Now, where did you wish to be let out?"

"At the Infirmary."

"Oh, yes, you have the remains of that unfortunate Colonel to deal with. What is the theory on that so far?"

"That his wife commissioned it."

"Dear Lord. Well, you and Major Vernon will be kept busy with that, but if you do manage some liberty, you will both consider coming to Holbroke, will you not?"

Chapter Twenty-one

Giles had just spread Kate's dress on Mr Fairfaxe's mahogany counter when the shop bell rang. He glanced behind him and saw Emma Maitland.

"This looks most intriguing, Major Vernon," she said, coming up and standing beside him. "What a beautiful dress."

"Certainly a nice piece of stuff, sir," said Mr Fairfaxe. "And a neat piece of work. What did you wish to know about it?"

"I am trying to find out some information about a dressmaker called Anne Waites. This is her work. I wonder if you had any dealings with her."

"Here in Northminster?"

"Yes."

"This is very superior work," he said, looking at the dress again. "There are only two, maybe three, women I know of working to this standard in Northminster – Madame Courtney, and Miss Blacker. Waites, did you say, sir?"

"Anne Waites. She works from Croft's Building."

"I have to say I have never heard of her. A shame, for ladies are always asking me for recommendations."

"Have you ever heard her mentioned, Mrs Maitland?" Giles said. "I know you have not been here long, but sometimes these things come up in conversation."

She shook her head.

"A Miss Blacker had been mentioned to me," she said. "I was going to order a dress from her, as a matter of fact." She had drawn off her glove and was stroking the silk. "This is the very quality I was after. Do you have anything in this weight, Mr Fairfaxe?"

"Certainly, madam. If that is everything for now, sir, may I attend to the lady?"

"Yes, thank you," said Giles.

Fairfaxe went in search of silk for Mrs Maitland.

"It was too much to hope he would know anything useful," he said.

"Not at all," said Mrs Maitland. "Linen-drapers usually know a great deal about everyone. Shopkeepers in general, I think." Now she smoothed out one of the flounces. "This is such a charming dress – these scallops must have been time-consuming."

"And expensive?"

"Yes. Do you know to whom it belongs?"

"Yes," Giles said.

Mrs Maitland now turned over the bodice and examined the buttonholes.

"But you want to find out more about its maker?" she said.

"Were you really going to order a new dress?" he said.

"Yes. I have been asked to Holbroke. I need a new day dress. It is something of an extravagance, of course, but needs must."

"You could help me, then," Giles said. "You might send for Miss Waites. She will not talk to me, but she might talk to you. This will be an excellent pretext."

She did not answer, but traced her finger again across the lilac silk.

"I wonder if that is wise," she said at length. "Wise for me, that is. I have no doubt I could be useful to you, but circumstances being as they are –"

"Then I will ask Dr Fforde, if that is –"

"That is not what concerns me," she said, lowering her voice. "He will not object. No, I think I must object on my own grounds. I do not wish to – oh, Heavens, must I spell it out to you?" she finished in a whisper.

Her discomfort brought a flush to her cheeks, which an objective observer might have found becoming. However, knowing that he was the active cause of her pain, Giles could not take any pleasure in it. He felt himself colouring also, and said, "No, no, of course not. Forgive me. I didn't mean to be so –" He broke off, for Mr Fairfaxe had returned, carrying half a dozen bolts of silk. Giles was obliged to whisk Kate's dress from the counter so that he could put them down.

"Oh, those look charming!" exclaimed Mrs Maitland, with relief in her voice. "Plaid – yes, that is exactly what I was thinking of, Mr Fairfaxe."

"These are the newest thing," said Mr Fairfaxe. "And I think, ma'am, this one in particular would suit your complexion."

Fairfaxe unfurled the bolt with practised flamboyance, and the plaid, a spirited mixture of greens and blues, flashed on the counter.

"I will leave you to your deliberations. Good day," Giles said, deciding the conversation was best ended at once. He bundled up Kate's dress with scant ceremony and left.

He had not got ten yards down the street when he heard her call out behind him, "Major Vernon!"

She was standing in front of the shop looking as if she were about to run after him, but could not quite bring herself to do it.

He walked back and said, "Yes?"

"What you suggested," she said. "I am too proud. And I know you would not have asked me if it was not important. Of course I must help you."

"Even if I am liable to be an ungrateful boor?" he said.

"I believe we can all learn from our mistakes, Major Vernon," she said. "What is it you want me to do?"

~

He gave his explanation as he walked her back to the Minster Precincts by way of Parker's Lane.

As they went along the lane, a cat dashed across their path which he recognised as the handsome tom Kate had lured inside to keep her company in captivity. He wondered what the cat was running from, and saw a huddled figure, swathed in rags, sitting in the recessed doorway opposite the narrow little house. He quickened his step a little and approached, for it was an odd place for a beggar to sit, and there was something that seemed familiar.

He drew close and saw it was Kate, only barely recognisable. Her head had been shaved and her face was riven with welts as if someone had taken a horsewhip to it.

She saw him, and stretched out imploring, shaking hands to him. She was attempting to rise but it seemed to be a desperate struggle for her, and in the end, he found himself crouching before her in order to catch her in his arms. She fell against him, gasping for breath, sobbing, desperate, jerking in his arms as he tried to get a better grip on her so that he could begin to lift her.

"In my right coat pocket," he said, for Mrs Maitland was bending over them, attempting to assist, "there should be a loose key. That will unlock the door opposite."

She found it and went to unlock the door, while he managed to gently lift Kate to her feet, and supporting her as best he could, they crossed the street and into the house.

They barely got across the threshold before she gave way and pooled onto the floor in a dead faint. As her wraps fell away, it was possible to see the extensive blood-staining down the front of her dress, as well as the tears to the fabric caused by a blade. He heard Mrs Maitland gasp.

"Shall I fetch Mr Carswell?" she said.

"He should be at the infirmary," said Giles. "Yes, if you could. And if you see a constable..."

She needed no more prompting and was gone in a

moment. Giles managed to move Kate into the room a little further, and sat down with her on the floor, taking her in his arms and attempting to loosen her clothing and stays to find where the wounds were, so he could at least attempt to staunch the bleeding by pressing on them.

She revived a little, her head resting against his chest, as he made these clumsy and probably futile investigations.

"Who did this to you?" he said.

"B..." she began but then dissolved in tears. "I shouldn't have –" She pressed her head against him, the whole of her body shaking and shivering. "I thought –"

"Hush now," he said, wrapping his arms about her. "It doesn't matter now. Help will be here soon. Save your strength. I shouldn't have asked. It doesn't matter."

He had no idea how long it was that he sat there on the floor cradling her in his arms, listening to her increasingly uncomfortable breathing. Time seemed to slow, and he was acutely aware that the fragile being in his arms had very little left. She had been cheated of everything.

Then, curiously, she seemed to find a little more strength and began to talk, in a hoarse, excited whisper.

"Johnny, Johnny, when will we go to America? When? Will we go to New York? It's a long time on the boat. I wonder if I will be sick. I wonder what the fashions in New York are." She gazed up at him blinking. "You're not Johnny," she said. "Has Johnny gone to New York? He said he'd take me."

"He told me to send you there when you are better," said Giles. "I'll take you myself, if you like."

"Johnny wouldn't like that," she said with a smile. "Colonel."

"Then you'd better go alone."

"I don't know if I'll get there," she said. "I don't know. I'm so tired..."

"Hush then," Giles said, and cradled her a little more

closely. At the same time she seemed to droop visibly, like a flower on the branch that was about to shed its petals. He held her against him, his mouth pressed to her head, feeling the stubble against his lips.

He closed his eyes, thinking of his dream of Lizzie and Laura, and found himself picturing that great drawing room again. There he saw Kate, ringleted and in her lilac silk standing at the threshold, fiddling with the long ribbons of her bonnet, looking about her, nervously. Looking for Johnny, he thought, and felt that her hand, which lay in his, was growing colder.

~

"Given the extent of her injuries," Felix said. "It is something of a miracle she survived as long as she did."

Major Vernon said nothing. He had said very little since Felix had arrived with a constable and Mrs Maitland. He had been sitting on the floor, with the dead woman in his arms, his hands covered in her blood.

Now in the gas-lit basement of the Northern Office, her body lay waiting for his examination and the Major stood over her, again holding her hand.

"From the depth and placement of the abdominal wounds," Felix said, "I think we can say that she was possibly restrained or incapacitated in some way when they were inflicted. But how she managed to get away and walk –"

"Perhaps they left her there for me to find," Major Vernon said at last, and gently laid her hand down. "This is my fault."

"How?"

"I did not protect her adequately."

"She ran away."

"I should have anticipated that. I have underestimated everything."

He turned away suddenly and began to retch into a pail. This was unusual, for the Major normally had a stronger stomach for such sights.

"Excuse me," he said. Felix offered him a cup of whisky but he waved it away. "No – it's just my head, that won't help." As he did so, Felix saw that he was screwing up his eyes against the light.

"Then you should go home," said Felix. "And sleep it off."

"It's not so bad," he said. "I will get some coffee. That will deal with it."

"Unlikely," said Felix. "You would be better –"

"There really is no time for that," Major Vernon said. "It is nothing."

~

It was hardly nothing, and by the time he had got to the cells at the Constabulary Headquarters and was scanning the list of prisoners, it felt as if chisels were being applied to the roots of his eyes.

"Where is Baxter?" he asked, as the names swam in front of him.

"He's gone, sir," said the Custody Sergeant. "Didn't you know? Gone at noon for committal for trial at Leeds, with these others. Here you are, sir, guilty plea before the Justices this morning."

"Leeds?" said Giles. "Why on earth to Leeds?"

"Because the circuit judges are there at present, I suppose, sir, and because he made a full confession to Superintendent Herrick and Captain Lazenby, they must have thought there was no point keeping him here. It happened last night, I think."

"Oh, did he?" said Giles, putting down the list. "Were you on duty then when this confession was made?"

"No, sir, it was Sergeant Bale. He's gone home now, of course. Can I help you with anything else, sir?"

"Not at present," said Giles. "Thank you."

He went upstairs to see Lazenby, feeling, as the intensity of his headache increased, a curious dislocation from his surroundings. The building no longer formed part of his daily life, and now seemed populated by strangers. Lazenby had brought in new men and new methods, which was understandable, but at that moment, struck with both acute pain and annoyance, he struggled to see the necessity of it.

He called in at the clerks' office first, to see if he could locate a copy of Baxter's confession, and having been disappointed in that, wondered how he was going to be civil with Lazenby.

He stood in the passageway a moment, closing his eyes, attempting to steady his mood, and found he could only think of Kate's wretched, wrecked form lying on Carswell's laboratory table.

He knocked on Lazenby's door and went in.

"Can you spare five minutes, sir?" he said.

"Of course, Major Vernon, of course!" said Lazenby, leaping up from his desk at the sight of him. "What can I do for you?"

"I wondered if you had a copy of Baxter's confession – if that is the name he gave you. I understand he also goes under Hopkins."

"Baxter, ah yes. That was quite a development. I have it here."

"And he has gone to Leeds?"

"Yes, the Justices committed him for trial there. To make a swift example of him. His confession is very detailed, as you can see, and he was determined to plead guilty. It's better the matter is settled quickly."

"I'm not sure of that," said Giles, taking the confession and glancing at it. He found the words swam on the page before him. "I would have liked to speak to him before he was sent to the Justices, given that I began the investigation."

"Yes, I do understand, but he was insistent, and you were out of town. He talked a great deal with the Chaplain, and that seemed to hasten his resolve to unburden himself. As you can see, it is a thorough account."

"Is there anything in this that can be corroborated? He lied persistently to me."

"I was there, Major Vernon, and I found it a satisfactory account. And there was no reason to delay his appearance in front of the magistrates. He is fully aware of the nature of his crime. That is enough, I think."

Giles moved away to the window in order to attempt to read the confession but his eyes again failed him, and he felt dizzy with pain. He reached for a chair back to steady himself for a moment and then decided he had better sit down.

"Excuse me –" he began.

"Are you unwell, Major?"

"I seem to be," he said.

"You should consider some furlough. I was looking at the records. You are long overdue. I think I should insist if you are not well."

"I must go to Leeds and talk to Baxter before they hang him."

"You will find all you need in there. I think you should go on leave."

"It's impossible. We have this business of Parham's death – the ramifications are complex, and there is another witness who has died in circumstances which –" He got up from the chair, and feeling ancient as he did so, thought it must show in his posture. So he pulled himself very straight and went on, "I cannot take any leave now. The situation is –" But Captain Lazenby was shaking his head.

"You are clearly not well, Major Vernon. I order you to take your leave. A fortnight."

"A fortnight?" he began.

Lazenby shook his head again and said, "You have good men under you. You must delegate. It is irresponsible to lay so much of the burden of this on yourself. That is not your role, sir, and you know it. Now, I know you have the instincts of a hunter, and you do not like to give up the chase, but that is what you must do in this case."

It was politely put but Giles sensed that he would not be persuaded otherwise, and so reluctantly agreed, hoping that a few days' rest and a good account of matters from Carswell would allow him to return.

"I will make arrangements tomorrow and be away by noon," he said. "But if I might take this?" he added, indicating Baxter's confession. "My men will need to see this."

"Yes, certainly," Lazenby said, and showed him to the door.

Chapter Twenty-two

"Did you sleep?" Carswell asked the next morning. He had come in while Giles was at his breakfast, and insisted on examining him.

"Very little," Giles conceded.

"After a substantial dose of laudanum. It was more severe than the last attack, then?"

"Yes, I suppose so."

"And you are still suffering?"

"But it is improving –"

"Because you are sitting in a dark room doing very little. I have to agree with Lazenby," said Carswell. "Some leave is in order."

"Very well," Giles said after a moment, realising there was little point arguing with Carswell. "Might I ask for one or two concessions, though – firstly, that I might go to Ardenthwaite for a few days? Given the place is lying empty."

"Of course," said Carswell, "if you like. So long as you will rest and have no ulterior motive in going there. You don't, do you? After all, it is still rather to the point in the investigation."

"Yes, it is, but I was not really thinking of that. It's merely that, despite everything, I find the place very agreeable." This was not entirely the truth, of course, and there was something about Carswell's expression that suggested he knew this too. But it had occurred to Giles that he could make some quiet progress with both his health and the case if he were there.

"Very well," said Carswell. "But I will join you there – I too am due some leave – though I am not entirely sure how I feel about the place at the moment. But perhaps I will find those damned mushrooms this time. And if you do attempt anything foolish, I will be there to prevent it."

"I will be good," Giles said. "I will send Holt on this morning, then?" Carswell nodded. "And I will go down later today. I have a few things that I must do before then."

Carswell looked doubtful for a moment and then nodded.

When he reached his office and started giving out orders, he began to feel the wisdom of Carswell and Lazenby's advice. He was struggling to function adequately – a mixture of angry grief and pain seemed to rob him of his usual sense of clarity and purpose. He sent out men to look for evidence and witnesses on the attack on Kate, but had no faith in their finding anything.

He had finally cleared his desk when he found Mrs Hughes' notes. Since he had to go to the Minster Precincts, he decided he would return them back to her in person, and give her a strong warning to have nothing further to do with Bickley.

It was about noon when he approached the Bishop's Palace, and it seemed that the brilliant spring sunshine was tormenting him.

He found himself standing on the steps, his hand on the bell, frozen for a moment in intense discomfort, while in his mind the image of Kate's scarred face and shorn head came to him unbidden and full of reproaches.

He was shown to the library and as before, found Mrs Hughes there, in lieu of her husband. However, she was not alone. George Bickley was there.

They were sitting together at a baize-covered circular table. There were books open in front of them and it was clear that Mrs Hughes was the teacher and Mr Bickley the pupil. Bickley was dressed on this occasion in his flash horse dealer mode, his expensive clothes suggesting the dandy of twenty years ago: a superbly cut, dark blue coat, beautifully polished riding boots and a jewel fixing his elaborately arranged cravat.

His snowy-white hair was immaculately swept back from his forehead, almost as if he were about to sit to have his portrait painted.

It was a little alarming to see his prey so exposed. In theory it was an ideal opportunity, but in truth, it felt like no opportunity at all, for he had as yet no hard evidence against the man, only a rag-bag of suspicions. He had not yet gathered enough weapons to launch an attack.

Neither, he realised, did he have a great deal with which to defend himself. He felt that he was the exposed prey, the vulnerable bird on the clearing on the hillside, a foolish, easy target.

Bickley looked up from his books as he came in, and although his expression said nothing overt, Giles knew there could only be appraisal behind it. Bickley would be very interested to know why he was there. It was therefore necessary to devise an excuse for this call.

"Major Vernon," said Mrs Hughes, on seeing him. "How good to see you again."

"I think I am interrupting something," he said.

"We have just finished," she said. "Now, Mr Bickley, for tomorrow, might I suggest you read the second book of Acts?"

Bickley nodded humbly and got up, closing his books.

"Thank you very much again for taking the time to help me, madam," he said.

"It is a pleasure," said Mrs Hughes.

"I am so unused to this kind of study. I'm lucky to have such a gentle hand to guide me."

He bowed, and began to gather up his books.

"You have a natural understanding of God's word," said Mrs Hughes. "I feel I am learning as much from you."

Bickley smiled becomingly and said, "I'd better leave you and this gentlemen to your business, ma'am." He began to move towards the door. "Major Vernon, is it not, sir?"

"You remember correctly, Mr Bickley," said Giles. "How fortunate that we should meet here. You see, I have heard the inspiring story of your conversion – it seems there may be hope for all of us," he finished, hoping he sounded in earnest. Indeed, thinking of his own faults, it was not difficult.

"Oh yes, Major Vernon, yes, there is always hope," said Mrs Hughes. "And I truly believe that Mr Bickley's experience is the harbinger of something extraordinary – a spiritual awakening in this city. Why, I do believe you are feeling it as well! The Lord is working in you, Major, that is as sure as sure can be!"

"Yes," said Bickley, and laid his hand on Giles' forearm for a moment, and looked levelly at him, apparently with perfect sincerity. "That may well be so. And we can all lay our burden down and find peace, Major Vernon, that's the great and simple thing. God's love is here for us all. We have only to open our hearts to it."

Again he laid his hand on Giles' arm and his ringed fingers caught the light.

Remember the man is a genius at cards, Giles thought, remember this man is a highly-disciplined fighter, who will do anything he needs to survive and succeed.

"I saw a woman die yesterday," Giles said. "She was the victim of a monstrous attack. It reminded me that death may come to us at any time. She never had a chance to acknowledge her Redeemer and to beg for His salvation. It struck me as a terrible warning."

"Amen," said Mrs Hughes. "She was attacked, you say? Here in the city?"

"Yes, here, ma'am."

"Why?" she said. "Was she robbed, or –?"

"That's a good question. From the signs, it was a prolonged, deliberate attack. She was, I think, being punished for something."

"What do you mean?"

He glanced at Bickley, who was standing there with his Bible and his notebook and wondered if it was he who had given the order to shave Kate's head before she was set upon in earnest. It was such a calculated and cruel addition to the rest of the barbarity.

"She talked to someone she should not have done and paid a very high price for it. There are people in this city, ma'am, who live shadowy, desperate lives, controlled by immeasurably cruel codes from which they can never break free. They are trapped like slaves in their wickedness. This poor woman was one of them."

"Slaves, in Northminster? Surely not?" she said.

"It is hard to understand what you cannot see," he said. "And this, because of its illicit nature, is well hidden. There is another man, sentenced to hang, who has made a false confession, and sworn an oath that it is true. He will not tell the truth, even though he is facing the gallows, because he is still too afraid of his master."

"Now, sir, we mustn't alarm the lady," Bickley put in.

"I think Mrs Hughes has a strong constitution," said Giles. "And her position is such that she ought to know the facts. However, I can reassure you, ma'am, that it is only a matter of time before we have rooted all this out and put a stop to it."

"I pray so!" said Mrs Hughes. "What you say is very distressing. May the Lord guide your endeavours, Major Vernon! And this poor woman – perhaps in her heart she knew and acknowledged her Saviour!"

"I was wondering if I could at least arrange a decent burial for her," Giles said. "Perhaps gather a few shillings here and there from friends. She was without any family."

"Yes, certainly, certainly," said Mrs Hughes, opening a drawer. "We always keep a little ready money here for such purposes."

"No, allow me," said Bickley and pulled one of the rings

from his finger and held it out to Giles.

"Will this cover it?"

Giles took the ring.

"More than enough. Thank you very much."

"I'm sure you will put the rest to an equally good purpose," Bickley said.

"How kind, how very kind," said Mrs Hughes, fluttering with pleasure, and Bickley basked in her approbation. He was enjoying being magnanimous, that was clear enough. That was a notable weakness, Giles thought as he put the ring into his pocket. "Shall I ask my husband to take the service?"

"Thank you, but that won't be necessary. And he must have a great many more important calls on his time."

"Yes, yes, he is busy, that is true. But I am sure time could be found, when he is at home, that is. He is travelling about the diocese. He intends to visit every parish and see what needs to be done."

"Then we will not trouble him with this," said Giles. "And since Mr Bickley has been so generous, there should be no difficulty."

He took his leave, and wondered what might be passing between Bickley and Mrs Hughes when they were alone.

But Bickley followed him swiftly from the library, and they were alone in the hall together.

"On second thoughts," Giles said, putting the ring down on the table. "I can't accept this. God knows where it came from."

"Nice little performance in there, Vernon," said Bickley, taking up the ring. "A few things you left out, of course. That you fucked the bitch, for example. Shall I mention that to my lady? I have her ear, after all."

"Just her ear?" Giles said.

"You need to tread carefully," Bickley said. "This is not your business."

"It is exactly my business," Giles said.

"I am giving you fair warning –"

"I should arrest you now."

"But you don't, do you, because you've nothing on me except the hearsay evidence of a dead whore, who you took your pleasure of!"

"I will have you hanged for what you did to her," said Giles.

"That I sincerely doubt," Bickley said, and strolled past him to the door.

~

Giles went back to The Black Bull, and took a generous dose of laudanum. Holt had already left for Ardenthwaite and he had planned to go himself on horseback as soon as he was able, but the state of his head made him realise he must delay and take the carriage. So he lay down on his bed, intending to rest for an hour or so, hoping the laudanum would do its work.

It did, after a fashion. He slept a little, albeit fitfully, and woke in a state of mild confusion after troubling dreams. There was a servant knocking at the door. He was carrying a note from Emma Maitland.

So a little after three he set out again for the Minster Precincts, and the Treasurer's House. She was waiting for him in the small drawing room. Sally and Lamb had already gone to Holbroke, but Celia and Tom remained, and they were sitting with her by the fire.

He stood in the doorway for a long moment, watching them, imagining for a moment he was the master of the house, returning early from his business to the pleasures of family and hearth. He drank deep this bitter-sweet fancy, finding in it a better remedy than laudanum for the pain that gripped him.

Then she looked up and saw him there. Her smile was unaffected and full of pleasure, and she flung out her hand towards him.

For a moment he felt he ought to turn and walk away, feeling that he had no place there, but he could not resist, for all the guilt he felt about it.

He came in and took her hand, and before he had thought much about what he was doing, he had bent over and kissed it briefly, carelessly perhaps, but enough to want to remain standing there, still holding her hand, savouring the warmth of it on his lips.

He let go, for Celia was scrabbling to her feet, toasting fork in her hand, demanding her usual embrace.

"You look like Britannia with her trident," he said, when he had hugged her.

"Especially if I put the coal scuttle on your head," said Tom, pretending to reach for it.

"Don't you dare!" Celia screeched, then conceded, "but it would make a good helmet, should I need one. If I ever get to go to a fancy ball."

"You will one day, I'm sure," said Giles, settling down in Lambert's favourite armchair.

"Lady Maria did say something about tableaux vivants at Holbroke," said Mrs Maitland.

"Yes, they have quite a theatrical wardrobe there. You must ask to see it if ever you are invited," said Giles.

"I certainly shall," said Celia, returning her attention to the toast. "Well, I shall ask Mama to ask, I think, yes?"

"Yes, that would be the thing to do," said Mrs Maitland. "You see, we are all going to Holbroke now. Lord Rothborough and Lady Maria were insistent that Tom and Celia should come with me tomorrow."

"I may see you there, then," said Giles. "I have been asked, and I have been told to take some leave."

"Oh, you must come, Uncle Giles," said Tom. "We are

going rook-shooting."

"Tom – you're burning!" said Celia, as Tom's piece of toast caught fire.

"Oh, bother!" said Tom, and attempted, rather ineffectually, to put out the flaming bread by furious blowing and fanning. In the end, Celia seized the fork from him and plunged it into the fire so that the bread fell into the flames. "What a waste of a perfectly good piece of bread!" he said.

"Better that than burn the house down," said Celia. "You can come with us, Uncle Giles. We will have room in the carriage."

"You are forgetting my Patton, Celia," said Mrs Maitland.

"Oh yes – I'm sorry," said Celia.

"I shall make my own way," Giles said. "If I come."

"But you will come?" said Celia.

"I don't see why not."

"Oh, that will be splendid!" said Tom, getting up. "I'm going to see Hughes for a bit. Are you coming, sis?"

"If you don't mind?" Celia said.

"No," said Tom.

"Even when you said I bored him?" she said.

"No, I think he likes you," said Tom. "Though why, I can't say. Come on, then."

"Why don't you take the toast with you?" said Mrs Maitland, indicating the plate on the hearth. "We will never manage such a quantity."

"Good thought," said Tom. "You take that, and I will take the butter," he added, picking up the butter dish and pocketing a knife.

"Does Lord Rothborough know what he has done?" said Giles, when they had gone. "Will Holbroke ever survive such an invasion? And to let Tom loose with a gun! My poor sister will be in agony the entire time."

"I think it is delightful of him to ask them. And you should have more faith in your own flesh and blood, Major

Vernon. Your niece and nephew are some of the most delightful young people I have ever met. Actually, I think it is Lady Maria who is behind it."

"That I can believe. She is truly the kindest of creatures."

"Quite," said Mrs Maitland. "In fact, I am glad that Charles has gone back to Oxford, for he was very taken with her, and I worry that if he sees any more of her, he will be head over heels."

"Is that such a bad thing?"

"No, but it would be sure to lead to disappointment. Charles may have his title, but he is still too threadbare for that family."

"I wouldn't be so sure. Lord Rothborough is not so rigid."

"But Lady Rothborough is, and I understand that Lady Maria has quite a fortune from her mother's family. So there would be objections, I'm sure. It's best he is kept away. And really he is far too young to be thinking of this sort of thing."

She busied herself with the teapot and refilled his cup.

"Thank you for yesterday," he said. "No one could have been cooler in a crisis, or more useful."

"What else could I have done?" she said. "I am sorry I could not do more. That poor, poor woman –" She broke off. "Why are you taking leave, if you do not mind me asking? In the circumstances, surely –?"

"Sometimes I have migraines; I had one yesterday," he said. "Mr Carswell and the Chief Constable have told me to rest."

"That sounds sensible," she said. "But difficult for you, I should think."

"Yes, but I still have various irons in the fire. You, for example. How did you get on with Miss Waites? Did she bite?"

"She did indeed. She came just after luncheon. I was quite surprised that she did come, after what you said. She was quite reluctant to take on any work, though, and said she was very busy, but I was insistent with her. It really was quite an interesting encounter, all in all."

"In what way?"

"She said she had more clients than she knew what to do with, but when I offered to pay her in advance, more than one usually would, and mentioned that she would never be short of work amongst the ladies of the precincts, and that they would pay very promptly, that seemed to sway her."

"Because you think she is being underpaid?"

"I think she is half-starved and exploited. And scared, just as you said, very scared. I had them put aside a plate from luncheon and she wolfed it down."

"That makes sense."

"And why is she operating out of such a dubious address when she is so skilled?" said Mrs Maitland. "She could have her own shop and hands, and be fat and prosperous. It makes no sense."

"That is what puzzled me," said Giles. "And she was glad to take cash?"

"Astonishingly glad. As if she never got cash payments. Is she a slave of some sort? Is that what you think? That dress you said she made – who was it made for?"

Giles could not help sighing. He leant back in his chair and gazed at the ceiling for a long moment.

"It was made for the woman who died yesterday," he said. "She made it for Kate." There was silence between them for a moment, and then he asked, "How much did you give Miss Waites?"

"Two guineas – and the length of silk. And a dress of mine to copy. She is to send it to Holbroke when it is finished."

"Ask her to bring it in person," said Giles. "As soon as she can. In fact, can you find room for her when you go tomorrow? I'm sure work could be found for such a person in that house, and she would be safe there."

"Safe?" said Mrs Maitland. "Is she in danger?"

"She may be. She certainly knows a great deal that may be of use to me, and that puts her in danger. If I can get her to Holbroke, she can disappear, in effect. And you can get her to talk – you have already made a good start on that."

"Oh, I think anyone can buy trust with ready money. That is not so difficult."

"You underestimate yourself," said Giles, getting up. "I must go now, though I could sit here forever."

"It is very pleasant, isn't it?" she said.

"I should have gone in for the Church and got myself a nice living like this," said Giles. She smiled at that. "And clergymen seem to get the best wives."

"You make me afraid when you say that," she said. "I have yet to prove myself worthy on that score, remember."

"I'm sure you will be a success," he said.

She got up from her chair and said, "It does feel something of a responsibility."

"All marriages are, surely?"

"Yes. But Edward is –" she hesitated and then said, rather quietly, "so very good. It makes one feel most unequal to it. Especially as he sees in me nothing but unblemished virtue when, as you know all too well –"

"I am sure he sees your faults but chooses not to remind you of them," Giles said. "He knows your conscience works hard enough, without him labouring the point, as other fools might."

"Oh, how I wish that were so!" she exclaimed. "But in his eyes I am a paragon and, therefore, I can only fail him. That is truly frightening! It makes me wonder if –" And suddenly she had laid her hands on his forearm and was looking up at him, imploringly. "Tell me, my dear friend, that I am not about to –"

He gently removed her hand as carefully as he could,

trying to ignore the warmth in her voice, the particular intonation of 'dear friend' and the closeness of her.

"Edward is no fool," he said. "He will have read you as you are. Otherwise, why else would he have asked you to share his life with you? He is too sensible to be clouded by fancy, and you are too open and unguarded for him to see you as anything else but as imperfect but adorable –"

"Adorable?" she said. The word had escaped him, like a bird evading a hunter's net. "Adorable?" she said again.

He stepped back a little.

"It has been his great good fortune," he said, "to be in a position to offer – he could have married anyone. He chose you, Emma, with his eyes open, I am sure."

She looked away, her head a little bowed, and he wanted more than anything to reach out and touch her cheek.

"I know it is the greatest good fortune for me," she said, "that my interests and my feelings should be so engaged. I ought not to hesitate, but –" She looked back at him imploringly. How tempted he was by that, by the doubt in her voice. It would have been the simplest thing in the world to press his advantage. She was inviting it, after all. That was clear enough. "But I do, still. I –"

"No sane person ever married lightly," he managed to say. "This is all part of the business of doing it well, surely? Your doubts do you credit."

When he had said this, he felt as if he had locked a puppy in a box to suffocate. It was a cruel necessity. He reminded himself he had nothing at all to offer her except self-indulgent desire which would no doubt dissipate when he found some other object.

The door opened, and Celia came in with the empty plate of toast and the butter dish.

"Full of crumbs, I'm afraid," she said, putting it down on the tea table. "Boys are such pigs."

"Even young Master Hughes?" said Mrs Maitland.

"He is a little better than Tom," said Celia. "But only a little. And I have horrid sticky hands now!"

"Then I will kiss you on the cheek and say goodbye," said Giles. She presented her cheek to him and dissolved in laughter when he put his arms around her and attempted to tickle her. She squeaked, half in protest, half in pleasure.

"I'm too old for tickling! Stop, stop, please!"

He did so and caught sight of Emma's wistful smile. Again the bitter-sweet fancy of another sort of life came over him, and he felt certain she was thinking the same thing.

"That was simply horrible!" Celia said.

"It was," he agreed. "I promise never to do it again."

"Good!" she said, and flounced out of the room.

Emma shook her head at him.

"Half a woman, half a child," she said.

"May she never change," said Giles.

"We never do, at heart," said Emma, "if we are careful," and she again put out her hand to him.

He resigned himself to merely shaking it.

Chapter Twenty-three

Sir Richard Blanchfort was buried three days later in the little parish church at Hawksby, a few steps from his handsome manor house.

As was customary, neither his wife nor his daughter attended the service, but neither did they sit together with the other female mourners at the house and read through the burial service. Lady Blanchfort remained at Hawksby while Eleanor, despite Lord Rothborough's strenuous efforts, remained at Holbroke.

"Was there ever such a pair of obdurate females!" exclaimed Lord Rothborough to Felix as they drove back to Holbroke after the service.

They had been in to pay their respects to the widow, and had been received with frosty correctness, or rather Lord Rothborough had been – she had not even bothered to acknowledge Felix. Lord Rothborough had taken the opportunity to urge Lady Blanchfort to come to Holbroke to make her peace with her daughter, but she declined, rather as if he had suggested something indecent. They had left after five minutes or so, five such strained minutes that Felix was relieved to find in the carriage the usual small but luxurious basket of refreshments. A generous measure of sherry in a silver-gilt cup and a chicken sandwich were like manna from Heaven.

"I think Eleanor will relent before her mother," Lord Rothborough said. "Or at least I pray that she will."

"Her position seems more than understandable to me," said Felix with his mouth full. "Lady Blanchfort is hardly a tender parent. Why should she want to return to that?"

"Did you forget to breakfast this morning?" Lord Rothborough said.

"Yes," said Felix. "And going to funerals always makes me hungry."

"We must devise some compromise that both sides will find acceptable," said Lord Rothborough.

"We?" Felix said.

"I think you have a measure of influence with Eleanor," said Lord Rothborough.

"I wouldn't say that," said Felix. "And why does it matter so much to you that they are reconciled? You are her sole guardian, and she evidently prefers you to her mother."

"Because she is her mother, Felix – have a little heart for the poor woman! She may seem stubborn and cold, that's true, but Eleanor is her only child. It would be highly remiss of me not to try to broker peace between them."

"And it won't look good if you don't, I suppose?" Felix said. "I'm sure she is the type of woman who will write a hundred letters to her friends and acquaintances saying how you have poisoned her only child against her."

"Naturally, I don't want to be branded the villain of the piece," said Lord Rothborough. "But that is not my principal motive. Family quarrels like these are dangerous for those involved in them – like some dreadful illness. Eleanor must make peace with her mother for her own sake – she is effectively my daughter now and her welfare is paramount. I will not have it on my conscience that I did not try. But what a business!"

"She will resent you as well if you try to force her hand," Felix said.

"That is the danger," said Lord Rothborough. "But I think with time, and the right influences, she will see and feel the good sense of it."

The carriage had now turned onto a narrow, ill-made track that marked the entry into the wilder, wooded upland country to the north east of Northminster. More specifically, they were where the far reaches of the Hawksby estate touched borders with the extensive woodlands that surrounded Ardenthwaite.

As they jolted their way through the woods, he wondered again where exactly it was he had first encountered Eleanor Blanchfort, and how far he had managed to stray from the house in his delirium. There were still scabs and scars on his feet and legs to remind him of that business, although the undergrowth he had stumbled through was now shimmering with bluebells.

They turned from the winding lane into a broader avenue of great elms, with the house in view at the end of it.

Approached from this angle, the place seemed quite strange to him, but as they drew closer, the familiar shapes of the roof became legible, and when he smelt the wood smoke in the air, he had an agreeable sensation, akin to coming home. This surprised him, especially given recent events in the house. How had the old place come to mean so much to him?

Holt had been sent ahead to arrange things and hire some additional servants and it was Holt, now in the guise of butler, who came out to meet the carriage. Felix might have expected Major Vernon to come out too, but Holt informed them he was resting.

"Then I will not disturb you any further," said Lord Rothborough. "We will expect you at dinner tomorrow!"

Felix went in and found Major Vernon sitting in an easy chair in the low-ceilinged, oak-panelled parlour. He was in a state of uncharacteristic lassitude, gazing into space, while Colonel Parham's pointers lay dozing on the floor beside him. Felix's entrance seemed to startle him for a moment, but he soon recovered.

"How was the funeral?" he said.

"Mercifully brief. But decently done. You seem very settled."

"I must look indolent," said Major Vernon, getting up and stretching.

"Indolence has its uses, especially if you have been ill. How is your head?"

"Clear since yesterday, thank God! A little distance from Northminster has done me good. I was about to take Hector and Hero out," he said. "Will you come with me?"

"Yes. I am stiff from the carriage."

"I was going to take them through the woods. I have been thinking –"

"I knew you were not idling just then," Felix said.

"There is some use in a state of cultivated vacancy," Major Vernon said. "Things occur to one that might otherwise –" He broke off. "And you can keep an eye open for deadly milk-cap."

They set off together through the gardens, the dogs happily rushing ahead towards the orchard gate.

"You see they are used to taking this path – they know where they are going," said Major Vernon. "We might assume this is where the Colonel used to go."

"Which helps us, how?"

"We need to consider exactly what happened on that last day – that may give us some idea who was involved. And also, the clearer we are about what may have happened, the better placed we are to look for witnesses. Someone will have seen something that will help us."

Felix nodded, and opened the orchard gate where the dogs were now waiting impatiently. It was at this gate that Holt had found him that morning. Then the buds had still been tight on the branches; now the place was a dazzle of pale blossom.

"I wish they had not killed him here," he could not help saying. "If I am to take up residence at some point, then the memory of it will always –"

"There is a risk of that," said Major Vernon. "But it may

be that you can remove the stain by the act of occupation. I have to admit that was half in my mind when I suggested we come here."

"You are like a riding master who makes you get straight back into the saddle after every fall."

"Precisely."

"There is sense in that," said Felix. "I do care for the place, despite everything."

They had reached the far side of the orchard where another gateway, this time with the gate ajar, led on to the ancient woodlands that formed much of the park at Ardenthwaite. There was a section of rough upland, but mostly there was a deep band of sheltering oak, beech and elms, carefully coppiced, with long shady drives through them: a delightful conceit at any time, and on that day, with the fresh greenery of spring and the great pools of bluebells here and there, it was particularly so.

"It would be hard not to," said Major Vernon, as they set out into the woods, following the dogs. The dogs stopped, and seemed to be waiting for them to catch up. "The trouble is, there are too many ways through these woods," he said. "Too many ways to go without being observed."

"It would help if we knew where they were heading, I suppose," said Felix. "And how they travelled."

"Quite. I am assuming they left, at least, by horseback – remember they took the Colonel's horses with them. And if they had any sense they would have gone off in different directions."

"Mostyn towards Swalecliffe?" Felix said.

"At least we have that fragment," said Major Vernon, setting off again. Seeing him do so, the dogs raced on.

"We are going somewhere that pleases them, at least," said Major Vernon.

They walked for some time, with the woods growing darker and cooler, but then the path turned and they came across a small cottage, with a neatly fenced garden, and set in a clearing to catch what sun it could.

The dogs were yelping with delight at the cottage gate, and as they approached they could see they were being greeted by a sturdy, bearded man dressed in the clothes of a respectable countryman.

He swept off his hat at the sight of Felix and Major Vernon, and came out through the gate and along the lane to meet them.

"Squire!" he said, bowing respectfully to Felix. "Glad to see you here, that I am!" Although he looked familiar, Felix found he was struggling to remember the man's name, and at the same time not at all comfortable to be so addressed. "Sam Webb, sir," he went on, helpfully. "Forester. You set one of my lads to rights last year when he slashed himself with a sickle."

"Ah, yes, I remember," said Felix. "He is quite well again?"

"Right as rain. Working for his Lordship over at Holbroke now and doing very well at it. Will you gentlemen come in and have a dish of tea? Mrs Webb has just boiled the kettle. We'd be honoured."

"Certainly," said Felix. "This is Major Vernon."

"Aye, that's right, so it is! Odd, though, what a look of the Colonel you have about you, sir – you might be brothers, God rest his soul! What a business!"

"Yes, that has been remarked on," said Major Vernon. "In fact, it would be very good to have your observations on that matter, Mr Webb. I think a constable may have visited you about the time we discovered him."

"Well mayhap he did, but we didn't see him, for I was up at Holbroke that week – I go and help out when I'm needed and Mrs Webb went to see her sister. I tell you, if we had been here, we should have seen or heard something."

"I'm sure. But you may be able to help us anyway," said

Major Vernon. "Clearly you had some dealings with Colonel Parham. His dogs seem fond of you."

"That they are. He used always to walk them down this way, and often enough we'd meet. Now, will you come in, sir?"

He led them to the front door, calling out, "Mary, Mary – I have the young squire here!"

They went into an austere but immaculate kitchen, where Mrs Webb was soon mustering her best cups and saucers, and talking with great gratitude about "Johnny's leg," before concluding, "It's the best of it you are back here, now, sir. The place shouldn't be in the hands of strangers, especially those that get themselves done away with!"

"But I'm a stranger, Mrs Webb," Felix could not help pointing out.

"Nay, Squire," she said. "Thee is a Haraald to thy fingertips, wedding vows or no, and it's better for the place that it should be yours. His Lordship knows best. When old Sir Robert died, well, who knows who might have taken the place over, if he had not. No, Mr Carswell, you're no stranger, and I hope you'll make a good long stay of it this time. Now, will you have a piece of tea cake? It's fresh."

"I can't promise you it will be for very long," said Felix. "Major Vernon and I have this business of the Colonel's death to clear up."

"What did you make of him, Mrs Webb?" Major Vernon asked.

"He was pleasant enough. I didn't really speak to him. Usually he only talked to Mr Webb."

"And did you ever go up and help at the house? Perhaps when Mrs Parham was there?"

"Aye, once or twice, but I never did again, because they never paid, did they? And she was not there for long. They were in a deal of trouble, those two, and she was off by Christmas. In a huff."

"You saw that?"

"Nay, Agnes Taylor told me – she was working there for longer than I was. She's working over at Hawksby, at the big house, now."

"Sir Richard's place?" Felix said. She nodded. "Miss Blanchfort's now, I suppose," he added.

"Oh yes, so it will be," said Mrs Webb. "Do you know her, Squire? Think you should, given you'll be such close neighbours. Happen you should offer for her."

"That's none of your affair, Mary!" said Mr Webb.

"He's of an age to wed," said Mrs Webb, with no trace of apology. "And should be thinking of it."

"So when did you both last see Colonel Parham?" Major Vernon asked.

"The day before I went over to Holbroke, which was on the – well, I marked it on the almanac to remind me when I was to go." Webb got up and took down the almanac from the shelf where it sat with the family Bible. He thumbed through it and found the place. "On the Monday. And you went away before that, Mary, on Sunday." She nodded.

"And how did he seem that day? Was he on his walk as usual?"

"Yes, with the dogs, and his gun."

"He did not seem troubled at all?"

Webb shook his head.

"And he never mentioned the house being haunted to you?" Felix asked.

"Haunted?" said Mr Webb. "Ardenthwaite?" He shook his head again. "Never heard anything like that about the place. Have you, Mary?"

"No," said his wife.

"And did you have anything to do with Mostyn, the Colonel's servant?" Major Vernon now enquired.

"Oh, do you have him fingered for it, sir?" said Mrs Webb.

"Why do you say that, Mrs Webb?"

"Because he's a thorough rogue! And you must talk to Agnes, and the other girls – most of them are at Hawksby now. He was a dirty pest, I can say that much."

"But that doesn't mean he'd hang his own master!" said Webb. "And that's just gossip, Mary, nothing more."

"But I shall go and talk to Agnes, certainly, Mrs Webb. There is often more truth in gossip than you know."

"There!" said Mrs Webb. "Haven't I always said the same thing, Sam, haven't I?"

They finished their tea, and set off with the dogs again.

"You will have to tread carefully at Hawksby," Felix remarked. "Lady Blanchfort is not of a warm and welcoming disposition."

"No, and she will be grieving in her own way for whatever her marriage was, I suppose," said Major Vernon. "But probably I will not even need to trouble her."

"If I were you, I would go by the book and abase yourself in the drawing room before you go questioning her servants. She is exactly the sort of woman who would object violently to that, even if one's motives were unimpeachable. This morning she was as cold as a glacier. There was no sign of emotion about her."

"She has great command of herself, then."

"On the day of her own husband's funeral –" Felix pointed out.

"Estranged husband," Major Vernon said.

"Then a little relief might have cracked her mask. Oh, it is no wonder the girl is so confused when her mother is such a marble monument!"

"Misery does harden people," Major Vernon said.

"She is calcified!" said Felix.

"Not an ideal mother-in-law?" said Major Vernon with a smile.

"Please, please – spare me that!"

"It will be talked about. You danced with her and helped her when her father was dying. Oh, and your lands march together. In a novel, that would be quite enough," he added.

"Heaven forbid!" said Felix. "No, never!"

"You will have to arm yourself against the speculation, then, Squire," said Major Vernon.

"And do not, in the name of merciful Heaven, call me that, I beg you!"

The dogs began to bark furiously. They seemed to be very excited by a heap of broken branches a small distance away – they were sniffing and scrabbling.

"Interesting," said Major Vernon, striding over to them. "What have you found there, Hero? What is it, girl?"

He began to push aside the branches. Felix came to assist him. Under the branches was a layer of bracken, and below that, spread like a tarpaulin over a shallow pit, was a dark green man's overcoat, exactly the same shade and style as that worn by the late Colonel Parham.

Major Vernon picked it up to reveal the contents of the pit, namely a battered old travelling box. He shook out the coat and hung it on a low-hanging branch. Hector went up to it and tugged and whimpered at it.

"Poor old boy," said Major Vernon, crouching and comforting the dog. "I'm afraid he's gone for good. But what a clever fellow you are to lead us to this, and you too, my girl," he added, pulling Hero close to him as well. "You shall get some nice scraps later for this, I promise."

"I wonder if it's locked," said Felix, getting into the pit to try the lid. "Yes."

Major Vernon handed him his set of keys and in a few moments Felix had successfully picked the lock.

"I shall have to get you a set of your own," Major Vernon said when Felix returned the keys. "You are far more adept that I am."

"Too tempting," said Felix. "I might turn to

housebreaking for a living. So what have we in here? Shirts, by the look of it."

But what lay beneath the linen was a good deal more interesting – a varied collection of small valuables: snuff boxes, miniatures, silver cups, a gold watch and some old-fashioned jewelled shoe buckles.

"Is all this the Colonel's, do we think?" Felix said, opening a double miniature of a man and a woman. "His parents, perhaps?"

"Hard to say," said Major Vernon, squinting at it. "But there was no trace of any of his personal effects in the house, so it is reasonable to suspect that Mostyn or whoever he was working with, gathered it all up. Strange not to take them with him given how portable they are, but there may be reasons for that. And to take books as well – these are your books, Mr Carswell, I think, rather than the Colonel's. They have the Ardenthwaite crest on them."

"Perhaps he fancies setting up a gentleman's library in his retirement," said Felix, examining the titles. "I should have never have missed these, I have to admit. What on earth would he want with them?"

"Perhaps they were taken to order for someone," said Major Vernon. "We may be able to find something useful from that. And now we know that our man will be coming back for his treasures. I shall have to organise a watch."

Chapter Twenty-four

The next day, as arranged, they presented themselves for dinner at Holbroke.

Carswell had begun grumbling about the necessity of this earlier in the day, and Giles wondered if he was worried about being forced into the company of Miss Blanchfort, a sentiment he entirely understood when he caught sight of Emma Maitland in an anteroom to the drawing room.

She was standing with her back to him, wearing the same fetching wine-coloured dress she had worn that night at the Treasurer's House. Beside her stood Celia, dazzling in white muslin, admiring the famous Holbroke Dolls' House. They were both wearing crowns of spring flowers, their heads bent together as they examined some tiny detail.

"What a pretty sight," Sally said, coming to his side.

"Celia is dining with us?" said Giles.

"Yes, Maria insisted. We are *en famille*, apparently. It's really so charming."

"As are these," he said, touching the flowers that also decorated Sally's hair.

"That was Maria. She and Celia have been making them all afternoon. Even one for Miss Blanchfort – and you might think that was quite wrong given her degree of mourning, but really it looks very right. I'm not quite sure how that can be – but it did make the poor girl smile when Celia gave it to her, which is something."

"What do you make of Miss Blanchfort?" said Giles.

"Interesting you should ask – I had quite a conversation with her this afternoon. She's a very clever young woman, certainly, but she's had such a mass of tutors and teachers. The intention seems to have been never to allow her an idle moment to herself. Every minute of the day prescribed for her as if she was not to be trusted with the slightest liberty. She has found it very odd to be here and not being told what she should do. Of course, children do need routines, but an overbearing system such as that – I think it must be damaging. Not that she is damaged yet, but she is a little like a pot about to boil over."

"It's as well she's been taken off the fire."

"Yes, this is an excellent place for her. Lord Rothborough could not be a better guardian and he is being strenuous in his efforts to reconcile her with her mother."

"And if he cannot manage that, who can?"

"Quite," said Sally. She glanced about her and at Emma and Celia in the anteroom. "Those two will have to be dragged away – that dolls' house is a wonder, though."

At this moment Emma Maitland turned away from the dolls' house and caught sight of them. She smiled and came out of the room.

"Miss Waites came with us," she said.

"That is good news," said Giles.

"She is with Lady Maria at the moment, adjusting a sleeve. You were right – there will be plenty of work for her here. Patton is keeping an eye on her downstairs. She is dining with the upper servants and generally being made a fuss of so that she will feel safe. I explained it all to Lord Rothborough, and of course he was most obliging. Anything in your service, Major Vernon. He is a great admirer."

At this point, the Rothborough spaniels came skittering into the room, heralds for the Marquis himself who was accompanied by his daughter and his ward. In their wake came Lambert, Carswell and Tom. The latter was all jaunty confidence in a new suit (so Sally informed Giles) and looked as if he had been frequenting great houses all his life, and intended doing much more of the same.

"He is going to be unbearable," Sally murmured. "He has shot five rooks."

True to form, Tom now bounded up to Miss Blanchfort and asked if he might take her down to dinner.

"Tom, dear," Sally said, "that is gallant, but it is for Lady Maria to decide."

"I think it will do nicely," said Lady Maria. "If Miss Blanchfort doesn't object?"

"No," said the young lady. "Of course not."

"Mr Carswell can take your sister in, Mr Fforde. I know they are great friends," Lady Maria went on. "And I will ask you for your arm, dear Canon Fforde, if you don't mind? And Mrs Fforde, you will go in with Papa. Leaving Major Vernon and Mrs Maitland. Oh dear, I did not mean you to sound like remnants!"

"Please, we are not remotely offended!" said Mrs Maitland. Giles could not help smiling, for all that it pained him to hear her speak for him, thoughtlessly and yet accurately. It made him wish that it was a commonplace.

They went into dinner, which although it was a small party, *'en famille'*, as Lady Maria had put it, involved all the usual splendour of Holbroke: a blaze of candles and silver, and many courses of complicated, delicious food that seemed to decorate the plates like sculpture. Yet an informal mood prevailed, much helped by Tom and Celia, who seemed to shine brighter than any of the candles. That Lord Rothborough was delighted by them was obvious, and Sally and Lambert naturally looked very gratified by this.

As the dessert came in, Celia turned to Lord Rothborough and asked, "Would it be possible, my lord – if I found a way to do it – to make some tiny books for the dolls in the Dolls' House? Mrs Maitland and I noticed that they have none."

"Yes, of course," said Lord Rothborough. "Would you write them yourself as well as making them?"

"Yes, I think I could. They would have to be nice stories. I shouldn't give them anything improper. But exciting, naturally."

"Naturally. There is no point in stories that are not exciting," said Lord Rothborough.

"I have some stories that I have written that might do. And I have a tiny hand," Celia went on.

"Then it should be a magazine," said Tom. "Like Blackwoods. That might be easier to make than a little book, Celia."

She considered it for a moment and said, "Yes, perhaps."

"If it is a magazine," said Canon Fforde, "then we all might contribute something. To thank our hosts?" He raised his glass to Lady Maria and then Lord Rothborough. "The Holbroke Digest?"

"Miss Fforde, nothing could give me more pleasure. A charming idea. Now tell me, who in your opinion writes the most exciting stories? Mr Ainsworth or dear Sir Walter?"

"Do you know what?" Tom said, "Edmund Hughes told me they are not allowed to read Sir Walter at the Palace."

"They don't have plum pudding at Christmas either," said Celia.

"The Bishop's family?" said Lady Maria.

"No plum pudding? How very strange," said Lord Rothborough.

"Perhaps the Bishop has a weak digestion," said Lambert. "Plum pudding can even seem excessive to me, and I'm a well-known glutton."

"I'm sure the servants have a nice one," said Sally.

"No, not even the servants," said Celia.

"That seems rather harsh," said Lord Rothborough.

"Our people would never stand for that," said Lady Maria. "Plum puddings are a great thing with us, though. We have a special larder for them, and a secret receipt. I have often thought if ever we lost our fortune, I should take it and open a plum pudding shop!"

"It would almost be worth losing everything to see that," said Lord Rothborough. "And I would sit in the back of the shop, smoking my pipe and being shockingly idle, reading nothing but the sporting papers, while my daughters worked themselves to the bone."

~

Tom Fforde was permitted to drink half a glass of port before being sent up to the ladies. This he did with relish and managed to make a nice compliment about the quality of the wine, which pleased Lord Rothborough enormously. Felix wondered at his social skills. He remembered the agonising awkwardness of being fifteen all too well. How on earth did Tom manage to be so easy in himself? Perhaps it was something one was born with.

When he had gone, Lord Rothborough said, approvingly, "He is going to go far, Canon Fforde."

"But in what field?" said Canon Fforde. "This idea of engineering is all very well, but I don't think he is ready to be apprenticed. It's a rough life, and he's still very young."

"Perhaps you should send him to Edinburgh," said Lord Rothborough. "Yes, Felix? A couple of years at the University would give him a solid preparation in mechanics and mathematics. That family you lodged with, are they still taking in undergraduates?"

"Dr and Mrs Hill?" said Felix. "I suppose so. I'm not sure Tom would stand for the food there. It was dreadful."

"Perhaps they have a new cook. I could make a few enquiries, if you like?"

"It's certainly an interesting idea," said Canon Fforde. "What do you think, Mr Carswell?"

"He would do well anywhere," Felix said. "But given he does have a mathematical bent, there would be plenty for him at Edinburgh. But then one might say the same for Glasgow. I have an acquaintance who is now an instructor there, and quite satisfied with it."

"This is all most interesting," said Canon Fforde. "I have no intention of sending him back to school. That business with the tattoos – he has been in silly, idle company. He needs something definite to occupy himself with, something that he is inclined towards. Latin and Greek certainly don't agree with him."

"It never did with me," said Major Vernon. "There is Woolwich as well. He mentioned that to me."

"His ears will be burning," said Canon Fforde.

"Oh, I doubt it," said Major Vernon. "I think he will be sitting gazing at Miss Blanchfort, just as he was during dinner."

"So long as he does not forget himself and attempt to flirt," said Canon Fforde, getting up from the table. "I think I had better go up now and encourage him to go to bed – if you will excuse me, my lord, gentlemen?"

"I will come with you, Lamb," said Major Vernon.

Felix was left alone with Lord Rothborough.

"You are not tearing yourself away to gaze at Miss Blanchfort, then?" said Lord Rothborough.

"No," said Felix. "Do you think I ought?"

"No, not at all. I merely wondered –"

"I have already been told, in no uncertain terms, to offer for her by Mrs Webb, the forester's wife."

"You do not want to cross her, Felix, I can tell you that," said Lord Rothborough, smiling.

"I'd better go and do it now then," said Felix pretending to rise. Lord Rothborough laughed, put out his hand to stay him and said, "No, I don't think so."

"Truly?"

"Of course not! I thought we understood each other

better than that."

"It was not so long ago that you were talking about that girl in Germany."

"And that was a mistake on my part, for which I crave your pardon."

"You do?" said Felix.

"Circumstances have allowed me to see what is important. I have no wish to force your hand. You look astonished – perhaps you believe that old dogs cannot learn new tricks?"

"No, no – yes, I am surprised, but grateful, of course."

"To be frank, there is no misery in the world like an unhappy marriage," Lord Rothborough said after a long moment. "It is a curious thing how long it took me to realise it; it was not until this last winter in Italy." He rubbed his face and sighed. "It is a terrible thing to know one is the sort of man who cannot find any love left in his heart for a sick woman, let alone pity. God forgive me, but I failed her. The mother of my darling girls, and I could not –" He broke off, rather overcome with his distress. He got up from the table and turned his back to Felix. "That is what I want to spare you, Felix. But you are a better man than I. I don't suppose you would fall into the same trap."

Felix got up and went to stand beside him.

"You did everything you could for her," he said. "And she is much recovered now. No one has said that you have been anything but exemplary."

"What one does and what one feels can be different things," said Lord Rothborough.

"She is a difficult woman," Felix said. "Sick or well, she is difficult. If you had done nothing, that would have been reprehensible, but you did everything you ought."

"Except feel compassion?" said Lord Rothborough. But then he reached out and squeezed Felix's shoulder for a moment. "Thank you though, for that. Now, we should join the others, should we not?"

Chapter Twenty-five

Giles rode over to Holbroke again the following morning and was surprised by Emma Maitland seeking him out as soon as he arrived, as if by previous arrangement. He had been going in to speak to Lord Rothborough, and she came dashing up after him as he passed through the great library.

"I have news for you," she said, laying her hand on his arm for a brief moment to stop him.

"Oh?" he said, startled, if also pleased, by the eagerness of her approach.

"I hope you don't mind – I have spoken to Miss Waites this morning, and got as much out of her as I could in the course of general conversation," she said. He nodded, and she went on: "Without arousing her suspicions unduly, that is. Although I think she is a little wary, all things considered, but on the other hand she seems equally inclined to accept a merciful providence for giving her a good dinner and a bed for the night as well as money in her pocket. I hope you do not mind. The moment presented itself, we were alone – and I thought –"

"No, of course I don't mind," Giles said. "Given you have begun the task, you may as well finish it. What has she told you?"

"I made some notes – I was not sure when you would be here again." She reached into her pocket and produced some folded papers which she handed to him. "I hope they make sense."

He could not help smiling as he began to study them. She had a clear hand and she had organised the material exactly as he would have liked it. In fact they were so thorough, and he became so absorbed for a minute or two in reading them, that he quite forgot she was standing there.

"I think I have made a note of everything that seemed pertinent," she said, breaking into his train of thought. "And then again, of things that might not be pertinent at all, but I do think you said on one occasion that it is often a trifle that can lead to the largest truth."

"Did I say that?" he said. "I think you have paraphrased me – no, improved on me. These are excellent. Quite –"

He broke off, aware that she was looking at him with an expression of ardent pleasure, which in turn quickened his own heart in a fashion that felt dangerous. Despite everything, she still provoked heady delight in him.

Carefully, he walked away down the library, looking down at the notes again, attempting to be indifferent.

"So she comes from Marlingford. Her father was the landlord of The Blue Bell Inn."

"Yes. Where is Marlingford?"

"A little to the south east of Northminster," said Giles. "Fast becoming a suburb."

"She was most keen to tell me she was respectable, that the family was 'highly respectable' – she said that several times. Of course, she may have been trying to vouch for herself. But even given the difference in our situations, it seemed to labour the point. It strikes me that truly respectable people never draw attention to their respectability. There is no need to. I felt she was trying to distract my attention from something disreputable, but that is only my instinct."

"A good observation. I have seen that for myself. We must let her get even more comfortable. And in the meantime, I think some enquiries need to be made in Marlingford. She is not intending to leave tonight, I hope?"

"No, she is engaged for a week at least. Lady Maria and Mrs Hope have got all manner of things for her to do. I think Mrs Hope is getting a new Sunday dress and there are some ancient embroideries that need to be remounted, or some such. Oh, the life of a great house like this!" she said. "It is like a walled city, is it not? And therefore a good place to hide someone."

"I hope so," said Giles. "There have been too many deaths already. We need to protect her." He could not help sighing, the image of Kate in all her dying wretchedness springing into his mind with painful clarity. "It is..."

"Tell me," she said, laying her hand on his arm again. "You are troubled, I think. It will help you to talk about it."

He had not meant to betray so much to her, and forced himself to smile.

"No, not really."

"Not really?" she said, her eyes ardent and searching, her hand still on his arm.

He removed her hand from his arm, but somehow their fingers knotted together and for a moment they stood, heads bent slightly together.

"I cannot lay that sort of burden on you," he managed to say. "Surely you understand –"

"I'm strong," she said, coming a fraction closer.

"Yes, yes, I know," he said, "but you're not mine. That's the difficulty. I can't presume when –"

"It would be no presumption."

"When you are going to marry another man?"

"I shall not marry him." She spoke quietly but fiercely, with a shake of her head. "I did not sleep a wink last night. I got up at six and started writing the letter –"

"And I hope you screwed it up and threw it in the fire!" he said, moving away from her. "You cannot break from him, Emma. You have given him a solemn promise."

There was a moment's silence; then she said, quietly, and with conscious control, "I cannot marry if my feelings are not engaged. I thought they were, and it seems they are not."

"You cannot throw away such an opportunity," he said.

"Not on a whim, because you think that –"

"How dare you!" she exclaimed. "To call it a whim, when you know that it is nothing of the sort!"

"Don't," he said. "Don't think you can put a loaded gun to my head. Don't threaten me with breaking with Edward."

He had meant to be harsh. Her ardour was too dangerous for both of them, and needed to be checked with force. Yet when he saw her expression, a mixture of anger and grief, he wished it could have been otherwise.

"It was not a threat," she said, and he could hear her suppressing the passion in her voice. "I am merely describing my situation. What you make of it is your own business."

She walked away down the long library, and then stopped and turned back to him.

"I have lived alone for all these years, after all," she said. "Perhaps being a widow has a great deal more for it than is generally supposed. After all, living men are awkward creatures at the best of times!"

Then she threw up her hands for a moment, turned her back on him again and continued her exit from the room, like a celebrated actress quitting the stage.

~

Giles had intended to ride to Marlingford and begin his enquiries there, but a little beyond the park at Holbroke the weather took an angry turn. A heavy fall of rain became a storm of peculiar vehemence, under a leaden sky, crazed and cracked with unexpected lightning, making it impossible to proceed. He turned into the woods about Ardenthwaite, seeking the fastest way back he knew, and rode on, soon wretched with damp and the lingering discontent of his conversation with Emma.

If she did break with Edward Fforde, there was only one reason for it, and that was because she was still in love with him. In some other life, that might have been a matter for rejoicing that she had seen the light and was still free, but it meant no joy for him. One thing was clear enough: though he might wish to marry her, he could not. He was not fit.

Through the deluge he perceived the figure of a girl in a green riding habit, standing under a tree. As he approached, he realised who it was. It was Miss Blanchfort, looking as if she had been thrown into a stream.

"Miss Blanchfort?" he called out. "Are you in difficulty?"

She did not answer. She was supporting one wrist in the other, and from her expression she looked as if she was in pain. "Did you fall?" he said, dismounting. "Where is your horse? Where is your groom? Have you sent him for help?"

"I don't have one."

"You were out alone?" Giles said. "Did you have permission from Lord Rothborough?"

"I don't need his permission," she said.

"I doubt that," Giles said.

"I can manage alone quite well."

"Is that what you told them when you went out? That you didn't need a groom? That his Lordship had allowed it?"

"What does that matter to you?" she said.

"I just think it highly unlikely that Lord Rothborough would allow it."

She glanced away, biting her lip and then said, "It would not have happened if it had been my horse. That mare was very bad-tempered – and then the storm came on, she threw me and went bolting off. I tried to catch her, of course, but – you didn't see her about, I suppose?"

Giles shook his head.

"And you've hurt yourself," he pointed out.

"I don't know. It's sore. But nothing's broken."

"Show me," Giles said. She put out her hand, still

supported by the other, and gave an involuntary gasp of pain as she did so. Her wrist looked suspiciously bent and was already quite swollen. "Mr Carswell will need to have a look at that. Fortunately we are not far from Ardenthwaite. Less than a mile, if I am not mistaken."

"I was simply waiting for the rain to clear," she said. "I will make my own way back to Holbroke, thank you."

He shook his head.

"I don't think so. That would be a wretched inconvenience for everyone, and you have probably caused enough already. They will be sick with worry at Holbroke, especially if the horse is found without its rider. You are far better coming with me to where a surgeon can look at you, without having to be sent for in a storm. Shall we...?" He indicated the path with a sweep of his hand, and began to lead his horse in that direction. She showed no signs of moving. "If you please, ma'am?"

She consented at last, and so they walked back to Ardenthwaite in very disagreeable circumstances. Giles decided he would deliver her to Carswell and then ride at once back to Holbroke to tell them what had become of her. As the rain was still sheeting down, this was not a pleasant prospect.

~

"Are you sure you won't take some laudanum?" Felix said, before he started.

"No," Miss Blanchfort said, and turned away to bury her face in her shoulder, "just do it, would you, and do it quickly!"

"Naturally," he said, and began as gently as he could to realign the bone in her wrist. Fortunately it was a neat break and would mean only a few minutes of agony for her. She stiffened, screwed up her face and bit into the sleeve of her habit.

"That's part one done," he said, reaching for a splint. She gave a gasp of relief, and met his eyes with a wild stare of exhaustion and pain. "You can have something in a minute. I advise it, really I do. There isn't any necessity to be brave, Miss Blanchfort."

She sank back in the chair, grey-faced now.

"Don't you think I deserve to suffer?" she said.

"No," he said.

"I think Major Vernon does," she said.

"He is going to get extremely wet, so he was entitled to be a little out of humour with you. But they will be so pleased to see him at Holbroke and glad to hear that you are safe and not lying in a ditch with a broken neck –"

"They will be angry too. Lord Rothborough will be."

"He will be relieved. And if he is angry – well, it is never for long."

"I suppose you would know that," she said. "Being what you are."

"Your mother drilled that into you, I suppose," he could not help saying, remembering how to the point Lady Blanchfort had been.

"Is it unpleasant?" she said. "That state of yours?"

"That's too complicated a question to answer when I am trying to splint up a broken wrist," he said. He wanted to add that it was impertinent as well. "Now, can you lift it a little while I fix the splints underneath?"

She obliged with a wince, and he set about immobilizing it as quickly as he could.

"How long will it be like this?" she said, as he finished the bandaging.

"Oh, quite a while. A month or two. No piano practice for you."

"Good."

"Nor riding," he added.

"I shall go mad," she said. "I swear I shall. If I cannot get out, then –"

"Then perhaps you should have thought of that when you picked out the wildest horse from my lord's stables and went careering off without anyone to see that you were safe," Felix said.

She closed her eyes.

"I shall go mad! I cannot bear it. I wish I had broken my neck! I wish I was dead! Then you could bury me with Papa and... and..."

"And what would be the point of that?" Felix said, needled by her histrionic tone. "Do you think the dead can see people crying over their tombs? Count the mourners at their funerals? Admire the flowers?"

"No! That isn't what I meant! You are so cruel!"

"I was only trying to make it clear that there would be no point in your being dead."

"I want to be dead," she said, "because I can't bear to feel. Truly I cannot. Everything is agony. You tell me to take laudanum for the pain. Well, that's just bodily pain. I can bear that. It's this terrible pain in my head, in my heart, in my very being..." She broke off and sighed. "But how can you understand that? What do you know?"

"A little. Only a little," he added, seeing her about to interrupt him. "But I know that you are dealing with a great grief, and that takes time to heal, just like this bone will need time to set straight again. Wishing yourself dead won't help you. You would be better finding something that will make you feel purposeful and happy."

"And are you happy?" she said after a moment.

"I don't know," he said. "But I try to be purposeful. And I think we need to get this arm of yours into a sling, and then you need to rest."

Somewhat to his surprise, she acquiesced. The pain had exhausted her, after all, and she allowed him to help her into bed. He had told Holt to have a bed made up for her in the bedroom where his parents had slept that summer. It was perhaps the pleasantest in the house, especially with a large fire going in the hearth. The afternoon sun had somehow got the upper hand over the storm and had filled the room with a comforting glow of golden light.

The bed was a high one, and she had to scramble up into it. Once installed, wrapped up now in his own dressing gown, she sat propped up on a pile of pillows, with her loose, damp hair falling down over her shoulders. She looked to him like an exquisite but old-fashioned wooden doll with brightly painted cheeks.

"Sit with me a while," she said, as plaintive as a child.

"Are you sure?" he said in surprise.

"I don't want to be alone," she said.

So he pulled a chair nearer to the bedside.

"You are sure you don't want any laudanum?" he said.

"No, I can bear this," she said, closing her eyes.

They sat in silence, and he listened to her breathing as it grew more steady. The fire spat and crackled and the wind moved through the young leaves on the trees in the forest beyond, taking away the last remnants of the storm. She seemed to sleep, and Felix sat there watching her, longer than he ought, finding it hard to tear himself away.

Chapter Twenty-six

Major Vernon returned from Holbroke in the early evening, with such a quantity of domestic reinforcements that it seemed he was relieving a siege of many months rather than seeing to the comfort of a girl with a slight injury, who might remain there but one night.

However, Miss Blanchfort was no ordinary girl. An heiress and the ward of Lord Rothborough could not be left to scramble in a borrowed dressing gown in a house of unmarried men. So Major Vernon was accompanied by Mrs Maitland as chaperone, Miss Blanchfort's maid, Mrs Maitland's maid and Jacob, one of the lesser footman. There was also a quantity of luggage and extensive provisions from the great larders at Holbroke.

"But not my lord?" Felix remarked, when he was alone with Major Vernon in the library, the women having all been taken to the patient. "I was sure that he would have come back with you."

"I told him exactly what you said about her condition – that she was in no danger, and then Mrs Maitland proposed herself as chaperone – very ably I have to say – then, he was content to stay by his own fire."

"Wonders will never cease," Felix could not help saying. "Do you know what he said to me the other night? When I told him that half the county seemed to expect me to marry her, he said he had no expectations of any kind about it! That he is done with all that! I can't quite credit it."

Major Vernon smiled at that, and yawned. "Please excuse me – I think I will have to make my excuses for dinner as well, if you don't mind," he said, rubbing his face. "I am more tired than I ought to be."

"How has your head been?"

"It has been clear, thankfully, but I think I need to rest or it will be with me again."

"A good plan. I'm sure Mrs Maitland and I will find plenty to talk about."

"I am sure you will," Major Vernon said, and then went to his room.

~

"Miss Blanchfort intends to dine downstairs," said Mrs Maitland coming into the dining room, "and will be with us shortly. If her physician allows it? I did suggest it might be conditional on your say-so, Mr Carswell."

"I don't suppose she took much notice of that."

"No, not really. But I can still go up and turn her back if necessary."

"Attempt to, you mean?" said Felix.

"She is not so wilful," said Mrs Maitland, with a smile. "Do you object? Ought she to rest?"

"I think she had better come down, especially if she is hungry," said Felix. "She has had too many people giving her too many orders, and she chafes against it."

"You may be right. There is a line it is not useful to cross when bringing up children, as you will find one day, no doubt."

"I cannot begin to imagine myself a father," said Felix. "It seems so –"

"Parenthood is a condition that is hard to imagine until one attains it. Even on the day my son was born I had no idea what was awaiting me. The theory is always very different from the practice."

"You are encouraging me to stay unmarried," Felix said.

"No, not at all," said Mrs Maitland. "You will be an excellent papa, I am sure. You have all the right instincts."

"I don't seem to have them when it comes to finding a wife," he said. "And that is rather a prerequisite."

"You are still ridiculously young, Mr Carswell. There is plenty of time for you to find her, whoever she may be. Now, where is Major Vernon?"

"Resting. He will not be joining us. He sends his apologies."

She frowned and said, "Oh dear, he's not ill again?"

"No, no. He's just being sensible."

"Yes, of course," she said. "Oh, good evening, Miss Blanchfort."

Felix turned and saw that Miss Blanchfort had slithered into the room as quietly as a cat. She was standing just inside the doorway, leaning against the wall. She was now wearing a black dress and someone had expertly replaced the linen sling he had provided with a square of red silk. "How striking you look! Did Patton do that for you? She is very good with slings."

"Yes," said Miss Blanchfort. "I shouldn't be wearing red, should I? But there was nothing else to hand."

"In the circumstances, no one could object," said Mrs Maitland.

Miss Blanchfort remained standing where she was, as if she were either paralysed by uncertainty, or using the wall to hold herself up.

"Now, where would you like us to sit, Mr Carswell?" Mrs Maitland said, reminding him of his duties as host. This was a responsibility he would gladly have delegated to her, for Miss Blanchfort's manner was highly distracting. It was as if he were again drugged and in the woods. She continued to stand there, with the tapestry-covered wall behind her. Against her ink-black dress, dull with crepe, the blood-red expanse of silk glistened across her chest like an unfurled battle standard. Her hair had been piled up to make a glowing crown and it seemed to him that she might have stepped out of the tapestry itself: she was a creature made from dreams, fancy and desire.

And he did desire her, just as he had that first time in the woods, when he had been astonished by her beauty. He felt it as they sat down to dinner, and with some force.

Mrs Maitland mercifully talked of this and that, and directed Holt and Jacob, just as he should have done, for he felt struck dumb, as if there were poison again in the food he ate.

He tried not to look at her, and to concentrate instead on Mrs Maitland and respond to all the sensible things she was saying. Yet he found himself stealing glances at her, like a boy in church bored by the sermon. When Mrs Maitland asked about the gardens and his plans for them, he attempted to punish himself by recalling conversations on that same subject with Sukey, so that he would feel again the wretchedness of a broken heart. But he could not remember it as sharply as formerly. The sting was fading, the scars healed. It did not provide the necessary lesson.

It was something of a relief when the dessert was finished and Mrs Maitland rose from the table, suggesting that Miss Blanchfort ought to go to bed again rather than sit up in the drawing room.

"I will be poor company for you," she said. "And you will mend faster with plenty of rest. Yes, Mr Carswell?"

"Certainly," he said.

"I am tired," Miss Blanchfort admitted. She went with Mrs Maitland to the door, before stopping and saying to him, "Will I have to go back tomorrow?"

"I don't know. I think you will be more comfortable at Holbroke."

"I like it here," she said, and with her uninjured hand, reached out and touched the tapestry.

"It is a beautiful house, certainly," said Mrs Maitland, passing into the great hall. "With many possibilities."

Felix followed them from the room. Miss Blanchfort crossed the hall and went to stand in the great oriel window, looking out. The full moon of the night before had only just begun to wane and its eerie brightness supplemented the candlelight.

"One would never know it was here," Miss Blanchfort said, "hidden away in its own forest. It is a wonderful secret of a place."

"It is quite a curiosity," said Mrs Maitland. "Do you know much of the history of it, Mr Carswell?"

"No," he said. "I am sorry to say I haven't taken the trouble."

"You have been busy with your profession," said Mrs Maitland.

"I can't even give you a ghost story for your collection," he said, "because we think the ghosts we saw were induced by mushrooms."

Miss Blanchfort spun round.

"You saw a ghost here?" she said.

"I saw –" he hesitated. "I saw some projection of my imagination, created by the poison. The Colonel told us a ghost story to prepare the ground, and that, with the mushrooms, made me imagine it all."

"You did not imagine me, Mr Carswell," said Miss Blanchfort, "when I found you raving in the woods."

"Goodness," murmured Mrs Maitland.

"So perhaps," Miss Blanchfort went on, "you did not imagine your ghost. After all, I am quite real. I have breakable bones to attest to that."

"The two parts of the experience were quite distinct," Felix said. "The part with the alleged phantom is imprecise in my recollection – sketchy, confused, like a dream, but my memory of seeing you is quite distinct."

"Just because it felt like a dream does not mean there might be no objective truth to it," she said. "You still might have seen something, you do not know."

"I think it is most unlikely," said Felix.

"I take it you are a believer in spirits, Miss Blanchfort?" said Mrs Maitland.

"Oh yes, definitely. And you, ma'am?"

"I like stories of such things, but I don't think I want to encounter one in reality. So I choose not to believe for my own peace of mind."

"I should like to see a ghost," said Miss Blanchfort. "Perhaps I shall tonight. After all, there has been a man hanged in the attic here, has there not?"

"I hoped you had not heard of that," Felix said.

"Why?" she said. "Are you worried it might disturb me? Do you think I am so easily scared?"

"It disturbs me," said Mrs Maitland. "And he will be in my prayers tonight. In fact, we should all remember him, and hope that he is at rest, poor man."

Felix nodded. The thought of the Colonel as a ghost was deeply unsettling.

"If he appears, I shall not be surprised," Miss Blanchfort went on.

"I think, for Mr Carswell's sake," Mrs Maitland said, "you should not wish that on his house. It is quite interesting enough as it is. Now, perhaps we should go up?" she added, taking one of the candlesticks and going towards the foot of the stairs.

But Miss Blanchfort did not take the hint.

"Do you know why he was hanged?" she asked.

"Not yet," said Felix. "It is proving very complicated. His wife may have had some part in it. He was not a good husband, certainly."

"He will be here," she said, glancing around her. "I am sure of it."

"Miss Blanchfort, it is unwise –" Felix began, but she put her finger to her lips to silence him.

"I saw my father, you know," she said. "Two nights before you came to see me and told me he was dying. I woke in the night and saw him in my room. He did not speak, but it was him."

"That was a dream, surely. And not uncommon, I think."

"He came to see me," she said, coming a little closer to him. "I am certain of it. Can you explain that away? I think not."

She did not allow him to answer but swept past him and started climbing the stairs. Mrs Maitland gave him a bemused shrug and followed.

Felix reached for his cheroot case. He went and sat down on the window seat to smoke, trying to steady himself. But it was as if her determined talk of spirits had lifted a veil, and all his own uncomfortable phantoms appeared to him, while at the same time his body ached for sensual release. A ghostly Sukey in her blue linen dress and straw hat, her lips stained with raspberry juice, taunted him with the memory of kisses, but at the same time, the girl in the black dress, standing by the tapestry, awoke in him a more urgent longing. Her bold stare and provoking manner left him hungry for more. He wanted to tussle and tangle with her, both with words and limbs, and then feel that struggle evolve into the sweetness of congress.

There was the sound of footsteps on the stair. He looked up through his cloud of smoke and saw Major Vernon coming down in his dressing gown.

He got up and extinguished his cheroot, glad to have a distraction from such tormenting thoughts.

"How are you feeling, sir? Did you sleep at all?"

"Very well," said the Major. "And I woke up with a few useful questions in mind. I wanted to look at the estate map. Have the ladies gone to bed?"

"Yes."

"And Miss Blanchfort – all is well with her?"

Felix hesitated.

"There is no trouble about her wrist. That will be straightforward, if she takes care."

They went into the dining room, where the map was hanging. Holt was clearing the table.

"Shall I leave the wine, sir?" he said to Felix.

"Yes," said Felix, taking up his own glass and refilling it.

"And some tea, if you would, Holt," said Major Vernon.

"You won't have a glass?" said Felix, when Holt had gone.

"Half," said Major Vernon, already absorbed with the map.

"I shall get some more candles," said Felix, and went out into the hall to fetch some.

He returned and set them down so that the map was properly illuminated. But even with the light, the dense complexity of the forest was evident.

"'A wonderful secret of a place,'" Felix said, quoting Miss Blanchfort.

"And not easy to find your way through without local knowledge," said Major Vernon, tracing routes with his fingertip. "Someone will have seen something. Tomorrow we will go to Hawksby and question the servants."

"And Miss Blanchfort will go back to Holbroke," Felix said, sitting down at the table, his back to the fire.

"That would be for the best, I think," said Major Vernon. "If she is fit for travel?"

"Yes, there is no difficulty in that."

"The sooner she is away, the better," Major Vernon said.

Felix did not answer.

"Surely?" Major Vernon said. "You said yourself she was dangerous."

"Lead us not into temptation!" Felix said. "Yes. And I suppose the same applies for her chaperone?"

"Yes," said Major Vernon, sitting down. "You might say that."

"Or then again, 'marry or burn,'" Felix said, refilling his glass and pushing the decanter towards Major Vernon who was still nursing his chaste half-glass.

"That is no possibility of that," said Major Vernon.

"You could make her break with Fforde if you liked," Felix said. "If that was what you wanted, I mean. She is, after all, rather an exceptional woman."

Major Vernon sipped his wine.

"Did she say something to you?" he said after a moment. "About me?"

"No. I was just considering the benefits of matrimony. It seems to be quite the fashion. Mrs Connolly is also to be married. O'Brien came and told me himself."

"That is good news, although it might not feel like it to you," Major Vernon said. "And it was bound to happen sooner or later, for she is very marriageable –"

"Like Mrs Maitland," Felix put in.

"Quite. Why else has Edward Fforde chosen her? She is –" he broke off and to Felix's surprise poured out another inch of wine into his glass. "Not for the likes of me." He raised his glass as if making a toast. "Ned Fforde! A better candidate entirely." He put down his glass again without drinking from it. "So, this general thinking about the benefits of matrimony, are you sure it is so general?"

"No," said Felix, and pointed at the ceiling. "She is..."

Major Vernon smiled. "A great temptation?" he said.

Felix pulled at his cravat and loosened his collar.

"It would be pleasant," he said, "not to be alone at night. If you know what I mean."

"All too well," said Major Vernon with a sigh.

~

Giles was making his way back to his room, candle in hand, when he came upon Emma Maitland in her nightgown. Wrapped in a dark shawl, her hair streaming down from beneath her night cap, she stopped at the sight of him, holding up her own candle.

The fact of meeting her, in such a state, in the same state of undress, seemed to push aside the curtains of decorum that had been hanging between them. He was exhausted with being cool with her, with being rational and restrained. All he wanted in that moment was to pull her close to him and let the tantalizing possibilities become something tangible.

She stood there, as if she could not take a step further, so he advanced on her.

"I am glad to have caught you," he said. "I wanted to apologise. This morning, I was –"

She put her finger to her lips and pushed open the door to what was apparently her room. That she meant him to follow her was clear.

She went in and set her candle down on a table, and he put his own beside it. Then she closed the door carefully behind her and stood there, wrapping her shawl around her.

"I was very sharp with you," he said.

"Perhaps I deserved it."

"No," he said. "You were struggling and I failed to understand it. Forgive me."

"There is nothing to forgive," she said. "Won't you sit down? There is some heat left."

And so, on chairs on either side of the tiny glowing remnant of a fire, they sat for a long moment in awkward silence as if they were a young couple artfully left alone for the first time by a scheming parent.

Eventually he said, "Might I explain? I was harsh because you unnerved me. I had not expected you to have got so far in your thinking. I knew you had your doubts about your engagement, but to be thinking of breaking it –"

"But you were right to be harsh. It would be wrong to break with him now. I must do as I promised, to the best of my ability..." She shook her head, her voice choking. "I made a promise to be his wife and I must..." She gave into her tears then, but covered her face and twisted away so he should not see.

He could restrain himself no longer and crossed over to her, and knelt by her, attempting to take her into his arms. For a moment she resisted him, and then she fell against him, her wet face pressed to his chest.

"But I don't love him!" she managed to say, and again buried herself against him. "I thought I did, but I don't."

She slithered from the chair and deeper into his embrace. They sat in an inglorious muddle on the floor, arms wound about the other, while she cried out her heart, and he felt his own tears leak from his eyes, as he kissed her forehead and felt her hands clutch at him.

"I have nothing for you," he said. "I cannot give you anything. I'm not a good man, and I'm not worth your tears."

"I would follow you barefoot around the world, Giles. I wouldn't care if I had to sleep on the floor or if – I don't care what you do, or don't do. I don't care even if you never love me! Only let me love you – that is all I want."

She had disentangled herself a little to say this, and he could see her face sticky with tears in the dim light.

"No, no, that I can't have," he managed to say. "If you give me your heart, I must give you mine in return."

"Are you sure?"

"Completely. That has been the trouble. You are already its keeper, that's the truth of it." He found her hand, and kissed her fingertips. "But that isn't enough. You are getting a poor bargain with me. I'm a dirty wretch, Emma, and I'm not fit to be your husband, no matter how much I want to be."

"That is for me to judge," she said. "And I believe you capable of redemption, as we all are. I absolve you of your sins."

"Without knowing what they are?"

"That is the whole point, surely?" she said. "Love is an act of faith. You do not know my sins either, and yet you have given me your heart." She swept her fingers across his hair and kissed him on the cheek. "I did not dream that you would say so much. I thought that –"

"How could I not love you?" he said, and kissed her on the lips. "How?"

Chapter Twenty-seven

Felix was woken from his shameful and lascivious dreams by Jacob noisily entering his room. For a moment he was entirely confused as to where he was, for only moments ago he had been on the verge of seducing Eleanor Blanchfort on the rickety chaise in his mother's drawing room. This had been occurring in the full knowledge that Sukey was waiting for him in the garden, talking to his mother about the apple harvest.

"Rain all cleared away now, sir," said Jacob. "Pleasant morning for a ride, I'd say. Major Vernon says that he'd like to be away by nine. I've polished your boots. Had to do them twice, as Mr Holt was being very particular."

Felix could not bring himself to respond to this cheerful chatter. He wanted nothing more than to go back to sleep and see where his dreams might take him. So he closed his eyes again and pulled the covers up a little.

"And Miss Taylor, that's Miss Blanchfort's maid, asked me to tell you her mistress was asking for you."

"What did you say?" Felix said, sitting up.

"Her mistress is asking for you," said Jacob.

"Urgently?" Felix said, climbing out of bed, at once concerned there had been some complication manifesting itself in the night.

"I don't know about that, sir," said Jacob.

"Where the devil is my dressing gown?" Felix said, looking about him.

"You're sure you don't want to dress first, sir?" said Jacob, handing it to him.

Felix did not trouble himself to answer and went straight to her room, fastening his dressing gown as he went. He stopped at the door, realising only then, to his shame and horror, that his silhouette betrayed the contents of his fevered dreaming. He was forced to pace the landing for a few moments, thinking the grimmest thoughts, utterly mortified that Jacob should have seen everything.

When he felt calm enough, he knocked at her door. The maid, Taylor, admitted him.

He was relieved to see that she was not tossing in bed, bathed in a putrid fever. Rather she was sitting up, her breakfast on a tray in front of her.

"Must I really have chicken broth for breakfast?" she said.

"Is that all you wanted to ask?" he said. "You are not feeling unwell?"

"I feel unwell when I have to drink chicken broth for breakfast," she said. "You ordered this for me, I think."

"I did," said Felix.

"Drink it up now, Miss Eleanor," said Taylor. "Her Ladyship would tell you that, I'm sure, and if the gentleman has ordered it –"

"Her Ladyship is not here, Taylor," said Miss Blanchfort. "I really detest the stuff, Mr Carswell. Must I have it?"

"If you cannot stomach it, then I suppose there is no point," Felix said.

"Take it away, Taylor. I would like toast and coffee."

"Coffee I cannot advise," Felix said.

"Then chocolate. Is that allowed?"

"Yes, that will do well enough. In fact, would you be so kind as to bring some for me as well?"

"Yes, certainly, sir."

"So you intend to take your breakfast with me?" she said, when the maid had gone.

"To make sure you eat yours," said Felix. "And to save time. I am going out with Major Vernon shortly. I need to check you over first. How did you sleep? Did you have much pain?" he said, taking her uninjured wrist and testing her pulse.

"A little," she said, "but I did not take anything to help me. But I slept, better than I imagined. In fact, I had the most interesting dreams."

"You did?" said Felix and found himself flushing.

"I saw Papa again – but this time it was most definitely in a dream. And most comforting."

"I'm glad to hear that," he said, touching her forehead and cheeks. "No feeling of fever at all?"

She shook her head.

"I am quite comfortable. And he is in Heaven," she said. "I'm sure of it. And he spoke to me in this dream, and he said such interesting things."

Felix lifted her wrist from the sling and checked to see that the splints and bandages were still all in order.

"Shall I tell you what he told me?" she went on. "I think you will find it interesting. After all, it does concern you."

Felix busied himself with rearranging her wrist in the sling, and then moved away from the bedside. If she did not have a fever, he certainly did. He went over to the window and opened the lattice.

"Dreams don't mean anything, you know," he said.

"Of course they do!" she said. "What are they for, then?"

"I don't know. Nobody does," he said. "Whatever he might have seemed to have said, well, it was only your fancy. I have dreams like that all the time, in which the things I want occur. Or rather things I should not want."

"You do?" she said. "And you think it is not significant that you should? You think they should just be dismissed as fancies?"

"Yes," he said.

"I cannot agree," she said. "Tell me what you dreamt, Mr Carswell, tell me what you dreamt last night."

As she spoke she began to climb out of bed and, because of her arm, had to struggle and stumble to do so, forcing him to cross back to the bed to stop her falling. He found himself with his arms about her, her flimsy nightdress becoming disarranged and revealing rather too much, and he had to quickly yet gently disentangle himself from her. He grabbed a shawl from a chair, and handed it to her.

"I would rather not. It is not –"

"Decent?" she said, not wrapping herself in the shawl as he had intended, but instead, standing there looking very directly at him, her gown slipping lower and lower from her shoulder. He found himself trembling with desire, and from the boldness of her stare, he guessed that the nature of her dream had not been dissimilar to his own.

"I dreamt," she said, in a whisper, "that you were my husband. That is what my Papa wanted."

The door opened and Taylor came in with the breakfast tray. Miss Blanchfort mercifully enfolded herself in her shawl and Felix took his leave, abandoning his cup of chocolate.

~

They had limited themselves to one kiss. There was too much that was uncertain in their future to risk crossing the threshold into an intimacy between them that might yet prove impossible to sustain.

In the first instance, she had to break with Edward, and then they had to deal with all the disagreeable feelings that would naturally arise when the cause of the break was known.

The business of actually terminating her engagement would be hard enough for her, and it was something she must, as she had pointed out, do entirely alone. He could have no hand in it. She must deliver the blow, and it would be a punishing one.

As he walked back to his room, having pulled himself from her arms with such difficulty, Giles knew the pain it would cause. As her victorious lover, he knew keenly that to lose such a treasure to another man would be almost unbearable.

Then, when the cause of the break became known, the Fforde family would surely be grossly offended. Lambert and Edward were devoted to each other, and no matter how highly Lambert might regard Giles, it was no small thing to have a blood brother slighted by a person who had been accepted and trusted as an intimate and an equal. Sally would surely side with her husband out of loyalty, no matter how much she might personally like the match – Giles could expect no less of her, and for her to go against Lambert in such a case would have shocked him. Their intention to marry would not be met with much rejoicing by anyone. Her son would not like it. Even if he had not already formed a partiality to Edward, he could not like it, when he saw how little in the way of material goods his prospective stepfather could offer his mother. He would seem a poor match in every respect.

Yet for all this, he went to his bed a happy man, and the next morning, as he waited for Carswell outside the house, he found himself looking up at her window and smiling, content that the trouble would be worth it. If they were to be tested, then so be it, and let them prove to the world the worth of their affections.

As if to justify his confidence, she appeared at the window, opening the lattice and looking down at him as he stood there, the reins of his horse in his hand.

"Oh, good morning, Major Vernon!" she said.

"Good morning, ma'am!" he said.

"We shall be gone before you are back, I think," she said. "Any messages for Lord Rothborough?"

"No, nothing," said Giles, unable to stop himself grinning broadly now.

"I hope it will not be long before we see you there," she said.

"I hope not."

He did not like secrets nor playing games, but this was a very innocent one and the pleasure of it in the mild morning sunshine was undeniable. He would have been a dead man not to enjoy seeing her smile down at him like that.

At this moment Carswell came out of the house, saying, "I am very glad you have things for me to do, for –" and then he broke off, seeing Giles looking up at Emma's window. "Oh, good morning!"

"Good morning, Mr Carswell! I think the weather will hold for you today. The sky looks promising. Do you have any orders for me?"

"Orders, ma'am?" said Carswell, looking puzzled.

"About your patient, Miss Blanchfort."

Carswell thought for a moment and said, "She ought to be made to rest as much as possible when you get to Holbroke, and if she will not take broth, try marrowbone or some such. Or even beef steak and porter."

"Are you quite serious?" she said.

"No – well, a little, because she is fussy and she cannot afford to be with a fracture."

"I shall tell her that," said Emma. "Good day, gentlemen!" she added, and closed the lattice.

"Not that she will listen," said Carswell, mounting up.

Giles mounted his own horse and they set off down the avenue together.

"Where are we going?" Carswell asked.

"Marlingford, and then Hawksby. We have a few enquiries to make."

"What is at Marlingford?"

"I am not entirely sure. With luck, the answer to a puzzle. Is your patient causing problems?"

"She is..." Carswell began. He hesitated and said, "I think it would do me good to talk of something else entirely. Tell me about your puzzle."

So Giles gave his account of what Emma Maitland had discovered about Miss Waites.

"I am sure she is connected to Bickley, intimately perhaps."

"And you think she can help you bring him down? Surely she will not be privy to all his secrets?"

"No, he's too careful for that. But she is so fearful, she must know something. The fact that she is working for nothing for them is significant."

"Perhaps they are using some indiscretion on her part as an excuse for that," Carswell said.

"That's possible. She did stress her respectability."

"That will mean a foundling somewhere," Carswell said. "Or some such."

The ride to Marlingford was accomplished without difficulty. The village, as he had observed to Mrs Maitland, was fast becoming a suburb of Northminster, due to its convenient position on the canal, with brickfields beyond. There were many recently-built terraces of small houses of the plainest sort, and the ancient village green was now a muddy midden, and home to a herd of miserable-looking dairy cows. There were several inns adjacent to the green, suggesting Marlingford had in the last century been a place of pleasant resort from Northminster. Now they looked wistful and run down, especially The Blue Bell, which was an oversized edifice, with elaborate half-timbering and a large yard in front. As they approached it was clear that this was now a piggery, and the inn itself had been divided into many dwellings. It reminded Giles of Miss Waites' Northminster residence in Croft's Building, with the addition of swine.

An old woman in a red bonnet was sitting with her knitting on a bench under one of the windows, enjoying, it seemed, the spring sunshine and the company of the pigs who surrounded her like a guard of honour.

"Fine animals, ma'am," Giles said, necessarily in a loud

voice, for they set up a bellowing as they approached. "Are they yours?"

"Yes, sir, that they are," she said. "Do you want to buy one? They make the best bacon in the county. I've a lovely crop of piglets. You came on the right day."

"I wish I could oblige you," said Giles. "Perhaps another time. Have you lived here long?"

"All my life, sir."

"In this house?"

"On and off."

"Do you recall a family called Waites?"

She considered for a moment, and then shook her head.

"So who kept the inn here, when it was an inn?"

"That was a very long time ago, sir," she said. "I can't say I recall who. Being old, you know, sir, I can't remember such things."

This was rather artfully said, and Giles felt she probably knew a great deal about the building's history and its occupants, but for some reason chose not to reveal it.

"Let's go and enquire at the church," Giles murmured to Carswell, turning his horse.

~

The elderly verger leant on his broom and considered Major Vernon's question.

"The Blue Bell Inn, sir," he said, "yes, well, that was kept by Mrs Waites for many a year. A widow she was, and a right fierce baggage I must say – not anyone you wanted to get on the wrong side of – just like her daughter, madam herself, that's up at the Manor now. My old father, he had his run-ins with Mrs Waites, and now it seems it's my turn." He gave a great sigh and shook his head. "I'm to lose my place because of her!" And he pointed at the canopied box pew which presumably was occupied on Sundays by the family from this hall.

"And her name is?" Major Vernon said.

"Bickley," he said. "Miss Bickley. She never married and never will, for what fellow would ever take on such a tartar, not for all her money and land!" he added, with some force.

A voice called out from the back of the church. "Green! I hope you are helping these gentlemen."

A young man in clerical dress came striding up the nave towards them. "I saw your horses outside, gentlemen. I am the Vicar here, Charles Mortlake. Can I assist you?"

"We were admiring your beautiful church, Mr Mortlake," said Major Vernon. "My name is Peters, and this is my associate, Mr Frazer."

Felix wondered why the Major thought it necessary to conceal their identity from the clergyman. Major Vernon continued: "I think we have an acquaintance in common – Miss Bickley? We were on our way to call on her at the Manor, but I can never resist an ancient church."

"Oh, you know Miss Bickley?" he said. "Such an excellent patron. My wife and I have not been here long, and she has been nothing but kindness. A very good Christian lady."

"When she's not threatening to take away a man's livelihood," muttered Green as he departed with his broom. He stood a little distance away and began sweeping ineffectually.

"Perhaps we should go into the chancel," said Mr Mortlake. "There are some picturesque old family monuments, if you have a taste for such things. I believe they are highly regarded by local antiquarians."

They followed him into the chancel and the Vicar began what was obviously a well-rehearsed speech about the marble monuments, which in truth were very dull and nothing to compare with the mortuary chapel at Holbroke.

"No Bickley tombs, though?" said Major Vernon, glancing around.

"No, I believe Miss Bickley came quite lately to the Manor. But she has had a long association with the village. The old lady who lived there before left the property to her, out of fondness. She was her companion at one time. This is her monument – Miss Elizabeth Hickman. Paid for by Miss Bickley, of course."

"A handsome design," said Major Vernon. "So the family at the Hall were called Hickman?"

"Yes."

"And this lady was the last of them?"

"I believe so," said Mr Mortlake. "This is the first of them here, this fine gentleman in the ruff: Sir Merriam Hickman."

Fortunately the Vicar had an appointment to get to, and Felix and Major Vernon were allowed to examine the crumbling old graves in the churchyard at their leisure.

"Merriam Hickman," said Major Vernon. "That's quite a coincidence, whatever way you look at it. Both unusual names. Why would our Mr Hickman call his business Merriam's if he did not have some connection with that family? What do you make of this story of Miss Bickley being left the property by Miss Hickman?"

"I don't know. It seems unlikely, if Miss Bickley is the sister of George Bickley, which I assume she is, since you have not said otherwise. Have you met her?"

"Yes, I have."

"As Mr Peters?"

"Yes – I thought it wise not to show my hand. She is his sister. She was running that large song and supper room in Bank Street, The Horseshoe."

"And now she is here," said Felix.

"She is, if anything, more assured than her brother. Well, you will see for yourself, for we shall have to call on her now."

"Isn't that rather dangerous? What if Bickley is there as

well?"

"That's a risk we shall have to take. What is certain is that Mr Mortlake will report on our appearance there and if we have not called, she will be very puzzled. But first I want to talk to Green again."

They found the discontented verger in the vestry, taking his ease with his pipe. He looked rather startled to be discovered so.

"You won't tell Mr Mortlake, will you, sir?" he said.

"Don't worry, please, Mr Green," said Major Vernon, sitting down beside him on the bench. "Now tell me all you know about The Blue Bell Inn, and the Bickleys and the Waites."

"But you won't speak against me to her up at the Hall, will you?" said Green. "Being friends of hers."

Major Vernon shook his head.

"Not exactly friends," he said. "Now, Mr Green, tell me about Mr Bickley, Mrs Waites' first husband. I saw his grave out there. Was he the landlord at The Blue Bell?"

"Yes, and he was as fine a man as you'd hope to meet. A real gent he was. The trouble was in marrying Peg Diggory, and after he married her he was never the same. She had her hooks in him and that was that."

"And that is the Mrs Waites we were speaking of?"

"Yes."

"Where did she come from? A Marlingford family?"

"Aye, one of us, but a dirty, low, trouble-making family – the Diggorys – always have been, always will be. And when she nabbed Bickley – told him she was with child by him, of course – his poor mother took to her bed and died with the shock of it. Not what she wanted for her boy."

"So they ran the inn together?" Major Vernon said.

"Yes, though she gave him a deal of trouble with his carrying on, always wanting bigger and better and never contented with her lot. And then he goes and dies, just like that, and well, it was talked about, that, for he was as fit and healthy as you and I, and suddenly he's dead. And whether it was the will of our good Lord or summat else less savoury..." Green shrugged and gave a long draw on his pipe.

"And the widow Bickley remarried Mr Waites?"

"No mister about him," said Green. "Strapping great fellow, ten years younger than she, some sort of cousin of hers, and no better than she."

"And they had children?"

"She had a couple more by him. Boy and girl."

"Who is the woman who keeps the pigs at the Inn now?" said Major Vernon.

"Old Betty, you mean?"

"I think so," said Major Vernon. "She told me she could not remember who kept The Blue Bell."

"Ha!" said Green and slapped his thigh. "She's as thick with them as any. She's a Diggory too, old Mother Waites' cousin, and she has the whole run of the house now, and makes a pretty penny letting out her rooms to all those sorry folk who come looking for work in the brickfields up the canal there. Now, here's a thing, sir, I heard it the other day, that those brickfields belong to George Bickley, their eldest boy that was. He were a few years younger than me, and I were only a strip of a lad when his parents got wed."

"And the younger boy," Major Vernon said, "the lad she had by Waites; what was his name?"

Green began to laugh and said, "Now that's a rum thing you should ask that, sir. She had him christened Merriam, after the old Squire. She said it was because he was the babe's grandfather. It were a good thing they were both dead, her old ma and the Squire, for they'd both have beaten her black and blue for such a slander. But she believed it, went to the grave believing it. Gave herself airs, and all the children too." He shook his head, laughing still. Then he sobered and said, "But who owns the Manor now? Her daughter; and the brickfields all round – her son."

"What happened to the younger children?" Major Vernon said. "Merriam and the girl? Was she called Anne?"

"Aye, sir, she was. That I cannot tell you. They were sent off to school or to learn a trade or something. Haven't seen either of them in many a year. Merriam probably came to a bad end. He was that sort. Always picking a quarrel or taking advantage. Like his mother." He gave a groan. "And my lady up at the Manor! Well, I shall not be forced out, no matter what slanders she pours in the ear of Mr Mortlake, for I have been verger here, nigh on fifty years, and my father and grandfather before me. I shall walk to Northminster and tell the new Bishop himself that, if needs be. I will not be put out, I tell you, sir, I will not!"

After that, Felix felt it was a great mercy to find that Miss Bickley was not at home. However, Major Vernon was disappointed.

"An interview with her would have rounded the picture out nicely, don't you think?" he said.

"From what you have said about Bickley's operations," said Felix, "indeed from what I have seen of them, I think we are best keeping our distance."

Chapter Twenty-eight

Lady Blanchfort was at home, but was not at all gracious in her welcome.

She at last came into the room where they had been made to wait for some minutes, holding a paper in her hand.

"I received this yesterday from Lord Rothborough," she said, addressing Felix and waving the paper under his nose. "And now you are here! Why, pray?"

It took him a moment to gather his wits.

"May I present my colleague, Major Vernon, ma'am? It was he who rescued your daughter from her accident." Major Vernon made his bow but she scarcely acknowledged it. "You will be pleased to hear she is in no danger now."

"I think she is in every danger," said Lady Blanchfort, "as long as you and Rothborough have her in your sights."

"I wonder if Miss Blanchfort would not be glad to see you at Holbroke now," Major Vernon said. "An incident like this may have made her see a little more clearly about things. An illness is often cause to remind us where our affections lie."

"And who are you, sir, to presume that?" said Lady Blanchfort. "An associate of Lord Rothborough, I don't doubt."

"Don't you wish to see her?" Major Vernon said.

"Naturally," she said. "But I must sacrifice my maternal feelings. That is what I have been driven into by Rothborough's manoeuvring – such a painful sacrifice! But I shall not be drawn into his plots. I have a message for you, gentlemen, which I trust you will accurately convey to Lord Rothborough: my daughter will be returned to me here. I shall not go and beg for what is mine by rights. I will see her here and on my terms. She will come back to her own house and her mother."

"Then you are lucky that the accident was not a serious one," Felix exclaimed, "if you are going to take such a ridiculous position, ma'am! What if I had come here to tell you she was at death's door, what would you do then?"

"I should not take your word for it, sir," she said.

"Then surely, ma'am," Major Vernon said, "you do not trust it now, and ought to see for yourself that she is well."

"I would send a physician of my choice to her. A reputable man I could trust. Not Rothborough's bastard sawbones!" she added, with a fierce glance at Felix.

"I think your distress is getting the better of you, ma'am," said Major Vernon, placing a chair to allow her to sit. "You have set yourself up an impossible task. To resist seeing your only child when she is ill, on a point of principle? A brave stand, but in all honesty, ma'am, I beg you to reconsider."

Felix, smarting from the blow of her words, could not help being impressed by Major Vernon's gentle but firm tone.

"Won't you sit down?" he went on, and to Felix's astonishment she did. "I have no children," Major Vernon went on, taking a chair and sitting down opposite her. Speaking quietly, he continued, "I can therefore only guess how hard this must be for you. And how hard it must be for your daughter to be without her mother at such a time. What we say and what we feel are often at odds. We wish to act according to reason but our hearts are sometimes crying to be heard."

She sat there, apparently considering what he had said, folding and unfolding Lord Rothborough's letter in her lap. She then turned and gave Felix a long appraising look, which made him feel most uncomfortable.

"Lord Rothborough has found a most eloquent advocate in you, Major Vernon," she said, turning back to the Major.

"That was not why we came, ma'am. We are not here to plead that cause. In fact I have come to interview some of your servants about Colonel Parham's murder. I spoke because I saw you were in distress and I wished to help you. Please excuse any impertinence."

"It is no impertinence," she said after a long moment. "I am not used to kindness, that is all." She stood up again. "My peculiar situation has made me –" She broke off, now looking at Felix again. There was something about her gaze that made him straighten a little. "How old are you?" she asked.

"Twenty-five," said Felix, somewhat astonished by the question.

"And you were brought up in Scotland by a clergyman and his wife?"

"Yes, ma'am."

"He is a minister of the Scottish Kirk?"

"No, my father is an Episcopalian."

She nodded and walked away down the room.

"And you wish to talk to my servants, Major Vernon?" she said.

"Only those that were working at Ardenthwaite," said Major Vernon. "I understand that some of the women came here after Mrs Parham left the Colonel."

"What a nest of scandal this neighbourhood is," she said. "I had thought it would be a quiet country place!"

"We will not keep them from their work for long," said Major Vernon.

"You must do what you need to do, I suppose," she said, ringing the bell. "I shall have the housekeeper find them for you. But tell me, does it not trouble you to find yourself in such a disagreeable line of work?" She glanced again at Felix. "For a man of good family, as I am sure you are, Major Vernon, do you not feel any loss of caste? Forgive my frankness."

"It is certainly not to everyone's taste," said Major

Vernon. "But it needs to be done and done well. And I think, as with medicine, the quality of a profession is improved by the quality of men who take it up. Yes, Mr Carswell?"

Felix nodded.

"How things do change," she said.

"If you ask me," Felix said, "that will be one of the achievements of our era – skill and talent will come to define a man's worth, not the circumstances of his birth. Any man may become Prime Minister, if he is good enough, or any woman, for that matter."

"Now you are spinning fairy tales," said Lady Blanchfort. "If a woman were to become Prime Minster – an idea which I find abhorrent, I must say – one may be certain that she would be very well connected, and that her husband would be a wealthy man. But really, what an extraordinary notion! You are as fanciful as my daughter, Mr Carswell."

~

"And will she stir herself to go to Holbroke, I wonder?" Carswell said, as they waited in the estate office to speak to the servants. "Though I don't suppose Miss Blanchfort will be very pleased to see her, whatever you might say about it. She is – they both are – well, what do you think?"

"I don't know. Neither are in the common run of women, certainly." Giles gazed about him at the neatly fitted-out office, with its many shelves and cupboards, many of them labelled with the names of the properties they represented. "The extent of this property must be considerable. She might use her intelligence by taking all this in hand, and then teaching her daughter to manage her own property. I wonder what went amiss."

"Lord Rothborough made dark allusions," said Carswell,

"to some wrongdoing on her part. He would not tell me what, but it must be –" He sighed. "But why on earth did she start interrogating me?"

"She was sizing you up," said Giles.

Carswell gave an exaggerated shudder.

"That's what I thought, though it's an odd way to go on after insulting me! I'm quite surprised she didn't ask me if I subscribed to all the Thirty-nine Articles," he said. "Oh Lord! Especially after what Miss Blanchfort said to me this morning –"

He broke off as the door opened and the housekeeper came in with the first of the servant girls.

"This is Grace Ellis," the housekeeper said. "She works in the laundry here for us."

"Sit down, won't you, Grace?" said Giles.

Grace Ellis was a tall, well-formed young woman of about nineteen, with a clear complexion and handsome features. As she sat down, she struck Giles as being in command of herself. She looked at him levelly, with no hint of deference.

"Mr Mostyn?" she said, in answer to his enquiry. "I didn't have much to do with him. And I'm not silly that way, not like some of them others."

"Silly?" Giles said. "By which you mean they were involved with him in some way?"

"You'd have to ask them about it. I'm just saying he didn't impress me."

"Why not?"

"What do you mean, sir?"

"What was it about him that didn't impress you?"

"Too full of himself," she said. "Thinking he was better than he was. Giving out orders like he was the Colonel himself. I don't care for that."

"Was there a particular occasion when he treated you like this?" Giles said. "That made you angry?"

She shrugged.

"Not in particular. Just his way. I didn't like it. That's all. Can I go, sir? I don't want to get behind."

He let her go, a little reluctantly. He felt she might be concealing something else behind her firmly stated dislike.

The next girl was Agnes Taylor.

"Mrs Webb mentioned you to us, Agnes," he said. "She told us that you had been unhappy at Ardenthwaite because of Mr Mostyn."

"Aye, sir, that's right."

"What was your job at Ardenthwaite?"

"Chambermaid, sir. That was the trouble, sir, I couldn't get away from him. He was one of those men – well, sir, I don't like to say it, but you know –"

"Mrs Webb said he was a pest."

Agnes closed her eyes and gave a sigh.

"Oh yes, sir, that's it. Had to keep my wits about me. Lizzy too – that's the other chambermaid. He was always at you – any excuse to be touching and kissing – and more – though I didn't let it come to that, of course I didn't – but then he'd act all offended and get you into trouble some other way." She gave a slight shudder. "I'm glad to be away from that, I can tell you."

"And you did not tell Mrs Parham about this?"

"She wasn't that kind of mistress. Then she left and we were all turned out, which was a good thing after all, for we got our chance here, and this is a good place."

"Did he bother Grace Ellis in the same way, out in the laundry?"

Agnes glanced at the door and leant forward.

"I saw you were speaking to her, sir," she said, in a quieter voice than before. "She is sweet on him, that's what we reckon, Lizzy and I. There was something going on between them, for certain, and I think she sees him still. She won't ever hear a word said against him, and only the other night I saw her slipping out when she oughtn't. She's a fool to do it because this is a place worth keeping, and if she loses it – well, that's her business, I suppose."

"Why do you think she was going to see Mr Mostyn?"

"She had tricked herself out – and she has some fancy things – fancier than most of us can stretch to – and where would she get the money for that except from him? Because he was as flash as you like, sir, probably stealing from his master as well."

She leant back now, as if exhausted by this burst of confidences. She then leant back in, resuming, in an even quieter tone: "You talk to Lizzy, sir. She saw them together, saw them at it." The last two words she did not speak at all, but only mouthed.

"We certainly shall, Agnes," said Giles and let her go.

"She could be going to see anyone," Carswell pointed out, when they were alone again.

"Yes," said Giles. "But there was something about her disdain that seemed very studied, don't you think? Let us see what Lizzy has to say."

"Yes, sir," said Lizzy, who was entirely unable to look Giles in the face. "I did see them together. In the linen cupboard. I only went up there to get some towels, and –"

"Yes?"

"I shouldn't have said so much," she said. "I shouldn't have told Aggie and she shouldn't have told you. She'll kill me if she finds out that –"

"Grace?"

"She's a hard one," she said. "And he said –" She broke off again, and then at last looked up at Giles. "They say you think he murdered the Colonel."

"That is just gossip at present," said Giles.

"I think he did," she said. "He could kill a man. He were that angry wi' me. I wish I'd never gone in there, and I wish I'd never seen them." She screwed up her face.

"Agnes seemed to think that Grace is still seeing him."

"She's right. He's hereabouts, I'm certain of it. When we were coming back from evening service last Sunday, I swear I saw him. There's a lane going down – I don't know where it goes, but we walk past the end of it and I swear I saw him standing there as if he were watching us. He was leaning on a wall, smoking and staring. I swear it was him, and then Grace goes off in her velvet bonnet, and Agnes and I wondered if – is this what you want, sir?"

"I want the truth, as well as you can remember it."

"I'm sure it was him. I was thinking it was me just being afraid of him and then seeing someone and thinking it was him, but it was him, I swear it."

~

"It's impossible to say how much of this is truth and how much speculation," said Major Vernon as they rode away from the house.

"Should you not talk to Grace Ellis again?" asked Felix.

"I don't want to alarm her unduly," said Major Vernon. "If she was lying and she is Mostyn's lover, then I want her to think she has got away with her lie. She will want to warn him of our interest, though, and that will be our opportunity. If he is still here, that is."

They were proceeding down the neat main street of the village.

"That might be too much to hope for," said Felix.

"Grace is a beautiful young woman. That can make the most calculating man behave irrationally."

"Yes," said Felix, thinking of Eleanor. "That tendency is a dangerous flaw in our design."

"And he has his stash to retrieve from the forest," Major Vernon said. "It will not do any harm to ask about the village if a man meeting his description has been seen. After an early dinner, yes?"

"Excellent. I am faint with hunger."

The principal inn of the village was called The Blanchfort Arms. The landlord at once recognised Felix from Sir Richard's funeral.

"Standing by his Lordship, you were, sir. And someone did say to me you were with Sir Richard at the last."

"I was."

"A shame he never got back here in time. He grew up in this village and when my lady and Miss Blanchfort came back, we had hopes that he would too – but God's will is God's will. What can I get you for dinner, sir? Roast lamb? A sweeter bit of meat you won't find anywhere in the county."

The lamb was as delicious as promised, and they ate sitting by the window of a private parlour that overlooked the village street, and then beyond to the long, tree-lined forecourt of Hawksby Hall. In the warm spring sunshine, after a glass or two of claret, while Major Vernon made his notes, Felix fell into idle musing on the nature of desire, and what the consequences of his most recent bout of that affliction might mean.

Major Vernon startled him slightly by pushing his open notebook across the table and saying, "A family tree. Stepbrothers."

Felix glanced down at the names and connections Major Vernon had sketched out.

"Stepbrothers?"

"Merriam Hickman Waites and George Bickley."

"I see."

"Is that the cause of it? The quarrel? Does it reach this far back? An ancient rivalry? Both in the same business. Now both in the same town. Bickley has his gin palaces and other enterprises. Waites alias Hickman opens his. Who knows what other turf he may be encroaching upon. He has certainly done well for himself in Swalecliffe. Perhaps he intends to do the same in Northminster."

"Knock his brother from the top of the tree?"

"Something like that. But Bickley isn't going to stand for it. So he has one of his men brutally assault one of Hickman's men. Ergo, Horatio Baxter murders our first victim. But –"

"Yes?"

"The swallow tattoo. What does that mean? Enemies marked with the same mark? Shouldn't they be different? Why kill a comrade?"

"Because he proves not to be one," Felix said.

"A false friend, yes," said Major Vernon. "Perhaps our nameless man was attempting to infiltrate Bickley's operation, and that was why he had to die. But why does Baxter have to hang as well? He is being punished by Bickley for something, that is clear enough."

"You think Bickley ordered Baxter to kill him, and then confess to it?"

"Yes, it's possible. Whatever, it has been done to send a clear message that traitors will not be tolerated. It also suggests that Bickley is unnerved by Hickman's encroachment. Bickley has not resorted to such naked brutality before. It's a show of weakness in some respects. He is under threat. And given the way he dealt with Kate –" Major Vernon sighed and rubbed his face. "That was savage."

He took the notebook back and looked down again at his family tree. Felix glanced out of the window and said, "Sir, look – that's interesting. Isn't that –?"

Major Vernon looked up.

"Grace Ellis, with her bag. We had better ask her where she is going."

Swiftly, they made their way out of the inn, crossed the road, and reached the gates of the Hall, just as Grace had come out onto the village street. At the same time, a covered gig coming from the direction of Northminster came trotting smartly along. It soon became clear that the driver was none other than Mostyn.

Major Vernon ventured out, at some danger to himself, and grabbed the bridle of the gig, forcing the pony to stop. Mostyn jumped down and began to run in the opposite direction.

Felix went after him. Somewhat to his amazement, he managed to catch up and hurled himself upon him, bringing him down on one of the broad grass verges that lined the street, a refinement for which he was heartily glad as they went crashing down with some force.

Mostyn put up a struggle, but it was in vain. The village constable had fortunately not been far off, and he was a marvellously burly individual, who on being told by Major Vernon in no uncertain terms that Mostyn was under arrest, finished the job nicely and took Mostyn off to the village lock-up.

Chapter Twenty-nine

"A strange way of passing your leave, Major Vernon," said Captain Lazenby. "Still, I can't say it isn't a good thing to have the fellow under lock and key."

"As long as we can keep him here," said Giles. "All he will admit to so far is stealing a few books from the library after Parham was murdered."

"And he says nothing about the murder?"

"He claims he was unconscious the whole time. That they came through the front door and knocked him out, and after that he observed nothing. I don't find that entirely credible. For one thing, there is no sign of any contusion – Mr Carswell feels that even after this lapse of time there would be some bruising – and it is far too convenient. And there remains the question of why he was seen taking money from Hickman in Swalecliffe. All he will say about that is that it was money that Hickman owed him – a long-standing debt."

"Do you think he will admit to more in time?"

"I hope so. We will work on him."

"And your leave?" Lazenby said.

"I have put Inspector Holland and Sergeant Coxe in charge of interviewing him," said Giles. "They are more than capable."

"I am glad to hear that."

Having brought Mostyn back to Northminster, Giles had at first been unwilling to make this concession. He had intended to work on Mostyn himself, and then, realising it was going to be a tortuous business, decided it was better to fully brief the Inspector and Sergeant and leave them to it. Holland had an austere demeanour and a steely manner which had seen some recent success in extracting confessions in unpromising situations, while Coxe was astonishingly quick-witted, and one of those recruits who had profited greatly from Giles' insistence on employing a schoolmaster for the men. He had an appetite for learning and self-improvement that had earned him rapid promotion.

"I am going back to the country today," he added.

Lazenby was satisfied with that, and Giles took his leave.

What he had not told Lazenby, of course, was that he had Anne Waites at Holbroke and that it was his intention to see if he could get her to explain to him in useful detail the nature of her peculiar family connections. Perhaps Emma Maitland had already got her confidence.

He met Carswell in the carriage by the Infirmary, as arranged. He arrived, a few minutes later than he had said, carrying a parcel which he threw down on the seat opposite as if it disgusted him.

"May I ask?" Giles ventured.

"It is a book. For Miss Blanchfort. But I shall probably not give it to her. I am not sure why I bought it, to be honest. I saw it and I thought of her, but now I think it would be more than foolish to give it to her. What do you think?"

"Perhaps it depends on the book," said Giles. "And also on the lady."

"That is my problem in a nutshell," said Carswell, reaching for the parcel and untying the string. "I do not think – well, what do you think? She has probably read it."

It was a nicely bound copy of Scott's 'The Bride of Lammermoor.'

"An excellent choice for a convalescent. And even if she has read it, it stands reading again. I am sure she will be delighted," he said.

"That is exactly the problem. I can't give it to her without implying something, can I? So why did I think I could?"

"Because you wished to imply something?" Giles said.

"I shall not give it to her," he said. "I will not allow myself to be put in this position again."

"What is the objection, if I might ask?" Giles said. "She is certainly not objectionable. She is young and rather contrary, of course, but that's nothing. She will grow out of it, and she is intelligent and charming."

"Her money, her position, her mother – everything!"

"But not the girl herself? If she had nothing and no connections, would you hesitate?"

"I can't believe you are encouraging me," said Carswell. "What do you mean? Surely I should hesitate? Surely you should be telling me to steel myself against such temptation."

"I don't think she will lead you to hell. She might save you."

"And also," Carswell went on, "you said, I remember distinctly, that you considered this profession of ours to be incompatible with marriage. Yes?"

"I was consoling myself," Giles said. "And you, if you recall."

"Has something happened?" Carswell said.

Giles hesitated for a moment, wondering how much he dare confide.

"It is early days, and this is to go no further, I beg you, Carswell, but Mrs Maitland and I did have a frank conversation the night before last, and –"

"She's going to break with him?" Carswell said.

"It is not going to be pleasant. My sister and brother-in-law are –"

"But you and she!" Carswell said. "Well, you may depend on my backing, no matter what. She is perfect for you – congratulations are in order, no matter what the circumstances throw up!" And he grabbed Giles' hand and shook it. "May I tell her that I know, or would you prefer I say nothing? I should like to tell her what an excellent choice she has made."

"Perhaps not just yet," said Giles smiling, "but I

appreciate the sentiment – and the support."

"I could not do otherwise," said Carswell, reaching out for the book again and turning it in his hands. "And what shall I do with this?"

"Give it to her. Treat it as an experiment for your feelings and her own. It cannot harm you to get to know her a little better. You might, as a result, find something out about her that quite cures you."

"Or else –" Carswell began. "I shall just have to risk it, shan't I?"

"It seems so," said Giles, and glanced out of the carriage window.

The conversation turned to other matters until they approached Holbroke.

As Giles climbed the great steps up to the portico, he had a sudden memory of the previous summer, and Lord Rothborough handing Laura out of the carriage and leading her up the same steps. She had glanced back at him with a nervous smile, wishing to be reassured, but now in his recollection he saw a look of reproach, as if she knew everything that he had done and that it had hurt her.

Death, her expression seemed to say, had not dissolved the vows they had made, and he felt all that comfortable certainty dissipate. He tried to recover it, especially as he came into the house, and saw Emma, standing arm-in-arm with his sister, a perfect picture of how he wished his life to be arranged.

It was fortunate that Celia demanded his attention almost at once, and he was dragged away to look at the tiny book she had been constructing. His signature was wanted on an article, devised by Tom, called, 'The Annals of Crime by One Who Knows, by Major V. of the Blankshire Constabulary.'

"How did you manage this?" he said, peering at it.

"With a magnifying glass on a stand. Lord Rothborough has lent us this one," said Celia. "It takes a little practice. You can practise here," she added, sitting him down at a table where the glass, paper and ink were set up.

"A good idea. I would hate to ruin it. In fact, might it be better if you forged my signature, Celia?"

"Oh no! I could never do that. Isn't that very wicked?"

"Then I will have to do my best," he said picking up the pen and attempting to scratch out his name in miniature, aware at the same time that Emma had followed them into the room and was watching, with her usual genial expression. He glanced up and now their eyes met, and he could not manage to return her comfortable smile.

At once she was at his side, murmuring, "Is something wrong –?"

He had no opportunity to answer. It was time to go into dinner.

~

"I have scarcely done anything but eat and sleep since I came back," Miss Blanchfort said.

Coming into the drawing room after dinner, Felix had found she was sitting apart from the others, or rather lying, on a couch by the fire.

"You are going to be quite tired for a while, so that is a good regime you have hit upon," he said, drawing a chair near, and making some pretence of examining her hand.

"I nearly did not come down for dinner, but I did not want to miss the Ffordes' last night. I wish they were not going tomorrow. They are such – oh, I don't know how to put it – I have never met people quite like them before. So kind and so warm. And interesting."

"Perhaps they will ask you to stay with them in Northminster."

"I have been asked and I shall go," she said. "If it is allowed, of course!" She gave a sigh. "Will I ever be able to make such decisions for myself, I wonder?"

"I'm sure Lord Rothborough will let you go to the Ffordes," said Felix.

"Yes, but I cannot count on being allowed to remain here. My mother will have her way, I am sure of it, sooner or later, and I shall have to go back."

"Lord Rothborough does not like to be prevailed over," said Felix. "He will fight your corner."

"Yes, and she will win. It is always the way."

"I saw your mother today," Felix said.

"How disagreeable for you. I expect she was unpleasant."

"A little."

"She insulted you, I suppose?"

"Yes, and then – well, it was a little peculiar; she started asking me about my parents and so forth. She wanted to know that I was not a Presbyterian."

"That is interesting," said Miss Blanchfort, leaning back on her cushions and looking at the ceiling.

"That I am not a Presbyterian?"

"Yes, perhaps, but mostly that she asked. How did she ask it?"

"As if she were interviewing me for a place as second footman."

Miss Blanchfort laughed.

"Don't you think I would make a very good footman?" Felix went on.

"Not up to her standards," said Miss Blanchfort, still laughing. "I can imagine it perfectly. Oh, I am so sorry, she is quite –" She broke off, suddenly quite grave again, and said quietly, "I cannot go back to her. I will not."

"I am sure Lord Rothborough will not let you be unhappy."

"That is not certain, although I know he means well. But

there is only one way I can be free of her, and I must be free of her. You must understand that."

"Surely in time –"

She shook her head.

"You told me it was wrong to call it slavery, and perhaps you were right. But it is... she is so cruel to me."

"Physically cruel? Does she hit you?"

"No – well, sometimes she has slapped me and I probably deserved that. No, it is the constant regulation of every aspect of my life. It is intolerable to be controlled to such an extent. You can have no idea of it. To be sitting here, just idling, and talking, that is such a novelty to me. I cannot believe it will last unless I make some drastic change to my state, because now I have had a small taste of freedom, I cannot go back to my prison, I cannot!"

She had grabbed his hand with her unbroken hand and was looking earnestly at him, with tears in her eyes.

"That dream I told you about –" she went on.

"Was a dream," he cut in.

"Yes, yes, I quite take your point. But you are not without pity. You are, I think, feeling something of what I am feeling, Mr Carswell. I know I should not say such a thing, but I truly think that destiny has brought us to this strange place. Ever since I saw you in the woods that morning –"

"Destiny?" he said, swallowing hard. "It's true, I cannot stop thinking about you." Her eyes widened at that. "But I do not want to be in love, Miss Blanchfort," he managed to say. "It is a dangerous state for me."

"Yes, yes it is – for all of us," she said. "It is a lake of fire to be crossed barefoot. My feet are already scorched, my hem is singed, and yet –"

Her words seemed to touch him like fingers. Her lips were parted in expectation, but there was of course no way in which he could kiss her there, no matter how much he might have liked to. Her hand was still clutching at his and he could scarcely bring himself to detach himself, but he knew he must. Gently he laid it back in her lap and got up.

"I should let you rest," he said. "Perhaps you should go up to bed?"

"There will be no rest for either of us, I think," she said, looking up at him, ostensibly so vulnerable with her wounded hand in its bandages and sling, but in reality he saw and felt the power of her magic over him. She was the Queen of the Fairies again, determined to drag him away to her kingdom underground.

And in a heartbeat, I would go, he thought as he walked away across the drawing room.

~

"Is there something wrong?" Emma said. "Giles, did I do something...?"

He had spent the evening avoiding being alone with her, but she had contrived it, and now they were standing together in the great drawing room.

He sat down on the chaise by the dwindling fire, feeling utterly tongue-tied and unable to find a ready answer. Now, Emma perched beside him.

"No, no, it's nothing you have done," he managed to say at last. He leant back and massaged his temple.

"Is it your head?" she said.

"A little, perhaps," he said. She reached out with her hand to touch his brow, but knowing he could not resist her touch, he caught her hand, and as gently as he could pushed it away.

"Giles –?" she said. He had been more forceful than he meant to be. The tremble in her voice was evident.

He pressed his hands to his face, and bent forward and away from her. "What is going on?" she said.

"It's Laura," he said. "She is haunting me."

"Haunting?" said Emma after a moment. "What do you mean?"

"I wish I knew," he said. "But she is – here, somehow, or other. I can't explain. It will sound as if I succumbing to madness, which perhaps I am."

"No, no, I am sure that is not the case. My dearest..."

Her hands were on his shoulders, turning him towards her, but he would not allow it.

"Please!" he said, as if that would make rejection less painful to her. "We cannot. We should not. We are not in a position to marry."

Emma straightened beside him on the sofa and for a moment they sat in silence.

"Listen to me," she said, in a quiet, calm voice. "You are tired and ill and overworked. My situation, which is difficult enough, is making things worse. It is no surprise that you should feel guilt about the manner of Laura's death. I have heard the details. It was a shocking business, and that will have scarred you, of course it will! You have more capacity for feeling than a hundred men, my dear, and such tragedies cannot be put aside lightly. You are not done with your mourning."

Now he fumbled to take her hand. She wrapped both of hers about his instead and went on, "You are under no obligation to me," she said. "I wish to be clear on that. I have enough entanglements of my own. We were a little foolish the other night, perhaps."

"But you are still going to break with Edward?"

"Yes, but for my own sake. I must be honest with him. And as for you and me, well..."

He could only nod in agreement. So they sat in silence again, his hand still wrapped around hers. He was aware that she was crying.

At length he pulled his hand away and got to his feet. He

looked down at her, sitting there, with her hands clasped in her lap, her cheeks wet, her eyes red. She sobbed openly and looked away.

He pulled her gently to her feet and folded her into his arms, and held her as she cried herself out, feeling his own face grow damp with his own tears.

"You still have my heart," he said, "whatever else happens or does not happen. That can't change."

Chapter Thirty

The next morning, after the Ffordes and Mrs Maitland had gone back to Northminster, Mrs Hope took Giles up to the sewing room, an airy room in the attics of the north wing where Miss Waites had been set to work repairing a set of embroidered bed hangings.

"She's a treasure, Major Vernon," said Mrs Hope. "We have been in great need of a clever woman like her. And I have work enough for her until Christmas, if others do not get there first – Mr Bodley, for example," she added with a frown, picking up a very fine linen man's shirt that was lying on one of the work tables. "Has Mr Bodley been up here, Miss Waites?"

"Yes, ma'am," said Miss Waites, glancing up from her work. "Just a little tear in one of his Lordship's evening shirts. It won't take me long to set right. Then I shall be back to the curtains."

She glanced warily at Giles and turned away to cut a length of thread. Then she took the shirt from Mrs Hope and spread it on the table in front of her, looking for the tear.

"I suppose this gentleman has something he wants mending," she said, still looking over the shirt.

"No, I just want to talk to you, if I might, Miss Waites?"

She shrugged.

"As you like," she said.

"Thank you, Mrs Hope, that will be all," Giles said, and the housekeeper left them alone.

"I've been wondering if I had you to thank for this," she said. "If thanks are what's due. Ever since that lady asked me to come here – well, I nearly didn't come, you know. I probably shouldn't have –"

"I am glad you did," said Giles. "And in the end you know it will be the right thing."

"Will I?" she said, looking up at him. "When they find I have gone, then –" She sighed and pushed away Lord Rothborough's evening shirt as if it disgusted her.

"But you came. What made you change your mind?"

"I heard what happened to Kate," she said after a pause.

"Who told you that?"

"I just heard it," she said, "and I thought, if this lady wants me to come out to the country, then maybe I should risk it. And then when I was in the carriage, it struck me you might be behind it, and I nearly turned tail and went straight back."

"Better the devil you know than the one you don't?" Giles said.

"Yes. It's not pleasant but it's kept me safe long enough."

"Playing by their rules?" She nodded. "But those rules have changed, and you decided to come here after all. I was with Kate when she died. I saw what they did to her," he said and saw her wince a little. "That isn't something anyone can accept."

"She was a silly girl," Miss Waites said.

"But she didn't deserve that, did she? Nobody deserves that. And who would be next? That's why you came here, after all. You can't trust your own kin any longer, can you, Miss Waites? What if they turn on you?"

"So you know who I am," she said, after a pause.

"Yes. I was in Marlingford yesterday."

She got up from the table, went to the window, and gazed out.

"Who did you talk to?" she said.

"An old aunt of yours. And the verger, Mr Green."

"Then it will be nothing but gossip."

"Perhaps, then, you should tell me the truth. Tell me

about your brothers and sister."

"Why should I?"

"Because they need to be stopped. Give me something I can use against them. Or if you don't know anything specific, make me understand them and what they are about. I need to know what is going on here. At least three people have been murdered over this, and I want it to stop. As do you, Miss Waites, yes?"

"And if I do talk, you'll protect me?"

"Yes," said Giles.

"And they won't need to know it was me?"

"That I can't guarantee. But anything you think you can bear to tell me, I can use, and that will help you, surely. The time for loyalty is past."

She gave a bitter laugh and said, "That's what my brother said."

"That would be George?"

She shook her head.

"Merriam."

"Merriam Hickman Waites?" Giles said. "Goes by Hickman, yes?"

"Yes," she said, sitting down again. "Always fancied he was the squire's grandson. Silly boy, but my mother encouraged him. She was convinced she was gentry, that we all were. She did give herself airs. It was mortifying. I was glad to get away from it. Had to beg her to let me go and be apprenticed. That was bad enough, for it turned out that they didn't have the money when they said they did, and I was left there in this shop in Leeds – she was a distant cousin on the Bickley side, and a very nice business it was – and it's a wonder she didn't turn me out. I had to earn my keep, and she kept me slaving at it, like I was plucked from the poorhouse." She sniffed and smoothed the shirt in front of her. "But I learnt the trade, and I could earn my bread by it – just – but I couldn't have my own business, which is what I wanted. And then Merriam came to Leeds, and started doing well for himself."

"In what capacity?"

"He was working as a clerk to a wool merchant. Learning the business. I thought he'd be steady enough, and take the straight path. He was a devil when he was younger, but I thought he'd grown out of it. And he was doing very well. Took a little house, and I went and kept house for him and began to have a few customers of my own. Began to build up something for myself, but –" She sighed. "I should have known better. I should have cut with him like I cut with the others."

"You mean your half-brother and sister?"

"Aye, George and Susan. I saw which way that was going, and I wasn't having anything to do with it. That was why I was glad to see Merriam. He'd been working for George and then when he came to Leeds he told me he wanted nothing to do with them, that he didn't like George's way of doing business. The fool that I was!" She began again to smooth the shirt. "Now, where is this tear?"

"That can wait," said Giles, "if you please. Why were you a fool?"

"Because Merriam was at the same game. Right from the start. No wonder he could afford that house for us and the fine furniture. No wonder my business did well when he told the other dressmakers to turn their best customers in my direction or else." She glanced away. "And I thought I was doing well because of the quality of my work. And when I found out, he expected me to be grateful for it! Told me I shouldn't be so proud, that he was just taking care of me."

"So he threatened these other women?"

"Put at least two of them out of business. And not just in my trade. He had a nice line in threats, and if they didn't pay for his protection, then God help them!"

"And he learnt all this from George?" She nodded.

"Pay me or else," she said. "And then he'd give them credit, and charge them even more, and then he'd push them into the hands of a money lender, who of course worked for him, and bled them that way. And with the money, he bought out their leases and their businesses, and made it all very respectable, and Susan helped him do it. In fact, it was all her idea in the first place. It was a wonder how the money piled up. And I was so blind. I didn't see it until it was too late for me to get out. And then when my Henry died –" She broke off and swallowed down a sob. "If he hadn't got a fever, we'd have been wed and gone to Canada. He would have taken me away from it all, but he died. Three weeks before our wedding."

She broke down and cried for some minutes. Finally she managed to speak again. "And the worst of it was, Merriam was so kind. I should have been lost without him. He couldn't have been a better brother to me in my grief. And how could I leave him then? He was all I had in the world to love, and to love me. So I stayed and I said nothing."

She got up from the table and turned away from Giles in order to dry her tears and compose herself. Then she sat down again to face him.

"No, I've never told a soul about all this," she said. "But there comes a time, and now Kate is dead – oh, that stupid girl! She was Merriam's mistress, after a fashion. I don't know how sweet they were on one another, but she was often at our house, and we became friends of a sort. And then George came to see us, and she went back to Northminster with him. Merriam wasn't happy about that, I can tell you."

"And why did George come to see you?"

"To talk business. Merriam was doing well, and of course so was George. Merriam had Leeds and George had Northminster. That was the bargain they struck. But of course Merriam had his plans and his schemes, and when Kate left to go with George, it piqued him. He'd already begun dabbling at

Swalecliffe. Even took me on a holiday there for my health. Gave me the deeds of one of those fancy houses he was building up on the hill – for my old age. If only he could have just left it at that, for he made plenty of money there, but he had to go back to Northminster. I think it was when Susan bought the Manor after Miss Hickman died, that was the last straw for him. He wanted that for himself. Always talking about how he would have bought the place, and set up a family there. So we went back to Northminster and he declared war."

"So how did you come to be living in Croft's Building?"

"Merriam set me up in a little shop and I was determined to make my way, quite on my own, and I begged him to let me alone, and I thought I was managing – though it was hard enough – when one day my sister comes in and says she wants me to make some clothes for her. I was surprised, naturally, for I thought I would be the last person she would ask, but she said she wanted to make peace, and it was up to us, the women of the family, to show the way, and I couldn't help but agree with her, for I was sick with worry that Merriam and George would come to grief, and it seemed that Susan felt that too. I was wrong, of course. She was using me. She wanted to know what Merriam was planning, and because I thought she wanted to make peace, I told her what I knew. God help me, I told her! And then of course Merriam found out, and that was that. He has a temper on him. He beat me black and blue and burnt the deeds of my house while I was lying bleeding on the floor. So I went back to Susan. What else could I do?"

"And she put you in Croft's Building?"

"She owns it. She said I'd be safe there, and could earn my keep. Making dresses for their whores. Earning her trust, for she said if I betrayed Merriam I can betray them. And I have now, haven't I? And what good will come of it?"

"You have done the right thing. These people may be your flesh and blood but they are no good for you."

"Sometimes I think I would have been better getting Henry's fever and dying with him," she said. "I'm a dead woman now, that's the long and the short of it. When they realise what I have done –"

"You were right to talk, Miss Waites. This has gone on too long. It has to stop."

~

Felix was both relieved and disappointed when he did not see Miss Blanchfort the following morning. He did, however, send her the copy of 'The Bride of Lammermoor', but by means of a footman and not with his compliments, and certainly not with any incriminating inscription.

"Give Miss Blanchfort this," he had said, meaning to be careless and peremptory about it. It was an amusement for an invalid and nothing else.

Lord Rothborough had an errand for him – he wanted him to come with him to visit the wife of one of his tenants, who was gravely ill.

It proved to be a sad and sobering case. Felix could not find any hopeful signs to contradict the medical man she had already seen, and he drove back to Holbroke with Lord Rothborough in a sombre mood.

"Such a good woman," said Lord Rothborough, "and bearing it all so cheerfully, though she must face the thought of leaving her children without a mother, and her husband alone. But what else can she do in the circumstances?"

"It makes one wonder why we ever risk our feelings," Felix said.

"Yes, but I think, on balance, the joys do outweigh the sorrows, though sometimes it is hard to see the account clearly. You should not be too cynical, Felix."

"No, I need to be more cynical," Felix said. "I am altogether too –" He broke off.

"You did appear to be having quite an involved conversation with Eleanor last night," said Lord Rothborough after a moment.

"My point entirely. She is too full of fancies and I am too susceptible."

"It's not a propitious time for her, certainly," said Lord Rothborough, "and I stand by what I said, but there may be something between you that might be built upon. You certainly looked very well together."

"That is not standing by what you said!" exclaimed Felix. "And how we look, surely that cannot indicate anything?"

Lord Rothborough did not respond to this and they drove the rest of the way in silence.

They returned to find Lady Maria, Major Vernon and Miss Blanchfort sitting in the morning room. Miss Blanchfort was looking more flushed than usual, as if a fever had set in, and he could not stop himself going straight up to her to see if all was right. As he did so, he was aware that everyone else was watching and he was soon as crimson as she was.

"You looked feverish," he said, having felt her forehead and cheeks. He took her hand and checked her pulse.

"It is warm in here," she said. "And I was playing with the dogs before."

"It is," he said, feeling himself that the room was oppressively hot. "Your pulse is quite as it should be."

Then he noticed, lying in the folds of her dress, the volume of Scott. Seeing this, she smiled up at him.

"It's a favourite of mine," she said. "Thank you."

"I thought you might need something to pass the time," he said.

He felt a strong desire to sit down and discover which scenes she liked best, and if her impressions matched his own. But at the same time, he was relieved to hear Major Vernon saying they must take their leave, and he was able to disentangle himself from this silken snare.

~

"So it is as you thought – a feud between two brothers?" Felix asked, when Major Vernon had told him all Miss Waites had said.

They had returned to Ardenthwaite and Major Vernon had spread a map of Northminster out on the large library table.

"It's about territory," said Major Vernon. "If Merriam Hickman had not decided to come back to Northminster, then Bickley would have carried on as before. But they are competing for the same business now, both legal and illegal."

"And which one will win?" Felix said.

"Neither, if I have anything to do with it," said Major Vernon. "But how are we going to achieve that?"

Felix was a little surprised at the bluntness of the Major's question.

"Well, if Mostyn can be got to admit he had a part in the Colonel's murder, and who paid him for it, then you can go directly after Hickman, perhaps?"

"If he does admit it," said the Major. "At the moment, he knows we have only flimsy, circumstantial evidence against him and if he gets an adequate counsel, he might easily get off. He has no reason to admit anything. And Hickman presumably could be prevailed upon to pay for his defence."

"Could you not arrest Hickman for his assault on his sister?"

Major Vernon shook his head.

"She will never testify against him." He walked over to the window and looked out, leaning against the embrasure.

"No, the only way we can do this is by finding those who will talk. There will be people, no doubt, who have lost everything through their racketeering and intimidation. If we can persuade them to speak – they have been silent so far. But perhaps we can find someone who has nothing left to lose."

Felix looked down at the plan of the city, and tried to imagine it as an anatomised body that had succumbed to the ravages of disease. Where were the most damaged and wretched people of the city to be found?

"We could try the workhouse," he said.

"That is an excellent suggestion," said Major Vernon, coming back to the table and looking at the map. "And the almshouse at St Benet's Gate gives out casual charity, and of course, the debtor's prison."

"That should keep us busy," said Felix. "Are you not supposed to be on leave?"

"You are going to give me a clean bill of health, Carswell," said Major Vernon, taking out his notebook.

At that moment there was the sound of a carriage drawing up outside. Felix went to the window to see who it was.

"It's Captain Lazenby," he said, in some surprise.

They went straight downstairs to meet him.

"I am glad to find you at home, gentlemen," said Lazenby. "I am afraid I must cancel your leave, Major Vernon. A serious situation has arisen. The Bishop's son has been abducted."

Chapter Thirty-one

"He was taken," said Mrs Hughes. "He would not leave of his own free will. He had no reason to run away. Another boy, yes, but not Edmund."

"Now, I know this is difficult for you, ma'am," Giles said, "and you have already given your account to Captain Lazenby, but could you bear to tell me again what happened? When was the last time you saw him?"

"Just after luncheon yesterday. I went up to the schoolroom to speak to him."

"About what?"

"Just to remind him to keep his journal up to date. He keeps it while his father is away, travelling about the diocese – it is so that he can see all has been well when he returns."

"So, just a simple reminder?"

"What do you mean?"

"You didn't scold him over it?" Giles said.

"No, no, of course not."

"Forgive me, ma'am, it sounds like the sort of thing my mother might have scolded me over when I was that age."

"No, I went to remind him because I had forgotten to mention it to him at luncheon. The fault was mine, not Edmund's."

"And after you had spoken to him, you left him to his books?"

"Yes."

"And his tutor was not supervising him at that point?"

"No, Mr Cooper was with the younger children at that point, giving them their lessons downstairs."

"And after that you went for your walk in the gardens?"

"Yes. For about an hour or so. There is a little summer house where I stopped for a while and read, and then I walked back."

"And went where?"

"To see the children downstairs. To hear them say their lessons. And at four we generally take tea. That was when Edmund did not come down. So I sent Fred to fetch for him – that is my second-eldest boy."

"And Fred came back without Edmund?"

"Yes. He said he could not find him in his room or the schoolroom. And that was when I began to worry a little."

"Because that was quite uncharacteristic of him?"

"Yes," said Mrs Hughes. "He is a good boy, very diligent, and it was odd that he was not there."

"And you would expect he was hungry and would want some tea, I suppose?" Giles said.

"Yes, yes, there is that," she said. "But mostly it is because we are very orderly here, Major Vernon. Things happen at their appointed hour, and we all like it that way." She gave a sigh. "And half an hour passed and he still did not appear. And so I asked one of the servants to see if he had seen him about – but there was nothing. I cannot tell you any more, Major Vernon. He had simply gone. It is as if he were stolen away."

"I doubt that very much, ma'am. When people vanish, it is most often through their own volition."

"But Edmund would not do such a thing. He had no need to run away or any such nonsense. He was taken, sir, I am sure of it!"

~

"Are you doubting Mrs Hughes' word, Major Vernon?" said

Lazenby when they left the drawing room.

"No, of course not," Major Vernon. "Just her reading of events. It's hard for her to imagine her son might have been rebellious enough to abscond. And what is more likely, do you think, sir, that the boy has run off somewhere or that he has been abducted by some nefarious individuals for reasons unknown?"

"But there was that case in London – Mrs Hughes actually reminded me of it – where two boys were taken from their beds and sold into degradation."

"Yes, I remember that case," said Major Vernon. "And you will forgive me, sir, but that was wrongly reported. I think it was put about in an evangelical pamphlet to promote the suppression of vice. A worthy cause, of course, but the facts were mistakenly presented. Those boys ran away to escape a violent stepfather and were reduced to selling themselves for bread. There was no abduction, and I doubt it very much in this case."

"That pamphlet was written by the Dean of Hornchurch," said Lazenby.

"Yes, sir, and he was, no doubt, wrongly informed. I shall not say he elaborated the story for effect, though I think the story was bad enough in the first place."

"So you do not find the idea of an abduction plausible at all?"

"Not at this stage. All we know is that the boy has gone. Why and where and how, that is all to be determined. Captain Lazenby, if you wish me to work on this case, you must allow me to do it in my way."

"Yes, of course," said Lazenby. "I only hope you will consider Mrs Hughes' feelings, Major Vernon. She is such a good woman."

This was too much for Felix. Lazenby's tone had been needling him.

"I think you may be sure that the Major will show proper

consideration for any woman, whatever her rank," he said.

Major Vernon smiled briefly at that, and said, "I want to look over his room. Mr Carswell, shall we go up?"

A footman took them to Edmund's room, which was located in a remote corner of the Palace. It was a north-facing attic adjoining his schoolroom and overlooking the kitchen wing.

"I should like to speak to Mr Cooper, the tutor," said Major Vernon. "Could you find him for me and send him up here?"

"Certainly, sir."

"So," said Major Vernon, when they were alone. "Edmund apparently vanishes into thin air from here. No one saw him leave, no one heard anything. It is very odd."

"If you assume they are telling the truth."

"Quite; we shall have to talk to the servants," Major Vernon said, looking around him. "I would imagine, all things considered, he has run off."

"From this house, yes, I would," said Felix. "No plum pudding and no novels."

"And being kept at home with a tutor, with no friends of his own age. Tom might know where he has gone," said Major Vernon, examining the bookshelves. "A dry diet." He turned to the writing table.

"I met him," said Felix. "He was with Tom and Celia, and they were playing with the rats, and then his tutor came and carried him off. He seems to have had very little leisure time."

"Perhaps Tom has stoked the fires of rebellion in him," said Major Vernon. "That isn't going to help matters, is it? Let us hope for everyone's sake that Edmund gets hungry and comes home soon. We have got better things to be doing at this moment than chasing after fifteen-year-old boys. This must be the journal," he said, picking up the notebook on the table. He flicked through it and grimaced.

"Nothing of interest?"

"Just a record of his lessons."

At this moment, Mr Cooper the tutor came in. A pale, underfed young man in clerical dress, he stood nervously in the doorway.

"You wanted to see me, sir?"

"Yes, Mr Cooper. Please tell us what you think has happened here."

"Well, as Mrs Hughes says, I think he must have been abducted. Otherwise I cannot account for it."

"You don't think he could have run off, as boys of that age sometimes do?"

"Edmund would not have run away, I am sure of that."

"Why?"

"He is a good, obedient boy, and he would not do anything to hurt his mother and father. Running off would not have occurred to him. Why would he?"

"He did not seem unhappy in any way?" Felix asked. "Sometimes young men conceal a burden of distress from those closest to them."

"No," said Mr Cooper.

"And he is never difficult or disobedient?" said Major Vernon.

"No. He is a model pupil. Very diligent and intelligent. There is no reason for his disappearance other than some evil hand at work."

"But you heard or saw nothing that would support that theory, Mr Cooper?"

"No. I was in the nursery downstairs with the other children. I saw nothing."

"But you agree with your employer?"

"Of course, sir – who would know a son better than a mother?"

"They are close?"

"As I said, he is devoted to his parents. This is a loving, harmonious household. It is full of the spirit of God's love."

"I believe you had to come and fetch Edmund from Canon Fforde's house the other day," Major Vernon went on. "Presumably he had absented himself from his lessons without your permission?"

"No. He was simply late coming back so I went and fetched him. I suppose he lost track of the time. That is rare with him."

"Tempted away by fancy rats," said Major Vernon.

"I'm sorry, sir?"

"My niece was showing him her fancy rats," said Major Vernon.

"Then he was being polite in not leaving when he should. That's all."

"Goodness. So you have no complaints at all about your charge, Mr Cooper?"

"Why would I, Major Vernon? As I have said, Edmund was –"

"Yes, thank you Mr Cooper," said Major Vernon. "That will be all."

The tutor left.

Felix glanced at Major Vernon. It was not like him to be so peremptory. Major Vernon went to the window and looked out.

"You think he is lying," said Felix after a moment.

"Can a fifteen-year-old boy really be such a saint?" said Major Vernon. "It was as if Edmund's reputation as a good boy was all that mattered to him. Not that he might be in danger or distress, or plain miserable. The mother was the same. It's interesting, don't you think?"

"What is it that you think has happened?"

"I've no idea, but I find it uncommonly odd how Mr Cooper is parroting his employer's theory of an abduction."

"I suppose he has too much to lose by offending her."

"Quite – given how many fat livings her husband has in his pocket. He must dream of preferment."

"And a decent dinner," said Felix. "He looked half-starved."

"Let's hope that the servants are more honest," said Major Vernon, pushing up the sash. "What build is Edmund?"

"Skinny and smaller than Tom," said Felix. "Why?"

"Might he have managed to climb out of here?"

Felix joined him at the window. "And out into the gardens?"

"Would you have risked it?" Felix said, looking out.

"At that age, yes, but if he is a paragon, then it is a moot point. But it is a possible means of exit, which would not have been noticed by anyone."

"It does look as if some of the moss has been knocked off. Look there, at those patches on the sill, where the stone is a different colour. It's not conclusive, but it does suggest someone might have gone out that way."

"We'll have a look at this from outside," said Major Vernon.

~

They found their way out into the gardens, and managed to identify the section of the building containing the window to the boy's room.

"Small and slight, you said?" Giles said, looking up. "He could easily have managed that. The downpipe is very well placed."

"Not to be undertaken lightly, though," said Carswell. "Hardly a soft landing," he added, pointing to the cobbled paving that edged the building. "He could easily have sprained his ankle, or worse." He crouched down. "There is some disarrangement of moss here too, as a matter of fact."

"Just right if he went down that downpipe," said Giles.

"If he came down in a hurry, he might have kicked it to one side on landing," said Carswell. "But then we may be seeing what we want to see."

"Yes. After all, I would certainly prefer that he was a normal boy in search of amusement and adventure," said Giles, "than the victim of a frankly implausible abduction plot. Humour me a little longer, Mr Carswell. Let's suppose he did escape down here. Where would he go next? What is his objective?"

"He wouldn't go back towards the house, because he might be seen," Carswell said. "If I were him I would head off into the parkland, and into town the back way, over the wooden bridge by the racecourse."

"That is what I would have done too," said Giles. "Shall we?"

So they headed into the gardens, through a dense area of shrubbery which seemed to have been planted to conceal the back of the house from open view, and then turned onto a broad path which gave a fine prospect of all the park.

"That must be the little summer house where Mrs Hughes stopped to read," Giles said, pointing out the temple-like structure in the distance. "Perhaps he went to see her."

"Then why climb out the window?" said Carswell.

"Because he was locked in his room?" said Giles. "There was a good lock on that door. Perhaps Mr Cooper and he quarrelled. Mr Cooper locked him in as a punishment and he wanted to appeal to his mother against the injustice of it. That might send him out here, don't you think?"

"In theory, sir, yes," said Carswell. "But this is all theory."

"It is less than theory, it is more like fancy," said Giles, looking around him, scanning the landscape. "For nothing here explains his vanishing into thin air. A little kicked moss explains nothing. And who am I, after all, to doubt the word of a Bishop's wife?"

~

"Did he say anything to you in confidence?" Giles asked.

"What's happened to him?" said Tom.

"We don't know. I'm clutching at straws here, Tom, but he might have said something to you that can help us find him. Was there anything he said to you that made you think he was going to run away?"

"No, but we did talk about climbing out of windows. He said he did that – climbed out of his window to come over here and see our rats. That time you were here, Mr Carswell, when he was here and his tutor came and got him – the next time I saw him he said he had done it by climbing out the window. I laughed at him because it seemed ridiculous and dangerous. I mean, it's a couple of storeys up! He could have broken his neck. But I know fellows do that sometimes. There was a boy at school – years ago – climbed out of a window and fell and died. They are always telling us that to discourage us. You don't think that could have happened to Hughes, do you?"

"No," said Carswell. "An accident like that would be – well, we would know about it, surely, sir?" he added, turning to Giles.

"Yes, we would," Giles said. "Let us say instead, he is adept at escaping – that is very useful, Tom. Now, was there anything else? What about family quarrels? Any scrap of gossip will do."

Tom considered for a moment and said, "I don't think he was very happy. He was worried because he wasn't saved yet, and that was all his mother and father seemed to care about, and he wanted to talk to Papa about it, whether you had to be saved, if there wasn't another way. He didn't want to go to Hell because he didn't have it happen to him, the saving I mean. I don't understand it, really, Uncle Giles, that's why I'm glad he wanted to talk to Papa about it."

"Did he talk to him?"

"I don't think so. It was just before we went to Holbroke. He was jealous about the rook shooting too," Tom said with a sigh. "He is going to turn up somewhere, isn't he, Uncle Giles? Can I help look for him?"

"You are helping. Do you know where he might have gone?"

"I wish I did. But I can't think of anything except the window thing and the saving. Oh, and Bickley."

"You talked about him?"

"He wanted to know if he was really saved. He found it hard to understand that he could be saved, because he doesn't trust him."

"He has good instincts," said Carswell.

"When did you have this conversation?" Giles asked.

"Just before we went to Holbroke. As I said, he wanted to go with me. Asked me if I could smuggle him in somehow – he could be my servant and I could give him three and six for waiting on me."

"And where did you talk?"

"In the gardens at the Palace. It was that time we took the toast and butter – you were there, yes?" Giles nodded. "We'd arranged to meet, and after Cissie went back and we were alone, he asked me if I knew what it looked like when a man was making love to a woman. He'd seen his mother with Bickley and he thought he was being disrespectful in some way. I said I didn't know." Tom went on, "I suppose if I'd seen someone like that going after Mama, I would feel pretty –"

"Insulted?" said Carswell. "Yes, so would I."

"He is only a horse dealer, after all," said Tom. "Not a gentleman."

"Even if he were a gentleman, it would still be aggravating," said Carswell.

"Do you think that this might have something to do with his going off?" Tom asked. "Is it something to do with Bickley?"

"I sincerely hope not," said Giles.

"May I help look for him?" said Tom. "There are a few places hereabout I think he might have gone, places you wouldn't think of, perhaps. Shall I go and look?"

"Yes, do that," said Giles. "And if you do find him, bring him back here, in the first instance. I want to talk to him."

Chapter Thirty-two

The exercise yard for the condemned prisoners at Northminster Castle was a small square, only half-illuminated by the afternoon sun. Hopkins, alias Baxter, was standing alone in the sunlit portion, his face turned up to the sky, his eyes closed.

Given the man had only ten days of sunshine left, Giles hesitated to disturb him. On returning to Constabulary Headquarters he had learnt that he had been returned to Northminster to be hanged.

"Shall I bring him in, sir?" said the guard.

"No," said Giles. "We will talk out here."

There was a bench against the wall, still in the sun. Giles sat down, and after a moment Baxter came and sat down beside him.

"I've nothing to say to you," he said. "I've said my piece and I will take what I deserve."

"I understand that, but I have news for you."

"What can you have to say to me that will make a difference?"

"It's true that I have nothing for you that can change your fate. But if you help me now, those who forced you into this place can face justice as they should."

Now he glanced at Giles.

"Who do you mean?"

"George Bickley. It was on his orders you killed that man, the man who has gone to his grave without his name, yes?"

"He had a name," said Baxter.

"Then tell me it. He was an associate of yours, I think. You both carried the same mark of a swallow, and Kate took it too, to show her love for you. Do I have that right, Mr Hopkins?"

"That is not my name now."

"Johnny Hopkins. Kate told me that was your real name."

"What does that matter now? She shouldn't have said that. She shouldn't have said anything. The daft –"

"She talked to me because she loved you. She wanted to help you."

"Loved?" he said, and then made a long, low groan. When he spoke again, he was struggling to speak. "Loved? Is that your news, then, that she is... Because if she talked to you, then she will be –" He turned away from Giles, hunching up his body as his emotions overtook him. "Is she dead?" he said, turning back to Giles again. "Tell me it isn't so, tell me!"

Giles shook his head.

"I'm sorry, I can't."

"What happened?" Hopkins said, after a long silence.

"She was stabbed by Bickley or one of his men. You probably know better than I who was responsible for it. I was with her at the end. She did not die alone."

"And her blood is on your hands! You made her talk, when you knew what would happen if she did."

"No, she chose to talk because of you. She sought me out. She loved you and wanted to help you. She wanted justice for you and the truth to be known."

"It's too bloody late for that. If she is dead and I am dead, what does it matter?"

"I need your evidence, Mr Hopkins, so that I can send Bickley to the gallows. He deserves it. You know that. You cannot defend him now, not when he has brought you to this place."

There was a long pause, then Hopkins wiped his face clear of his tears and said, "He does deserve it. Plenty of times I have thought of doing it myself, just to get clear of him and that life."

"Then help me."

"We wanted out of it, Matty and Kate and me, that was all. We decided it, and that was the trouble, because once you are in, you can't get out. These shackles here, this prison here, it's nothing like that, once you're in it. Death is the only way out. They get you and that is it."

"Matty?"

"Matty Jones. We were blood brothers. Known him since I was a lad, since I first came to Northminster, and we were in a gang together. Just stealing to stay alive, and then this woman comes along and offers us food and a decent place to stay, and tells us we are likely boys and we won't want for anything, if we just do as we are told. And that she'd protect us from your lot."

"This was Susan Bickley?"

"That's right. The bitch. And she fed us well, and gave us decent clothes, made us learn to read and count, and of course we had to be grateful and do exactly what she wanted, or she sent her brother to thrash the living daylights out of us. So we did what she wanted, and what he wanted. There was always plenty that had to be done."

"Such as?"

"A lot of labouring in the yard. Mucking out horses, that sort of thing, and he taught us to fight. Sometimes we'd have to fight each other, like dogs, and he'd run a book on it. Or we'd have to go with gentlemen, who liked boys better than the whores. Matty more than me, for I wasn't pretty enough. It wasn't so bad, because you were never hungry, and I'd been hungry before, and I could stand the work well enough and even thrashings and the dirty gents, after a while. And then when we got to be men, we went out on the main business, collecting the money, and doing what had to be done if they wouldn't pay."

"And you never got a cut?" Giles asked.

"We got our clothes and our food, as before, and our pick

of the whores and liquor as we wanted. But nothing to put away. Nothing to let you build something for yourself. That wasn't on the cards. Times were I thought of selling my coat and boots and making a dash for it, but that would mean leaving Matty, and then I fell in with Kate and I wanted to make her my wife –" He broke off. "Just like some ordinary lad. I wanted to wed. So that's when we started to think of it, getting to New York and starting again, while we were still young enough. And so Matty went and talked to Hickman. Oh Christ, I wish he hadn't. But he said it was the only way to get the tin we needed."

"What did he do?"

"He gave titbits to Hickman. Nothing that could really hurt the Bickleys, but that wasn't the point. It was the doing of it. But Matty was getting good money from Hickman, real tin, and we were going to go to America, Kate, the three of us. Try our chances in New York!" He laughed bitterly. "New bloody York. What fools we were, to think that we wouldn't be found out." His laughter turned to tears again. Eventually he resumed: "I had to kill him. That was my orders, and so I followed my orders, even though I knew it would lead to the gallows. Well, it's a fool that would disobey Bickley or that bitch of a sister of his. I reckoned I'd rather take the risk of swinging on the racecourse than the certainty of being cut into a hundred pieces and left in an alley. So I did as I was told and I killed him. Beat him with a poker until – until –"

He broke down utterly again.

When he recovered a little, Giles said, "Thank you for being so frank."

"It needed to be said," said Hopkins. "Will it help bring them down?"

"Yes," Giles said. "I will need you to repeat it all to one of my men, so it can all be recorded properly." Hopkins nodded. "Just tell me one more thing – the swallow tattoo – why?"

"It was Matty's notion. A mark to bind us, like brothers. We were blood brothers, you see. And I killed him and he died knowing it."

~

Giles returned to the Northern Office, and had been in his office for no more than ten minutes when he heard the sound of Tom's voice in the outer office. He was a trifle out of breath.

"I must speak to my unc– I mean, Major Vernon, at once!"

Giles came out from his room.

"Yes?"

"I found this," said Tom rushing forward. "At the ice house in the Bishop's Park. It's his, I'm sure of it!"

He thrust it at Giles. It was a white handkerchief, heavily stained with blood.

"It has his initial on it," Tom added, pointing to the corner where a clumsy 'E' had been embroidered with some labour but little success. A present from one of his little sisters, Giles thought.

"Let's show this to Mr Carswell," he said.

~

The ice house was set in a distant corner of the park, conveniently located for the river and a footbridge to the race ground beyond. Lying in a secluded, almost invisible hollow, it was evident that it had not been in use as an ice house for some years, and the top of the mound was heavy with brambles and ivy. However, the rusty gate opened with ease and when Tom led them down the tunnel and into the domed chamber, it was obvious that it had been used for purposes other than storing ice. There was a distinct tang of urine in the air, and the walls were decorated with obscene drawings created with smoking candles.

"And where did you find the handkerchief?" Major Vernon said.

"Here, by the wall," said Tom. "I put that stone there to mark the spot."

"Excellent work," said Felix, squatting down with a candle in his hand and peering at the floor. But there was little of interest to be seen.

"Here's something," said Major Vernon, who was making his own survey. "A cigar stub, I think. But that proves nothing in itself."

Felix went and examined it.

"It looks quite recent," said Felix. "And there is a scrap of the band left here. That means it's an expensive one, from Cuba."

"Bad habits have their uses," said Major Vernon with a smile. "So we might be able to identify where it was bought?"

"Certainly. I think the place I buy my cheroots in St Anne's Street might have them."

"And you and Edmund weren't in the habit of smoking expensive Cuban cigars down here, Tom?" said Major Vernon, taking a sheet of paper from his notebook and folding the cigar stub up inside it.

"Of course not!" said Tom, and then realised he was being teased. "Oh, I see. No."

"Who knows what has gone on in here over the years," Major Vernon said. "I think the Bishop ought to invest in a lock for the gate."

They emerged from the ice house and Major Vernon stood scanning the landscape.

"Tom, that path goes up into the woods there, does it

not? Where does it come out?"

"By the summer house," said Tom.

"You know this place like the back of your hand," said Felix.

"We have always treated it as if it were our own," said Tom. "The old Bishop was quite happy that we should."

"So, in theory, if Edmund had been at the summer house," Major Vernon said, "and was running away from something unpleasant, he might have come that way, perhaps in order to hide at the ice house?"

"Yes," said Tom. "That's why I showed it to him in the first place because it is a good spot for that. And that's why I went looking for him there."

"Now, please don't take this amiss, Tom," said Major Vernon. "You have been a great help to us and to Edmund, but I am sending you home now, and you are to stay there until further notice."

"Must I?"

"I'm afraid so."

Tom left, albeit reluctantly.

"That sounded rather grave," Felix said as they took the path down to the river and the footbridge.

"It was a precaution," said Major Vernon. "I don't want him with us if we turn up anything –"

He broke off and left the path to go down to the river bank, where the grass had been worn away to form a small, muddy beach. "There would be no problem bringing a boat alongside here, wouldn't you say?"

"To what end?" Felix said, joining him at the water's edge.

"To remove someone discreetly."

"Are you subscribing to the abduction theory now, sir?" said Felix.

"It is easier to tell the truth than lie," said Major Vernon. "Perhaps that was a partial truth from Mrs Hughes. He has been abducted, someone has told her so, and she can therefore speak with perfect sincerity about it."

"Bickley, you mean? He has told her that he has taken her own son and she has acquiesced to it? That cannot be right, not even to save her reputation, surely?"

"Bickley has made a fortune from intimidation. It is his modus operandi. And she appears to be emotionally and perhaps physically in his thrall – after all, who knows what Edmund may have seen when he blundered into the summer house. A woman in such a state might agree to anything."

"So what do you think happened?"

"Edmund has been removed somewhere. I think he ran away to the ice house. Perhaps Bickley came after him and gave him a good hiding, possibly to the point of leaving him unconscious. Or worse, God forbid – but we must be clear about what we are dealing with here. So the boat is fetched to remove Edmund in whatever state he might be in, and Bickley tells Mrs Hughes that he has been abducted, perhaps for his own good."

"So the boy could be anywhere," said Felix, looking downriver to the towers and chimneys of Northminster, wreathed in grey smoke and the looming dusk. "Alive or dead."

"If he is dead, then Bickley could use him to frame Hickman," said Major Vernon. "If he's alive, he is being battered into silence somewhere. And then perhaps Bickley intends to 'find him' and restore him to his mother, proving what a saint he is. I don't like either theory. I wish he had just run off to cut loose, but I don't think that is the case. Come, let us go and see if that cigar stub can help us."

~

They made various enquiries, but with little success. Then, as they were walking back toward the Northern Office, a carriage drew up alongside them, the window was pulled down and a woman looked out and addressed Major Vernon.

"Oh, Mr Peters, it is you!" she said. "I thought it was, but I wasn't sure – but it is! How very fortunate!"

"Can I help you, ma'am?"

"I don't know – perhaps. I was going to the Infirmary to get a surgeon. There is a young Scotsman there, I understand, who is very talented."

"Mr Frazer?" said Major Vernon.

"Oh, is that his name?" she said. "I didn't know. Do you know him?"

"Oh yes, ma'am; in fact, you are in luck. It is this gentleman here with me. May I present Mr Frazer, Miss Bickley?"

"Goodness! How extremely fortunate. Sir, could you possibly spare an hour or two? I have a poor soul under my roof in dire need of professional attention."

"Of course, ma'am," said Felix, trying not to sound too astonished at the mention of this name.

"Then we had better go at once," said Major Vernon, opening the carriage door and propelling Felix inside. He found himself sitting opposite the woman while Major Vernon sat down beside her. "You do not object to my coming too, ma'am? I may be able to help in some small way."

"Not at all," she said. "How kind you are, sir."

They drove at some speed to Marlingford and arrived at the Manor House a little after five.

A respectable old manservant was there to open the door to them, and they went into an ancient panelled hall, well-lit with candles.

"How is he?" Miss Bickley asked the butler. "This is Mr Frazer, the surgeon. Do everything he tells you, Stevens."

"Of course, ma'am. He's no better, no worse. Rose is

with him," said Stevens.

"This way, if you please, Mr Frazer," said Miss Bickley, starting to climb the stairs. He followed her up and then along the passageway into a large, comfortable bedroom. Here, lying in the canopied bed, was a slight boy. It was Edmund Hughes.

Chapter Thirty-three

Carswell glanced back at Giles with an expression of surprise mixed with confusion. It was clear that he recognised the boy, and that given the circumstances, the boy could only be Edmund Hughes.

He appeared to be in a wretched state, his face black with bruises. Carswell began to examine him at once, and Miss Bickley seemed inclined to hover at his side, like the most tender and anxious of relatives.

"We should leave him to his work, ma'am," said Giles to Miss Bickley. "Yes, Frazer?"

Carswell waved them away, and Giles led Miss Bickley out of the room and closed the door. They stood in silence in the passageway for a moment.

"You are right," she said after a moment. "It's just that I am fearful for him. He looks so delicate."

"And how did he come to be here?" he asked.

"Perhaps we should go downstairs?" she said, clearly not ready to give her answer.

She took him into a pleasant sitting room and ordered tea to be brought in. If he had known nothing of her background, seeing her presiding over her tea table, in her comfortable sitting room tastefully furnished with old pieces, he might have taken her good sense and respectability entirely at face value. Even the well-behaved pair of terriers, who lay curled up in their basket near her chair, spoke of it. It was hard to believe that it had been built on a sordid base of brothel-keeping, crooked card games, slave labour, intimidation, fraud and usury.

"It's a curious business," she said, when she had sat down

by the fire and taken one of the dogs onto her lap. "I don't quite know how to begin to explain it. But I think I may rely on your discretion?"

He sat down opposite, wondering how he should respond. He sensed she knew exactly who the boy was, and why it was important. At the same time he felt even more sure that she knew he was not Mr Peters.

"Of course," he said, and saw her smile, and felt this confirmed that she did not want him to be discreet. She wanted the facts on the table.

"How well do you know my brother?" she said.

"Not as well as I would like."

"I am glad you do not know him well," she said. "Oh, Mr Peters, I'm so ashamed of him, I cannot begin to tell you!" She sighed and glanced away.

There was certainly a talent for theatricals in this family, Giles thought, leaning back in his chair and considering her words.

"His misdeeds will not taint you, surely?" said Giles.

"Oh, I hope not," she said. "But he has done such terrible, terrible things. That poor boy –"

"You think your brother assaulted him?"

"I am sure of it. He did not deny it, after all."

"You've spoken to him about it?"

"I was down at the brickfields. It is a joint venture of ours and I had gone to speak to him about a point of business. It was only by chance I saw the lad. He had left him lying on a pile of sacks in a store room, having, it seemed, vented his anger upon him."

"Did your brother say who he was?"

"He implied that he was the Bishop's son. How he came to be at the brickfield is another matter entirely. I fear that there is some sordid intrigue behind all this! Of course, I tried to find out what his intentions were, but George would tell me nothing. In fact we had a most disagreeable scene."

"And how came the boy to be in your care? I am surprised you were allowed to remove him."

"It was only by chance that I could – a merciful chance. George was called away to town on business and I was able to take him then. Fortunately I have some authority with his men. If I had not been able to rescue him, I dread to think what might have happened to him."

"Do you think it was his intention to leave the boy to die?"

"I rather fear so. I suppose he knows something that he should not."

"He is in good hands with Mr Frazer."

"There have been too many deaths already," she said. "I could not bear another. This must stop now. I think you understand me, sir?"

He nodded, then ventured, "You think your brother has other blood on his hands?"

"Yes. I hoped it was not true, of course, but I fear –"

"Was he provoked in some way?" Giles asked, wondering what she might say about Hickman.

"Perhaps, perhaps; I do not really know what brought it on," she said.

"If you were to try to find the cause of it," Giles went on, noting a small degree of fluster in her last reply, "it might bring some relief to you. An explanation is not a great comfort, but it is something, perhaps?"

"I really do not understand what you mean," she said. "I do not wish to look for causes. It is painful enough as it is, to be faced with a brother who can behave so violently."

"Forgive me," said Giles, sensing the full force of her deflection. She was, he concluded, anxious to condemn Bickley and Bickley alone. He supposed she was motivated by those joint business ventures she had mentioned. She would presumably profit if her partner were hanged. It was all very convenient.

"Assuming the boy recovers," he said, after a moment, "what do you intend to do with him?"

"Ah, you see," she said, "that is why I was so very pleased to see you, Mr Peters. I was hoping you might help me – help him, in fact. I get the impression that you have certain connections that might be of use in such an affair, where discretion is paramount."

He nodded, certain now that his true identity was known to her.

"I will do what I can," he said. "But you must understand, ma'am, there may be limits to how I can help you."

"Of course," she said. "So what would you advise?"

"I think we should wait to see what Mr Frazer says," said Giles. "I'll go up now and see what progress he is making."

She let him go, and it was with some relief that he found Carswell alone with the boy. He had just sent the servants away for supplies and was sitting on the bed gently cleaning his wounds.

"We shall be done in a moment or two," said Carswell. "And then the laudanum will help you."

Edmund nodded, gulping down his pain and then looked enquiringly at Giles.

"This is Major Vernon," said Carswell. "Tom's uncle."

"But Mr Peters, while we are here," said Giles, drawing up a chair to the bedside. "I know you don't want to talk much now, Edmund, but can you tell us anything of what happened? Who attacked you?"

"It was Bickley," Edmund said and then grimaced at the memory. "I wish I had never – but he was – he was kissing her and –" he went on, breathing hard, and struggling with the words. "I could have just run away but it made me so angry!"

"Your mother?" Giles said. "He was kissing your mother?"

"It was more than that. It was – well, I think you know what I mean. It was vile. So I tried to stop him and he just threw me on the ground and kicked me and started at me with his riding crop. And my mother didn't say or do anything to stop him. She simply stood there. Why didn't she do anything? I don't understand it. What did I do wrong?" He was almost in tears now.

"You didn't do anything wrong, Edmund," said Giles.

"And then," Edmund went on, "when I managed to get away, I ran to the ice house, but he still followed me, and then –" His distress overcame him and he broke down.

"You should rest now," Giles said. "We can talk again later."

Carswell finished dressing the boy's wounds, and they left him to sleep.

~

Standing on the landing, Felix outlined Edmund's injuries to Major Vernon. Necessarily, they spoke quietly.

"He's got a couple of cracked ribs, as well as extensive bruising, and welts – he will recover, if he is carefully looked after. But should he be here?"

"That," said Major Vernon, "is the question."

"Does she know who you are?"

"I am pretty sure she does. But she is pretending she does not. That suits her better. She was anxious to point the finger at her brother, though."

"Why?"

"She senses her ship is sinking? She is salvaging what she can. She thinks that rescuing the boy will buy her credit and put her in a good negotiating position with us."

"And will it?"

"What do you think?" Major Vernon said.

"No," said Felix.

"Quite right," said Major Vernon. "But it will do no harm to give her the impression that something might be done for her. I need a great deal more from her anyway, and the more pliant she is, the better. She's not said a word about her half-brother, which I find interesting."

"Do you think she may have taken his side?"

"It's possible," said Major Vernon. "Now, about Edmund – could he be moved somewhere, and if so, when?"

"Tomorrow morning, perhaps, assuming there are no complications overnight. Where should we take him, though? Given that the mother does seem complicit, we can hardly take him back to the Palace. To allow your lover to assault and abduct your own child – it really does beggar belief!"

"I wondered if we might take him to Ardenthwaite, at least in the first instance. But perhaps somewhere in town might be safer. Whatever, he needs to be away from here. I can't think it will be long before Bickley comes to see his sister and have it out with her."

"Holbroke?" said Felix.

"That's an excellent idea," said Major Vernon. "And we will concoct a story for the parents that he was found injured in the park having run away from home. Perhaps he was even trying to find his friend Tom – remember how they talked of his going there?" Felix nodded and Major Vernon went on, "We want Mrs Hughes to think she has got away with it for now. Miss Bickley will like that, and so will Bickley for that matter. Yes, it will help us along greatly to have a little subterfuge. Now, I had better go and report to the lady of the house, and you had better see how your patient is!"

~

Before he returned to Miss Bickley, Giles wrote a couple of

messages and went into the servant's hall, wondering how easily he could persuade any of them to carry them. If they were afraid of Miss Bickley, it was unlikely. Fortunately, he had ten shillings on him, an adequate bribe for the very young housemaid he found darning her stockings by the fire. She was happy to run an errand for him for such a sum.

If she did betray him to her mistress, it was not such a calamity. For surely Miss Bickley would have suspected he would take the opportunity to send for reinforcements. Perhaps, indeed, that was part of her plan to bring her brother down.

"Mr Frazer will be able to join us for dinner, I hope?" said Miss Bickley, when he returned to the drawing room. "I usually eat at eight. I have sent Stevens to ask him."

"He would be glad to, I'm sure. The boy is a great deal more settled now," Giles said, "and not in any danger."

"Oh, thank goodness!" she said. "May I offer you a glass of wine?"

Giles declined, feeling he would need to keep his wits as sharp as possible.

"You are not worried your brother will come looking for the boy?" he said, when they had settled down by the fire.

"No, George never comes here," she said.

"Never? Even in such exceptional circumstances?"

"I don't think he would dare," she said. He wondered if the opposite was the case, and this was all an act of provocation.

"I do not like you to take such risks," Giles said. "I am going to arrange for the boy to be taken away from here tomorrow morning. Mr Frazer thinks he will be able to travel."

"Taken where?" she said.

"Holbroke."

"Lord Rothborough's place?" she said with a note of surprise.

"He is a friend."

"You must be a very intimate friend to take such a liberty."

"Mr Frazer also has a connection with the family that goes back some years."

"Oh, Mr Frazer, yes," she said with a smile. "What a very handsome young man – and so talented!"

"I thought," said Giles, "given that this business seems liable to make a great deal of unpleasant noise, as the boy is from such a prominent family, that in order to keep the scandal to a minimum, another story be put about as to how the boy came to be at Holbroke. An innocent one, where there is really nothing to blame other than young Master Hughes' adventurous spirit."

"An interesting idea."

"You asked me for discretion," said Giles.

"I did," she said, and sipped her wine. "What sort of story?"

"That he ran away from home to find his friend who was visiting Holbroke. That he was found injured in the park by Lady Maria Haraald herself."

"That is quite a tale," she said. "Are you sure such a thing could take?"

"I think so, if it comes from me. And I'm prepared to do it, to protect the reputations of the various ladies involved. Mrs Hughes, of course, but more importantly that of Miss Bickley. What you did for the boy was noble, and I don't want you to suffer for that. You have told me yourself the monstrous nature of your brother's character. This falsehood will pacify him and make your part in it seem inoffensive. He will be happy, don't you think, to hear himself distanced from all this?"

"True," she said. "It is prudent not to rouse his ire. I'm honoured by your concern for me, as well, sir."

"It is the least I can do," he said. "I worry that your honesty and compassion has made you vulnerable."

"How gallant," she said.

"It's not gallantry," he said. "To be frank, ma'am, given that you perhaps know what my business is" – she nodded – "you will understand it is my job to maintain peace in Northminster. There are lines that ought not to be crossed, as you yourself have pointed out, and these lines have been crossed recently due to a dispute between two parties."

"You are very perceptive, sir."

"But there are other matters, which, if they are conducted in an orderly way, are beyond my remit," he went on. "I have no interest in upsetting unnecessary apple-carts."

"I read you correctly, then," she said. "I had heard differently, but when you presented yourself the other day, I felt –" She smiled. "That you might be able to help me."

He felt relieved that his bait had taken.

"Of course, I would expect a little discretion from you on the matter," he said.

"Yes, yes, of that you can be certain. Are you sure you won't have a glass of wine, sir? I feel we should be drinking a small toast to our new association," she said, getting up and going to the decanter. He shook his head again. She herself took a small glass and then flitted over to the window and looked out.

"Are you expecting someone?"

"I did ask someone to call, yes," she said. "I hope you don't mind," she added with a flutter. "He will be of great interest to you, I think."

Giles smiled, but felt uneasy. He wondered who she meant, and a most unpleasant idea occurred to him who it might be. He found himself glancing about the room wondering what he might use to protect himself if necessary. He was not armed, but he was certain that whatever visitors arrived that night would be. He thought of Carswell and Edmund upstairs, and wondered if he could get the boy to safety sooner than the next morning. Perhaps the Vicar might take them in. He hoped that the young housemaid had not been dilatory about delivering his letters, and that their contents were being acted upon. The potential for this situation becoming a bloody trap was not lost on him.

"Would that be your half-brother, ma'am?" he ventured.

"You are perceptive!" she said, laying her hand on her breast, as if he had solved a clue in some parlour riddle. As she did so he noticed that the tip of her ring finger was missing, and he realised where he had seen such a thing before. It had been her hand curled about Kate's door, trying to see who was in her room. "Yes, we have a little business to talk over."

"How interesting."

At that moment, there was the sound of a horse outside, and she went again to the window and looked out. Then, without another word, she left the room and went to meet her visitor in the hall. Giles remained in his chair, and tried to cultivate the manner of a police officer who was prepared to turn a blind eye when it suited him.

She returned a few moments later with Merriam Waites, alias Hickman. Seeing Giles lolling in his chair by the fire, he said, "What the devil is he doing here?"

"So you two gentlemen know each other?" Miss Bickley said.

"What has he said to you?" Waites said.

"Don't worry, Merriam," she said. "He is quite in our corner. Now, will you have a glass of wine?"

"In our corner?" Waites said. "How?"

"Now, Merriam, we agreed, did we not, that if we are to bring matters to the conclusion we desire, then we must turn where we can for help. And Mr Peters" – Waites snorted with disgust at that name – "is being very obliging."

"You're a fool, Susan," he said. "A very great fool."

"Wait until you hear what I have to say," she said. "Sit down, won't you?"

He glanced warily at Giles.

"I'd listen to her, if I were you," Giles said. "Given the trouble you are in. It's only a matter of time before Mostyn or the widow Parham start talking. This may be your last chance."

"There," said Miss Bickley, rather as if one of her dogs had performed a neat trick.

So Waites sat down, or rather perched on the edge of his chair, and Giles wondered whether he was carrying a knife or a pistol, or both.

"So?" he said. "Get on with it."

"I have made a new will," Miss Bickley said. "Entirely in your favour, Merriam. This house and its land, the brickfields, my properties in Northminster, which as I am sure you know are quite extensive."

"Very nice," said Waites. "But what good is that to me? You will probably live to a hundred."

"Then your children may have the benefit of it. If you were minded to marry and have some children. After all, it would not be difficult to get a nice little wife if you were living here."

"I'm not living here with you," he said.

"I thought I might go to the continent," said Miss Bickley. "For my health. And leave the house safely in the hands of my heir. Yes?"

"All the property?"

"Yes. I should want an income, of course, but the business would be yours."

"A fine tale," said Waites. "George would never let –"

"George has –" she began and then sighed. "George has –"

"You're giving him up?" Waites said, and jerked his hand towards Giles. "To him?"

"Regrettably, yes," said Miss Bickley. "Hence the need for new arrangements."

"I see," said Waites, sitting back and considering. "Well, it's an interesting proposition."

"I know how much you have always loved this house," she said. "And I have improved it a great deal. Furnishing and fittings included."

Waites looked again at Giles.

"And he will cost me something, I suppose?"

"Naturally," Giles said.

"You can come to an amicable arrangement in time, I dare say," said Miss Bickley, getting up and filling a wine glass. She took it to her brother. "Wouldn't it be charming for you to be the master here? I remember how you used to break into the gardens and steal the flowers."

"One-off lump sum, not a percentage," said Waites, getting up and strolling across the room. He stroked the marble chimney piece with an appreciative hand. "Those are my terms. I'm not putting myself under any long term obligation." He drained his glass and went to refill it.

Giles got up and said, "That may not be possible. As I said, there is plenty of evidence of your hand at work, and it's never cheap to bury the truth. You may have to take what you can get, and your sister's offer is more than generous given the circumstances."

"And what's to say I won't cut your throat this very minute and bury the truth that way? Much cheaper."

"That would be extremely foolish," said Giles. "I'm sure we can come to some sort of arrangement."

"I don't know, I don't know," said Waites. "This is all too –" He broke off and refilled his glass again.

"I am glad you like my claret, Merriam," said Miss Bickley. "The cellar here is excellent for keeping wine. I should show you over the house."

"You've really changed your will?" he said.

"Oh yes. Signed and sealed. All in order. Would you like to see it?" she said, going to an ornate cabinet on a stand and unlocking it. "I keep it in here, with all my important papers."

Despite everything, Giles found he had to admire her

audacity. Waites was looking intensely at her as she calmly sorted through the papers and brought them to the table, like an animal watching its prey. Giles could not help remembering the stench of the attic where the Colonel had been strung up. Had Waites been there to supervise the Colonel's execution?

"There you are," said Miss Bickley, turning up the lamp on the table.

Waites sat down at the table and began to read through the document. Miss Bickley glanced over to Giles and smiled, as if extremely pleased with him. He managed to smile back, though he did not much feel like it, realising that this appalling charade utterly depended on her belief in his corruptibility. That she had taken him so readily at his word had surprised him, but perhaps in this shadowy world of hers, there were no moral boundaries that money and power could not erase.

As Waites read, and she walked about her drawing room showing off her figure, perhaps as she had been instructed to do at her finishing school all those long years ago, Giles took the time to survey the chess board as she had arranged it. She had lured Waites there to tempt him with a gift of her property and her power, and it seemed that he was succumbing fast to the idea. She had Giles on show as the turncoat policeman, to protect her in the short term and to show Merriam the business was safe in the long term. Upstairs she had the Bishop's son, and although she had assured him that Bickley would not come to the house, he now felt certain that was her intention all along. Edmund was bait.

Chapter Thirty-four

Felix lay on the couch at the end of Edmund's bed. The boy had drifted into a comfortable sleep and Felix, stretched out by the fire, felt drowsy himself. The old butler had come in to tell him he would fetch him when dinner was served, and he presumed that Major Vernon would soon come upstairs to see how Edmund was. In the meantime he closed his eyes, and found himself thinking of Eleanor Blanchfort with her nightgown half falling off, telling him in a husky whisper that she had dreamt he was her husband. It was the most intoxicating memory and in his relaxed state, he found himself transforming it into a fancy, where he gathered her up into his arms and carried her to bed.

The sound of the door creaking open made him wake, and realise he had been asleep. He sat up quickly, startled and confused as to where he was. He twisted about to see who had entered and saw a white-haired man looming over the bed with a blade glinting in his hand, bending over Edmund, his arm raised and about to attack.

Felix sprang up in alarm and launched himself over the foot of the bed, throwing himself across the bed in a wild attempt to protect Edmund from attack. The man roared with surprise and fury, and grabbed him by the collar, and in another instant, Felix found himself locked in a fierce grip, with the blade of the knife pressed against his neck.

"Give me one good reason why I shouldn't cut your throat?"

Felix could not think of any.

Edmund, groggy with laudanum, was now awake and sitting up. He was gazing at them, as he was unable to tell if this was reality or a nightmare.

"Yes?" said the man, tightening his grip so that Felix felt he would soon be unable to breathe. "What do you say?"

"If you kill me, you will hang," Felix managed to say. "You don't know who I am or who my friends are, but I warn you they will show you no quarter. Are you ready to hang?"

He had meant to sound defiant but at the same time felt certain that this was the worst argument he could have come upon, and that his delivery sounded less than convincing. He closed his eyes and tried instead to determine whether, if the man did slit his throat, there was any way he could save himself.

"Oh, fine words," he said.

"Don't kill him, sir," Edmund said in a dry little whisper. "He doesn't know anything, Mr Bickley – I haven't said anything to them, I swear it!"

"Why would I believe a filthy little runt like you?" Bickley said. "No, first I'm going to kill him, and then I'm going to kill you. Oh, your mama, she will cry and cry, won't she, when she hears you are dead!" Edmund began to struggle out of bed. "No, no, don't try anything, boy, or I shall make you die slowly, and then you will be sorry. Stay where you are!"

"Do as he says," Felix said. He could feel the pressure of the blade more firmly against his skin. He was glad to see Edmund obediently retreating back into the bed and drawing up the covers over him.

"Downstairs," said Bickley. "I want a word with my sister."

He began to manoeuvre Felix towards the door, and Felix felt he could do nothing but go along with him. He felt his body to be quite devoid of strength, and his mind was equally empty of any useful ideas that might help him extricate himself.

As they shuffled out across the threshold and onto the dark landing, it occurred to him that he was quite unable to bear the thought of death, and so he began to struggle in an attempt to free himself, but with little success. All this earned him was a violent kick in the back from Bickley's knee, which left him groaning and winded.

But when he opened his eyes again, having screwed up his face in pain, down the passageway he saw a moving light and heard the sound of footsteps hurrying up the stairs.

It was Major Vernon carrying a lamp. As he approached and saw him locked in Bickley's grip, he carefully set down the lamp, and with his hands up, took a few more steps towards them.

"Let him go," Major Vernon said. "It isn't worth it, Bickley. Let him go."

"Or what?" said Bickley. "I've a mind to fillet him and then you! I have had enough of your nose in my business!"

"George, let him go," said Miss Bickley who had come up in Major Vernon's wake. "Let's all be civil, I beg you."

"You beg me, do you?" said Bickley. "Oh, very nice. I'd like to see you begging properly, sister, that I would –" And then he broke off, seeing another figure appearing at the top of the stairs. "What the devil is he doing here?"

It took Felix a moment to recognise him. It was Merriam Waites.

"Business, George," said Miss Bickley. "Just business. Now let go of Mr Frazer and come downstairs. I've a very nice Madeira."

Merriam Waites began to laugh.

"Oh Christ, Susan, you are the –" Waites said, but could not continue for his amusement.

"What's so funny, Merriam?" said Bickley.

"You!"

"What the devil do you mean by that?" said Bickley, letting go of Felix. He began to advance on Waites, knife blade flashing. "Explain yourself!"

"I'm not sure I can be bothered," said Waites, moving

nimbly out of his way. “You senile old goat. Pretending you are saved to get a fuck from a Bishop’s wife!”

At the same time he whipped a blade of his own from a pocket, which he flashed and flourished in front of his brother with all the calmness of a flamboyant barber about to shave a customer. The two of them squared up to one another, performing a sort of dance, each with their knives ready to seize the slightest opportunity to take the advantage.

“So was she worth it?” Waites went on, grinning.

Bickley gave a muffled groan of fury and moved closer to his brother. Felix could see that Major Vernon was moving discreetly forward to attempt to intervene and disarm Bickley, a risky endeavour in a knife fight. He felt his stomach churning violently at the prospect of a bloody and possibly fatal outcome, and willed the Major to take care.

“I will kill you,” said Bickley. “I will. I should have done so long ago.”

From the corner of his eye, Felix noticed Miss Bickley retreating into the shadows, and he saw that Major Vernon had noticed this too. Suddenly Giles turned, caught her by the arm and pulled her forward to face her brothers. She gave a little shriek of surprise, and the two fighters were for a moment confounded.

“Put down your weapons!” Major Vernon said. “She is the source of all your trouble. Can’t you see, she has brought you here to make you destroy each other. Don’t fall for it!” With which he pushed her a little closer to the two men.

Bickley turned and looked at his sister, with a long quizzical glance. Miss Bickley was now struggling in Giles’ grip.

“Nonsense,” she said. “Will you let go of me!”

“She brought you here with something you both wanted. You, Waites, get the fake will and you, Bickley, get Edmund.”

“Fake will?” said Waites. “What do you mean –?”

“Did you really think she would leave you all this?” said

Major Vernon. Bickley snorted with amusement.

"I was in earnest, Merriam," said Miss Bickley. "Of course I was!"

"And when has she ever been straight about anything?" said Bickley. "Dear God above, I see it all now –"

"Don't listen to him, George," Miss Bickley went on. "How can you take his word against mine?"

"Because, sister, I know you. And I have been sold! And after everything I have done for you, after all these years –"

"Done for me?" exclaimed Miss Bickley. "Oh, I think you will find, George, that without me you would not have a coat to put on your back, let alone such a fancy one! No, indeed, you would have been dead from the drink and the gambling long ago. I have saved you, so many times, I cannot begin to count them. There would be nothing if I had not worked for it, if I had not seen to all the details, if I had not imposed the necessary discipline. If I had not taken you in hand when I did, then the Lord only knows what would have become of you. You owe me everything, my boy, everything!"

Waites was now laughing again.

"Oh, that's telling you, George!" he said.

"Hold your tongue, Merriam," said Miss Bickley. "A little gratitude from you would not go amiss."

"When you are palming me a fake will?" he said, his amusement turning to anger.

"That is nonsense," she said.

"It is not," Major Vernon said. "Put down your knife, Waites. And you, Bickley. It will make it all go better for you."

But Bickley shook his head. He stood for a moment examining his blade, and then before anyone could do anything he lunged towards Miss Bickley and the Major.

Major Vernon dragged her out of the way, and attempted to shield her, but he was too late – the blade went in at her neck, catching the carotid artery, and she collapsed onto the floor, blood cascading from her throat.

Felix dashed over, and threw himself onto his knees, ripping off his cravat in order to improvise a tourniquet, but even as he leant over her he knew it was too late. She was dead.

He glanced up, aware of a fierce scuffle going on. Waites was retreating down the stairs, attempting to run away, but Bickley had dashed after him, and pushed him to the ground on the half landing. Leaving Miss Bickley's corpse on the floor, Felix ran to assist Major Vernon, who was attempting to stop him attacking Waites.

A terrible struggle began as they tried to pull away Bickley, who was crouching astride Waites and stabbing him repeatedly in a frenzy that suggested years of frustration. Waites lay writhing on the floor and then ceased to move entirely. At last Bickley stopped resisting their attempts to pull him back, and wilted in their grasp, leaving his knife stuck in Waites' body. He crumpled in a dead faint, bleeding copiously. Waites had managed to stab him back.

"Can you save him?" said Major Vernon, as Felix pressed his hands to the wounds he could discover.

"With any luck," said Felix. "Is he –?"

Major Vernon crouched over Waites, checking for signs of life. He shook his head.

~

A little before midnight, still in their bloodstained clothing, Giles and Carswell found themselves sitting by a dwindling fire in the late Miss Bickley's drawing room, eating bread and cheese and drinking strong tea. Carswell looked utterly exhausted.

He had done everything he could to keep Bickley alive, and had apparently succeeded, although he had been the most difficult patient. Giles had had to assist him by holding him down as the wounds were stitched and dressed. Eventually opium had worked its magic on him and he lay upstairs, in a satisfactory state. How long it would be before he would be available to be charged and then tried, was another matter.

Reinforcements had eventually arrived from Northminster, and the bodies of Susan Bickley and Merriam Waites had been moved to the village lock-up and were waiting to be transported back to the city for post-mortem. All in all, it would create a very strong case against Bickley and there was no doubt that he would hang, but Giles felt the full weight of failure on his shoulders, as he sat there watching the embers. Again and again he turned over in his mind what he had said and done, and wondered if there might have been some better way that would have led to three prisoners in the Marlingford lock-up, instead of two cadavers. If he had only moved Miss Bickley out of Bickley's reach, if he had reacted more promptly and anticipated his fury, then...

"I want a clean shirt," Carswell said, breaking the silence. "And a decent bath and a brandy. And –"

"Holt will be here tomorrow first thing. And Peterson. I think you should take a day or two's leave."

"I should go and check on Edmund," said Carswell.

"He was sleeping soundly when I went in a quarter of an hour ago."

"Then I should go and see Bickley," he gestured towards the door and sighed. "I have never felt less enthusiasm about keeping a man alive," he said. "I have no pity for him. After seeing what he did... Thank the Lord, Edmund stayed in his room. If he had seen all that..."

"You did all you could for Bickley," Giles said. "There is no need to reproach yourself. That is my business, I think."

"No," said Carswell. "How else could it have played out? She lit the spark by bringing them both under the same roof. Something was bound to happen. That is what she was counting on, surely, and you saw it."

"When it was too late," said Giles. "And perhaps I goaded him. Did I?"

"They were all beyond the point of listening to reason," Carswell said, heaving himself up from his chair. "They evidently all loathed each other at heart, and perhaps it was just a matter of time. The truth is that you have brought them all down, and if Bickley survives to stand trial, then you will be perfectly vindicated. So I shall go and make sure he is comfortable, though it sticks in my craw!"

Chapter Thirty-five

At first light the next morning, lacking any other horse to hand, Giles rode George Bickley's superb grey into Northminster. He had left it in the stables at Marlingford. He took him to The Black Bull, where the combination of a beautiful horse and his own sorry, blood-stained appearance caused much astonishment in the stable lad and Mr Wilkes.

Having washed, shaved and changed his clothes, he went up to the Minster Precincts, stopping first at the Treasurer's House.

On his being announced, Sally, who was sitting frowning over her paperwork, leapt up at the sight of him.

"We have had the strangest news from Oxford," she said, and resisted his attempt to kiss her, in a most uncharacteristic manner.

"Oh," said Giles. "I think I know what that might be."

"You do?" she said. "You know about Edward and Emma?"

"Tell me, what is the news?" he said.

"Have you a hand in this? Have you and she –"

"What was the news?"

"That it is broken off! And Lamb is – oh dear, well, he is not happy. You are lucky he has gone out. I have never seen him so – I tried to defend her, to defend you, of course, but it clear that Edward is miserable. Oh, Giles, what have you done?"

For a moment he could not speak. Sally stood there, her arms folded, waiting for his confession, and he could think of nothing to say. All he could think was how wretched Emma would be.

"Are you engaged to her?" she said.

"No," he said. "All we have decided is that she would break with Edward. That was all."

"All? 'We have decided'?" she said. "That sounds as if you have quite committed yourself."

"Yes, I have, after a fashion. I don't pretend that we know whether we can marry. After all, I'm no position to marry, and she understands that."

"And you have made her break it off on such terms?"

"That was her decision."

"How could it be? You have put pressure on her, of some sort. You must certainly have made love to her, and goodness knows what else. I know what you are like!"

"No, Sally, nothing like that. But we have been frank with each other. Truly, I'm sorry you have found out this way. I was going to tell you, in time, but it seems –"

"Why are you not engaged to her, then?" she said, throwing up her hands. "Did you not offer? To make a woman throw over such an eligible match and not offer marriage? I don't understand."

"I told you: I'm in no position to marry and she understands that."

"So what was your intention?"

"I don't know," he said. "Truly I don't. I can't expect anyone else to understand, and I know this seems so shabby, and I know how painful for you and Lamb it must be, for which I can only apologise, but she is –"

"You do love her, then?"

"Dear Lord, yes," he said. "More than anything. And she loves me, poor creature. Her judgement is usually rather better."

Sally twisted her fingers together for a moment and then stretched out and gently put her hands on his shoulders, as if searching for support.

"There will be such a storm. Such a storm."

"I know. I'm sorry."

"Lamb will come round, I dare say," she said. "But it is going to take time."

"I know. I will talk to him. You do not have to defend me. You must take his part, that is as it should be."

She squeezed his shoulders a little and almost shook him in her agitation.

"Oh Giles, I do wish it could have been any other way –"

"I know, I'm very sorry, but I cannot give her up."

"Even if you will not marry her? How odd this all is! But then, you are odd, Master Giles, you always were and you always will be. I remember old Nancie saying that of you. She thought you were a changeling." She broke from him and walked across the room. "What will be, will be!" she said with a great sigh, her back to him, as if she could not quite bear to turn and look at him.

"I must go," he said. "I only looked in to say that we have found the Bishop's son. Could you tell Tom and Celia that he is quite safe?"

"Well, that is something, I suppose," she said.

He left, feeling the chilling breath of Sally's displeasure and disappointment, a far worse thing than the momentary sting of her anger. At the same time, he wished he could at once make his way to Oxford, go to Emma and take her into his arms and comfort her. He ached for her, as he had never done before. It felt as if the first great trial of their affections had begun, and he was by no means certain that they would survive the trial, no matter how strong their feelings were. The whole world seemed set against them.

He had scarcely got through the door of the Palace when the Bishop came hurrying out of his library to greet him.

"You have news, sir?" he said.

"Good news. We have found Edmund and he is quite safe. A little worse for wear, but –"

"Oh, thank the Lord! But what happened – do you know?

What has he said? I take it he did run away for some reason."

"You do not subscribe to your wife's theory?"

"That he was abducted? She is very distressed. I don't think she was thinking straight when she said that to you. I talked to Mr Cooper, his tutor, and it seems they had some sort of argument. Cooper confined Edmund to his room and I suspect he must have climbed out of the window – though how he avoided breaking his neck, I can't imagine – but he is safe! Where is he?"

"Perhaps we should give the news to Mrs Hughes first?"

"Yes, yes, quite. This way, if you please."

They went back into the library. Mrs Hughes was sitting hunched in a chair by the fire, a brown shawl of great ugliness wrapped about her, covering her customary black dress. She looked up at Giles fearfully.

"Do not be afraid!" said the Bishop, his hand raised. "Edmund is found! Deo gratias!"

"Oh, oh!" she exclaimed and leapt up from her chair, and grabbed Giles' hand, and to his horror, attempted to kiss it, rather as if he were some papal prelate. "Thank you, thank you! Where is he? Is he quite well?"

"A little rough around the edges," Giles said. "But he is in good hands, and will, I hope, be able to come home soon."

"Very soon, please, Major Vernon," she said, grabbing his hand again in both hers. "Please?"

"I think we need to talk a little first, ma'am," he said. "If you would sit down?"

"I don't understand," said the Bishop.

"A few facts need to be clarified. Yes, ma'am?"

She nodded, avoiding his gaze, and he handed her back to her chair, where she seemed to shrink, even as she sat down. Her husband went and stood protectively by her.

"I will keep this brief," said Giles.

"Thank you," said the Bishop, who seemed wary.

"May I sit down?" Giles said, pulling up a chair.

"Of course," she said.

"Now, Mrs Hughes, the Bishop has just told me that Mr Cooper confined Edmund to his room on the day in question and that he feels he probably climbed out of the room and ran away somewhere."

"I don't know, I really don't," she said, glancing up at her husband. "If my husband says so, then –"

"Then, after he had climbed out of his room, my feeling is that he came to see you. To air his grievances."

"I'm sorry, sir, what do you mean?"

"You were, I think," Giles said, taking out his notebook and consulting it, "in the summer house."

"Yes, I told you that."

"You did indeed. And it is your custom to go there each day at that time?"

"Yes."

"Now this is where it gets a little confused. Edmund tells us that he did indeed climb out of the window and go to find you. He was angry with Mr Cooper, and he wanted to talk to you about it. A rather rash thing to do, but understandable."

"Quite," said Mrs Hughes.

"So can you confirm that you saw him at the summer house that day?"

"No, I did not see him."

"Although he told me he was there. He went there and spoke to you. Is he lying?"

"I don't know. He is not one to lie but, in this case, I think he must have. Perhaps he is not straight about what happened."

"He seems very clear about it to me. And quite distressed at the same time. Can you tell me why?"

"I really don't understand what you are asking me."

"Perhaps I should rephrase that, ma'am. Edmund went to see you at the summer house, saw you there and was distressed by what he saw. Have you anything to add to that?"

"He is confused," she said after a moment. "He must be, because there was nothing there to distress him."

"So he did see you there, ma'am? He is not lying about that, I think?"

She glanced up at her husband who looked puzzled.

"I am sorry, Major Vernon, what is the end of this?" he said.

"I need to know exactly what happened. This is not a simple case of running away, you see. Now, ma'am, will you confirm to me that you did see Edmund that afternoon at the summer house?"

"Perhaps," she said.

"My dear," said the Bishop. "That is not the answer to such a question. Did you or did you not see him?"

There was a long pause and she said, "I did."

"Then why did you not say so before?" said the Bishop. "What on earth –"

"Mrs Hughes was not alone," said Giles. "That was the difficulty."

"How dare you say that!" she exclaimed.

"I am simply saying what your son told me. He has no reason to lie about this, but you, ma'am, have every reason."

"What are you saying, sir?" said the Bishop.

"Edmund told me he saw his mother and a man engaged in congress."

"What!" exclaimed the Bishop.

Mrs Hughes leapt up from her chair.

"Where is he? Where is Edmund? How dare he say such things? He must have lost his reason. What on earth would make him say such a thing about – where is he, sir? I demand to see my son!"

"I'm afraid you won't be able to see him for a while. And I think his reason is quite intact. He saw what he saw. He is not an imaginative boy, given to fanciful stories."

"He truly said that to you?" said the Bishop. "Truly?"

"He did."

"And you deny this, Margaret?" the Bishop asked, turning to his wife.

"Of course! Of course! He is lying."

The Bishop looked at her for a moment, and then turned away, clearly thinking hard.

"He is not a fanciful boy," he said, "and I have never known him tell a lie."

"And have you ever known me tell a lie?" said Mrs Hughes. "This is nothing but wicked slander. The devil has got hold of our boy, John, that is the cause of it. That he could say such a thing about me, his own mother –" She sank back in her chair, her hands pressed to her face, apparently sobbing.

"You did just lie about his seeing you there," said the Bishop. His voice had a dry, staccato quality to it, as the reality of the matter began to affect him. "At the summer house. Why would you be so equivocal, unless you had something to hide, Margaret? Can you explain that?"

"I forgot that I saw him," she said, looking up at her husband. "One does forget things."

"On the day your son goes missing?" said the Bishop. "What else did he say, Major Vernon? Who was there with my wife? Was it someone Edmund knew?"

"It was George Bickley."

The Bishop closed his eyes and looked heavenwards, as if asking his maker for strength and guidance.

"You warned me against him," he said at length. "You told me and I did not see it. And I trusted you, Margaret, I thought that you –" Words deserted him and he walked away and sat down in a far corner, his head bowed, his hands pressed to his face.

"Edmund is lying!" she screamed, jumping up and pursuing him. "Of course he is! Of course!"

"Silence!" exclaimed the Bishop, standing up and towering over her. "I have seen all the signs. I knew there was something going on, I knew, but I could not bring myself to accuse someone I thought – I don't know what I thought. That I was prey to delusions, that my wife could not, would not descend to such vile wickedness as this! But my own boy who cannot lie, who has never lied – he saw the truth and now, oh God help me, now –" He reached out and gave Mrs Hughes a shove. It was rather feeble but full of very evident repulsion. However it was enough to make Mrs Hughes fall to the floor bawling.

"He assaulted me!" she screamed. "That was what Edmund saw! Have pity on me, for the Lord's sake, John. I had no choice!"

"So that was why you stood silently by and let him horsewhip your son until he was unconscious?" said Giles. "And let him drag him away to goodness knows where and then cry abduction on his command? That is not the usual reaction of a woman who has been assaulted, ma'am!"

"I had no choice," she sobbed.

"I think you did, Mrs Hughes, and you chose your lover over your son."

"He was attacked?" the Bishop said.

"He has a couple of cracked ribs where Bickley kicked him, and welts from the whipping. But he has been well patched up, and is perfectly able to recall what he saw and what happened to him. I have no reason to doubt him as a witness. He has nothing to hide."

Now the Bishop found his strength and grabbing his wife by the shoulders, manhandled her into a chair. Then, taking another chair, and pulling it up to her, he grabbed her chin and said, "Look at me, Margaret, and remember that all your sins are clearly laid before the Lord and that you will be judged accordingly. Tell me the truth. Did he in fact rape you? Or are you his lover?" She said nothing. The Bishop proceeded, his voice colder and quieter now: "If you do not tell me the entire truth now, I will have nothing more to do with you and I will take your children from you, and you will be turned out like a beggar into the world! So be honest, for their sake, Margaret."

"My lover," she said softly, after a moment. "Yes, my lover, John, and I have never felt so loved as when in his company. I have never felt this way in my life before."

The Bishop looked away, as if he had been struck. The ardour in her voice had been undeniable and without any note of apology.

Giles found himself remembering what Emma had said to him that night at Ardenthwaite, the same fervent tone, and he felt ashamed of what he had wrought in her and of the destructive power of strong affections. Mrs Hughes had thrown everything away for Bickley, while he had made Emma give up her secure and prosperous future. For what?

In that respect, was he really any better than Bickley?

~

Having briefed Peterson on the state of his patients, Felix was glad to find that Holt had taken his usual efficient command of the situation. He found him in a dressing room, laying out his clean clothes. There was hot water too, in a shallow tub, so he stripped off his filthy clothes and started to sponge himself down.

"I shall need a shave, Holt," he said.

"Certainly, sir."

"And then I am going to Ardenthwaite."

"Not to Holbroke, sir?" said Holt, handing him a towel. "I thought you might want to see the young lady, sir. See that her wrist is setting straight."

"That is none of your business," said Felix.

"Given that Mrs Connolly is getting married, there's nowt to stop you now, sir," Holt went on, quite unconcerned.

"Did Major Vernon mention that to you?"

"He did, sir," said Holt. "And I told him what I am telling you now. It is better for you both to look elsewhere. Christian marriage is a fine institution."

"And what do you know about it, Holt? You're not married."

"I may be, sir, sooner rather than later. Especially if we go to Holbroke."

"Oh, so you have an object there, do you?"

"Met her last year. We've been biding our time, but now it is the courting season."

"Have you told Major Vernon this?"

"No," said Holt, and added with a trace of nervousness, "not yet. Shall do, soon enough, when I have my answer."

Felix wondered if this meant he intended to look for another place, more compatible with married life.

Felix put on his clean shirt and sat down so that Holt might shave him.

"So, you think we should go to Holbroke?" he said, when Holt had finished.

"Like I said," Holt replied, dragging a comb through Felix's hair. "It's courting season."

~

"Holt?" said Lady Maria. "Major Vernon's man? Oh, how delightful. Who is the young woman?"

"Mary-Ann Fuller. I think she is a still-room maid," said Felix.

"He has a sweet tooth, then," said Lord Rothborough.

"And this courtship is the only reason we have the pleasure of your company?" said Lady Maria, with a playful smile.

"No, I thought I had better see how Miss Blanchfort's wrist was faring."

"Oh, but of course," said Lady Maria, "her wrist. That must be of the greatest concern to you."

"Maria, really," said Lord Rothborough with a frown. "Remember what I have said on this subject? That sort of imputation is most unbecoming."

"How can I resist, Papa?" Maria went on in the same playful manner, apparently not at all feeling the sting of his reproach. "When she will have me play nothing but arias from Donizetti's Lucia for her? I think she has cast her Edgarro –"

"Maria, enough!" said Lord Rothborough. "Have a care, for goodness sake!"

Felix was glad of this, for her words had disturbed him. That she should speak so plainly was mortifying, and it must have shown, for she glanced at him and said, "Oh, I have made you uncomfortable! I am very sorry, truly, Mr Carswell. Can you forgive me? I was only teasing, but I have hurt you, I see."

"Of course you have not," he said. "It does not matter."

"Go and find yourself something profitable to do, Maria," said Lord Rothborough. "I wish to speak to Mr Carswell alone."

Maria went, but not before she had kissed them both by way of apology. Seeing her bright but contrite eyes, Felix felt heartily sorry for her.

"She only meant to be kind, I think," he said, when she was gone.

"When I have expressly told her not to speculate on that matter?" said Lord Rothborough. "The trouble is that she does not have her sisters here to keep her in check. Eleanor is a strange companion for her. She seems to have unsettled us all, in truth."

"You might say that," Felix said, thinking of the disturbing dream he had about her only the previous night, when he had been sleeping on the couch at the foot of Edmund's bed.

"And you are feeling something of a fascination," Lord Rothborough went on. Felix nodded. "But there is no need to act upon it, at least in the short term. In fact, I would advise you against it. As I said before, I want to see you well settled, but not at the expense of your happiness."

"So you think she cannot make me happy?"

"I don't know. That is for you to determine: if the fascination you now feel means something more, if it might form the basis for a more profound association. It is in your hands."

In that moment, Felix rather wished that his hands were completely tied and the decision was Lord Rothborough's to make. He felt it would have been simpler to accept that, whether he were to forbid it utterly or endorse it entirely.

"Perhaps I should not stay here," Felix said.

"No, stay," said Lord Rothborough. "You need to test the matter, surely? And as I said, there is no need to act in haste. She is still in mourning, and you are both young. You have time, and you should tailor your actions accordingly."

Felix had a strong desire to be very frank about the state of his passions, and how he ached for consummation. The idea of pursuing a slow, decorous, courtship seemed to him quite impossible. It was not in his nature, and he was quite certain it was not in hers. After all, how could one discover the true nature of the ocean by standing gingerly on the shoreline, retreating each time the water threatened to splash one's boot tips? The only way to know was to wade in and immerse oneself.

But of course, that way, there was a considerable risk of drowning.

Chapter Thirty-six

Miss Blanchfort had gone for a walk. Given that the gardens at Holbroke were extensive, and the park beyond vast, there were a hundred places she might be. Without any more specific knowledge, to attempt to find her seemed futile. Therefore Felix decided to wait until she returned, and made his way to the library.

Lord Rothborough had the excellent habit of always seeking out what was new and interesting in literature, and Felix found lying on a table a couple of freshly published books on scientific subjects. He took them and settled down to read.

Unfortunately the first book was not nearly as good as the reviews and advance mentions had promised, and Felix soon found himself annoyed by it. So he put it aside and began the other. A few pages of this were enough to irritate him excessively and he took to pacing the great library, wondering what on earth he was doing there, and if he would not be better leaving at once. Lord Rothborough's advice and Lady Maria's hints had confused him utterly. He wanted very much to see her, and at the same time the thought of it terrified him.

It was nearly noon and the spring sunshine had grown intense. A footman came in to adjust the blinds, so that the light should not spoil the books, and not liking to be plunged into shade, Felix left the room by the small garden door and went outside.

A few steps and a turn of the corner took him to the terrace, which looked down on the geometric beds of the great parterre. It was bristling with crimson and yellow tulips, while the great fountain was playing, its three jets spouting and sparkling from the mouth of a giant gilded sea creature. Walking about the basin was Miss Blanchfort, a slight figure in black. Her shawl and black bonnet lay abandoned on the grass nearby, and her copper hair was falling down too. Occasionally the breeze grew stronger and caught the water jets so that they threw their spray over her. Instead of recoiling, she seemed to revel in this, like a bird splashing in a puddle.

Felix ran down towards her and then stopped on the far side of the fountain basin, so that they faced each other across the silver-grey expanse of water. He saw that she had got herself quite wet and that the effect was extremely becoming. Then, as he stood quite lost in admiration, the breeze, like a mischievous spirit, turned and threw the water at him.

He exclaimed at it, jumped back and heard her burst out laughing.

"Isn't it delightful?" she said.

"Yes, yes, it is," he said. "You are not feeling so tired now?"

"No. I must be mending fast. I'm hoping you will tell me that this horrible thing can come off," she said, tapping her splinted arm, which was resting in a now sodden black silk sling.

"Not for a while yet, I'm afraid," he said, walking round to her side. "But I may be able to replace it with something a little less clumsy. The joiner here could make some more delicate splints, perhaps. And I suspect you have just got the bandages soaked –"

"No, it is covered in oiled silk. See," she said, taking it from the sling. "This is Mr Bodley's notion. He had Miss Waites sew a sleeve for it."

"Bodley is extraordinary," said Felix, admiring the black silk casing.

"He told me all about you," she said, and Felix wondered what on earth had been said, and indeed who had raised him as a subject of conversation.

Before he had a chance to answer, the fountain decided to deposit upon them both, and with some force, as if it had now turned spiteful. She did not object at all when he took her elbow and steered her from its range.

"It's quite taken agin us!" he managed to say, once he had mastered his laughter.

"Yes, I think so," she said and gave a shiver, for a raft of pewtery clouds had drifted in and blocked the sun. He went to pick up her shawl and bonnet.

"Perhaps we should go inside," he said, and put the shawl, which was brightly checked and made of delicate silk, about her shoulders.

"Do you like my plaid?" she said, adjusting it. "Or is it not a proper plaid? I have been wondering what a proper Highlander's plaid might be like."

"I'm afraid I don't know. It's very pretty, though it would not keep you warm in Pitfeldry. Nor here, if that cloud is anything to go by. Shall we go and find a fire?"

She nodded, and they went back into the house by the library door. Here they were met by Lord Rothborough on the way to his study, which was reached through the library.

He looked them over as they stood there, with their wet faces. Felix was holding Miss Blanchfort's bonnet, as if he had plucked it from her, causing her hair to fall down in the process.

"I didn't notice it was raining," he said.

"It was a very particular rain-shower," said Miss Blanchfort, and she and Felix both burst out laughing.

"Excuse me?" said Lord Rothborough.

"The fountain," Felix managed to say. "The breeze conspired against us."

"That would be very charming if you were both still in the schoolroom, but you are both a little old to be –" He broke off and glanced around him with an air of irritation. "Could you please both go and make yourselves respectable? We have important business this afternoon. Eleanor, your mother has finally yielded to my persuasion and will be here shortly."

"I shall not see her!" said Miss Blanchfort.

"Eleanor, we have been over this," Lord Rothborough said. "You must make your peace."

"No, no, no!" exclaimed Miss Blanchfort, shaking her head, "I shall not see her!" She ran past him and out of the room.

"Eleanor!" said Lord Rothborough going after her, but the door was slammed in his face. Turning back, he said to Felix, "Well, don't just stand there, go and talk some sense into her!"

"What on earth can I say to make her change her mind?" said Felix.

"A woman in love will listen to her lover when she will listen to no one else."

"In love? Do you think that she is –?"

"It would seem so." He sighed. "Go and get some dry clothes on and then talk to her. If this match is to be brokered then she must absolutely submit to her mother. Otherwise your cause is lost. So it is in your interest to persuade her. Yes?"

"But this morning you said that there was no haste and now you are talking –"

"That was before you were cavorting in the fountain with her."

"We were not in the fountain, and we were not cavorting," Felix said.

"You may as well have been. The effect is the same. And that was hardly the measured approach I was suggesting."

"Nothing at all happened."

"No, of course not," said Lord Rothborough. "Even I know that you would exercise restraint in such circumstances. But for a girl like Eleanor, the slightest favourable attention adds up to something significant. And you have now become significant. It is a good thing that it seems to be mutual and you are at present free of entanglements. You're lucky, my boy, to have such a prize as Eleanor Blanchfort within your reach, and to have those around you who will support such a suit. Now go and get changed, will you?"

Felix was happy to be dismissed.

Chapter Thirty-seven

Lady Blanchfort was already an hour late. Miss Blanchfort had also failed to come downstairs and wait for her arrival, despite being sent for on several occasions.

"I am very sorry, my lord," said Taylor, Miss Blanchfort's maid. "But she says she will not come down. She says she has a headache."

"You do not quite believe in this headache, do you, Taylor?" said Lord Rothborough.

"That isn't my place to say, my lord," said Miss Taylor.

"It is just as well that we have a medical man at our disposal," said Lord Rothborough. "Mr Carswell, go and see if you can assist her."

So Felix went upstairs to Miss Blanchfort's dressing room. This was a generous room, hung with green damask and with a fine prospect of the park. Miss Blanchfort was sitting in one of the window seats, wrapped in her plaid silk shawl, her face half buried in it. She looked miserably up at him as he entered.

"Mr Carswell, miss," said Taylor. "For your headache."

"Thank you, Taylor," she said. "That will be all."

Taylor, who was a middle-aged woman of sober appearance, gave a disapproving sigh and seemed to consider the point at some length before she finally went into the adjoining room and closed the door behind her.

"Do you have a headache?" Felix asked, going to the window and sitting down beside her.

"Yes," she said. "Of sorts."

"A poultice with Eau de Cologne might help," he said.

"What would help –" she began and broke off.

"Do you have some Eau de Cologne?"

"On the dresser there."

He went and found the flask and soaked a handkerchief in it, before coming back to sit beside her. He pulled down the blind to reduce the light, and taking her chin in his hand, tipped back her head so that he could press the folded cloth to her forehead. She leant back, accepting the attention without any resistance, closing her eyes and sighing slightly as he did so. He leant a little closer, wondering if this was a sign of her inclinations towards him, or mere relief. That she yielded so easily to his touch was both delicious and alarming. If he had awoken a passion in her, then it only served to fuel his own desire for her.

They sat there for some minutes in silence, and then he gently took off the poultice. She caught his wrist and opened her eyes to him, as well as parting her lips, as if daring him to kiss her. He would have done so, but with some effort managed to resist. He moved away a little with the scent of the Eau de Cologne hanging between them, sweet and sharp, as enticing as the girl herself, and then he found he could no longer hold back, and pressed his lips to hers.

It was more than pleasant, and it left them giddy.

"That," she said, "is an excellent cure for a headache."

"I think I need to complete the prescription," Felix said, and kissed her again. In truth he wanted far more than kisses, and from the fierce little movements she was making against him, and the strength of the grip of her undamaged arm about him, he could tell she was as hungry as he was. But of course, that was impossible.

So as gently as he could, he disentangled himself, and moved a little distance away to a chair next to the window seat.

"All in good time," he murmured, giving her one final kiss, and she nodded, and they sat, composing themselves.

He smiled across at her, drunk with happiness. Her ardent eyes were fixed on him, as if he were the source of all meaning and happiness in her life. He was, just as Lord Rothborough had said, extremely lucky, and in that moment any last hesitation receded. Any difficulties could be surmounted, he was certain. All he knew was that he must take his chances with her.

He reached out for her hand and kissed it at some length, before looking up at her again and saying, "I don't know how I begin to ask you this, after such a short a time, but it feels that there is a congruence, a purpose, a rightness to it, for all the difficulties we will undoubtedly face. Everyone will no doubt call me presumptuous to even consider you as a potential wife, since I am nobody in particular."

"You are not a nobody to me!" she said. "Do you think I care for any of that?"

"I have nothing. You have everything."

"You have a house. Surely that is all that anyone needs? I like your house, Mr Carswell. I should like to be mistress of it, if that is what you are trying to say to me," she said.

"That is exactly what I have been trying to say," he said, laughing now. "Would you like to be mistress of Ardenthwaite, Eleanor?"

"Yes, yes, I would. Very much."

He moved back onto the window seat and began to kiss her again.

"Oh, I hope we can be married soon," she said.

"We shall have to be," he said, breaking from her, anxious that he should not go too far. This time he got to his feet and walked away. She too got up and stood, shaking out her shawl and her skirts.

"I was supposed to persuade you to come down," he said. "You have to talk to your mother. In fact, *we* must talk to your mother."

"Very well," she said, with surprising cheerfulness. She came over to him and pressed herself against him. "As you wish."

"Are you sure?"

"What can she do to me now?" she said. "I shall be married and that will be that. She cannot put me back in her prison. You have rescued me. I have been rescued!" With this statement, she turned her face up for another kiss, her head thrown back. Felix could not resist, and he wrapped his arms about her, feeling her collapse with the pleasure of his kiss. He felt faint at the thought of the hours of conjugal pleasure that awaited them.

There was a loud cough. Taylor had come back into the room and was standing at the doorway looking as if she wished to horsewhip him.

"I think you should leave now, sir," said Taylor. "And Miss Eleanor, don't think I'm not going to tell her Ladyship about this."

"Oh, be quiet, Taylor!" said Eleanor. "Come, Mr Carswell, let us go downstairs!"

~

Lord Rothborough, Lady Maria and Lady Blanchfort were sitting in the small drawing room. Eleanor and Felix went hand in hand to the closed door and then stopped before it.

"Shall we?" he said. She nodded and then they went in, still holding hands.

It was Lord Rothborough who saw them first. Lady Blanchfort had her back to them and was some distance away. Lord Rothborough had risen from his chair and seeing their knotted fingers, made a brief chopping gesture, to make them break apart. When they did not, he repeated it again, with a fierce shake of his head, which counselled Felix to prudence. Felix let go of her hand, and Lord Rothborough's countenance now assumed a genial welcoming smile. He stretched out his hand to greet his ward.

"Ah, there you are, Eleanor," he said. "I hope your headache is better?"

Eleanor glanced at Felix, and he gestured that she should go to Lord Rothborough. She did, and even kissed him on the cheek.

"Here she is, Ann," said Lord Rothborough to Lady Blanchfort.

Felix remained by the door, feeling like a footman, and waited for his own summons. Lady Blanchfort had not risen nor turned.

He watched as Eleanor made a perfect little curtsey to her.

"Eleanor," Lady Blanchfort said.

"Mama."

"You look flushed," said Lady Blanchfort.

"That will be the remains of the headache," said Lord Rothborough. He gestured to Felix to come forward. "Is that the case, Mr Carswell, that a slight fever can persist after a serious headache?"

"Yes, my lord," Felix said, coming and standing by Eleanor. "Good afternoon, Lady Blanchfort," he said, making a slight bow. "You can see she is doing very well here. Her wrist is mending as it should, and there have been no complications."

"How fortunate you have been at hand to treat her," said Lady Blanchfort. "You must remember to send me your bill, Mr Carswell. And as for complications, I can see there has been a major one. What has been going on?"

"Mr Carswell has asked me to marry him, and I have said yes," said Eleanor.

Lady Blanchfort rose from her seat, and said, "Do not be silly. Now, would someone ring for a servant? We must fetch your wraps. It might be rather cool in the carriage. There is no real warmth in this spring sunshine, I find. We do not want our precious patient to catch cold, do we, Mr Carswell?"

"Mama, did you not hear what I said?"

"Yes, and it was not worthy of remark."

"We are engaged, Mama," said Eleanor.

"It is true," said Felix, taking Eleanor's hand and kissing it. "Miss Blanchfort has done me the honour of consenting –"

"Done you the honour?" said Lady Blanchfort, shaking her head. "There is no honour in this. This is barefaced machination of the most vile description. But you will not succeed, sir, in your pretensions."

"Sit down, Ann," said Lord Rothborough. "I think you and I need to talk. The young people can go elsewhere. Maria, why don't you go with Eleanor and Mr Carswell into the music room?"

~

"Can this be true?" said Maria as they went along the passageway. "No wonder you looked so sore when I teased you this morning, for which I am more sorry than I can say! Oh, how very exciting!"

They went into the music room, and Lady Maria insisted on kissing them both.

"The way my mother looked just then," Eleanor began, "it may be impossible –"

"Oh, but Papa is for it, I'm sure," said Maria. "He is able to achieve the most extraordinary things is that not so, Mr Carswell?"

"I can vouch for it."

"How can she object when you make such a fine couple?" Maria went on, putting their hands together and performing a mock betrothal.

"Because I have nothing?" Felix said. "And you know

who I am?"

"You are my brother," Maria said, "and no one shall ever stop me from thinking of you as anything else, and as you are my brother, then how can you be unequal to anyone? It is true that fate has made things awkward, but the fact of it remains! Dear Eleanor, I could not be more happy to have you as another sister, and I know Papa will be doing everything to accomplish this for you."

This show of sincerity and enthusiasm was profoundly touching, and Felix kissed her again, and the three of them walked about the great room. Lady Maria began on the subject of wedding journeys.

"You must go to Scotland," she said, "surely?"

"Oh, yes, to the Highlands," said Eleanor. "Might we?"

"I should think so. We will have to go and see my parents, I suppose." With a slight shock, he realised he had not thought at all about what they might make of this marriage.

"Mr and Mrs Carswell!" said Maria. "Oh, they are the sweetest people imaginable, Eleanor. I met them last summer when they were at Ardenthwaite."

"I hope they will like me," said Eleanor, glancing at Felix with some apprehension.

"I am sure they will," he said, but did not add that he was sure they would dislike her fortune and her connections. But then the thought of showing her the country near Pitfeldry, which he felt would be greatly to her taste, and sharing with her all the pleasures of a Highland summer, made him dismiss any difficulties. "We must certainly go to Perthshire!"

Maria rushed to the piano and started to play a reel. Felix was about to make Eleanor dance with him, when Lord Rothborough came into the room. He stood looking rather grave, and Maria stopped playing at once.

"You are both quite settled on this?" he said. "Felix, Eleanor?"

"Yes, my lord," said Felix. "Quite settled."

"Eleanor?"

"Yes, my lord," she said.

He nodded and said, "Lady Blanchfort would like to speak to you, Felix."

"Not me?" said Eleanor.

"No, not at present," said Lord Rothborough. "You wait here."

Felix left the room with Lord Rothborough and when they were outside, he said, "Well, you exceeded my expectations there. Good Lord! A little decorum would have made things a great deal easier for me. Really, did you have to be quite so intemperate? I did not send you upstairs to get engaged to her."

"I could not have done otherwise," Felix said. "It all became very clear when I went up. And she loves me. You said I was lucky, my lord – I am. I see that now."

"You certainly are," said Lord Rothborough. "Lady Blanchfort was something of an obstacle, but I think I have managed that for you."

"By using thc mattcr that you said was discrcditablc about her?" said Felix.

"Yes, and I hesitated to do it, but seeing you and Eleanor – it seems my sentimental nature got the better of me. I think you are well suited, and it is better that you are married sooner rather than later, even though she is only seventeen. You are both passionate creatures. Marriage will settle you."

"She is only seventeen?" Felix said.

"Did you not realise that?" said Lord Rothborough.

"No," he said. "We have not discussed it." He realised how little they had discussed in the course of their strange, slight acquaintance. "She does not seem that young."

"She is just a touch younger than Maria," said Lord Rothborough. "Does that disturb you?"

"I don't know," said Felix. "What do you think?"

"As I said, you are a pair of hot-heads, and apparently

violently in love. The match is advantageous for both of you. It could be that she is too young to be a mother, but you and I both know that is a situation that can easily be postponed until she is ready for such a responsibility. Indeed, until you are ready. Now, will you go in?"

He had thought Lord Rothborough would accompany him, but it seemed he was to face the lady alone.

She was standing and staring down into the fire. Whatever Lord Rothborough had said, it seemed to have chastened her. There was a bow in her shoulders and she looked unhappy rather than angry as she turned and sat down.

"You wished to talk to me, ma'am?" Felix ventured.

"This is difficult for me," she said, after a moment. "I hope you appreciate that."

"I do," said Felix.

"Eleanor is still so young," she went on. "And her character is not entirely formed. We have lived quietly, as I think that suits her temperament. The glitter of society would not suit her, and I had decided that she should not be brought out as girls usually are. I had hoped that, two or three years hence, some suitable candidate would present himself to us. He would be a man of rank and solid fortune, who would bring assets equal to the enormous advantages she would bring him. I did not conceive of marrying her at seventeen to a man who has scarcely established himself in a profession I find distasteful, and who has nothing to recommend him except a small estate that he has come by only because of the peculiar circumstances of his birth."

"I agree, ma'am, I'm no catch," said Felix. "But I love your daughter and she loves me. It is the most curious thing. It's not what I intended. Ordinarily, I would never have presumed, but we have been thrown together, and it seems that it must be, that *we* must be. I am certain of that much. And I do not care about her fortune – in fact, I should rather she had nothing to her name!"

"That is a pretty speech," she said. "But I do not know you well enough yet, to know if you are sincere."

"I have friends, ma'am, who would speak for me. Major Vernon, my employer, for example –"

She held up her hand to silence him.

"But the fact remains that you stand to gain a great deal by such a marriage. It is often the case with natural sons of great men that they work to legitimise themselves by making brilliant marriages."

"I do not care about that! I never have. My relationship to Lord Rothborough is an entirely private one and I do not seek to get any advantage from it."

"So you say," she said. "But to me your actions seem suspect. Pursuing my vulnerable daughter when she is under this roof, when its mistress is unhappily absent? Lady Rothborough, were she here, would not tolerate the freedom with which you treat this house. You have established yourself as an equal here. You have presumed to offer for a young woman who is far above you in rank and fortune."

"You may doubt my motives all you like, ma'am," Felix said, "but nothing could be further from my mind. I have never presumed to be anything other than I am, and frankly, as far as I am concerned, your daughter's position and fortune is an irritating inconvenience."

"Yet you behave as if you are the legitimate heir, as if you were indeed the Viscount Avonside and not mere Mr Carswell. And that, of course, is a name you may only bear because of the charity of your adopted parent. If it was charity, that is, and not due to my lord's ever-generous purse. Clerical households can be uncomfortably threadbare, especially in the wilds of North Britain, and even the greatest saints among us are not immune to temptation."

"That madam," he said, "is a slander. My parents took nothing from Lord Rothborough. They refused absolutely. Now, you may insult me all you like, but I shall not allow you to insult them!"

She stood up, and for a moment he thought she was about to terminate the interview.

"Very spirited, and very proper," she said instead, in a tone which he could not place as either sarcastic or sincere. It was impossible to read her. "Do you truly love my daughter, Mr Carswell?" she now said, looking hard at him. As she did, it was hard not to see the striking resemblance between her and Eleanor, and to imagine how Eleanor would look twenty years hence. There was a formidable power in that extraordinary cast of beauty that they shared. In Lady Blanchfort it had grown into something majestic, and if he were frank, for all her insults, she was still impressive.

"Yes," he said.

"She will not be an easy wife, you do understand that?"

"Why would any man want an easy wife?" he said.

That produced a faint brief curl of her lips, suggestive of a smile.

"Explain yourself," she said.

"A man who expects an easy wife might as well employ a good housekeeper and keep a mistress. When a man and a woman marry it ought to create something greater than two individuals can achieve as separate beings. They are equals joining in a great endeavour – in ideal circumstances, that is."

"And those ideal circumstances are –?"

"When they choose each other for love and for temperament, without regard to worldly considerations."

"That is quite a philosophy," she said.

Felix was astonished by his own eloquence on the subject, but at the same time he was thoroughly enjoying his boldness. It was as if Eleanor's admission of devotion had given him a sharp sword to defeat the dragons.

She walked away to the window and stood looking out for a moment.

"If I give my consent," she said, "there will be conditions

attached. Please understand that."

"Conditions, ma'am?"

"Given that my daughter is so young and unformed, there are two ways that we may approach this. Either you wait to marry until she is of age, or if you marry now you will both live with me. When I think she has reached sufficient maturity and when I am sure of you, Mr Carswell, you may form your own establishment without me. That is your choice."

"Ma'am, I do not think –" he began, utterly confounded by this.

"That is your choice," she said again.

"That is not consent," he said, "that is –"

At this moment there was a knock at the door, and a footman came in with a message for Felix. It was addressed in Major Vernon's distinctive hand and the contents were, as usual, to the point.

"Bickley has taken a turn for the worse. Peterson desires your immediate assistance at Marlingford."

Chapter Thirty-eight

Carswell had arrived at Marlingford, in the speedy comfort of Lord Rothborough's travelling carriage drawn by four superb chestnut horses. Carswell went straight into the house, leaving Giles on the steps.

"That must be a very important patient, sir," remarked Forbuoys, the head coachman, to Giles. "I took my beauties faster than I should have liked, for this is a young team, which we have only just got under harness, but Mr Carswell insisted we get here as soon as we could."

"The stabling is more than adequate here," said Giles. "You will find all you need, I trust."

Forbuoys led his magnificent equipage round to the stable yard, while Giles went back into the house.

Carswell and Peterson were already deep in conference by the bed on which Bickley lay. He was now almost as pale as his mane of white hair. He lay staring up at his physicians, clearly too weak to speak.

"I cannot staunch the bleeding," Peterson said. "He is fading fast."

"There is something we might attempt," Carswell said, when he had finished a brief examination. "A transfusion – you know Blundell's work?"

"I do, but I have not seen it done."

"I have – Mr Harper has had one or two notable successes with it and, although I have not yet performed it myself, I have bought the necessary instruments. I've been wondering when a situation might arise. It's a most ingenious process, and I think Mr Harper may even have improved on Blundell's technique. Hardly surprising, given how deft he is."

"He certainly is that," said Peterson.

Carswell had already thrown off his coat and was unpacking his bag.

"I think this," he said, holding up a narrow tube, "will become commonplace before long. This ensures the regulation of the stream from vein to vein. And this part here fixes on the patient's forearm. The stream of blood from the donor enters the funnel with the regulating cock here, supported by this bracketed arm. Major Vernon, if I might ask you – could you lay that stool alongside our patient here, so I can put it in place?" Carswell fixed the arm to one of the legs of the stool, and used the arm to hold the silver tube perpendicular to it. He then took up a scalpel and made an incision in Bickley's forearm. Bickley groaned and protested, but Carswell went on regardless. He fixed a metal tourniquet-like cuff over the incision, and attached the silver tube to it. He then put the receiving funnel at the top of the tube.

"All ready," he said. "Blundell calls it a gravitator, because, as you can see, it uses gravity to send the blood in a steady flow into the patient."

"And who will be the donor? You?" said Peterson. Carswell had rolled up his right sleeve and was tapping at his veins in the crook of his arm with his fingertips.

"Yes," he said. "Can you make the incision for me, Peterson? Just there? Just as if it were a venesection."

"Of course," said Peterson.

"This may work," Carswell said, catching Giles' eye as he stood on the far side of the bed, "or it may not."

He screwed up his face as Peterson made the incision, which caused a lively stream of blood. Carswell then moved and stood with his arm outstretched so that the blood fell into the little funnel at the top of the tube.

"Open the cock when there is an inch or so in there," said Carswell.

"Extraordinary," said Peterson. "And as you say, very

ingenious."

"The funnel holds about two fluid ounces when it is full. I can stand to lose about twenty-four in the first instance."

"Twenty at most," said Peterson, turning the cock.

Silence fell as Carswell's blood drained from his arm and into the funnel and then vanished down the tube to trickle into the veins of the dying man. Although he scarcely knew what he should be looking for, Giles found himself staring at Bickley who was gazing up at him, helpless, lost and confused. His hand clawed at the covers, and then after some minutes he opened his mouth as if attempting to speak. But no sound came out, only a dry sigh.

"His pulse is improving," said Peterson.

"Excellent," said Carswell.

"And you are not feeling faint?" said Peterson.

"Not yet," said Carswell.

At this point Bickley began to writhe, and threatened to unsettle the equipment, so Giles put his hands on his shoulders to still him. As he did, Bickley breathed hard into his ear and said, "Damn you!"

"It is definitely having some effect," said Peterson and at the same time, Carswell staggered back and fell to the floor in a dead faint. Peterson rushed round to attend to him, while Bickley, quite lively now, began to resist Giles' restraint.

"You shall not have the satisfaction –" he rasped. "You and your –" He hauled in lungfuls of breath. "I will not leave here alive."

"Tell me, then, did you order Matthew Jones' murder?"

"Yes, he was a dirty traitor."

"And Kate?"

"She needed a beating."

"Ruthless even in death," Giles said.

"She was a traitor. She deserved it. Like my sister and bloody Merriam. And he killed my friend."

"You mean Colonel Parham?"

"Aye, with the help of that little blaggard Mostyn!" Bickley went on, in a fearful, rasping tone that made his words practically unintelligible. But he seemed determined to say his piece. "I told him not to trust him, but he wouldn't listen. Didn't see what he was until it was too late. Didn't keep him in check as he should. So make sure you hang him, Major! He's a dirty, clever one, with his filthy mushrooms. You had a little taste of his tricks, I think."

"I think so," said Giles.

"His idea. I told the Colonel not to trust him. Poor fellow, poor –" He gazed up at Giles. "You look just like him. Never saw that before –" and then he seemed overcome by the pain completely and began to groan. At the same time he tried to push away the transfusion apparatus. "Let me die!" he managed to say. "God in Heaven, just let me die!"

He was gripped with the most fearful agitation, and went from deathly pale to a violent red, sweating profusely. At the same time he began screaming as if all the devils of Hell were leaping upon him. For some five minutes this persisted, despite all Peterson's efforts to calm and sedate him. Bickley was suffocating before their eyes, and a few minutes later, he expired.

Carswell, who had managed to get back onto his feet for the final moments, was staring down at him, his teeth chattering and a bloody bandage pressed to his forearm.

"So much for justice," he said.

"No one can say we did not try," said Peterson, and began to disassemble the transfusion device.

"Brandy," said Carswell. Then he turned and walked out of the room.

Giles followed him, for he looked most unsteady on his feet, and he had to be helped to a chair in the drawing room – the chair in which Miss Bickley had sat.

"It was scarcely a pint," he said.

"Perhaps that is why you never recommend old-fashioned

blood-letting," Giles said. "You cannot stand it yourself."

"Others can. I have seen people relieved of twenty-four ounces without blenching. But scarcely a pint – to no effect. Well, hardly that, either, because he's dead now, and it would be quite easy to point to my intervention as the cause. Not to mention my blood. Unless that is the problem." He sat up a little, as if possessed by an idea. "Perhaps one man's blood is not like another's. Perhaps when the procedure works it is because there is a compatibility there that we do not yet understand. Perhaps my blood was a sort of poison for Bickley. Your blood or Peterson's might have done the job better. We might have kept him alive."

"Try to postpone such speculation," said Giles. "Recover yourself fully first, before you launch into an exhausting investigation. Here," he said, handing a glass to him. "Sherry, I'm afraid, not brandy."

Carswell swallowed down the contents of the glass in one gulp, and sank back in the chair.

"What time is it?"

Giles consulted his watch.

"A little after seven."

"I should go back. I need to go back."

"It's too dark now, and you have already exhausted those horses. Why do you need to return, anyway?"

"Because –" Carswell broke off and gave a slightly hysterical laugh. "Because my fiancée will be waiting for me, and I have left her to do battle with her mother, and that I cannot allow. So you see, I must go."

"Congratulations," said Giles. "I take it the lady in question is Miss Blanchfort?"

"Yes," said Carswell. "I have plunged into the great matrimonial ocean and caught my silver salmon. She fairly leapt into my arms, in fact!"

"And naturally you want to go back. But I think you should allow Mr Peterson the last word on it."

"I fainted, that is all," said Carswell, and attempted to get up from his chair, but he wavered badly as he did, and ended up sitting down again. "Well, perhaps I should not go anywhere quite yet."

Giles went and fetched Peterson, who bound up Carswell's arm and told him he ought to lie down and rest.

"Then you should eat a decent dinner," he added.

"We shall have to make the best of things here," said Giles.

When Carswell had gone to rest, Giles went back to the room where Bickley's corpse lay. Peterson had covered him with a sheet, and Giles hesitated for a moment to draw it back and look at him. That he was dead and unable to do any more damage was in practical terms an excellent thing, but there remained the irritating feeling that the old devil had cheated justice.

~

Felix did as he was bid, and was surprised to find how easy it was to sleep. The old butler, Mr Stevens, woke him with a jug of hot water and the news that dinner would be served shortly. He had been asleep for nearly two hours, and had developed an appetite.

Major Vernon and Peterson were waiting for him in the dining room. The meal was by no means an extravagant one, but Miss Bickley's handsome taste in china and silver made it elegant.

"What will become of this house now, I wonder?" said Peterson.

"Miss Bickley had a half-sister," said Major Vernon. "She suffered at her hands, so there would be some justice if it came to her."

Having taken a glass of wine, Peterson excused himself and went to bed, leaving Felix and Major Vernon at the table.

"Perhaps we should drink a toast?" Major Vernon said, having added a scant eighth of an inch to his glass, and then pushed the bottle towards Felix. "To the future Mrs Carswell."

"It may be some time before that becomes a reality," Felix said, filling his own glass. "There are conditions. Either we must wait four years until she is of age, or her Ladyship lives with us until such time as she thinks it is appropriate to let us alone! And because your note came when it did, I have not had a chance to discuss this with Eleanor."

"I apologise, then."

"It is hardly your fault. No, I shall blame the late Bickley. He has caused us enough trouble, him and his wretched family!" Felix sipped his wine.

"I still think a toast is in order, whatever you decide," said Major Vernon, raising his glass. "It is good news. I hope you both will be extremely happy."

"So do I!" said Felix. "But with that woman in the house, I cannot begin to imagine – Eleanor is violently against her and for a host of very good reasons. But I do not think I can bear to wait, and I am sure Eleanor will not want to. For I could be dead in four years' time. I nearly was the other night, after all."

"Only if you decide to keep in this line of work, of course."

"What else would I do?" said Felix.

"It may be that your future wife has other ideas. That is another thing you must discuss with her."

"No, no, she will fall in with it. It's true she probably does not quite understand what it entails, just yet, but she is no fool, as you know."

"Certainly. But be prepared for her to be uneasy."

Felix nodded, feeling the good sense of this. He drank a little more and said, "And what of your prospects, if that is not an insolent question?"

Major Vernon did not answer for a moment, and then said, "I wish I had equally pleasant news for you, but I fear –" He broke off, and drew a pattern with his fingertip on the table cloth, seemingly thinking deeply. "I know I'm hardly the person to give you advice, but if I were you, I would seize my chance and marry now, her mother notwithstanding. I'm sure she can be worked on and made into a friend, not an enemy. You have the conviction of strong affections and the prospect of much happiness, even in such conditions. Why on earth would you wait?" He got up from the table. "Now, I have to begin on my reports."

Epilogue

Midsummer's Day, 1841

At a little after ten in the morning on Midsummer's Day, Giles left Carswell pacing the Chapter House at the Minster and went in search of any other members of the wedding party who might have arrived. This was a slightly futile quest, for the ceremony was not due to take place until eleven. However, in his agitation, Carswell had insisted on their arriving no later than ten. Giles did not like to point out that no bride in history had ever arrived early and that it was in fact considered unlucky to do so. It was better not to contradict him, given the mood he was in.

Carswell's anxiety was to be expected. The road to that morning had not been an easy one. The lawyers on both sides had decided that they could not resist taking the most adversarial stance in the matter of the settlements. Lord Rothborough had taken Carswell's marriage as an opportunity to rearrange the disposition of those parts of his assets that were not entailed. He had been determined that Carswell should not go empty-handed to the table, but with expectations. It was matter of personal pride for him that it should be so. Yet, Carswell had come back from these meetings with lawyers in a state of embarrassed bewilderment.

"I am afraid of what people will say – not for my sake, but for his. I do not want people gossiping about him."

The result of it was that Carswell would one day inherit a nice parcel of ground rents in London as well as shares in various commercial and industrial exploits, in which Lord

Rothborough had invested. The Blanchfort side had received this with little grace and had demanded apparently draconian conditions to protect Miss Blanchfort's fortune from her future husband, far more than was usual. This had enraged Lord Rothborough and the negotiations had stalled for some time, causing Carswell great misery, who was certain that at any moment the whole thing would be called off for good.

At the same time, Lady Blanchfort would not permit the lovers to see each other except under her supervision. Another condition of the engagement had been that her daughter would go back to Hawksby until the wedding. Giles had accompanied Carswell on one of these visits – Carswell had thought he might have some influence on Lady Blanchfort, or at least act as a distraction, but Lady Blanchfort had not wavered in her steely chaperonage. The young couple had been reduced to sitting in the corner, their heads bent together over a map of Scotland, planning their wedding journey, while Giles attempted to draw Lady Blanchfort out on some inoffensive subject. It had been exhausting, to say the least. She was as difficult as she was beautiful.

Even the choice of venue for the wedding had been a painful struggle. Lady Blanchfort had wanted the wedding in Hawksby for the sake of discretion, while Miss Blanchfort and Carswell had declared they wished to be married in the Minster by Canon Fforde. It had been settled, eventually, that Miss Blanchfort should be married from Lord Rothborough's house in the Minster Precincts. Lord Rothborough had managed to argue that this would be as discreet as any wedding in the country, as the gates to the Precincts could be closed, and only those on a special list allowed into the Minster itself. Lady Blanchfort wanted no idle gawkers.

Giles was surprised, then, as he made his way to the north door – the only door open at that point – to see a woman sitting in one of the enclosed chapels at the East End. She was sitting with her back to him, facing the altar, and a pierced stone screen partially obscured his view of her, but her outline was familiar. He paused a moment, deciding he was only seeing what he wanted to see, rather than what was possible. But then she turned, as if she were aware of him standing there at the entrance to the chapel; he saw it was her, and he found himself both shaking his head and smiling.

It was Emma, rising from her seat and putting out her hands to greet him.

"Carswell wrote to me and asked me to come," she said. He took her hand and kissed it. It was as much as he could manage not to fold her into his arms. "I hope you don't mind? I am breaking our rules, I know, but a wedding is a wedding, and I could not resist. It was such an eloquent letter, I thought he might even have written it at your request."

"No, but I'm very glad he did," Giles said.

They sat down together, and he reached for her hand. "You look very fine. A new bonnet?" he added, touching her striped ribbons.

"It is. Patton trimmed it. It cost me almost nothing. You also look handsome. Quite equal to the task." She, in her turn, touched the nosegay of roses and myrtle in his buttonhole. "The new coat is most becoming," she added, her gloved hand resting on his lapel for a long moment.

He had mentioned the coat in a letter. They had tried to be frugal with their correspondence, having agreed they ought not indulge themselves with it, but lately he had found himself writing more often and at great length. Her replies, sent from the Dower House at Woodville Park where she had exiled herself, had matched his. By way of letters they had slipped into an unplanned level of intimacy, and if this had pricked his conscience previously, he knew in that moment, on seeing her, and feeling the instant, settled comfort of her presence, that they had learnt much by it. He felt now that he knew his own mind perfectly about what the future might bring them.

He reached for her hand again, and squeezed it.

"It was in my mind, once this was over, that I would ride down to Whithorne and –"

"Bring me a piece of wedding cake?"

"Something like that." He smiled and saw in her expression that she knew exactly what he meant.

"How is Mr Carswell?"

"Anxious, very anxious. He sent me to look for guests. You should come and speak to him – it would do him good."

"Then of course."

"He's in the Chapter House."

They went together and found that Carswell was no longer alone. He had been joined by Canon Fforde and Tom. Lambert was sitting next to Carswell on one of the stone benches that lined the great octagon, his arm about Carswell's shoulder, giving him whispered counsel, while Tom was guarding a basket of wedding favours.

Tom jumped up when he saw them, rushed across to Emma and threw his arms about her.

"Guten Morgen, meine liebe, schöne Dame!" he said.

At this, Lambert looked over at Giles and Emma, his expression rather uncomfortable.

It could not be said that relations between them had been easy for the last couple of months. They had been polite, of course, but always guarded, and it was clear enough that Lambert had been gravely offended. The loss of their former intimacy had been a great grief, and although Giles had sought to conceal it from Emma, he knew she had sensed his unhappiness and borne it as if it were her own. Seeing him then, Giles wondered if things would ever be right with him again.

"You may blame it all on me!" Carswell said, getting up and going to shake Emma's hand. "I asked her to come. I thought – oh, God knows what I thought! But I'm glad you are here, ma'am; thank you for coming!"

"I know exactly what you thought, Mr Carswell," Tom

said. "It's not that it wouldn't have been excellent if she'd married Uncle Ned, it's just that, well, Papa, anyone can see, it surely, that –"

"Hush there, Cupid," said Lambert and came over to them. "Ma'am," he said to Emma, and then added, "Giles," with a nod of acknowledgement. "This is –" Then after a long pause, he suddenly grabbed Emma's hand in both his and said, "The thing is, I am always telling people that bearing grudges is the most dangerous poison – and what have I done but – oh, forgive me, won't you?" and he bent and kissed Emma's hand. "If you can?"

"There is nothing to forgive," Emma said rather quietly, her voice breaking as she spoke. "The fault was all mine. I did not know my mind properly. I made a foolish judgement and I hurt a good man."

"But he's quite recovered," Lambert said. "I was in Oxford last week. Ned and I had a long talk about it. I think it was not meant to be, whereas –" he gestured towards Giles. "Tom is – and I scarcely like to say this, for we must not encourage him – absolutely right!"

Now he took Giles' right hand and put it into Emma's.

"There," he said, smiling. "You are one of us now. And if I cannot have you married to one brother, then it will have to be the other. For this fellow here," he went on, laying his hand on Giles' shoulder, "is as good as a brother to me, and as fine a man as you could hope to get for a husband."

Emma glanced at him. There were tears in her eyes and Giles felt his throat constrict.

"If one is prepared to deal with crusts and uncertainty?" he managed to say.

"That has been somewhat usual with me," said Emma, with a shrug.

"Then that is that," said Giles.

"And God bless you both," said Lambert, now laying his hands on their heads for a moment. "Sally will be pleased with me!"

"Lambert, I'm so sorry; we have caused so much pain –" Giles began.

"Enough, enough," said Lambert, shaking his head. "This is not the day for such talk. Come, Emma, let's see if we can find Sally and Celia. You too, Tom; and you, Giles, can tell Carswell what a splendid fellow he is, and how although it may seem a little terrifying just now, when the moment arrives, he will quite understand what he is about!"

~

"She did say," Major Vernon said to Felix when they were alone together, "that it was a fine letter that made her break our agreement – I'm in your debt."

"You should have seen the letter she wrote to me first – about our engagement. I could not refuse her anything after such a letter."

"She asked to come?"

"No, of course not," said Felix. "It was simply that I felt she had to be here. For my sake, as much as anything. And would you not have – sooner or later – broken that agreement yourself?"

"I was intending to go to Whithorne after you had left for your wedding journey, yes," Major Vernon said.

"I thought right, then?"

"You did indeed."

"Then I am capable of reason and good judgement," Felix said, with a sigh, looking up at the vaults. "Although it feels at the moment as if I am nothing but a quivering jelly who has not one speck of sinew. Why the devil am I so afraid? It is absolutely what I want, and Eleanor is the most wonderful creature on the face of the earth, and I want nothing more than for her to be my wife, and yet –" He took several deep breaths. "What if I fail her?" he said. "What if I make her unhappy?"

"You will not," said the Major.

"How do you know that?"

"She is devoted to you."

"Yes, but after what happened with –"

"This is very different," said Major Vernon. "You will have time together as man and wife, and the world will see you as such. There will be nothing clandestine. You will be together and you will grow together. And you have learnt from your previous mistakes, I'm sure of that. This hesitation you are feeling now shows it."

"I wish I had your faith in myself. How can one know, though, truly –"

"One cannot," Major Vernon said. "And of course a woman's devotion is a powerful, even a terrifying, thing, and we are wise to be humble in the face of it, but it is only half the business. Your feelings for her will keep you straight, I'm sure."

"Nothing will be the same after this," Felix said, "that is for certain."

"No," said Major Vernon. "But otherwise, surely we would grow stale?" Felix nodded and began to tug his cravat, wishing he might be free of it. He was not wearing a stitch of comfortable old clothing – everything was new for the day, and it felt very strange, even the wedding shirt his mother had sewn for him. "And soon enough, you will be giving me good advice in a similar situation, if you would care to, that is?"

"I should be honoured, and I dare say you'll have less of a fuss about settlements and so forth."

"I have not even told my brother yet. I suppose Sally may have hinted something to him."

"He's not likely to object, is he?" said Felix. "How could anyone object to Mrs Maitland?"

"John is a strange fellow at the best of times," said Major Vernon. "One can never tell how... but I'm sure you are right, if anyone can charm him, it is" – he paused for a moment and smiled – "my future wife. Speaking of which, had we not better go and find yours? They ought to be at the north door by now, and Lady Blanchfort will be waiting for you to escort her to her place."

"To put her in her place, that would be more the thing," said Felix, with a slight grimace. "I think she is the real cause of my anxiety – I do not truly believe she will allow it to come off! There will be some insuperable objection thrown up even as I am putting the ring on Eleanor's finger."

"Or she may be quite overcome."

"Unlikely," said Felix. "Yes, let's go and find them!"

Major Vernon was right. The wedding party had just come in at the north door: Lady Blanchfort in her weeds, Maria and Celia in their bridesmaid's finery, and then behind them, Lord Rothborough with Eleanor on his arm.

She seemed to Felix to be smaller and slighter than ever. Her features were obscured by a close bonnet and a long veil of patterned lace, and she carried a huge bouquet of flowers that was almost as big as she was. He hastened to remind himself that she would be eighteen next month, still likely to grow a little taller, and that she was also far stronger in character and intelligence than she was in physical form. He also had to fight the temptation to march up to her, throw aside the ridiculous flowers and fling back her veil so he could see her.

"I think we are all here now," Canon Fforde was saying. He had put on his surplice and bands. "I shall go up to the altar now, and wait for you all."

So they formed a little procession, according to custom, with himself in the lead, taking Lady Blanchfort to her seat, while Lord Rothborough and Eleanor came last of all.

When they had reached the altar rails, and had arranged

themselves in their proper positions, Celia took away the flowers, and Maria helped her fold back the veil; he could at last see her. She turned and gave him a brief nervous smile, and he smiled back broadly, feeling that his expression must be unbecoming. But he did not really care. He was elated. To think that she was shortly to be his! Just as Canon Fforde had said, he was now quite himself again, and he was certain that he would learn to be a better man for having such an extraordinary wife.

~ THE END ~

Dramatis Personae

Northminster

Major Giles Vernon: Chief Superintendent of the Northern Investigation Office

Felix Carswell: consultant surgeon to the Northern Office

Inspector Rollins: senior officer at the Northern Investigation Office

Captain Lazenby: Chief Constable of the Northminster and County Constabulary

Mr Peterson: Police Surgeon to the Northminster and County Constabulary

Very Rev Dr John Hughes: The new Bishop of Northminster

Mrs Hughes: the Bishop's wife

Edmund Hughes: the Hughes' eldest son

Canon Lambert Fforde: Minster Treasurer

Mrs Sally Fforde: Canon Fforde's wife, and Giles Vernon's sister

Tom Fforde: the Ffordes' son, aged 15

Celia Fforde: the Ffordes' daughter, aged 11

Dr Edward Fforde: Master of Salvator's College, Oxford and Lambert Fforde's brother

Mrs Emma Maitland: widow of Colonel Maitland, old acquaintance of Giles Vernon, and engaged to Dr Fforde

Lord Milburne: her son, a University of Oxford undergraduate

Sir Richard Blanchford: owner of Hawksby Hall

Lady Blanchfort: Blanchford's estranged wife

Eleanor Blanchfort: Blanchford's only daughter and a great heiress

Mr James Harper: Chief Medical Officer at the Northminster Infirmary

George Bickley: horse dealer

Miss Bickley: George Bickley's sister

Horatio Baxter

Kate: a woman of the streets

Anne Waites: a skilful dressmaker

Ardenthwaite

Colonel Parham: Felix Carswell's tenant at Ardenthwaite

Mostyn: Parham's manservant

Holbroke

Lord Rothborough: Felix Carswell's natural father

Lady Maria: Lord Rothborough's youngest daughter

Mrs Hope: Lord Rothborough's housekeeper

Swalecliffe

Mrs Parham: wife of Colonel Parham

Mr Hickman: landlord and proprietor of gin palaces

About the Author

Harriet Smart was born and brought up in Birmingham. She attended the University of St Andrews, where she read History of Art, and married a fellow student. She now lives with her husband in an eighteenth-century house in Northumberland.

Harriet has an M.A. in screenwriting. She has published twenty novels as well as helping to design the creative writing software Writer's Café and the e-book editor software Jutoh.

She has been writing the Northminster Mysteries since 2010.

You can follow Harriet at www.harrietsmart.com and BookBub.